Thank you so much for
your support!
Gedya & Alisa x

Georga Wellerd has been a registered childminder for 8 years. *Community Chest* is her first novel. She lives in the beautiful North Essex countryside with her husband, three teenage sons and their beloved dog Lottie.

Georga is donating 20% of the profits from the sales of *Community Chest* to the Smile of Arran trust set up in memory of Arran Tosh, the son of one of her close friends who died last year, aged 13, from a brain tumour one week after being diagnosed.

Georga Wellerd

Community Chest

Cover Design by Dani Rainer

I dedicate this book to Stephen, Alison, Chloe and Abbie Tosh

In loving memory of Arran

27th September 2000 – 7th June 2014

With special thanks to Tracy Rainer and Diane Pawsey.

Dear friends to both Alison and myself and childminders in the early years to both Arran and my sons Oliver and Harry.

You were both a mum to our sons when we weren't able to be.

Thank you isn't enough.

Acknowledgements

Thanks first and foremost to Shanaz Daly.

Without your experience, encouragement, generosity, support and belief in this book I doubt I would have ever published it.

A big thank you to my 'Dream Team'; Shanaz, Angie, Sophie, Diane, Tracy, Geraldine, Abbie, Alex and Sue who all kindly agreed to read the first draft of *Community Chest* and feed back their thoughts and ideas on changes to the story line, plots and characters over wine and more wine.

Thank you to Anne Everitt for her wonderful baking skills, to Alison and Liz for listening and supporting me over the past three years and to Jacqui Betts who has been so generous with her knowledge and contacts on social media.

Thank you to my husband Ben for his quiet support and input into the book and to my three sons, Tom, Harry and Oliver for those car journeys when you were trapped in the car with me with no escape and had to listen to plot lines and character profiles.

I feel I should single out my youngest son Oliver for a special thanks who (usually) without a grumble, would let me use his brand new laptop to write *Community Chest* on when the 'a' fell off mine one day, never to be found again, and then one morning, in protest, a third of the way through the book, my poor, ancient, weary laptop rebelled and refused to start up at all.

A huge thank you to the extremely talented Dani Rainer, for designing the book cover, produced from some brief ideas by me on a tiny Post it.

I chose your first design. It was perfect.

Thank you to Leading Edge Graphics Ltd for their signs for the book launch and thank you to Vanessa Giles for agreeing to proof read my first attempt at a book. I hope it wasn't too painful.

Thank you to Poole Farm in Great Yeldham where I buy all my boots from, essential for the busy childminder and dog walker that I am and finally, a huge thank you to all the parents that I have had the pleasure to work alongside over the years and their wonderful children. You have all been so supportive over the past three years and for that I am very grateful. Thank you.

When history repeats itself...

His formidable mother stared down at him, challenging the tears to fall.

He blinked furiously, refusing to release the tears of pain and humiliation that demanded to be given their freedom.

His dominant hand, his right hand, chosen purposefully to ensure pain and discomfort with every chore undertaken, throbbed with the ferocity of today's correction.

He had failed the twice daily wardrobe check.

A coat, unzipped, on its hanger.

A teenage oversight on his part.

He straightened his back, squared his shoulders, and mentally shut out the pain, now radiating up his forearm, as long blisters began to form from the swollen, red welts in his palm.

To show emotion was to feel emotion.

A weakness.

It left one open to failure.

In the Whitehall household, this was not an option.

1

Sally pulled up at the battered rusty gates that led up into the teacher's car park of St Michael's Church of England primary school and pulled on the handbrake.

"Right children," said Sally, as she opened car door, "I'm just going to unlock the gates. I won't be a minute!"

Sally Slater, mother of three boys, wife to Nick, a Fedex department manager, for twenty years and childminder for nearly six years, hauled her weary body out of twelve year old seven seater Zafira and walked around to the front of the car, unlocking the padlock which secured the gates.

Sally parked on the school site with permission from Mr Young, the Headmaster. A youthful fifty something man who even with all the Ofsted restrictions regarding security, did his best to ensure the school was as accessible to as many parent/carers as possible. This enabled Sally to deliver her charges of various shapes, sizes and temperaments to school without having to risk life and limb on the precarious country lane leading to the school.

Her heart felt heavy. Christmas had gone off reasonably well; the boys had seemed genuinely pleased with their presents. This was a relief for Sally and Nick, they were all getting older and the 'wow' factor was gradually getting harder and harder each year to achieve. Nick had seemed really chuffed with the Queen Memorabilia book Sally had bought for him and the turkey had behaved itself and not been too dry. She could have just done without the letter that had apologetically dropped on to her front door mat three days after Boxing Day.

Simon, a child Sally looked after before and after the school day, would not be returning after the Christmas holidays. Unfortunately, Simon's dad had been made redundant just after the school broke up for the holidays.

2

This situation was every childminder's nightmare. It offset all the benefits of the job. Being at home for your children when they were unwell, being there when your children left and returned from school, arranging your work around deliveries, the gas and electric man, repairs to the washing machine. The benefits of working for yourself as a childminder were endless, but the sudden departure of a child due to redundancy was an issue that was talked about at night, in hushed tones, with her long suffering husband, who, for better or worse, held on tight and rode the financial rollercoaster that was the lot of a childminder's income.

Two hundred pounds down and the year had only just started! Sally never charged a month's notice if a parent had been made redundant and didn't know a childminder who did. It just didn't seem morally right. Sally sighed, got back in the car and drove up the slight incline to park the car. She turned the engine off and shifted around in her seat so she faced the six, slightly anxious looking children who filled her car.

She put on a bright face,

"Ok children, here we are, how exciting! A new term, new things to learn and you can tell all your friends about your Christmases."

"My drink's leaked!" squealed Tabitha, a little girl in reception, from the back of the car.

"It's gone all over my new Ben 10 bag!" cried George, a boy in Year 1, who promptly burst into tears.

"I hate school!" spat Jimmy, next to Sally. Jimmy, a boy in Year four whom Sally had minded since he was in the reception class, found school a challenge and Sally knew better than to try and reason with him first thing in the morning so she changed tack.

"Jimmy, have you got a tissue as mum thinks you're starting a cold?"

"No!" replied Jimmy, in a surly tone.

"Here you go then." Sally swiftly produced a tissue for Jimmy, a wet wipe for George and his bag after reassuring him it would soon dry, then secured the lid of Tabitha's drinks bottle.

"Rightiho! Let's go!" Sally declared with forced brightness. She then unclipped seatbelts, allocated book bags, lunch boxes and P.E kits to the appropriate child and off they all trooped across the playground, trepidation, nervousness and apprehension hanging like a cloud above the little group, including Sally.

"Bye bye love, have a good day and I'll see you at home time." Sally turned back to wave at Tabitha and was relieved to see her friend Ellie admiring her new hair bands, the drinks bottle incident thankfully forgotten. Sally hurried out of the classroom, her mind on the next child she was collecting that day when she saw Phoebe, mum of Portia, a little three year old Sally looked after on a Tuesday, disappearing into the adjoining class room where the local playgroup was held.

Phoebe and Sebastian, if ever there was an uber couple then they were it. Phoebe's husband, Sebastian, was incredibly handsome. Women couldn't help but follow his tall fluid frame with unadulterated longing. Immaculately presented, Phoebe and Sebastian together as a couple were a vision of glamour and wealth. They simply oozed confidence, success and sophistication. Phoebe was also a great mum to work with. She was punctual with payments and never took Sally for granted. The only slight hiccup was Phoebe's interpretation of old clothes. Being the only child of Phoebe's who herself was an only child; Portia had an expensive and extensive wardrobe of boutique and designer clothes.

Every Tuesday, Sally would gaze hopelessly at the layered gorgeousness that Portia would be adorned in. She would mentally picture the paints, glue, glitter, chalks and bottles of bubbles that were lurking in the depths of her cupboards and would inwardly groan at Portia's sequinned covered organza tutu that she favoured and which refused to be covered by Sally's aprons.

Sally smiled to herself for the first time that morning at the richness and depth of the human experiences which touched her on a daily basis.

Life was, if a little stressful, certainly never dull.

Sally rounded the corner of Class 1 and was about to cross the playground back to her car when she saw Anna, the other childminder in the village, bustling her group of children towards Sally on her way to the reception class.

"Happy New Year!" They both said in unison.

"Did you have a good one?" Anna asked, bending to catch a dummy hurled from the rear of the tandem she was pushing and with the other hand expertly pulling up the blanket at the front which threatened to end up being tangled beneath the wheels, dirty and wet.

"Oh well rescued, Anna!" admired Sally, "Far too early in the week for the washing to start and yes, lovely thank you. How about you?"

When Sally had first registered as a childminder the increase in her washing had come as a bit of a shock. The blankets and sheets for nap times, a separate set for each child. Sofa covers that needed washing every other week simply due to the amount of human traffic that sat on them on a daily basis not to mention the rugs which saved Sally's carpets from trodden in dropped breadsticks, rice cakes and the occasional toilet accident.

"Not too bad, it's all over so quickly isn't it?...... are you going to toddlers this morning?.....alright Jake, off you go and don't forget to hand your dinner money in, I'll be there in a minute!" Anna ran her hand through been her hair and sighed. "I really could have done with another week....I feel shattered before I've even started the week."

Sally thought how drawn and tired Anna looked. Five years older than Sally she walked everywhere. Sally knew from when her own experience of being temporarily without a car, how tiring it was to walk two school runs a day, plus a midday nursery run whilst pushing a tandem pushchair in all weathers.

"I know just how you feel," Sally agreed, reminded of her financial situation and how mentally draining it was. "Yes, I'm planning on going, I'll see you there and we can catch up then."

Anna smiled wearily,

"Will do, see you later." And she expertly negotiated the tandem through the milling parents and disappeared amongst the throng.

Sally hurried across the playground as she was meeting Julia, Fin's mum, at the car park gates and Spencer was being dropped off at her house at 9.15am.

It would be good to catch up with Anna later on.

They were both in a similar position. The income they earned equated to half the family income. Their money was essential for the survival of their families. Both mothers had sons turning eighteen later on in the year which would be an added expense for both of them. John, Anna's husband, was self employed and his work could be very up and down as, whilst although Nick was employed, his salary just about covered their direct debits and one week's food shop. The rest was left up to Sally.

On reaching her car Sally heard an unmistakeably familiar sound.

She turned to see Julia and Gabe's Land Rover vehicle struggling to manage third gear, failing, and then being forced to stay in second. Its gear box complained with every attempted manoeuvre, along with the engine, which, over the years, seemed to accept its fate. Week in and week out it dutifully coped with the daily abuse its owners, Julia and Gabe inflicted on it.

Sally broke into a jog to open the school gates ready for Julia to drop off Fin before she carried on up to the farm to continue her day of trying to do at least half of the jobs on her to do list that day. Sally unlocked the padlock and pushed open the gates.

"Hey Sally, Happy New Year! Got to dump and run, I've got the accountant coming at 9.15 to go over the figures for the grain yields." Julia called, hurrying up the driveway to the gates with Fin bouncing in her arms, beloved backpack on his arms.

Julia was a warm friendly woman with green eyes and auburn hair which was scraped back into the busy mother's ponytail. Sally took her hat off to her. Although Sally herself regularly worked a twelve hour day she knew Julia's day was far longer. Not only did she have five children to ferry around, she now looked after the business side of the barn since Gabe's dad had passed away suddenly the previous year, as well as often being called upon by Gabe to round up sheep, field walk, deliver lambs, harvest and bale.

"No problem Julia, I'll drop him off at the usual time. Will someone be there at three?"

Julia pulled a face, thinking.

"Uh, yes....yes, if not, Sue will be at home. Thanks so much Sally, have a good time Fin."

She leaned over to kiss Fin then in a flash was back in the Land Rover, grimacing at Sally as she turned the key in the ignition. It dutifully roared into life and Julia's face broke into a broad relieved grin. Sally laughed, gave a thumbs up, then turned to go back up the slope to her car with Fin in her arms.

'Right Fin, let's get this day started....we've got Spencer today and we're all going to toddlers so you're going to have a lovely, busy day."

Sally opened the rear door and peeled the back pack from a reluctant Fin's back.

"I'm not taking it away Fin," reassured Sally, noting the worried expression growing on his little face. "I just need to pop it on the seat next to you whilst I strap you in, ok?"

Fin looked dubious whilst Sally worked like greased lightning to put his arms in the correct straps and clip them together all before Fin started to cry.

8

Fin took a deep breath.

"MY BAG!!!" he bellowed.

"Done!" triumphed Sally, "there you go Fin."

She quickly delivered the bag into the lap of the rapidly pacified Fin.

"What a good boy you are patiently waiting for your bag while I made you safe in my car, mummy would be so proud of you, Fin. Well done."

Fin, a mirror image of his mother and elder brother, Giles, green eyes and brown hair, clasped his precious back pack to his chest as though it had the most valuable treasures in the whole world in it which, of course to Fin, it did!

Anything that caught Fin's eye, however seemingly insignificant, went in his bag. Julia had apologetically returned, on many a morning, Sally's missing T.V remote control, coasters, a framed photograph of one of Sally's children and various toy farm animals to name but a few. In return, Sally had made many a frantic phone call to Julia.

"Did you know Fin has got your....Bobbi Brown lip gloss, mobile phone, Katie's IPod, Gabe's keys....the list was endless.

Fin was an incredibly easy child to mind. The youngest of Julia's five children he fitted in with any group of children Sally had and was kind and nurturing to the younger children. This, Sally was sure, was the influence of Julia's three girls, aged from eleven to seventeen.

All were inept at running the kitchen and day to day life if need be in Julia's absence. They really were a lovely family thought Sally as she drove home.

She pulled onto her drive, a three bed roomed semi on the main road which went through the village when Fin piped up with a cheeky smile.

"Look Sally, Daddy's glasses!"

Sally looked in the rear view mirror at Fin, trying to put on Gabe's glasses upside down, and groaned.

Yet another telephone call to Julia.

Julia pulled up into the farmyard and turned off the engine.

She sat there, decompressing for a few minutes after not one, but three school drop offs.

Her phone beeped a text. Her accountant was running late and wouldn't be at the farm until 10am.

Not wanting to waste her unexpected extra hour she thought she'd pop round to see her mother in law, Sue, who lived in the main farmhouse on the farm and have a cup of tea with her.

Julia lived for her husband, Gabe, and her five children and truly loved her life, but the logistics of running the farm, the labourers, their wages, disputes, machinery when it broke down and organising the ever growing social lives of their children as they grew up was a military operation. It worked well enough if everyone played ball and were ready to leave or be picked up at the time they were meant to leave or be picked up, but if they weren't, or a vehicle that had Gabe left Julia with for the day as the farm workers were using the others, broke down, which was a frequent occurrence, then the whole day could quite easily go pear shaped.

She rose at 5.30am every morning to make five packed lunches then take her eldest daughter, Lucy, to the bus stop a mile away to catch the 7.15am bus to the grammar school fifteen miles away. She then returned home and fed the remaining four children their breakfast, took three of them to the school in the next village, as was their family tradition, then met Sally at the gates of St Michael's to drop off Fin.

A whirlwind of activity and the day was only just starting.

Julia had hated the initial thought of leaving Fin, although only for three short days a week, but Gabe's dad dying had forced her hand.

She simply couldn't do it all.

She had known Sally for years as Sally's eldest, Chris, now seventeen, had attended nursery with Julia's eldest daughter, Lucy and they had often seen each other at toddler groups and discussed niceties such as sleep patterns, (theirs, not the children's), money worries and what bugs were doing the rounds, all over a coffee that wasn't made by them, heaven!

Using Sally as a childminder had actually been suggested by a neighbour of Julia's, Fleur, who lived down the lane from Julia.

Many an evening, Fleur had had to phone Sally to say she would be late due to road works, a car accident or a school club that needed to be covered due to staff sickness. She knew Tristan would be safe, warm, fed and snuggled under a blanket on Sally's old, threadbare but comfortable sofa on top of cushions and cuddling a chosen soft toy watching 'Come Outside', a firm favourite, alongside Sally or one of Sally's boys who were always on hand to reassure a child if a mum was unexpectedly delayed.

Over coffee one morning with a tearful Julia she had suggested seeing if Sally could look after Fin for a few hours one day a week so she could get her head down and do some paperwork. Julia had blown her nose and agreed that maybe that would be the most sensible option for her sanity so, after a chat with Sally outside Fleur's one evening, it was agreed that Sally would mind Fin one day a week from 9-3.

Much to Julia's relief Fin loved going to Sally's and often had his bag packed ready for the day asking Julia if he was going to Sally's that day. It was a good sign that Sally was doing what Julia paid her to do, care for and mentally stimulate her child with play, activities and stories in his mother's absence.

Slamming the door of the Land Rover shut, she gave it an extra shove to make sure it was securely shut then walked briskly past the stables and out of the farmyard bearing left.

She passed a yard filled with farm machinery then through a pair of large wooden gates which led onto the drive to what was the original farm house.

Julia spotted her mother in law at the rear of the property, an old straw hat on her head, walking slowly down the garden, pushing an old petrol lawnmower which she simply refused to upgrade.

"Sue?...Sue?.." Julia called but Sue couldn't hear over the droning of the ancient mower. Not wanting to startle her she waited until Sue paused to turn the mower to return back up towards the house. The mower came to a quiet tick over as Sue did a slow awkward 180 degree turn so Julia tried again.

"Sue, hi there!..Sue!"

Sue looked up quickly and her sixty six year old face broke into a welcoming smile. She lifted an arm and waved.

"Julia, darling! How lovely to see you. I thought the accountant was visiting this morning? Are you stopping for a cup of tea?" Sue briskly moved towards Julia who in turn was striding towards her mother in law with open arms.

"That would be lovely, Sue, but after I've finished the lawn for you." Julia firmly took possession of the handle of the lawn mower which by now had stalled and was silent. "Perhaps you could rustle up a couple of chocolate biscuits too, I haven't had any breakfast yet?" cajoled Julia.

"Oh tsk, tsk," exclaimed Sue, "you can't start the day on an empty stomach young lady! Right I'll make the tea and rustle up some cake while you finish the lawn, so kind of you darling. It's always bigger than I think when I set out to mow it." And she turned on her heel and walked towards the house to provide sustenance for her daughter in law, just like she used to for her beloved husband and children, now passed on and all grown up.

Julia quickly finished off the lawn and pushed the mower to the open door of the shed that sat in the far left hand corner of the garden. She made a mental note to speak to Gabe about the mower. It absolutely terrified Julia. She was sure she could persuade Gabe to offer to mow the lawn one day and discover it was 'broken'. She shut the shed door and turned around to head back up the path to the kitchen where a welcome cup of tea and some home baked delight would be waiting.

"All done" Julia stopped in her tracks in the door way leading through into the farm house kitchen.

Sue was lost in thought, slowly stirring a cup of tea, staring at a photograph that stood on the low kitchen window sill.

It was of Sue and her late husband, John, laughing together at the camera, a glass of red wine a piece, looking together like one, two halves that didn't look quite right unless they were together.

Forty two years of marriage did that to a couple.

Their marriage had produced two sons, a daughter, ten grandchildren to date and a profitable working farm, that they had run together as a team. Sue had helped out with all aspects of the running of the farm be it delivering piglets in the middle of the night or organising a new tyre for the combine harvester mid harvest, as John had done umpteen school runs, doctors' appointments and read stories in the middle of the night to feverish children.

They had been a team....one.

Julia could only try to imagine the empty hole that ached inside Sue now. The twilight years, spent by yourself after a lifetime of togetherness. Julia had, at night, often tried to put herself in Sue's shoes. No Gabe, the children all grown up and moved on, treasured pets passed away, and she just couldn't. To her, in her late thirties, the loss seemed unimaginable.

Sue suddenly yawned, shook herself and gave a last quick stir of the spoon. Julia then carried on into the kitchen.

"Late night, last night Sue?" she asked, and carried on without pause at the sight of cake by the mugs of tea. "Ooo, coffee cake! Wonderful! Just what I need!" and with that Julia scooped up a generous wedge of coffee cake with butter icing and bit into it hungrily.

"Not too late, but it's the third night I've been slug catching. It's been so wet I'd thought I'd get ahead this year and look under the rockery where they hibernate to try and cut back on the hoards we seem to get every year."

Sue took a sip of her tea and smiled wistfully at Julia. Julia nodded and gently offered.

"Are you managing or would you like some happy helpers? I'm sure my lot could take over on a rota basis if it's too much for you."

"That's kind darling, is your cake alright? It's a couple of days old."

"Gorgeous," answered Julia truthfully, "just what my stomach ordered."

She finished the cake, wiped her fingers on a piece of kitchen towel and turned her attention to her mug of strong sweet tea and exhaled. She really could stay here all morning. Although only just around the corner from her house, which was two workmen's cottages knocked into one to accommodate her growing family, it had an air of calm and peace which were two words that could not be said of her home.

"Seriously, Sue, we can all take it in turns slug hunting. If we have a couple of glasses of wine while we're at it, get tipsy and fall over we could probably kill quite a few in one go. That was John's tactic if I remember rightly," Julia laughed.

Sue shot her a look, dropped her eyes, took a sip of tea and sighed.

"It certainly was...."

Sue's gaze turned to the window that was adjacent to the rear window of the house. It looked over the vegetable patch that she and John had tended over the many years of bringing up a family. Again, her thoughts wandered. Each year, as the children had grown bigger along with their appetites, the small vegetable patch had grown bigger and bigger and held a wide variety of vegetables to accommodate the children's favourites. Each year, normally in spring when night fell they would venture out into the garden, torch helmets on and a cup of salt in one hand, red wine in the other, would dispose of the slugs that loved to feast on fledgling leaves doing untold damage to the year's crop.

Julia walked quietly past her mother in law to the teapot to refill her mug and waited patiently for Sue to mentally return. Once more, Sue's thoughts returned to the present day.

"Goodness me, being tired is making me very day dreamy! Cut me a piece of that cake, Julia, there's a pet. I need the sugar..... right!" Sue announced decisively, stabbing the piece of cake with a fork. "We'll have another cup of tea and then I must get on. I've got some errands I need to run in the village. Do you need anything posting dear?"

Julia poured some milk into the bottom of Sue's mug.

"No, I'm good thanks, I'll drink this then wait for the accountant, he's due at ten."

She glanced at the clock; it was a quarter to ten. Better drink this quick, she thought and maybe take a slice of Sue's cake to offer, she'd used the last of hers in the five lunch boxes she'd packed this morning.

It never hurt to offer cake, especially to someone who you want to save you money.

As if Sue could read her mind she said,

"Take the rest of the cake with you dear, it really needs to be eaten up today."

Walking back around to her family's cottages, Julia reflected on Sue's pensive mood.

John's passing had been quick after a short illness last year in the early hours of the morning. The whole family had been rocked by their mainstay's passing. Gabe, Sue's eldest son, took charge, handling the funeral plans, informing his father's wide circle of friends and contacts but Julia knew his world had imploded.

Gabe, very like his father, had quite simply worshipped him.

From a very young age, John had been the only person that had influenced him. Sue had loved and nurtured them all but it was to John that he told his every action, his every experience lived, tried and experimented with. Gabe had taken on board his knowledge, advice and constructive criticism and acted on it.

Julia had entered the kitchen late one evening three weeks after John's funeral and found Gabe sitting in their faded armchair next to the fire, a glass of brandy in his hand, staring into the flames, silently crying.

Julia had quietly turned around and climbed the old battered staircase to bed.

Sometimes, the grieving, the remembering, needed to be done alone.

She had turned off the electric blanket and lay waiting for Gabe to eventually come to bed and into her arms, so they could remember together.

Sally

Sally left the downstairs bathroom after helping Fin wash his hands, walked through the lobby which housed the washing machine, tumble drier and fridge freezer and into the kitchen to pop the kettle on.

She opened the cupboard to get two mugs down when the door bell rang. That will be Spencer, Sally thought as she hurried to the front door.

Spencer was the second child of Mrs Banks, the reception teacher at St Michael's, who Sally had minded from the age of five months. Her first son Hugh, although intelligent, an early crawler, early walker and talker, had not thrown anything at Sally that she hadn't seen before on the child development front. Spencer, however, had completely re-written the book. Not only had he crawled, walked and talked early, he had climbed....before he could walk. Not content to leave it at that, he was a problem solver as well which had left Sally, at times over the past year and a half, a complete frazzled wreck after a Spencer day.

Climbing a sheer wall to reach an object on a far reaching shelf or on top of a cupboard posed no obstacle for Spencer. He would simply survey his surroundings and find a large object that could be pushed, pulled or shoved to the wall to enable him to reach the desired object.

Sally's need to colour her hair had really started, she remembered with a wry smile, when she found Spencer, before he could walk at eight months, on his hands and knees on her kitchen table, clutching the target that morning, a banana! He'd looked so proud of himself and looked at Sally as though she should too! Watching Spencer later that day Sally realised he had pulled himself up on her church pews by sheer strength, determination and willpower with absolutely no fear for his safety or Sally's Ofsted registration!

After having settled Fin and Spencer at the table with some Playdoh cutters and various tools, Sally sorted out the children's bits and pieces.

Daily diaries, to record their day at Sally's, were out ready on the worktop, camera and pogo printer were switched on to use as photographic evidence of any developments in their learning that day and lunch boxes were popped in the fridge. Looking at the clock in the kitchen Sally decided against a cup of tea, she would wait for the one that would be served at the Ladybird's toddler group later that morning.

It was one of Sally's favourite toddler groups as it was spread out over three rooms, which were very light and airy being a modern building and which had a great assortment of toys, puzzles and ride ons. They had a nursery rhyme session half way through the morning followed by a drink and biscuit for the children and a mug, not a cup, of tea or coffee for the mums and carers. It was a lovely start to the week.

Sally had just finished squeezing a Peppa Pig and Tractor Ted lunch box into the fridge when the phone rang. Sally glanced through to the conservatory and saw Fin and Spencer pressing beads into Playdoh as cakes.

"Dis ones for yooo Fin!" lisped Spencer, his big blue eyes filled with worship for his older Monday companion.

"I don't like cake, only my mum's cake!" declared Fin. Spencer looked crestfallen. Sally intervened quickly, phone still ringing.

"It's only a pretend cake and how kind of Spencer to make it for you! It would be really kind to say thank you to Spencer, Fin."

Fin looked very sceptical whilst Spencer's wobbling lip threatened to give way to a wail. Sally answered the phone.

"Hello, could you hold the line please, I won't be a moment?"

She turned to Fin again.

"Fin, please say thank you, Mummy and Granny would want you to." Fin looked defiant, Sally tried again, "and Giles your big brother....." she trailed off waiting. At the mention of Giles, Fin's six year old elder brother, Fin looked at Spencer and said begrudgingly,

"Thank you."

Spencer looked appeased and with a flourish of goodwill said,

"Me make Fin another cake!"

"Hello, hello... sorry about that?"

Sally went back to the phone call whilst standing in the doorway to the conservatory to keep an eye on the boys.

"Hi Sally, it's only me..."

'Me' was Sally's friend, Millie. Sally didn't mind for Millie, they had met at a toddler group a few years ago when Millie's youngest son, Drew, was still at nursery. Although the women had different ideas on child rearing they respected each other and each helped the other laugh at their flaws.

"Hi Millie..."

Sally looked at the clock; she really had to get a move on. "Is everything alright?"

"Yes Sally! Couldn't be better! I know you can't talk now but last night I stumbled across this article on Chinese mothering..." Sally closed her eyes, leaned against the wall and inwardly groaned. "... and I feel that this way of parenting is the perfect vehicle for Jane and Drew to achieve their full potential." Millie paused for breath.

"Crikey, Millie! I've heard about it, but isn't it a little, well, intense?"

"YES! Yes it is!" Millie sounded triumphant. "That's the beauty of it, anyway, I won't hold you up any longer, you're probably off to toddlers in a mo, but we must catch up soon, when can you manage?"

Sally turned and scanned her diary.

"That sounds lovely, Millie, can we say maybe next week though, the first week back after the holidays is always a bit hectic?"

"Lovely Sally, sorry to take up your time, have a good week and keep those stress levels in check now."

"Bye Millie, speak soon."

Sally replaced the phone in to its charger and drew a deep breath. Chinese parenting. Well, Millie did love to have a project on the go but Sally couldn't really picture her as an all out Tiger mother! She mentally put a seat belt on. She felt that maybe this term, she was going to need it.

Millie

Millie had put down the phone from Sally and was now sitting at her kitchen table, laptop open, scanning the books section on Amazon.

There it was, 'Battle hymn of the Tiger Mother' by Amy Chung. This was going to be her Bible from now on. She had no doubt that this book held all the answers to all the questions she had on raising motivated, obedient, educated children. This way of life was the way forward, the route to success, the yellow brick road to top set positions and A*'s.

Millie paused, her index finger poised to click the 'Buy now' icon. She thought back to Sally's brief comment. Intense was the word she'd used wasn't it? Millie had a fleeting moment of doubt about her new venture which was then gone as soon as it had arrived.

The Chinese didn't seem to worry about a child's happiness or self esteem. In fact the opposite was true if the article in last week's newspaper was anything to go by.

Millie suddenly had another thought and frowned to herself. She hoped getting Darius, her husband, on board with the change in lifestyle wasn't going to be too much of an issue. She made a mental note to next visit the Ann Summers website. Maybe she would buy a Chinese influenced all in one corset with all the extras that men, including Darius, never failed to be aroused by.

Undaunted, she firmly clicked 'Buy' and felt a wave of satisfaction flood through her. She sat back, picked up her coffee cup, and thought back to her own childhood.

It had been idyllic. An only child, she had been worshipped by both her parents who, unashamedly, had spoilt her rotten. Her parents had been so grateful to finally be blessed with a child in their early forties, when they had all but given up, that they had expected nothing from her academically at all. They were just thrilled that their only child was growing up able bodied, healthy and with an easy going nature.

The fact that she was extremely attractive was a bonus she was eternally grateful for. She possessed thick, dark wavy hair which could easily be straightened, piercing blue eyes and a naturally slim but curvy figure.

Just as well, thought Millie to herself with a wry smile, as she rose to pour a fresh mug of coffee before she started browsing the Ann Summers website. Her brain might not have been the reason that kept Darius captivated after their initial meeting, but her smile, wit and willingness to go the extra mile in the bedroom had certainly helped clinch the 'ring on the finger' deal in her mind.

What Millie failed to grasp was that Darius had became her husband because he had completely and utterly fallen in love with her the first time he had laid eyes on her.

Millie had met Darius at a bar she had been moonlighting at one Friday evening. During the day she worked at an estate agent which she absolutely loathed initially. The men in the office were obscenely competitive and would literally barge Millie out of the way with aggressive elbows as they leapt out from behind their desks, desperate to be the first negotiator to greet any potential homebuyers that walked through the door. They all had mortgages to pay, young families to provide for and every commission earned on a house sale helped boost their meagre salaries.

It was just not in Millie's nature to be ruthless. She had applied for a job as a secretary but the manager had other plans. At Millie's interview he could see what a visual asset Millie would be to the front office and had persuaded a reluctant Millie to cover a negotiator on maternity leave.

It had been a quiet time of year and house sales were thin on the ground. With Millie's lack of competitiveness and being paid a very small basic salary, her funds were running low so it had been necessary to supplement her income working weekend evenings at a trendy wine bar, 'Eve', which was conveniently situated around the corner from the estate agent.

The night she'd met Darius she'd felt wrecked. It was the second day of her period, her hair felt lank and lack lustre and she'd finished late at the office due to a no show viewing. Millie had waited around for half an hour. Fruitlessly, she repeatedly tried the mobile phone number she had for the client; it just kept going to voicemail. Millie felt powerless. She was desperate for a sale, the office was desperate for a sale and the vendors were desperate for a sale. After thirty five wasted minutes, Millie cursed under her breath and admitted defeat. It was pointless going home now; she may as well go back to the office, have a coffee, reapply her makeup and go straight to Eve's. Millie got back in her car, leaned back in her seat and wished for the millionth time she hadn't dreamt her way through secondary school.

A couple of hours later, Millie's shift at Eve's was in full swing. The wine bar was packed with smart young professionals eager to say goodbye to their working week. Millie felt confident she would be finished in another hour or so when she could finally escape home to a hot bath and a glass of red wine before bed.

"Millie?" called Mike, the young bar manager who thrived on the slight hysteria of the weekend trade, "drinks for table eight are ready, you'll have to come back for the bread and olives, Susie's just plating them up."

"On my way, Mike!" Millie hurried to the bar, weaving in and out of the suited bodies muttering 'excuse me' and 'sorry' as she went. She picked up the chit to double check the table number then gingerly turned with the tray, taking care not to spill the large glasses of red wine.

Two men were sitting at table eight, top buttons undone and ties loosened, typical Friday night attire. They both looked up as Millie approached, smiling. She started to say,

"Two glasses of red wine?" but she stopped..... still.

Both men had looked up but Millie only saw one.

Their eyes locked.

Time stopped.

Millie felt as if she had been hit by a force with such intensity she couldn't move.

Her surroundings seemed muted.

She could not tear herself away from staring into the eyes of their owner.

Brown eyes so deep that Millie felt she was falling into them.

Millie forced herself to shut her eyes and purposefully shook herself out of the trance she had been momentarily trapped in.

She opened her eyes and found the owner of the brown eyes smiling and now standing in front of her, reaching to take the glasses of wine from the tray.

"Thank you," he said gently, but with a tone of wonderment, as though he was actually seeing and processing the information at the same time. He put his glass down on his table, handing his colleague the other, and held out his right hand to introduce himself. "I'm Darius; I'm an interior designer and work just around the corner from here. If you would allow me, I would like to take you out for a drink so we can discuss what sort of wedding you would like and how many children we should have."

His eyes held hers.

Steadfast.

With no hint of humour behind their gaze.

Millie robotically lifted her hand to shake his outstretched hand, struggling to take on board what she had just heard.

Their hands touched, clasped.

A jolt of electricity flooded her entire body.

Darius's pupils involuntarily widened.

He had felt it too.

Millie tried to maintain a calm, dignified persona and act as though being proposed to was a regular Friday night occurrence.

"Ha!....very funny! Ok, right, I'm just going to see if your olives and bread are ready..."

Millie withdrew her hand, completely unnerved by her body's reaction to this complete stranger and turned to go.

"Wait, I'm serious!" Darius was now in front of Millie, blocking her path back to the sanctuary of the bar. He whipped out a business card and pen from his rear trouser pocket. "Please.... may I have your telephone number?" He flipped over the card, pen poised.

Millie just stood there, overwhelmed with the strength of her feelings and felt a wave of nausea ride over her.

I really should have eaten something with that coffee earlier, she thought to herself then everything went black.

Millie smiled to herself as she poured herself another mug of coffee and went back to the laptop. She let herself indulge in the memories of that first night that Darius had come into her life and laid claim to her.

After Millie had come round from her mortifying fainting spell, Darius had insisted on taking her home. Suzie, the other waitress who was working that night, who watched more than was healthy of NCIS, insisted on accompanying them in the taxi on the way to Millie's flat. Once there, Suzie reluctantly accepted that a kidnap, rape, murder situation wasn't about to take place, after Darius had willingly confirmed various personal and contact details verified by his bemused parents, and took the taxi back to the wine bar, paid for by Darius, much to the relief of the now frantic Mike who had suddenly found himself two waitresses down on a busy Friday night, not the best way to start the weekend!

Darius had taken Millie's key from her and opened the door to the flat. He took Millie's hand and led her down the hallway, and pushing open the first door he came to, led Millie into her own sitting room. He led her to the settee and they sat down.

"Well, I know your name is Millie," Darius said softly. He leant over and gently kissed her on the lips. Millie let herself be kissed. Darius leaned back. Millie felt she was floating up, looking down on herself, watching a scene play out in a film she was starring in, very surreal.

"As I said, my name is Darius, I'm twenty nine years old and as you already know, thanks to Suzie's very thorough interrogation, I am one of three sons to my Mum and Dad, Jane and Graham. I'm an interior designer and thoroughly enjoy what I do. I'm hoping to set up on my own some day." Darius paused, shifted closer to Millie and leant forward looking earnest. He continued, "I'm a one woman man. I've had two fairly serious relationships whilst at university, a few not so serious ones in the early days. I have never asked anyone to marry me," he paused again, "until now." Darius took Millie's hand, "Millie, I don't play games, we are meant to be together and if you give me a chance I will prove it to you."

Once again, his eyes held hers, confident, self assured but not arrogant and full of, could it be possible, love?

Millie just stared back, completely shell shocked and, not that she wanted to admit it to herself during this incredibly moving, life changing moment, absolutely starving!

Darius appeared to have read her mind.

"Right, first things first!" he said practically. He pulled down a blanket from the back of the sofa. He scooped her legs up onto the sofa and deftly shook out the blanket and covered her legs with it. He gently pushed her back against the arm and propped a cushion behind her back.

"Won't be a minute," and in the blink of an eye Darius had left the sitting room. Seconds later Millie heard bath taps running, footsteps then went into her kitchen. Cupboards were opened and closed, the fridge delved onto and glasses chinked.

Minutes later, the smell of eggs cooking wafted through into the sitting room where Millie's stomach was now growling loudly with hunger.

"Right, this should hold off any further fainting spells for the rest of the evening," and with that Darius placed a tray of ham and tomato omelette and a glass of red wine onto Millie's lap. "I'll just turn the bath off." He flipped a tea towel over his left shoulder and turned and left the room.

Millie followed his movements, subconsciously taking in his frame, tall, lithe, but not wiry, with nice shoulders. He had an easy grace and seemed to blend into her flat as though he had always been there.

Millie turned her gaze to the omelette. It was beyond belief. Here she was, sitting on her settee having had her supper cooked for her by a complete stranger! It was crazy! Absolutely crazy. Then why did it feel so normal?

She cut a piece of omelette and put it in her mouth. Good lord, she really should make omelettes more often.

Darius hovered in the doorway.

Millie lowered her fork.

"This is great Darius, thank you so much. You've been very kind....." Millie ventured shyly, she trailed off. Their eyes held.

"I'm going to go now." He said quietly.

Millie nodded.

"May I take you out tomorrow night?"

Millie nodded again. Darius walked over to the sofa and crouched down so they were now face to face.

"I meant what I said earlier. Can I pick you up at 7.30?"

"That would be perfect....and thank you again, for tonight." Millie replied softly.

His eyes, liquid brown, look deep into hers and with that parting comment he leant over and kissed her for the last time on the first time that they had met.

Millie's eyes filled with tears as she remembered.

It had quite simply been a fairytale romance.

Ten months after dating, Millie meeting his parents and Darius meeting hers, they had married at the village church near where her parents lived. A simple but stylish wedding, Millie's idea's had deftly been put into action and made a reality by Darius, his eye for detail gently polishing her ideas.

Millie typed in Anne Summers on the laptop and waited for it to load.

Deep down Millie felt that she just wasn't quite good enough for Darius, that one day he would wake up, come to his senses and realise that she wasn't as captivating as he had originally thought and walk out of her life as abruptly as he'd entered it.

By embarking on this 'Chinese mothering' way of parenting, Darius couldn't help but be impressed by her mothering skills and realise how seriously she took her role as a mother.

Still, it wouldn't hurt to have some oil, in the form of night time attire, to pour over any potential troubled waters that may arise in the early stages of her Chinese project, so Millie spent the hour filling her online basket with exotic underwear and accessories so that Darius would find hard to refuse her anything, or so she hoped.

Nick heard Sally call out, "Bye love," and shut the front door. He walked out of the bathroom, across the landing, into Jack's room, which was at the front of the house, and opened the window.

'Bye love, see you tonight,' he called. Sally turned, looked up at Nick, smiled and waved and got in the front seat of the car and shut the door. Nick just heard Spencer saying,

'I will be thensible Sally, I promise.'

Nick smiled to himself. Spencer was a little poppet; you just had to have one eye and ear on him all the time. Nick knew that Sally was certainly kept on her toes with him.

Back in the bathroom Nick looked at himself in the mirror to see if he could get away with not shaving today and decided he could. He reached for the toothpaste and his thoughts turned to Sally and how childminding had turned their lived around for the better.

Previous to becoming a childminder, Sally had spent six years working as a teaching assistant in a primary school. She had thoroughly enjoyed the job and it had fitted in perfectly with family life as she had the school holidays off.

Things started to unravel though when their middle son, Jack, started Year Eight. He would develop headaches, become lethargic and just sleep all the time. A 'virus' the doctor had said after all his blood tests came back clear. It was of course wonderful news that it was nothing serious but it meant that Sally would end up having four or five days off every half term.

Although her school had been very supportive Sally would feel riddled with guilt so, after one particularly stressful half term, Sally had declared during tea one Friday evening that she was going to hand in her notice and register as a childminder.

Nick, he remembered, hadn't been keen at first on other people's children stomping in and out the house, coming and going every day and he tried his best to talk her out of her seemingly sudden decision. What Nick hadn't realised was that Sally had been thinking about registering as a childminder for several months. Anna, Sally's neighbour two doors along from them, was a childminder and had come round that evening and over a glass of wine had helped Nick see that it would really be a positive move for the whole family.

First and foremost, Sally would be home for their three boys whenever the need arose, if they were unwell, or if the school had a non pupil day. Not to mention being around for deliveries and repair men. The benefits were endless for a mum with a family, who needed to bring in an income and who, of course, enjoyed working with children. Financially too, the rewards could be great. The previous year, Anna had grossed over £22,500. At that, Nick's eyebrows had shot up. Anna had laughed and informed him that that figure was achieved working five days a week from 6.30am until 6pm.

Thanks to Anna's input, Nick had gradually come round to the idea and now fully sung the praises of Sally childminding. The flexibility it gave their family was invaluable, especially now Chris was at college. He needed picking up at 5.15pm from the nearby town of Folkstead so Sally just popped the children into the car to collect him and if needed, dropped children off home on the way back.

Nick walked downstairs to make a cup of coffee before he left for his late shift. It had been a bit of a shock losing Simon just after Christmas. Things would be more tight than usual this January as they, like many families, had overspent at Christmas. Perhaps he could pick up some extra shifts at work. Fedex had been his dream job ever since he was a seven year old boy. A Fedex van had delivered to him a present from an Aunt in Australia and the moment his mother had handed him the parcel with one hand and signed for it with the other, Nick had been captivated and utterly mesmerised with the mystical prowess of the Fedex man and his van. To bring that much joy and wonder to someone had convinced the seven year old Nick there and then that that was the career for him.

A bit daft now he was forty eight, he thought to himself with a wry smile.

Nick spooned the coffee into his mug and poured in the water, then the milk. As he stirred his coffee, lost in thought about disillusioned childhood dreams, his mobile phone beeped. Tonight's driver was calling in sick. Nick sighed. He took two slugs of his coffee and poured the rest down the sink. Better get in early and try to get a head start. It would probably mean he would end up covering the shift tonight, oh well; the money would come in useful he thought to himself. He walked through the house to the front door to put his boots on, bracing himself for a day dealing with driver's absence, lost parcels and van breakdowns.

Phoebe Whitehall turned around to double check their bathroom before she turned the lights off.

Her eyes scanned the blind.

It was perfectly aligned with the fourth tile from the top of the window. The cord twisted four times in a figure of eight around the hook hanging to the right of it. Colour co ordinate towels hung folded to a width of 40cm each. The ruler to measure and check the towels was kept in her bathroom cabinet above her sink.

Phoebe frowned, the bathroom cabinets!

She hurried over to the elegant slim line bathroom cabinets above hers and Sebastian's basins and opened them.

The toothbrushes were facing to the right in their glass beakers, no water marks on the beakers and the toiletries stood grouped together in fours.

Phoebe exhaled with relief.

She didn't want a repeat of last month's outcome from her failure to check the cabinets. The bruise on her thigh had just about disappeared but the memory of its cause hadn't.

Surveying the bathroom one last time, she walked slowly backwards towards the door. Finally satisfied, she reached up for the light switch, turned off the lights and shut the door.

How had she, had her life, got to this stage?

She turned around and called across the vast landing in the direction of her daughter's bedroom.

"Portia, darling! Let's go!"

Negotiating the narrow entrance of the drive to the local village hall, Sally slowly drove up and swung right, onto a parking space.

'Tobblers!' shouted Fin

Spencer craned his head towards the church, a modern building which was not only the venue for the Ladybird toddler group but also for 'Coffee and Scones' on a Thursday morning and a flourishing Farmers market every fourth Saturday of the month.

The toddler group was run by the village vicar, David Carson and two church wardens, Joy and Bessie. It was run like clockwork by the trio and if a mum or carer needed to change a nappy they would ensure the sibling was kept an eye on in mum's absence. After nursery rhymes, coffee and cake, Joy and Bessie would set up a seasonal craft activity, making sure every child had a turn and went home with a piece of craft they had (almost) done by themselves. It was a firm favourite with Sally, Anna not to mention the other mums, grannies and carers in the village.

Sally got out of the car, swung her 'toddlers' bag over her back and velcroed the straps together across her body. The toddler bag was used by Sally throughout the week to carry changes of clothes for whoever she had that day along with nappies, cream, wipes, disposable gloves, drinks, bread sticks, travel first aid kit, nappy sacks and Sally's mobile phone, purse and keys.

It was less cumbersome than taking two or three changing bags everywhere and had stopped the tiresome scenario of Sally leaving her phone, purse or both in a child's changing bag and not realising until the evening when she needed to fill the car with petrol or buy last minute essentials from the Co op.

She unclipped Spencer and Fin from their car seats then, firmly holding their chubby little hands, they all walked into toddlers for a morning of play, craft, singing and socialising.

"Good morning Sally! Good morning Spencer and Fin, lovely to see you. Now let's go and find your names on the board shall we? Then we'll know you're here!" boomed David with a warm smile. He was a well rounded sixty something man with white hair and a bushy white beard who vaguely reminded Sally of Father Christmas.

"Thank you, David," Sally smiled back, unstrapping her bag, "I'll just sign in and pay."

"No worries, come on boys..."

Fin and Spencer happily went with David, content and secure in the familiarity and safety of their Monday morning routine.

Sally found a spare chair and shoved her back pack underneath and sat down with a 'humph.' She surveyed the main room for her charges. Spencer and Fin were both engrossed with the Early Learning Centre garage comprising of three storeys, a working lift and umpteen cars. Wonderful! Sally sat back in her chair and her eye caught Anna coming through the door. Anna quickly scanned the room, saw Sally, waved, paid and signed her name in double quick time and was sitting down next to Sally in the blink of an eye.

"Phew! I didn't think I was going to get here!" exclaimed Anna, 'Jamie did a number two just as we were leaving, Chloe tripped over thin air just as I was changing Jamie so I had to fill in the accident book, then John phoned to tell me there's no work today so he's coming home! Another day's wages not coming in!" Anna took a deep breath and sighed deeply, "I didn't know whether to spend the £2 on coming here."

Sally knew exactly how Anna felt.

"Oh Anna, I'm so sorry, there's always something isn't there? Did you hear Simon's not coming to me anymore?"

Anna looked shocked.

"No! When?"

"I found out three days after Boxing Day," replied Sally. It was now Anna's turn to look sympathetic, she knew only too well the effect a child suddenly leaving could have on the family finances.

"God, Sally, I am so sorry!"

Although John's work was up and down, he did have the potential to earn really good money if the work was there and he didn't mind doing a six or seven day week, whereas Nick's job, although fairly secure, had capped overtime with no real scope for promotion, unless Nick was prepared to uproot his family to follow it, which he wasn't.

Nick's own father had been in the Royal Air Force and it was not uncommon for Nick not to see his dad for six months at a time. Nick attended boarding school, which although he said he enjoyed at the time, he knew when Chris was born that that wasn't the sort of father he wanted to be. He wanted to put his children to bed every night, read them bedtime stories and stand on the sidelines at football to cheer them on.

"It's just never ending! We seem to go one step forward and two steps back," Sally paused, "or maybe we just try and do too much with the money we do have coming in?" Sally grimaced.

She tried not to moan, she really did, and she knew how lucky she was in the big scheme of things. She had a husband who was fit and healthy who came home to her every night, three healthy sons and a roof over her head. It just felt like sometimes she was walking through treacle in big heavy boots, just to get through the month.

Anna nodded in agreement.

"I know just what you mean, we have just paid the last instalment for the car last month and we thought, great, we can start reducing the overdraft and then at the weekend, the boiler started to leak." Anna pulled a face. "I just keep emptying the bowl underneath and hope it will stop."

Sally had a thought.

"Anna, have you phoned Phil down Boulders Terrace?"

Anna shook her head.

'No, John's going to look at it today, now he's coming home. If he can't fix it, we'll ring Phil."

Sally knew from experience how expensive boiler repairs could be. Two years ago their boiler had been declared null and void three days before Christmas to the tune of £1900. Fortunately, they had an offset mortgage and enough of a facility to borrow into. The bank had been sympathetic and the person Sally spoke to exclaimed, 'Ouch!' when Sally told him the amount to transfer and what it was for. Ouch indeed, Sally had thought at the time.

They had given each other I.O.U's that year for Christmas. A back rub for Sally and a night's viewing of football for Nick, uninterrupted by Sally or the boys unless it was to get Nick a beer or refill his peanut bowl.

"Sally! It's thong time!" shouted Spencer excitedly from across the room.

"Songs!" Fin screeched and they both ran in their stompy preschool way through to the next room. Sally smiled and got up from her chair.

"Coming boys," she turned to Anna who was now undoing little Daisy's body warmer as steam was literally coming off her.

"I'm not hot!" declared a red faced Daisy, who looked most indignant at being derobed from her body warmer and brand new Hello Kitty cardigan.

Sally took one look at Daisy's bright pink cheeks, smiled at Anna and said,

"I'll see you in there."

Anna rolled her eyes and replied,

"Hopefully!"

Sally hurried through the doorway to the middle room where twenty or so expectant little preschool faces of varying shapes, sizes and colours were waiting for song time to begin. Joy, who was lead nursery rhyme singer today, sat in her chair with a bright red song bag on her lap. Sally sat down in a spare chair opposite Fin and Spencer and felt a wave of contentment wash over her and was reminded of why she loved being a childminder, which she sorely needed at the moment. Their eyes were fixed on Joy and the red bag which held nursery rhyme cards and various toys which helped bring the nursery rhymes to life. The leaders were so well prepared. They had numerous ducks, frogs, spiders, cotton reels and other props to ensure every child had a turn of holding a toy through an enthusiastic rendition of 'Five Little Ducks,' 'Incey Wincey Spider' and many more songs.

Anna finally came through, just in time to join in with the last of the songs carrying a downcast, though cooler looking Daisy, who looked on the verge of a fresh flood of tears. Joy, as astute as ever, swiftly delved into the song bag and fished out a handful of ducks.

"Ah Daisy, lovely to see you! Here, we're going to sing Five Little Ducks before we do the Hokey Kokey, so you can take this one."

"Thank you" Anna mouthed to Joy and sat Daisy, her Hello Kitty cardigan incident temporarily forgotten, next to Fin and Spencer and plonked herself down next to Sally, worn out already before lunchtime on a Monday from financial worries and a reasoned tactical debate with a three year old over the suitability of wearing a cardigan indoors, albeit one with a Hello Kitty logo on it!

The rest of the toddler session passed off with little drama. Fin wet himself , unusual as he was toilet trained, but Sally had learnt through experience that when a child hadn't been with her over the holidays, the new routine and excitement of seeing old friends made bodily functions low down on the list of priorities.

"You must listen to your body, Fin,"

Sally gently reminded him as she pulled on her disposable gloves and pulled out a nappy sack, gingerly placing the wet clothes inside.

"I did Sally, but I couldn't hear it saying anything coz I was playing with Spencer at the Playdoh table!" His big green eyes were so earnest in delivering his 3 year old logic.

Sally smiled to herself.

"Alright love, don't worry, we'll soon have you in dry clothes and you'll all be set to carrying on playing."

Two minutes later, Fin was back with Spencer at the Playdoh table, not fazed at all by the slight delay in his play.

The rest of Sally's first day back after the Christmas break was soon over. She didn't have any children after school on a Monday so, after dropping Fin back at the farm to and delivering Spencer to school for Mrs Banks, Sally stopped off at the Co op for some potatoes and mushrooms to go with tonight's sausages. She'd refrained from doing a Tesco shop so soon after Christmas and in the light of Simon leaving. If there were any sausages left over she'd put them in a risotto for tomorrow night's tea, and maybe add a couple of rashers of bacon to bulk out the meat content for her four carnivores at home.

Sally was ashamed to admit that Nick and the boys thought that unless a meal had meat in it, and fish fingers were just about accepted in this category, it just wasn't a proper meal. She remembered the night she'd produced stuffed peppers for their evening meal, after Anna had given her a Slimming World recipe to try, which her husband and boys had raved about. At Sally's table there were four pairs of raised eyebrows then silence as they reluctantly began to eat. The cavemen in her family had accepted their fate in suffering the offered vegetarian penance, but Sally never made them again, it had just been too painful a meal time.

Later on that evening, another driver having picked up the extra shift, Sally and Nick were doing their nightly ritual of washing up together after the evening meal. As Sally reached for the last of the glasses she glanced at her diary to double check who the minded children were for the next day.

"Busy tomorrow, love?" Nick asked, picking up the entire cutlery in one go and expertly drying them in his thorough fashion.

"Not really, four before and after school and two during the day, you know what I'm like though at the beginning of a new term!" Sally picked up the plates, put them in the bowl then started methodically washing, rinsing then putting them to drain. "The nursery sessions change from the afternoon to the morning, or they do extra sessions and a couple of mums have changed their hours around. It takes me a couple of weeks to get into the swing of things and I'm terrified of turning up at the wrong time or forgetting to pick a child up! People would think I was losing the plot!"

Nick raised his eyebrows and smiled. Sally threw some bubbles at him.

"Oh ha, ha, well I know you know I have but I'd like to leave it until I retire before people discover the chaos that reigns inside my head."

"Crikey!" exclaimed Nick, "can you hold it off till then?" Nick feigned mock horror and was answered with a withering look from Sally.

"Hi Mum," Eddie bounded into the kitchen, their youngest son aged twelve. Eddie had initially struggled with Sally becoming a childminder six years ago. At only six years old and being the baby of the family he hadn't liked his mummy caring for other little children in their house, she was his mummy. He found the constant noise and hectic comings and goings after a busy school day too much for his little brain and one afternoon, six months after Sally started childminding Eddie had a meltdown. Too young to maturely process and verbalise what he was feeling he had shouted at Sally in desperation one evening after Sally had had to remind him to clean his teeth. His little body shaking with pent up rage and six year old fury he yelled that he hated her, hated school and he hated her being a childminder.

Sally had been shocked to the core. She had scooped up her little boy into a bear hug, full of shame at how she hadn't seen this coming, and carried him through to her bedroom, hugging and kissing him as Eddie had sobbed and sobbed. Guilt ridden at how Eddie was obviously struggling Sally had reassured him that she loved him more than anything in the whole world and when he had calmed down, Sally gently reminded Eddie of all the good things that happened through Sally being a childminder.

After lots of cuddles and chat Sally and Eddie came up with a plan. If Eddie needed some peace and quiet, he was to go up to his room, by himself, shut the door and just relax. Sally didn't child mind upstairs so he wouldn't be disturbed. Over time, Eddie adjusted and now found it too quiet if Sally didn't have any children.

"Sorry mum, I forgot to remind you again at tea, it's 'Learning to Learn' tomorrow so I need those ingredients, ok?" and went to leave to grab his last twenty minutes on the XBox.

Sally groaned and looked back at her diary. There, under Monday, squeezed in blue ink between the minded children's names in red, were Eddie's ingredients.

"Yep, ok Ed, sorry, my fault, I'll pop out now." And she started to pull of her rubber gloves.

"For Christ's sake Eddie!" snapped Nick, "It's five past eight, the Co op's shut and the garage is so bloody expensive!"

Eddie stood rooted to the spot, his mouth opened, then closed, wordlessly. He was stunned by the outburst from his usually mild mannered dad.

Sally shot Nick a worried look and realised with a pang of guilt that she wasn't the only one feeling the stress.

"It's ok Ed, off you go," Sally smiled reassuringly. She turned to Nick, "Love, I did know about the ingredients, it's completely my fault, I went to the Co op earlier today and I forgot."

Nick gave an unconvinced 'hmmph,' picked up another plate and resumed the drying up.

"I'll go and see him in a minute and say sorry, ok?" he offered.

Eddie slunk off, wishing he hadn't been the reason for making his dad cross. It wasn't hard these days since mum had suddenly stopped minding Simon. He reached for the Turtlebeach headphones and picked up the handset.

"Ok guys, I'm back, I've got twenty minutes left."

Sally reached into the under stairs cupboard for her coat when her middle son, Jack, came galloping down the stairs, sixteen years old and already six feet tall.

"Going up the shop, mum?" he looked hopeful as he landed with a thump after jumping the last two steps.

"Yes love; just getting some emergency bits for Ed for school, do you want something?" Sally replied, shrugging her coat on.

41

"Chewits would be great thanks, if they're not too expensive from the garage." Jack's ever present sweet tooth needed satisfying.

Sally gave Jack a wry smile.

"I know we've lost Simon love but I think we can stretch to a packet of chewits, ok."

Jack gave her a faux punch, teenage affection Sally knew, and jogged past her to the kitchen to inhale what food was left in the fridge after the weekend.

"Awight Dad?" twanged Jack as he bounced into the kitchen, also throwing Nick a punch for good measure as well. Jack was in last year of G.C.S.E's, studying and playing hard. Blonde hair and blue eyes, he took after Nick's father's side of the family. Calm, easy going, even natured, he was able academically but didn't rest on his laurels; he was just diligent and steady.

He opened the fridge door and expertly surveyed the contents. He reached in and selected a boiled egg, mini pork pie and a bowl of sliced pineapple, closed the fridge door and turned to Nick.

"Dad, can you pick me up from the sports centre tomorrow afternoon? I've got lifeguard practice and they reckon we'll finish about 6ish. Mum said she can do it but she'll still have 2 minded children so I just thought I'd see if you're around." Jack popped the pork pie into his mouth whole and chewed hungrily. Nick paused drying the stray spoon from the bottom of the utensil holder as he mentally checked what the next day was and what shift he was doing. Tuesday, an early shift. He would be back in time.

"No problem, son." Jack turned to leave but stopped having remembered something.

"Oh, and we need to contribute five pounds towards the petrol for the college mini bus and Miss Dunstable reminded everyone that tomorrow is that the last day for the final payment of ninety pounds for the lifeguard training."

Jack scanned his dad's face for any sign of worry but found none.

"No problem, Jack," Nick opened the utensil drawer to put the last, now completely dry and polished spoon back. "I'll write you a cheque now."

Reassured, Jack left the kitchen and once Nick heard him bounce back up the stairs he threw the tea towel onto the radiator and slumped down in the old comfy corner chair in the kitchen, head in hands, and sighed.

Maggie tied her long blonde hair back into a high ponytail then efficiently twisted it around and secured it with three hair pins into a no nonsense bun. It would be out of the way for the day of cleaning that lay ahead of her. She didn't want it coming undone over the many toilets that she faced that day so stuck another one in for good measure. She went next door to the bathroom to her daughter's bedroom and turned on the lamp. She leant over and gently roused her Adele from her sleep.

"Adele?..Adele love, come on, it's six o'clock..."

Maggie watched as her seven year old daughter stirred and rolled on to her back, her long dark hair tied up in a ponytail to stop it getting tangled during the night. She felt a stab of guilt at her enforced early mornings.

"Ok mum, I'm awake," her eyes still shut, Adele stretched her arms above her head and yawned.

Maggie kissed her on the forehead.

"You're such a good girl, love, well done; I'll get your cereal ready."

Maggie walked up the hallway, past the bathroom and into the lounge area of the one bedroom flat. She walked around the pullout sofa bed where her husband Dean was sitting up drinking a cup of tea that Maggie had made when she had got up, round into the open plan kitchen.

"Are you going to drop Adele at Sally's or am I?" Maggie asked Dean, opening a cupboard and reaching in for Adele's cereal bowl.

"Can you take her?" answered Dean, swinging his legs off the bed. "I want to make headway this morning. There are two sets of traffic lights on the road between Huntsdon and Stentbridge and I want to be at my first appointment by quarter to eight."

He reached across to the little table and chairs rammed up against the corner of the wall for his clothes and hurriedly got dressed. The dark January mornings brought a chill to the flat.

"Do you want me to help you fold the bed up?" Dean asked, reaching for his coat and keys and walking towards the doorway of the sitting room.

"No, you're fine, I've got time," replied Maggie, without looking up and placed a spoon beside Adele's bowl.

"Bye love!" Maggie heard Dean go into Adele's room, "see you later." A moment later, he was gone. The door to the flat closed, and then the muffled thud as the main door to the entrance foyer swung back in its place.

Maggie leaned against the work top and sighed. She felt trapped. She was pretty sure Dean felt the same way.

She had two cleaning jobs while Dean worked as a driving instructor. They were desperately saving for a house but to move from a one bed roomed flat to a two bed roomed house would mean a hefty increase of at least sixty thousand pounds. They had applied for a larger mortgage but the application was taking forever to process. Dean earned fairly good money but had to work long hours and at the weekends to offset the ever rising cost of petrol and still remain competitive.

Maggie took a sip of her coffee. She just wasn't sure she wanted to make such a large financial commitment with Dean when things were so tense between them.

Adele came through to the kitchen, dressed and her hair redone in a plait.

"Hi mum, I'm done."

"Well done love!" I wish I was as good as you at these early morning starts." She hugged her daughter close and kissed the top of her head. "Come on, let's get your breakfast inside you and we'll get you to Sally's."

Maggie carried Adele's breakfast over to the little dining table and pulled out a chair for Adele to sit on, then turned around on the spot and bent to start folding the bedcovers up ready to fold away the bed for the day.

Twenty minutes later at 6.20 in the morning Maggie and Adele knocked on Sally's door.

"Good morning Maggie, hello Adele, come on in," greeted Sally, far more cheerily than she felt.

When she'd first starting childminding her earliest arrival was at 7.30am which Sally had thought very early to start your working day, but she soon got used to it. Twenty past six was a tad early but whenever she felt it was too much, (usually on a Friday morning,) she'd think of Maggie who would be cleaning toilets ten minutes after dropping off Adele.

"Hi Sally," smiled Maggie, "bye Adele love," She bent and kissed her daughters cheek, "Thanks so much Sally, see you tomorrow."

"Will do, Maggie, have a good day."

Sally shut the door while Adele turned around and sat on the bottom step of the stair to take her boots off.

Maggie hurried down Sally's drive and back to the car, engine still running. School first, then straight on to the hotel. Maggie worked for two hours at the local secondary school from six thirty to eight thirty in the morning then drove seven miles to a small family run hotel where she was employed as a housekeeper for four hours a day. When she'd finally finished work for the day she had just enough time to drive home and have a cup of tea and a sandwich before picking up Adele from school.

Tax credits paid most of Sally's bill and that was with Sally reducing it to £3 an hour from her usual rate of £4 an hour for before and after school children. Sally had reassured her she had reduced the rate because Maggie used ten childminding slots a week, Monday to Friday, morning and afternoon, but deep down Maggie suspected it was because Sally knew how desperately Maggie wanted to move to a house with a small garden, so Adele could play outside.

Wanted to move, but with Dean?

She arrived at the school car park and turned off the engine. She exhaled heavily and slumped against the seat. She was becoming tired of Dean's temper outbursts. They scared Adele and in her view were childish. Every time they occurred the love that Maggie felt for Dean diminished, little by little.

46

Anything could trigger them, running out of milk, the bread bin being empty, a teenager cancelling a lesson at the last minute, frustrating, yes, but it didn't warrant a full blown hissy fit from a grown man! Maggie would just signal for Adele to go to her room, try to calm Dean down, then go and comfort Adele by reading her favourite book or colouring in together on Adele's bed.

Dean was never violent and Maggie never felt threatened or intimidated, just....tired and worn out living like it. She got out of her car and locked it; it was still dark and trying to rain.

Things need to change, Maggie thought as she ran across the car park. Enough's enough.

Suddenly feeling empowered, she pulled open the glass entrance door to the school and made her way along the corridor to the cleaner's cupboard. She gathered her cleaning equipment for her morning's work and headed off for the boys toilets.

Five minutes later, her head over the first of numerous toilets she would have to clean that day, Maggie started to plan the conversation she would have with Dean that night.

Sally picked up the remote for the television. She turned to Adele who was sitting on the sofa with a blanket over her.

"Do you want CITV on, love?"

"Yes please, Sally," replied Adele and wiggled her bottom down the seat a bit so she could rest her legs on Sally's old pine blanket box that they had bought for their first home when Chris was eighteen months old. It was filled with toys, as was every available cupboard and drawer in the house, not to mention stair gates behind the sofa which kept company with a pop up tent and fold up tunnel and travel cots under the bed. That was part and parcel of being a child minder, your home became an extension of your job and that's just the way it had to be.

"Luke will be here soon, and Pippa and Peter, so you won't be by yourself for long, ok" reassured Sally

Adele nodded, her eyes now fixed on the television. Adele loved to craft and to play with Playmobil but at 6.35 in the morning she needed time to come to, so she snuggled under the blanket and there she stayed until the day had properly started.

Dean closed the door to their one bed roomed prison behind him, pushed open the foyer door and stepped outside. He zipped up his worn leather jacket against the cold and reached into his inside jacket pocket for his mobile phone. He quickly scanned it, no cancellations....yet.

He unlocked his car, got in and started the engine. He looked back at the flats he and Maggie called home and felt suffocated. He could see no way to get Maggie and Adele to where they needed to be, in a two bed roomed house with a garden, so if Adele wanted to use her skipping rope at seven o'clock in the morning, she could.

Dean stared blankly ahead, his chest heavy with seemingly no prospect of change in their circumstances. They would be better off apart. Maggie would receive more benefits for herself and Adele, so they would be ok, he reasoned, and all he needed was a place to lay his head after a mind numbing day, trying to teach the human race how to drive.

He drove out of their cul de sac of flats and turned right onto the main road that ran through the middle of the village, all the way to Stentbridge. He hoped the house share he was going to view was better than the previous two he had seen, he could then start the process of dismantling his current situation, tread water for a few months until things were on a more even keel and then try to move forward.

He loved Adele and wanted to be part of her life, be a good father but he just felt at the moment he wasn't providing adequately for her.

He loved Maggie, he just didn't know if he was in love with her any more. They were always both so tired, so edgy, they had nothing left to give each other.

His phone buzzed, he glanced across at his phone positioned in its holder on the dashboard.

Fuck, his ten o clock had just cancelled.

Enough was enough.

He hated being a driving instructor, sitting next to people all day, stinking of take out, fags, B.O and weed.

He'd use his part of the small profit from the sale of the flat to go back to college and study carpentry. He'd been good at woodwork at school. With a new sense of purpose and direction, Dean drove to view house share number three.

Sally walked into the conservatory that joined the sitting room in an open plan layout and changed the day of the week on her pin board to Tuesday. The jury was out on the weather so she decided to let the children decide when they arrived. She did a quick visual assessment as she'd done a thorough sweep and check the afternoon before, when she'd finished early.

Sally didn't mind any babies at the moment so the pressure was off slightly regarding chokable pieces hiding under chest of drawers or sofas. Plug sockets were a nightmare! Sally checked these religiously as Nick would often forget to replace the plug cover in the extension lead after he had used it to mow the lawn, or the boys, in their self absorbed teenage world, would forget after they had plugged in their laptops downstairs over the weekend.

Sally opened the conservatory door which opened onto her garden and went out and double checked the side gate was closed and locked. The rest of the garden was enclosed by a six foot fence, so completely safe regarding potential escapees.

Ten minutes later, Sally was just getting out the Hama beads, a firm favourite at the moment, when the door bell sounded.

Sally unhooked the keys from the hook, unlocked the door, and greeted Luke, a six year old boy and his mum, Rosie.

"Hello Luke, Hello Rosie," welcomed Sally

"Hi Sally, how are you? Good weekend? Hop in Luke, you're letting all of Sally's heat out!"

Rosie, a forty something, highly efficient, no nonsense, secondary school teacher, stepped into the hallway and shut the door. Slender in build, she had a razor sharp blonde bob and brown eyes that held a ready smile.

"Mummy, have you got my trains?" Luke asked, taking off his shoes and fleece. He then yanked up his trousers high round his waist and wiped his nose on the back of his sleeve.

"Luke! For goodness sake, use a tissue!" exclaimed Rosie. She pulled a clean tissue out of a pack of an individual pack she had in her coat pocket and wiped Luke's nose.

"Mummy! I don't need your tissues, I have my own pack!" and with a dramatic flourish, Luke pulled his own little individual pack of tissues out of his trouser pocket.

Rosie rolled her eyes at Sally and whispered.

"Boys!"

She bent down to kiss Luke and said;

"Well, next time perhaps you could use your tissues and not your sleeve!"

"I'll try Mummy...bye," and he raced into the sitting room and jumped onto the settee next to Adele.

"Look, Adele, these are my new trains..."

Sally had minded Luke ever since he was two years old and now counted Rosie as a friend. They had been to each other's houses for wine evenings and coffee mornings, to moan about husbands, money and to generally put the world to rights.

Rosie respected Sally as a childminder and for her other roles as a wife and mother. She was very mindful that Sally had her own family and commitments and she never telephoned or texted at the weekends if she could help it.

They had met at a toddler group in a neighbouring village. Rosie had initially only wanted one day a week to enable her to get some uninterrupted housework done. She had decided not to return to work after having Luke but once she realised Sally had some vacancies and that Luke was so settled she made some enquiries and was now working three days a week as an English teacher at the local secondary school.

Luke was a bright articulate boy and was a joy to mind. His imagination was vivid and when playing with either with Lego, Playmobil, Bionicles or dinosaurs, an adventure would always happen. Like the Pied Piper, he would draw in a timid child, or a child that had arrived upset to join in, unable to help themselves, into the magic of his play.

"Right, Sally," said Rosie, "here are your vouchers for the month, got to rush, oh and I've got a meeting after school today so it will be John picking up Luke."

"No problem, Rosie, drive safely and have a good day."

Sally shut the door behind Rosie, locked the door and hung the key back up on the hook. She placed Luke's shoes next to Adele's, their lunch boxes and book bags neatly on the old pew she'd found in a second hand shop and went back in the sitting room to be with Luke and Adele and wait for Pippa and Peter to arrive.

Back in the car, Rosie checked her hair and makeup in the rear view mirror. Satisfied, she turned the ignition and started the engine. She glanced at the clock inset in the dash board. 7.15 am. She was making good time. She put the car into first gear when her briefcase caught her eye on the front seat.

A niggle.

Had she put her diary back in her briefcase last night after she had finished adding the last details to this morning's meeting? She quickly put the car back into neutral and flicked open the catches to her brief case.

"Damn it!" Rosie said out loud in frustration. Great start to the day she thought to herself and pulled off Sally's drive, now in a hurry and potentially late.

She could have really have done without a return trip home. The secondary school she worked at was only ten minutes away but she hated to be rushed, which she now was. She'd wanted to double check the power point presentation that she was going to use to help familiarise the two new members of staff in the English department with the following term's targets and assessment criteria.

Now she wouldn't have time to do it. Bugger!

Rosie pulled into the drive to the side of her two bedroom cottage, next to John's black Golf.

Strange, he hadn't left for work yet.

The cottage was a typical chocolate box affair with a double frontage, thatched roof, leaded windows and climbing roses growing up either side of the front door, threading and weaving through a white metal arch. Lavender bushes framed the base of the house and a No.1 white, Farrow and Ball painted picket fence finished off the look.

Rosie hurried out of the car and went through the side gate that led into the front garden from the drive, along the gravel path that ran along the front of the garden to the front door.

It was Rosie's dream house.

She had saved and saved from the age of fourteen, ever since her mother had tried to win such a cottage by religiously cutting out the tokens every day from the Daily Mail, for weeks on end. Her mother would describe in detail, every Sunday lunch, as on a Sunday, there were two tokens so her enthusiasm was heightened, how the inside would be. A faraway look in her eyes, she would reel off, as though she was standing inside the cottage itself,

Low beamed ceilings, uneven floors, window seats at the windows, open fireplaces and best of all....best of all would be a country kitchen. A kitchen large enough for a large old wooden table which could seat extended family and friends, an Aga, which her mother would then whisper conspiratorially, as though it may jinx her luck, that she had no idea how they worked but she'd find out before the competition closed, and all finished off with a quarry tiled floor.

Living there, her mother had fantasised, would be like coming home every night to a warm hug. Her father would roll his eyes good naturedly, whilst chewing his roast beef, at his ever optimistic wife, but Rosie's imagination had been completely captivated.

Their own family home had been a three bed roomed semi detached house on a housing estate. A perfectly nice, functional family home, but Rosie knew she wanted more from a home.

She wanted the home her mother had described so she had started saving as soon as she'd started her paper round at the age of fourteen. At sixteen, she got a job at McDonalds which also gave her extra hours in during the school holidays.

She wasn't really interested in clothes, preferring the classic, tailored look which she dressed up or down with jewellery and scarves. And although she'd learnt to drive at seventeen, she'd never bothered with a car initially, preferring public transport and cycling.

She'd attended a local university to keep costs down and kept her job at McDonalds whilst studying. By the time she had finished her teacher training she had saved up, with the help of birthday and Christmas money, a healthy deposit to put down on a cottage but she would still need a large mortgage and to take in a lodger to help pay it.

Ten years ago, she was still living at home with her parents rent free, as her mother wanted this dream cottage for Rosie as much as Rosie did. She was in her second year working as an English teacher at the local secondary school and one Saturday morning, Rosie had been doing her weekly traipse around the nearby town's estate agents. She paused outside Markham and Son's, the third agents that morning when she spotted a new listing.

Rosie froze.

The words jumped out from the listing.

'Thatched cottage 2 bedrooms, downstairs bathroom, court yard garden, set back from the road.'

Rosie dared herself to look at the price.

£147,000.

Rosie felt sick. It was a joke wasn't it? Her eyes scanned the description again, feeling sure she'd missed something and there it was.

Above the photo, in the top right hand corner of the listing Rosie spotted the dreaded words.

'Needs modernisation.'

How much modernisation? Rosie wondered as she found herself walking into the estate agent's in slow motion and sitting opposite a female negotiator with dark curly hair and deep blue eyes. She was on the telephone. She smiled at Rosie and mouthed,

"I won't keep you a moment."

Rosie's mind raced. If it was subsidence, forget it, anything else she could manage. She held her breath while the negotiator brought the telephone conversation to an end.

"This afternoon at 2 o'clock, see you then, Mr Wilson."

She replaced the receiver and stood up behind her desk and extended a hand to Rosie.

"Hello there, sorry to have kept you waiting, my name's Millie, how may I help you."

Rosie's words tumbled out in a torrent.

"Ummm, new listing, cottage," she pointed behind her at the glass fronted office where all the photos of the properties hung.

"How much modernisation? Is it subsidence? Can I view it.... today...please?" Rosie stopped and just stared at Millie who was smiling broadly at her.

"Yes I know the cottage you mean. It came on the market on Thursday and the photograph went in the window yesterday afternoon. It doesn't have subsidence but it does need extensive work done to it. Damp proofing, rewiring, replastering, new central heating installed," Millie paused, "to be honest it needs completely gutting! I'm actually taking someone to see it this afternoon."

Rosie's jaw dropped. She shook her head; she had to see it first.

"No..no, I have to see it first, please, I'm a first time buyer with a 20% deposit and I will pay the full asking price! I just HAVE to have that house." She finished in desperation.

56

Millie laughed out loud.

"You haven't seen it yet!" she exclaimed, taken with Rosie's honesty and directness.

Rosie looked Millie in the eye and said quietly.

"I've been waiting for this house nearly ten years."

Millie's smile slowly left her face and she nodded. She sat back in her chair and studied Rosie, her mind whirring.

The guy this afternoon had sold his property but his buyer still had yet to sell.

She desperately needed a sale.

For once, Millie thought to herself, I'm going to act like a negotiator.

"I'll get the keys, let's go."

Rosie was on her feet in a flash, barely able to contain her rising excitement.

"Thank you so much! Really, thank you."

Millie stood up, pushed her chair back and picked up her handbag. She went over to the key cupboard that housed the keys for vacant houses and vendors on holiday and selected a set. She turned to a young nervous looking young man who Rosie assumed was the Saturday junior and said,

"Take names and contact details of anyone who phones or comes into the office and the price range they are interested in. I'll be back in two hours."

The office junior sat in his chair, stunned, not quite sure what had overcome the usually laid back Millie.

Whilst Millie drove the twenty five minutes to the village of Chudley, Rosie filled Millie in on the background behind the search for the perfect chocolate box cottage.

Millie sat quietly and listened, nodding now and then. She completely understood Rosie's desire and drive to find her perfect home. She had seen it time and time again, people's lives enriched or seemingly devastated by succeeding or failing to buy their dream house. Rosie's story about her mum buying into having the perfect life if only she had the perfect house was what motivated many house buyers.

"Anyway," finished Rosie, "I will do anything, absolutely anything....as long as it's legal of course," She laughed nervously, glancing sideways at Millie who was now indicating left and turning down a country lane just outside the village. Rosie was suddenly a little embarrassed that she had just offloaded to a complete, although very friendly, stranger.

Millie came to a stop next to a five foot overgrown hedge.

"Here we are." Millie pulled the handbrake up and turned the engine off. She turned to Rosie. "I hope it's everything you want it to be." She said gently. "Ready?" She turned and opened the driver's door, taking her phone and property details with her.

Rosie nodded and slowly opened the passenger door. She got out of the car and straightened herself up. She could just make out the top of a much worn looking thatched roof through the forgotten hedge. She shut the car door and followed Millie, walking another five feet along the hedge, stopping at an old, what used to be white painted, gate which although was still hung, the latch had long gone through constant use so now just swung freely in the breeze.

The two women walked through the gate, Rosie closed it as best she could, in line with the hedges that stood either side of it. She loved the balance, the symmetry, and when she turned back to take in the front of the cottage she saw the gate and the hedges mirrored the double frontage of the cottage.

Front door in the middle.

Cottage windows either side.

She stood still and exhaled, she felt her shoulders drop and a calm sweep over her.

It was just what she had envisaged. She didn't see the rotten window frames, the broken and cracked window panes and the exterior plaster missing in chunks.

Rosie just saw potential.

Millie fished the key out of her coat pocket and placed it in the lock. With a twist and a push she opened the door into a cool dark hallway which played host to a pungent, musty damp smell. Wallpaper hung off the walls giving away the dubious condition of the walls underneath. A room led off from the hallway on both sides where Rosie noted original fireplaces, tiled hearths and original picture rails which gave a lovely character feel to the cottage. The stairs were situated halfway down the hallway, walking past the stairway then led on into the kitchen.

The kitchen housed an old oven, fridge and a sink with a work top one side. An old picnic table was pushed up against one wall with two old chairs tucked under it. A door to the right housed the old pantry, whilst a window above the sink looked out over the overgrown courtyard and a door to the left led to the bathroom, whose suite had definitely seen better days.

Millie placed the door key and her phone on the old picnic table and scanned the property details.

"Right, that's it for downstairs. Two reception rooms, kitchen, bathroom, obviously no central heating." She reached for the keys on the table and put the second key into the back door, turned the key and pushed.

"Out here is the garden area," as an afterthought she added, "the shed is staying if that's any use to you." Millie went through the back door, and surveyed the garden. It was the first time she'd viewed it as she hadn't valued it, though it was quaint, it was, to use estate agent jargon, a money pit.

She turned back to Rosie who was walking in slow motion through the back door towards her.

"Well, what do you think?" Millie asked, "a bit too much work to be done; now you've seen it?"

Rosie slowly shook her head and stared at Millie, her eyes shining with excitement and disbelief.

"It's simply perfect! I'll take it!"

Millie laughed for the second time that day.

"Whoa there! We haven't been upstairs yet! Shall we just go and check that there actually is one?" She smiled.

Rosie laughed at herself and put her hands up in mock surrender.

"Ok, ok, I'm sorry, of course we should go and look upstairs and I know you think I'm mad but as long as the survey comes back that it is structurally sound, I am buying this house!"

She nodded at Millie to make sure Millie understood how serious she was and nodded towards the back door.

"Let's go and see the upstairs then."

It was Millie's turn to raise her hands in surrender.

"Come on then, let's go and show you the upstairs to your new home." She said, playing along. Millie wished she could be as captivated by something that was able to inspire and motivate her that much.

She led Rosie back through the kitchen, down the hall then up the stairs which, although old and shabby, they looked solid and safe. Upstairs there were two windows with pitched ceilings and a window to the front and back aspect. Rosie went from one room to the next, then back again, taking in the peeling walls, precarious floor boards and the damp in the corner of one room.

She'd made up her mind. Rosie turned to Millie who was checking her phone for messages and said.

"Millie, I would like to put in an offer on this cottage for the full asking price. Would you call the vendor now please?"

Millie stared at Rosie, negotiator hat off for the moment.

"Are you really sure Rosie?" her blue eyes filled with concern. "The first viewing of any property is always the 'rose tinted glasses' viewing. Are you sure you don't want to sleep on it and view it again tomorrow?" Millie trailed off.

Desperate for a sale, but human enough to care that Rosie didn't make a mistake she may regret in the future.

Rosie shook her head. She looked so self confident, so self assured Millie thought.

"I have never been surer of anything in my life. Please tell the vendor I will pay the full asking price and in return would ask that they take it off the market immediately. I will have no trouble getting a mortgage."

Millie could tell Rosie was serious and stopped acting like a surrogate big sister.

"Right, I'm on it! If all goes well I'd better phone Mr Wilson to cancel his viewing this afternoon."

Rosie pulled a face.

"Sorry about that."

"Not at all!" replied Millie, breezily. "All's fair in love and house buying!" she said, phoning the office for the vendor's contact details. Putting the phone to her ear she smiled and winked at Rosie then turned her back as her call was answered by Phil.

"Phil? Hi, is everything ok?" Millie paced up and down the upstairs from bedroom to bed room and back again. 'Great, can you get me the contact details for the vendor of the property down Thistle Lane? It's priced at £147,000....yes I'll hold...what was that?....oh, ok, are you alright?...ok," Millie rolled her eyes at Rosie and staged whispered, 'He tripped over the bin!'

They both giggled. It broke the tension a bit.

Rosie turned and gazed out of the bedroom facing the back garden. She felt strangely calm. She was doing the right thing, she knew it.

Millie could hear Phil making his way back to the phone. Her commission, if this sale went through, would be very welcome in her pay packet.

"Yes, I'm still here, hang on, right fire away....ok, got it! Thanks Phil, I'll be back shortly then you can go to lunch, ok?"

Millie hung up and starting punching numbers into her phone. Before hitting the call button she paused and looked up at Rosie.

"Still sure?" she asked.

"100%," Rosie reassured Millie with a steady gaze of determination.

"Right, let's do this!"

Millie got through to the daughter of the man who had previously owned the house and started the preliminary greetings.

Rosie, although outwardly calm, was now unable to bear the tension. She left the bedroom and walked the few steps along the landing to the top of the stairs. She slowly walked down them. Although the downstairs was in desperate need of work, Rosie could see the potential. Her mind started to plan. Knock that wall down there, open up the kitchen into one of the reception rooms to make a large, open plan space, replace the windows, put in a new damp proof course, install new central heating, put in new ceilings, re plaster all the walls. The list went on and on.

Rosie mentally hugged herself, hardly allowing herself to think the unthinkable that she may....may, very soon, actually own this cottage.

She heard boots bounding down the stairs.

"Rosie?....ROSIE! Where are you?" Millie was now at the bottom of the stairs.

"In here!" Rosie quickly turned and hurried to the door of the reception room. Millie rushed in, almost colliding with Rosie.

"You've got it!!"

Rosie gasped, tears jumped to her eyes. Millie was beaming like a Cheshire cat and hurried towards her engulfing Rosie in a professionally inappropriate hug, but on a human level, completely appropriate.

"Well done, you!" Millie exclaimed, "She's agreed to have it taken off the market immediately on the condition that you have your survey done within seven days." She turned to get the keys from the little kitchen table. "Right, let's get back to the office. I've got some work to do and you've got a mortgage to arrange."

Now it was Rosie's turn to hug Millie.

"Thank you so much!" She said with genuine warmth, "You'll never know how much this means to me."

Millie pulled back and smiled at a flushed and starry eyed Rosie.

"I have a fair idea...come on, let's get back to the office. Phil's stomach will be complaining if it's left without food for too long."

Rosie ran up the stairs to fetch her diary from the office when she heard a draw slam shut in their bedroom.

"John? You're cutting it a bit fine this morning aren't you?" Rosie called, pushing open the door of their bedroom. She found her husband, John, hurriedly buttoning and zipping his trousers, looking flustered.

"I know, I know. I couldn't find a damn pair of matching socks without a hole in them."

Rosie caught sight of a foot of a pair of tights hanging from her underwear drawer. She walked over and opened the drawer slightly, tucked it back in, then shut the drawer firmly.

"Well you won't find a pair in my underwear drawer, silly," she grinned, "socks are in the third drawer down, you know that!"

John laughed nervously.

"I was panicking and just went through every drawer. What is it about socks? They're sold in pairs, worn in pairs and washed in pairs, but when they go through a cycle they mysteriously lose their partner and develop a hole!" he finished taking a deep breath.

Rosie frowned and looked at him.

"Are you ok? You seem a bit jittery."

John hurried over to her and gave Rosie a quick peck on the cheek.

"I'm fine love. I'm gonna miss my train if I don't shoot!" he called back over his shoulder, "Look, whoever's home first starts the tea and has a glass of wine waiting for the other, ok?"

John was now half way down the stairs. Rosie called out,

"Ok, bet you I win! I've got a meeting tonight after school so don't forget to pick up Luke from Sally's."

"Will do," came his distant reply.

She heard the door slam. She quickly retrieved her diary from the desk in the office and after quickly checking everything was turned off in the kitchen, Rosie finally left for work, only fifteen minutes behind schedule.

John arrived at the station with minutes to spare. Once on the train he sat back, breathed in and exhaled deeply.

That had been a close call back home. He really needed to be more careful in future. He turned his head and looked out of window, colours and objects of the landscape blurring into one as the train picked up speed.

His thoughts drifted back to Rosie. He loved her so much. She really was his soul mate. He never wanted to hurt her or make her question his love for her.

His mind went back to summer nine years ago, the summer they first met. Rosie had been struggling to lift a bag of plaster in the local Wicks when John had walked past the aisle. Seeing her struggle he had offered to help her load it onto a trolley. He had made a joke about how she was pretty enough and didn't need that much foundation and, after much laughter and blushing from Rosie, she had explained that she was doing up a cottage she had bought and plastering was the next job.

John had been completely wowed by Rosie's practical, no nonsense attitude. Contrary to his joke, Rosie wore no makeup that day; her hair was scrapped back in a tiny ponytail, she wore old jeans and a dirty shirt with cement covered boots finishing off her ensemble.

John thought she looked just great. He held at his hand to introduce himself properly.

"I'm John, if you ever need any help at this cottage of yours, I'd be only too happy to help. It's a bit of a hobby of mine, DIY..." he paused, "Do you mind me asking where this cottage of yours is?"

John shook Rosie's hand and fumbled in his pocket for a pen and scrap of paper. He found an old receipt that would do.

"Um, well it's down a country lane, in Chudley." replied Rosie, a little flustered about receiving a phone number from a stranger, although quite a nice one, in her local Wicks.

John stopped, halfway through writing his name and number down.

"A country lane? Would that be Thistle Lane by any chance?"

Rosie was stunned.

"Yes! How did you know that?"

John just stared at Rosie, his brain whizzing back six months.

"You have got to be kidding me!"

It was a statement, not a question.

His eyes widened, and then he shook his head and smiled. He repeated, "you have just GOT to be kidding me!' He stood back and crossed his arms across his chest. "I'm Mr John Wilson....Mr Wilson that a year ago had his viewing cancelled because a young woman had viewed that morning and made the owner an offer they couldn't refuse."

He paused, with a small smile playing around his lips, and waited for the penny to drop.

It dropped.

Rosie gasped.

"No way!" She clamped her hand to her mouth, eyes wide with shock. It was her turn to say,

"You're kidding me, right?"

"Nope!"

"My God!"

Rosie was dumbfounded. What on earth were the chances? She put her hands on her hips, struggling to process the coincidence.

"What can I say? I'm so sorry..." she attempted, rather lamely.

John carried on smiling as he finished writing his details down on the worn receipt. He handed it to Rosie.

"You owe me a drink I think, don't you?"

Rosie was in a corner and knew it.

"Well, it IS the least I can do I suppose." She replied smiling sheepishly, embarrassed at how quickly things had escalated.

"What about if I pop over tonight with a bottle of wine and a ready meal lasagne from the deli and you can show me how you are getting on redecorating my nearly house?"

"Uh, ok, that sounds great," she replied shyly.

"Right now, how many more bags of foundation do you need?"

John dodged a playful punch from Rosie.

John loaded another two bags of plaster onto the trolley and helped her through the checkout. He pushed the trolley to her car and helped them load them in. As Rosie was shutting the boot, John was already walking back to his car, waving and calling,

"See you at 7!"

John had never left that evening.

After reheating the lasagne in the microwave and opening two bottles of Pinot Noir, Rosie and John spent the evening talking about their careers, their families and their dreams.

At 5 o'clock Sunday morning, John had carried Rosie up the bare stairs to her bedroom and there, on the sofa bed, surrounded by plaster board, floor boards and bags of plaster, they had stayed until Sunday evening.

Renewed in his love for Rosie, after remembering with warmth their clandestine meeting, he vowed never to give in again.

He would have to try harder to resist.

Sue walked over to the kitchen sink and looked out of the window. The newly mown lawn which Julia had finished off for her yesterday looked just how it used to when John had done it. Perfect stripes, neatly edged.....Sue sighed, dropped her gaze, pulled on her rubber gloves and began to run the hot tap. She squirted some washing up liquid into the bowl and, as the bubbles began to form, she began to wash a coffee cup.

She had never understood how people thought a dishwasher saved you time. The pre-rinsing, loading, unloading..it seemed such a task. She found washing up therapeutic and a natural end to a meal. When the last utensil was put away and the tea towel was hung up to dry, that meal was finished, whereas the dishwasher had to be emptied at the end of the day, or first thing the following morning. What a job!

Sue shook her head, listen to yourself, Sue! she said to herself, you're sounding like a grumpy old woman, set in her ways. Truthfully, she missed the togetherness that she and John had shared for many years doing the washing up together.

Sue washing up, John drying.

So much was discussed during their evening ritual.

Lambing, harvesting, the weather, what farm machinery had broken down, the children...

Everything.

Sue kept rubbing the coffee cup.

Today was a bad day.

She just couldn't shake off this melancholy feeling.

It all seemed just a little more unbearable this morning.

She'd dreamt of John last night.

They had been snuggled up together, under their ancient duvet and crochet blanket. John, in his beloved wool pyjamas and she in her long nightgown and cardigan, complete with woolly socks. Chatting and laughing softly, John had kissed the side of her forehead and she had snuggled into him, tightly. We're so lucky to have each other, she'd thought, in her dream. When she has woken that morning, for a few seconds, she'd thought that John was beside her, breathing deeply, warm and comforting.

Then the ice cold wave of reality washed over her.

The emptiness in her stomach that had become part of her daily existence seemed to fill her whole being today, seemed to spread out throughout her entire body, threatening to encompass her like a heavy, dark, veiled cloak, suffocating her every thought and feeling.

Sue let go of the mug.

The ache....the void inside her was unbearable.

Overwhelmed with a grief that carried only blackness; Sue leaned over the sink, forehead on her soapy arms and broke down. The kitchen became filled with her desperate, animal sobs. She became utterly consumed with the pain for the loss of her darling John and for the times that had passed, never to be recaptured again.

She missed him so much, she didn't know if she could go on. Nothing would ever be the same again. She had never loved anyone else, ever. John had been the one. She had had her children with him and in her eyes that was it, what her life had been about, had focused on and around, and now it had gone. She didn't want another life; she wanted her old one back. Robotically, she straightened up and pulled off her rubber gloves. Exhausted, empty, spent, she walked to the back of the kitchen, through a low door, which hid one of two staircases in the house, and climbed the steps to the bedroom she had shared all of her adult life with her husband.

She pulled back the crochet blanket and duvet and climbed into what had been John's side of the bed, pulled the covers over herself and closed her eyes.

After dropping Pippa and Peter at their school in the next village and Luke and Adele to their classes, Sally whizzed around to pick up Spencer from Mrs Banks, who was busy greeting and answering queries from anxious parents.

"Hi Sally," Mrs Banks smiled. "Spencer's bag is by my desk and I think he's in the woody area."

She rolled her eyes,

"Sorry!"

Sally grinned.

"No problem, I'll go and fetch him, see you at home time."

Sally weaved in and out of the throng of mums, retrieved Spencer's bag and lunch box and went in search of Spencer.

After locating Spencer, hiding in the branches of the low lying trees that boarded the reception class and nursery area, they made their way back to her car. At 9.15 am Sally was expecting Phoebe with two year old Portia. Strapping Spencer into his car seat she hoped that Phoebe had remembered to dress Portia in old clothes as Tuesday was Messy Play at the Sunshine Centre.

"Excuse me, hi there....sorry, could I just have a word please?" a voice called from a distance.

Sally straightened up to peer over the roof of her car. She saw a mum she recognised, but didn't know the name of, hurrying across the playground towards her.

"Yes of course," smiled Sally, handing Spencer a lift the flap farm book to keep him occupied. "Is everything alright?"

"Yes, yes, fine thank you." The woman stopped and caught her breath. "Sorry, I really shouldn't be running at my age!"

Sally laughed.

"I agree, it's completely overrated!" She smiled warmly at the woman. "How can I help you?"

"Well, I was just wondering if, by any chance, you had any before and after school places available for my little girl in Year 2," she paused, "Oh sorry, my name is Jenny."

Looking anxious, Jenny shook Sally's hand and zipped up her coat against the cold January breeze.

Sally's heart leapt but she remained outwardly composed.

"Actually I do have one space, how many sessions are you looking for?"

Sally held her breath; she really needed another child to make up for Simon leaving.

"Every day if possible please. Monday to Friday before school, from 7.30, and then after school until 5.30pm." Jenny started to look hopeful. "My husband's just got a new job after having been made redundant and been out of work for six months so it's great news but we're now a bit stuck for childcare."

Sally's heart soared. She whipped a business card from out of her coat pocket and handed it to Jenny.

"Jenny, I'm sure I can cover those spots but I just need to double check my places." She glanced at her watch. "I have a mum dropping off a child in ten minutes so I've got to go now but if you give me a call one evening we can arrange a time for your family to visit, see my home and how I work."

Jenny was now beaming.

"Oh that's brilliant Sally! Thank you... thank you so much!" Relief was literally pouring out of Jenny. "Is 6.30 a good time to call?"

72

"Perfect, lovely, Jenny. I'll say bye for now and look forward to your call later."

"Thank you again, Sally, speak to later," and a less anxious Jenny hurried back across the playground.

Sally made her way home feeling elated. She must text Nick; hopefully it would take away some of the financial worry for him. She drew up on to her drive and got Spencer and his bags out of the car and into the house. She'd just taken her coat off when there was a knock at the door.

"Hello Phoebe, hello there Portia, how lovely to see you."

"Good morning Sally," smiled Phoebe

Portia looked suitably unimpressed with Sally's greeting, whilst Phoebe bent to take off her shoes, and looked past Sally's legs to see who else was visiting Sally today.

"Fin!" she screeched and ran past the two women in her three year old toddler way.

Phoebe stood up and smiled at Sally.

"What a little madam! I will work on her manners, I promise!"

Sally thought Phoebe looked a little strained today.

"Everything alright with you, Phoebe?" Sally gently asked.

Phoebe flashed Sally a look and like a light bulb, a smile was put in place.

"Gosh, yes, yes, absolutely fine Sally, couldn't be better, are you and your family well?" she asked, keen to take the focus away from herself.

"We're all fine thank you," Sally replied. Phoebe started to rummage through a large Gap carrier bag she had brought in. Sally couldn't put her finger on it but something was amiss with Phoebe. Over the past two years that Sally had known Phoebe she had seen her slowly change from being outgoing and gregarious to a more tense and private young woman.

"Good, good, right Sally, after our conversation about clothes for messy play, I did an online shop at Gap and bought three outfits, two coats, a raincoat, matching hats, scarves and gloves, pumps and wellington boots. Would be ok if I left them here? I was thinking you could change her whenever you think it's necessary and have her back in usual clothes for home time."

Sally paused for a split second then answered,

"Of course Phoebe, what a great idea!" and she took the offered bag from Phoebe.

Phoebe had obviously given a lot of thought to Sally's simple suggestion of casual clothes for messy play. Sending Portia to Sally's, the one day she was with her, in an old tracksuit was evidently not an option. Oh well, thought Sally, we're all different.

Phoebe herself never dressed down.

Five foot ten inches tall, whippet thin, jet black straight shoulder length hair with a delicate oriental look, thanks to her grandparents originating from Hong Kong, Phoebe had an exotic look that made whatever she was wearing look straight off the catwalk. Every day, without fail, she wore four inch heels; she made walking in them seem effortless.

She walked, strode, trotted, pirouetted, and drove in what Sally privately thought were the fashion world's joke on women. In projecting this vision of perfection Phoebe left Sally and every other woman in the village feeling ever so slightly saggy and frumpy when they talked to her. She would have made perfect gossip fodder at the Pampered Chef and Jamie parties if she wasn't so friendly, down to earth and completely unaware of the visual impact she created.

What Sally and the other envious women in the village didn't realise and would definitely find hard to fathom was the criteria that Phoebe had to dress Portia to; Sebastian, Phoebe's husband's, exacting standards.

Sebastian expected Portia to be as immaculately turned out as he did Phoebe, no exceptions. In his eyes, Portia was a reflection on Sebastian, on his parenting and fathering skills and his ability to provide for his family. It was imperative to him that appearances were upheld to the outside world at all times.

"Are you still alright for our girls' night out at Rosie's?" asked Sally. A look of angst flitted across Phoebe's eyes, and then disappeared.

"Yes of course! I'm really looking forward to it," her fixed, bright, smile, back in place. Once again, Sally felt Phoebe was hiding something, but what was it?

After Phoebe left, Sally changed Portia into a brand new GAP track suit and carefully folded the cashmere twin set and silk tutu that Portia had arrived in and placed them in the carrier bag and hung it up under the stairs. And that's where you're going to stay until fifteen minutes before home time; Sally thought to herself and firmly shut the cupboard door. She turned and walked through to the conservatory to find Spencer and Portia happily playing with the Little Tikes Mountain railroad and various vehicles and animals. Sally sat on the floor with them.

"Children," began Sally, "after our snack today we're going to the Sunshine Centre to see Fay and all our friends, and do some messy play. How does that sound?" she finished brightly.

'Yeaaah!' yelled Spencer, who loved anything that involved the possibility of glue, paint and glitter, and rightly so. Portia, on the other hand looked unsurprisingly dubious.

"Don't like messy play, me not like messy." Sally leaned forward and took both of Portia's little hands.

"You'll love it Portia! We can put paint on one hand and do a hand print for Mummy, or we can explore the glue and see how it dribbles everywhere, and then we could sprinkle some sparkly glitter on it and make it look like your beautiful tutu you came in this morning." Sally smiled as positively as she could at Portia .

Portia wasn't convinced and her bottom lip trembled.

"No! I not like painty hands!" pointing to her chubby little palms and burst into tears. Sally scooped her up in her arms and reached up for the tissue box that sat on the nearby chest of drawers, wiped Portia's tears and kissed her cheek.

"Portia, my lovely," Sally reassured, "you don't have to do anything messy if you don't want to. There will be lots of toys for you to play with as well, ok? I promise."

Portia looked slightly appeased and wriggled to turn around and face Sally.

"Me play with toys at Thunthine centre,....not get messy." Portia repeated, checking she had got her facts straight.

"I'm doing messy play!" said Spencer determinedly. "I LIKE messy play!"

Sally smiled at his enthusiasm and made a mental note to put an apron on Spencer with long sleeves. Spencer and hand painting generally turned into Spencer leaning over the table, using his hands, the entire length of his arms, and for good measure, his chest, to create his masterpiece. He certainly investigated the properties of paint. Bless him, thought Sally, now standing up to fetch the antibacterial spray and kitchen towel.

"Right, I'm just going to clean the table and then we can have our fruit and breadsticks."

"Can I clean the table Sally?" Spencer asked, climbing up onto one of Sally's benches.

"Me clean too!" seconded Portia, doing her best to pull herself up alongside Spencer.

"Well, that would be a great help, thank you Spencer, thank you Portia," replied Sally, bending to lift Portia's stray leg up so she could join Spencer.

"Now children, you can have three squirts each and then with a piece of kitchen towel I want you to rub the table top to get rid of all the germs." Sally turned the nozzle to 'on' and helped Spencer clasp the trigger and press it.

"One, two, three!" said Sally as they pressed together. Spencer looked very pleased with himself when a fine spray came out of the nozzle and on to the table.

"Well done Spencer!" praised Sally, "Now start rubbing to get rid of those germs."

Spencer started rubbing in a very determined manner.

Sally did the same with Portia whose eyes lit up in wonder at the spray seemingly magically coming from the nozzle.

"Well done, Portia! Now do what Spencer's doing and get my table clean please."

Portia started rubbing in little short strokes, glancing at Spencer's efforts, checking she was doing it correctly.

"Brilliant!" exclaimed Sally theatrically, "What would I do without you two!"

"Germs make you sick, Sally." Spencer said solemnly, fixing Sally with his big blue eyes, still rubbing the table, the kitchen towel threatening to become shreds with every rub.

"That's right Spencer, they can, that's why we should clean the table before we eat, then wash our hands. Shall we wash our hands now and then we'll be ready for our fruit." The trio went to the downstairs cloakroom and using antibacterial hand wash, Sally supported them following the four pictures above the sink.

Soap, rub, rinse and dry.

Sally made sure they washed their little hands thoroughly. Spencer desperately wanted to work the hand pump by himself but the bottom kept slipping from under it when his chubby little hand enthusiastically pushed down on the pump. Sally washed her hands and tore off a couple of pieces of kitchen towel each for the children and some for herself. She kept a roll in the cloakroom on a holder as she found it far more practical than having a named, individual towel for each child. Sally had fifteen children on her books in total; she couldn't quite imagine how she would keep on top of all the washing if all the children had individual towels. She knew a couple of childminders that did and she took her hat off to them!

Back up the table, Sally gave Spencer and Portia a banana each in its skin and breadsticks and raisins on a plate each. The benches had been Nick's idea when their children had been toddlers. Nick had bought them from a local business in the village situated at Tide Farm run by a lovely man called Matt, who happened to be the husband of Sally's friend, Jill, from her days as a teaching assistant. These particular benches, Matt had pointed out, were brilliant for young children as they were designed like church pews with high backs and sides so falling off them was virtually impossible and under the seats was a deep storage area which was much needed in Sally and Nick's home.

"Have we all finished?" Sally asked, leaning forward and wiping mucky hands and faces.

"Ok Spencer, off you go to the toilet before we go to the Sunshine Centre. Remember to put the seat up and Portia, let's check your nappy."

"Not poo," offered Portia, helpfully.

"Ok my love, we'll just check and see if it's a bit full then." Sally fetched a pair of disposable gloves and Portia's changing bag, quickly put a clean nappy on her, and then went to check on Spencer.

"Look Sally! I did it all by mine self!"

Spencer, standing on the toddler step with the pump action antibacterial hand wash standing over the plug hole, was thumping the pump down with a well aimed 'thump!' whilst his left hand overflowed with blue hand wash.

Sally looked at the new, now half full, bottle of hand wash, then back to Spencer, and her heart sank.

Forcing herself to focus on the positives about Spencer's progress in using the pump action hand wash, and not the waste of hand wash his development has caused, she exclaimed,

"Oh Spencer, that's very clever of you, but you only need a little bit to wash your hands with." Sally quickly unscrewed the pump from the bottle and tried to scoop some of the excess hand wash back into the bottle.

"But I'm a clever boy aren't I?" questioned Spencer, frowning

"Yes Spencer, yes you are, but in future just use two squirts, ok?" Sally replied. She screwed the pump back on and popped the bottle on the side of the sink.

"1,2,3,4,5,6..." counted Spencer, "I can count to six, I'm a clever boy aren't I?"

The wonders of the hand pump were forgotten for now.

"You certainly are!" reassured Sally, making a mental note to get basics handwash next time she did a big shop.

"Right Spencer, we must go otherwise Messy Play will be over before we get there.... let's go!"

"Ok Sally, let's go!" mimicked Spencer, counting also now firmly forgotten as the lure of Messy Play beckoned.

Phoebe sat in her black, top of the range, this year's model Land Rover and sighed. She had enjoyed meeting with the girls initially but each time she went along and listened to their stories of life at home, the more she began to realise that maybe all was not how it should be within her marriage. Then, for the second time that morning, she checked her to do list.

Sebastian forwarded to her phone every morning a list of errands he wanted carried out, any shopping she required and a suggestion for supper that night.

Except it wasn't a suggestion.

Phoebe had learnt to her cost to cook and serve Sebastian's suggestions.

'Duck breast, organic potatoes, organic salad, no dressing, five new shirts, silk boxers, shaving foam.'

At noon, she was meeting her mother for their monthly lunch date, then an afternoon of shopping for Sebastian and herself to replace items which he felt had lost their 'structure'.

Her phone beeped in her hand. Sebastian.

'An addition to your list. Silver evening shoes. Heel height, four inches.'

Phoebe sighed.

She must have four hundred pairs of high heeled shoes. Sebastian wouldn't let her wear anything else! Even at home, be it cooking, eating or relaxing reading the papers, Phoebe had to be immaculately dressed and made up to perfection, heels included.

Phoebe started the engine. It just wasn't an option not to buy a new pair of shoes using the excuse she had run out of time, or there weren't any available. She swiped across to her shopping list and added 'shoes'. Popping her phone in her bag she quickly checked her appearance in the rear view mirror. She must remember to stop by the Estelle Lauder counter; Sebastian had commented that her perfume bottle was only a quarter full and she would be wise to replace it soon.

She checked her mirrors and pulled away from Sally's. She was looking forward to seeing her formidable mother but hoped she wouldn't do her gentle probing on the state of her marriage. It was getting harder and harder, every time they met, to sound convincing when she reassured her mother that everything was harmonious on the marriage front.

Sally watched Phoebe drive away.

"I wouldn't mind swapping places with Phoebe," she thought wistfully, as she turned around to go through to the conservatory.

"Just for twenty four hours."

"Good morning children," trilled Fay North, the enthusiastic centre manager who never failed to lift the spirits of the weary mums and carers that filed through the doors.

The centre doubled at night as the village youth centre and was situated on the site of the local secondary school.

"Good morning Sally," Fay continued. "Are we ready for some messy play?" Fay threw her arms open, an enthusiastic, attractive dark haired lady with warm brown eyes and waited for a cheer of 'YES!' from the children. She was duly rewarded by Spencer yelling yes in reply but Portia clung to Sally's left leg, terrified at the prospect of messy play and all the messiness it would bring.

"Portia's going to start with the toys first, if that's ok?" Sally asked, trying to unpeel Portia from her leg to take off her coat.

"Yes of course it is, my pet, come on Spencer, let's get your coat off and I'll get you an apron."

"Thank you so much Fay. One with long sleeves please if possible," Sally said hopefully, finally managing to take Portia's coat off.

"No problem." Fay turned and winked knowingly at Sally. Fay hurried after Spencer who was hurrying as fast as his little legs could carry him to the painting table.

"Spencer? Spencer! Apron first!" puffed Fay, diverting Spencer with a coaxing arm to where the aprons were hanging. Skilfully negotiating Spencer's arms and head into his apron she called over to Sally.

"Sally, Tamara Jones telephoned this morning. She wants to run a childminder drop in, a week Friday, to introduce them all to the Speech Therapy team. Can you make it? There you go Spencer, all done, off you go and have fun."

Spencer rushed off to join the other children at the painting table whilst Fay straightened up.

"Ooo, I'm getting old!...so do you think you can make it?"

Sally took Portia's hand and guided her over to the half of the room set up with toys.

"That should be fine, Fay." Sally did a mental scan over next week's diary. "Friday's a good day for me as there are no toddler groups on so it will be a good focal point to the day."

"Brilliant! Tamara's going to email everyone but if you could mention it to Anna and Sarah if you see them that would be great. Not everyone is checking their inboxes regularly." finished Fay. She looked over Sally's shoulder out of the window that looked out on to one of the school's car parks. "Wonderful, here's Anna now, right, I'm going to put the kettle on for coffees, is everything ok, Julie?"

Julie, a work experience student from the local college, was bravely elbow deep in glue, feathers, paint and glitter. She looked up shyly.

"I'm fine, thank you. They're all being very....creative." She added tactfully.

"Ah, creative, one of Department of Education's favourite words along with investigating, code for 'trashing'." Fay laughed gaily and starting opening cupboards, clattering mugs onto the work surface of the little kitchenette, just off the main room.

"You're not wrong there," Sally agreed, smiling, and walked over to the heavy entrance door to hold it open for Anna.

"Morning Sally, thank you, come on everyone, Sally's opened the door for us, how kind, can we all say thank you please?"

Anna bustled through the door with four children, two in a tandem and two holding on either side.

"Thank you, Sally." They all chorused.

"You've gained an extra one today Anna," noted Sally looking puzzled.

"Well, poor James here is recovering from chicken pox, he's not contagious any more but just not 100% in himself, bless him, and Mum can't really take any more time off of work." Anna explained.

This was a common occurrence for childminders in general. Childhood diseases could take a chunk out of parent's holiday allowances, and they often resorted to taking unpaid leave. However, with everyone feeling the effect of the recession, parents were reluctant to take any more time off work than necessary, paid or unpaid.

One of the benefits of using a childminder was that they were far more homely than a nursery or day care centre and offered a smaller ratio of adult to child. Childminders had to meet the same stringent time frames regarding contagious diseases, but once the infectious stage had passed a child could recuperate at their childminder's, which was often viewed as a second home by the child and their family, curled up on the sofa under a blanket with a favourite teddy, whilst watching television or quietly looking at books.

Sally knew that she and Anna were fortunate to have good connections with their local nursery which was attached to the primary school. Carol, the nursery manager, always recommended that parents use the services of Anna and Sally as well as attending the nursery so they were then first in the queue for cover for non pupil days and school holiday cover when the nursery and school were shut.

"Well, hello James, if you feel up to painting you can come with me to get an apron on so you can start straight away whilst Anna gets everyone's coats off."

Sally smiled encouragingly at James, and held out her hand to him. James nodded shyly and took Sally's hand. Sally glanced over to the toy table and saw that Portia was engrossed with the dolls' house and all its contents.

"Thanks Sally, right, let's get everyone's coat off then you can all get your aprons on too!" Anna quickly and deftly de-coated her remaining three charges and, after popping on aprons, joined Sally, James and everybody else at the painting table.

"Francesca, we'll just tie your hair back before we start." Anna pulled a hair band from her pocket and gently gathered the little girl's hair into a ponytail, safe from waving paintbrushes and glue sticks.

"Wook Sally, I've painted a fish with a coat on!"

Spencer beamed at Sally and held up, by one corner, a paint sodden piece of A3 paper, with not an inch of paper showing and what looked like a pot of blue glitter on top of it. The excess was now cascading off the paper like a shimmering waterfall on to the floor.

"Well that's just fantastic, Spencer! Your fish looks absolutely beautiful; I'll just take a picture of it to send to your mummy," replied Sally, whipping her camera out of her pocket.

Spencer frowned,

"It's not bootiful Sally, it's a boy fish!"

"Well, boy fish can be beautiful too Spencer," Sally said weakly. Spencer didn't look convinced but was now trying to pick up the fallen glitter and press it with both his pudgy hands on to his masterpiece, muttering to himself,

"Boys not bootiful. Girls are bootiful. Boys are boys!"

A welcome distraction intervened.

"Coffee time, ladies!" Fay called, rescuing Sally from a debate she knew she wouldn't win. A caffeine boost was sorely needed.

"Julie, ten more minutes, then if you could start thinking about bringing the activity to a close and start washing hands etc, the children can then have some free play before song time. Biscuit, ladies?"

Sally, Anna and the other mums gratefully took a chocolate digestive and sat in view of all the activities, but safely by the kitchen area so as to keep the hot drinks away from the children.

"How's the boiler?" Sally enquired, dunking her biscuit in her coffee.

"Ok, thanks, John thinks he can fix it, so fingers crossed!" Anna paused to sip her coffee, "honestly though, if I could write this week off I would. I found Tommy had managed to pull the plug cover off the sitting room wall and was trying to poke a pipe cleaner in it he'd found in the craft box! Can you believe it, the little monkey!"

Sally's eyes widened.

"Crikey, he's strong! I struggle to get mine out when I want to do the ironing," she said, taking a sip of her coffee.

"I know!" agreed Anna indignantly, "they're not easy and do you know what he said when I asked him why he did it?"

"Go on," grinned Sally, reaching to put another half a teaspoon of sugar in her coffee.

"He said...." Anna paused for effect, "that he wanted to give it to the Borrowers that lived under the house because they could make something for their home with it!"

Sally burst out laughing,

"Oh Anna! Bless him!"

"Bless him, my auntie!" humphed Anna, "All I need is an electrocution entry in my Accident and Incident book before Ofsted visit!"

Sally, still grinning, said in a mock serious tone.

"Well, I suppose during this activity you observed Tommy's fine motor skills at pulling the plug cover off and duly noted it in his daily diary so you could plan for his next steps." Sally dodged Anna's elbow aimed at her ribs.

"Oh, ha, ha!" Anna couldn't help herself as she finally saw the funny side of the situation.

"I just can't turn my back for one minute. Roll on September when he starts school, my nerves are in shreds!"

Sally sympathised with Anna but then became serious.

"Look, Anna, it wouldn't have been your fault, you've risk assessed your home, you had the plug cover in place and Tommy's parents know what he's like."

Anna agreed,

"I know, I know....his mother only told me yesterday that the weekend she found him flushing cornflakes down the toilet so the Borrowers could try his breakfast!"

"That films got a lot to answer for!" rued Sally

"You're telling me!" grimaced Anna

"Look at my picture I've painted, Anna," called Tommy

"That's lovely Tommy," Anna rose, popped her cup on the side and went over to the painting table to admire the painting close up. "Tommy, what lovely colours you've used. Did you know there are bigger sheets of paper just here," she said, picking up some A3 sugar paper in various colours.

Tommy shook his head and held up a postcard size piece of paper with three blobs on it.

"No, I wanted this piece. It's me, mummy and daddy; it's for the Borrowers to hang on their wall so they know who their neighbours are."

Tommy's brown eyes looked so caring and so full of warmth.

"That's very thoughtful of you, Tommy, I'm sure they'll love it," smiled Anna. Tommy decided a bit more paint was needed for his masterpiece whilst Anna made her way back to Sally.

"I'd better warn his mum," said Anna under her breath, "just in case he tries to pull up his bedroom carpet and deliver the painting between the floorboards.

"Good idea!" replied Sally, "especially if the paint's not dry!"

87

"Anna, has Sally had a chance to mention next Friday to you?" Fay was now washing up coffee mugs.

"No I haven't yet Fay, sorry, but we were discussing activities that fulfilled areas of development in the revised EYFS."

Sally winked at Anna who rolled her eyes at Sally.

"Oh very good, you two are so diligent! Well Anna, Tamara is visiting next week..."

"It's ok Fay, can I stop you there," Anna apologetically interrupted Fay, "Tamara caught me just as I left the house this morning, but thank you Fay, and thank you for the coffee. It's so lovely to have one made for you and to be able to sit and drink it!" Anna popped her empty mug on the counter.

"Oh wonderful and you are very welcome Anna," Fay said, now drying the mugs and popping them away in the cupboard for next week.

"Shall we help Julie clear away, bless her, she's looking a bit overwhelmed!"

"You're right," agreed Sally, "I'll help them wash their hands."

Within ten minutes the children's pictures were hanging up to dry with the date and their names on ready to take home next week, the table was cleaned with the pots and brushes washed and little hands were all washed and dried.

Sally took Portia and Spencer's hands and sat them on floor cushions that were set out in a semi circle and waited patiently for Fay to fetch her song bag for nursery rhyme time.

In no time at all the children had finished their song time and were pulling on their coats, hats, scarves and gloves to wrap up against the January chill.

Portia looked relieved to be going back to the familiarity and security of Sally's and held Spencer's hand patiently whilst Sally did his coat up.

"Thank you Fay, thank you Julie," called Sally to the duo who were tidying away now tidying away the toys and had disappeared deep into the depths of the walk in storage cupboard.

"Thank you, bye," called Anna

"You're very welcome," came a muffled voice, "see you next Tuesday, if not, next Friday."

Sebastian Whitehall, six feet tall, dark-haired with unreadable blue eyes, scanned the Financial Times whilst the 6.45am train carried him to London where he worked as an investment banker.

He had risen at 4.45am that morning, as he did every morning, and showered. He then worked out in their basement gym he had had installed, for precisely thirty minutes, even though his company offered as a perk to its employees, a heavily discounted full membership to a prestigious gym located only a few steps away from his work. He would then shower for the second time that day. He would eat breakfast for fifteen minutes, precisely, which, without fail, consisted of half a sliced avocado on toast with fresh coffee, dress, and then drive to the station.

Sebastian's life was planned to the minutest detail. Every minute of every day was accounted for. Even time with Phoebe and Portia was scheduled. It enabled him to ensure his marriage to Phoebe was manageable and stayed on track on a day to day basis.

Theatre visits, art exhibitions, special occasions, planned spontaneous dinners were all planned with precision detail and timing, to allow him to accommodate his wife in his life. He would inform Phoebe of the month ahead's social engagements, with suggestions for the outfit she should wear, down to her shoes, underwear and jewellery. Except for the planned, spontaneous dinners. He planned these into his schedule as a 'reinvestment in their relationship' evening as apparently women appreciated these tedious occasions, he had heard at work, to self-evaluate themselves and the marriage status quo.

Sebastian viewed, and treated his wife, like a sophisticated pet. He'd needed to acquire a wife as it was conducive to his position at work. Three years ago he had been in danger, being in his thirties and unattached, of being perceived as homosexual, which, to Sebastian, was abhorrent. He therefore decided that within the year he would be married. He began to frequent art galleries and exhibitions, scanning the attendees for potential mates. His requirements were simple. She had to be young, educated and malleable.

He had spotted Phoebe on the third week of his project. Tall, dark, exotic looking and whippet thin, she turned, holding a glass of sparkling water and caught him looking at her. Sebastian wasted no time, he was on a schedule. She was in her second year of studying art history at university and had had only one boyfriend. This was important to Sebastian, he didn't want spoiled goods. She was more gregarious and outspoken than he would have liked, but that could be changed over time he had reasoned.

Within four weeks they were sleeping together, four months later they were engaged and ten months after their first meeting, they were married.

Sebastian was mentally exhausted by the time they were married. He was an astute man and knew his way of existing was a little exact, so he had made a supreme effort to be upbeat and relaxed whenever Phoebe visited and threw her shoes in the corner of the hall, flopped her clothes over the bedroom chair or left crumbs all over the worktops in the kitchen.

If Sebastian were perfectly honest with himself he would prefer to be single and use prostitutes. High class ones of course and always with protection. No need to waste time training them to your behaviours or ways of living. They offered a service; you paid for it. No emotional involvement needed or expected.

It had certainly been tiresome getting Phoebe round to his way of being. He had been careful not to use his preferred method of achieving results until after the birth of Portia, nine months after their wedding night. He calculated that Phoebe would have a moral as well as emotional investment in the marriage with Sebastian now the father of her child. He knew how much she valued family life coming from such a close knit family, as had her parents. It was all she knew and fully expected their union to be the same.

Sebastian closed the newspaper as the train thundered along, now nine minutes and forty seven seconds away from its destination, and looked out of the window, his mind now on the day's meetings that lay ahead.

He didn't enjoy correcting Phoebe, however, nor did he feel guilty. He wanted his life to run as efficiently and smoothly as possible and if he achieved the desired behaviour from Phoebe through his methods then it was clearly successful. Hence the need for tedious social events, the obligatory date nights and the gifts of jewellery, which offset the results of his corrections. It was a tiresome, but necessary, game for him to play to maintain the living conditions at home in a state he could function in.

Sue opened her eyes, the afternoon sunshine streaming through her bedroom window and onto her bed.

She lay there, coming to.

The blackness that had engulfed her that morning had subsided. She thought back to the last time it had reared its ugly head.

Countdown.

John's favourite programme.

He would come into the farmhouse during the summer months, watch Countdown with a mug of tea and a slice of Sue's homemade cake, and then go back on to the farm to spray the fields. He wasn't particularly good at Countdown, only forming three or four letter words and not once did he solve the mental maths challenge, but he loved the adrenaline filled thirty minutes in the middle of his afternoon.

It was a welcome contrast to the practical demands that being a farmer entailed.

Its signature tune had filled her low beamed sitting room early last week one afternoon and she had frozen, paralysed with grief.

In a trance she had walked over and turned the television off. She'd collapsed in the chair nearest to the television, clamped her arms around her middle, and rocked backwards and forwards, reeling with raw pain.

Enough! Sue purposefully pulled back the duvet and the crochet blanket and swung her legs over the side of the bed. 'Pull yourself together, Sue,' she said to herself, 'stop feeling so bloody sorry for yourself.'

She felt ashamed of herself thinking back to this morning. She reminded herself she'd had a long and happy marriage, she'd had three healthy children, numerous grandchildren and was as healthy as any sixty year old woman could expect to be.

She had a quick shower, and then formed a plan of action for what was left of the rest of the day.

She needed to pop into the village for some groceries and she would give Julia a ring and see if she could pick up some of her children for her, make her workload a little easier.

Twenty minutes later, Sue was in her Land Rover, driving down the narrow country lane away from the farm and into the nearby village. She felt positive and calm.

Long may it last, she thought ruefully.

Sue pulled into the Co op's tiny, awkward car park. Walking into the shop through the automatic doors, Sue fished from her pocket the list of essentials she needed.

Flour, butter, sugar, teabags, milk and eggs. She bent down to pick up a basket.

"Oh hello, Sue," a voice called.

Sue looked up and saw Sally, Fin's childminder, pushing a tandem pushchair with two sleeping children in it.

"Well, hello Sally," smiled Sue, "how lovely to see you. You've been keeping them busy I see," pointing at the sleeping toddlers.

Sally grinned and nodded.

"Job well done I'd say, they've had a pretty hectic morning at Messy Club and they're just recharging their batteries for this afternoon," Sally laughed.

Sue laughed as well, remembering from experience the restorative qualities of the power nap to a toddler. She thought how genuinely happy Sally seemed to be whenever she saw her out and about with her little ones. She remembered Julia had mentioned once that you knew where you stood with children. They were upfront, direct and honest. If they were upset, you knew it, if they were happy, you knew it, they called a spade a spade and, unlike adults, had no hidden agenda.

"How are you, Sue, keeping busy?" Sally enquired gently.

"I have good days and bad days," Sue replied simply, "I'm looking forward to the better weather so I can get out in the garden more."

Sally leant over the tandem to adjust Portia's blanket.

"Sue if you need any help digging over your vegetable patch, Nick and the boy's would be only too happy to help," Sally offered.

Sue was genuinely touched.

"Sally, that's very kind, I'll bear that in mind."

"I mean it, Sue, it would be no trouble at all," Sally paused, she'd just had a thought. "Sue, speaking of vegetables, I could really do with some advice on vegetable growing, my lettuces are alright but every year my tomatoes are a disaster. I have three or four red ones if I'm lucky and I never know which leaves to pinch out."

"Well, I'd be happy to Sally, just let me know when a good day is for you and I'll pop round."

"That sounds great, Sue," enthused Sally, "Mondays are a good day for me but I can fit in with you." Sally looked hopeful.

"Mondays are fine for me, Sally. When it's time, I'll bring round a tomato plant and I'll give you a hands on lesson in how and where in the garden to grow them and which leaves to pinch out, how does that sound?"

Sue felt a warm glow inside her. It felt good to be of use, to be needed, as though she still had something to contribute. She would actively seek out to do more of it! She wanted to keep the blackness she'd experienced this morning firmly at bay and going out of her way to keep active and involved might just do the trick.

Sally looked relieved.

"Brilliant, Sue, thank you so much! I'm not the world's most natural gardener and I don't know anything about pest control so any advice you have I'd be very grateful to hear it!"

"That's settled then, now, I'd better hurry," Sue glanced at her watch, "I've promised to pick up the children from school so I mustn't be late."

The two women said their goodbyes and went their separate ways. Sally paid for her apples and bananas which she was forever buying, and started the mile long walk to pick up the after school children.

Who did she have today? It was Tuesday, so Luke, Jimmy, Maisie and Hannah. She was keeping Portia until 4.30pm and dropping off Spencer to Mrs Banks at school. Tuesday meant it was sausages, mashed potatoes, carrots, broccoli and gravy for tea and, with a bit of luck, she should be finished work by 6.15pm.

Sally reached the school gates five minutes before the end of school bell sounded and greeted Mr Young, the Head teacher, who was holding open the gate for parents.

"Good afternoon, Sally, keeping busy I see," smiled Mr Young, tall, grey haired, unflappable.

"Good afternoon, Mr Young, busy enough for me, I'm not getting any younger!" Sally bantered.

Mr Young gave a faux grimace,

"None of us are, are we? I've really felt the cold this year in my bones."

He stopped and laughed. "Listen to us both.....Hello Mrs Peters; Mrs Jenkins....how's your puppy?"

Sally carried on into the main playground and waited near the hall entrance where the children came out, full of tales, after their day at school.

Sally had wanted to ask Mr Young how his wife had been over the Christmas holidays but the school gate wasn't the place when he had his 'Head Teacher' hat on. She'd catch him at another, more appropriate time.

It was so sad, so cruel.

Mrs Young, a gentle, slight, unassuming woman, also in her late fifties, had been diagnosed eighteen months ago with an aggressive form of Motor Neurone Disease.

The prognosis was poor.

At the Christmas play in early December last year, to the dismay of all the parents who knew her, she wheeled herself into the hall to sit along the edge of the audience in a wheel chair.

Mrs Young didn't teach at the school. She had worked as a Reception teacher in a primary school in a nearby village. She had been unable to have children so had devoted her life to the wave of expectant and nervous little ones that arrived each September and to supporting her husband at all the outside school hours events such as serving the teas and coffees at Parents evenings and helping out back stage during school plays. She had retired at the end of the previous summer term on medical grounds when her illness had begun to speed up its relentless claim on her body.

A week before last year's summer fete a letter had gone home to all the parents outlining Mrs Young's condition and informing them that this year's raffle proceeds would go to the Motor Neurone Disease Association. Although people were feeling the pinch, just over £1000 was raised. Sally herself had bought £10 worth of tickets and donated a bottle of wine as a prize.

Everyone had been shocked at someone they knew being diagnosed with such a debilitating disease with no cure. Sally was sure she wasn't the only one that night who, after reading the school's letter, gave the members of their family an extra big hug before they went to bed that night.

The Hall door opened and each class teacher came out with their class and waited until each child had spotted the person that was meant to be collecting them. The child would then hop down the steps to greet them and make their way home.

Sally saw Maisie and Jimmy, waved and smiled. Maisie was a Year four pupil with long brown hair fashioned into two plaits, big blue eyes, freckles, who loved horses and reading and was as bright as a button. She spotted Sally and ran down the steps to Sally. Jimmy, on the other hand, just scowled and walked as slowly as he could to where Sally was waiting.

"Hello Maisie, good day?" Sally asked

"Yeah, ok, can you hold my stuff please?" Maisie asked hopefully, flicking her plaits back over her shoulders.

"Well, let's see," answered Sally, bending down, "I can pop them in the basket, underneath the pushchair, here we go, there!" Sally straightened up.

"Thank you, Sally," said Maisie with a big smile, blue eyes shining with child like energy, "Jimmy's grumpy isn't he?"

"Yes, well, my house isn't his favourite place, I'm afraid," replied Sally

"He just wants to go home and play on his Xbox," said Maisie.

"I hate coming to your house!" Jimmy grumbled as he finally reached Sally and Maisie.

"Jimmy, everyone would rather go home to their own house but it's not THAT bad at my house, is it?" reasoned Sally, "I've got a television so you can relax and watch Horrid Henry or Top Gear DVD's, I have Lego and Playmobil, your two favourite things to do and you have a snack, a chocolate biscuit and before you know it Mum or Dad is picking you up."

Jimmy looked down at his feet and shuffled them.

"Well it's ok, I s'pose," he said begrudgedly

Give Jimmy ten minutes and he would have thawed out and be genial and chatty. It was just the initial greeting; he was the same in the mornings. Monday's were his hardest day as it was after a weekend of family time. One particularly cold Monday morning after the October half term, Jimmy had arrived in a foul mood, clearly not wanting to be at Sally's. He had turned around and shouted in frustration at the passing cars and bemused dog walkers,

"I hate Sally's house! Do you know it's a PRISON!!!"

Jimmy's poor mother was mortified and had bustled Jimmy into Sally's hallway. Sally had been quite literally stunned by Jimmy's unscheduled and somewhat negative advertising of her childminding business. She recovered herself and reassured Jimmy's mother that these things happen, waved her off to work and ever so gently, shut the door behind her and counted to ten.

"Here comes Luke, Sally," Maisie said

"Luke, Luke, over here!" Sally called. Luke spotted her and beamed.

"Jimmy, GREAT! You can see my new car I brought this morning,"

"Luke!" shouted Jimmy, "YEAH! I LOVE coming to Sally's and seeing Luke!"

Jimmy was now all smiles, Maisie turned to Sally, rolled her eyes and smiled,

"Well, at least he's happy now!"

"Right children, let's pop around to the Reception class, pick up Hannah and drop off Spencer."

They all trooped round to the other side of the school where Reception came out separately.

"Maisie!" called out a little blonde girl.

It was Hannah. Maisie's younger sister.

Sally thoroughly enjoyed looking after the girls, as she did Adele. As long as Sally's craft box was full she rarely heard a peep out of them. They gave a lovely round feel to the after school sessions and balanced out the once boy heavy sessions nicely.

Mrs Banks, Spencer's mum, came to the gate.

"Sally hi! Thank you for sending me the picture of Spencer's fish, he looked like he was having a wonderful time."

"You're very welcome, Sarah, it's still drying so we'll pick it up next week. Right, I've jotted down Spencer's day in his daily diary, there haven't been any problems today and he's had an hour's sleep this afternoon. He just woke up in the bottom playground so might be a little grumpy, bless him." Sally unclipped Spencer and he flopped into his mummy's arms.

"That's lovely Sally, thank you and I'll see you Thursday."

"Will do Sarah, bye Spencer, right children, let's all turn around and head back up the path and let's get home. Those sausages won't cook themselves!"

Maisie, who had been skipping along ahead of Sally, plaits bouncing on her shoulders, came to a halt, turned around and announced,

"Oh, I'm a vegetarian now!"

Sally, trying hard not to give a visual reaction, was momentarily caught off guard.

"Uhh..okay...um...right. Maisie, when did you become a vegetarian love because last night you had chicken and pasta at my house."

"Today....I've been thinking about it for a while now and I decided today, after eating my ham sandwiches, that I didn't want to eat animals anymore."

Well, thank you for deciding that on my watch, thought Sally to herself.

"What are you going to do with the sausages I've got for tonight's tea?" asked an intrigued and slightly bemused Sally

"Leave them on my plate!" replied Maisie, matter of factly.

Great! thought Sally,

"Ok love, I'll just give mum a call when we get home to see if it's alright for you to have cheesy mash with your vegetables. Will you still want gravy with it?

100

"Are their animals in gravy?" questioned Maisie, holding the gate open for Sally.

"Um..I don't think so, I'll have to check the packet. Right, let's get a move on then, those clouds don't look too promising."

The little group hurried back to Sally's. There's certainly never a dull moment in this job, Sally thought to herself and headed home.

Sally had now been home an hour. They had all bundled in through the front door and tripped over Eddie's size 9 shoes, back pack and blazer which had been thrown on the floor in his hurry to get to the fridge. Lunch boxes and book bags were now lined up on the hall bench with shoes sitting neatly in pairs to the side of it and the children were all playing in the conservatory. She had phoned Maisie's mum who had confirmed cheesy mash was absolutely fine for Maisie's tea and had apologised profusely on behalf of her daughter. She knew how manic Sally's day was and to have a last minute menu change could be done without.

Sally, her professional hat firmly on, had reassured her it was no problem at all and respected Maisie's decision. It showed at the tender age of eight she was developing her own feelings and opinions about animal welfare. Privately Sally knew that by next week Maisie would probably be tucking into pepperoni pizza by Wednesday.

Portia had just been picked up by Phoebe, dressed again in her cashmere and sequins, when the phone rang.

"Hello?" Sally answered, just wanting some peace and calm to reign on her and her day.

"Hello?..is that Sally Slater?" asked a voice

"Yes is it, whose calling please?"

"It's Sandra Peckham from Ofsted. Could you tell me what days you are childminding next week so I can come and inspect your setting."

Sally's mouth formed a silent 'O' and her eyes widened in disbelief. You have got to be kidding me, she thought wearily to herself.

Ofsted!

Sally exhaled as quietly as she could down the phone and hurried through to the conservatory to check her diary.

That evening, the last child gone, Sally put the oven back on for her own family's tea of sausages and mashed potatoes. She peeled the potatoes and cut them into small pieces so they cooked quickly and put them on to boil. She opened two packets of sausages, popped them onto a baking tray and took two cans of beans out of the cupboard.

Tea under way, Sally went through to the conservatory to tidy up the last remaining toys and sweep the floor ready for the next day.

Ten minutes later the front door opened and in trooped the rest of Sally's family. Nick with Jack, hair still wet from lifeguard training and Chris, who had just got off the late bus from college.

"Hi guys, everyone ok?" Sally called through from the conservatory.

"Yeah, s'all good!" Jack replied, now in their sitting room having dumped his bag in the hallway. "What's for tea mum? I'm starving!"

"Sausages love, they'll be fifteen minutes," she nodded towards Jack's bag, "is there wet washing in that bag?" knowing full well there was. Jack sheepishly went back and picked up his bag,

"Er, there might be," he smiled and slunk past Sally to empty his wet washing into the washing machine.

Chris came through and fell into an old, worn armchair.

"Good day, Chris?" Sally asked her first born, dark like herself, medium height and living life to the full, like most eighteen year olds.

"Yeah, so, so, the bus was twenty minutes late....again! It's always a

Tuesday as well! Apparently the bus driver had to replace a windscreen wiper! Why they don't do it at the end of the day, I just don't know! I was

ten minutes late for college!"

"I'll phone the bus company tomorrow, always a Tuesday? Are you sure?" asked Sally

"Yep! If you ask me, the driver just fancies an extra ten minutes in bed!" pondered Chris, probably not far from the truth. "Did you say it's sausages for tea? I'm starving!" finished Chris, repeating Jack's plea for food. He got up and walked through the kitchen to the fridge. "Anyone want these wedges and cold pizza?" he asked hopefully.

"You can have them, love," Sally called from the hallway, now rescuing lunch boxes and water bottles from everyone's bags to wash and refill with food, ready for the next day. It was never ending.

Nick emerged from their bedroom, having changed out of his work clothes and into his favourite old jeans and jumper. His once black hair was heavily flecked with grey.

Sally heard her husband's footsteps.

"You ok, love?" she called

Nick came into the kitchen and kissed his wife's cheek.

"Ok, yeah, bit of a day. A driver called in sick but Pete wanted to pick up an extra shift, otherwise I would have done it, we could use the money." He walked over to the kettle and started filling it. "Tea love?"

"Oooo...on that note, oh yes please, tea would be lovely. You'll never guess what?" Sally turned to face Nick, eyes shining with pure relief. "A mum stopped me today in the playground and wants ten sessions of childminding. Ten! Before and after school, can you believe it? It will cover Simon's money and a little extra!"

Nick's eyes widened and he smiled broadly.

"That's great, love, really great!" Nick was genuinely relieved.

The boys were getting older and more expensive to keep, what with Chris's bus fare to college which was nearly a thousand pounds for the year and Jack's extracurricular hobbies, and he reflected on the cheque he had written last night for lifeguarding.

"Something always seems to turn up, doesn't it, when things are going a bit pear shaped."

He leant over and kissed his wife on the lips.

Sally grimaced and continued hesitantly,

"Yes...... it's certainly taken the edge off the phone call I received this afternoon."

Sally trailed off and looked nervously at her husband who had now stopped making the tea and was looking questioningly at his wife.

"Ofsted are coming next week."

Nick's face fell.

He turned, leant forward with both hands on the worktop, dropped his head and exhaled heavily.

Not Ofsted.

He didn't know if their marriage could survive another Ofsted visit.

Sally watched her husband's reaction to her words.

Guilt and shame flooded her body.

"It won't be like last time Nick....I promise..." Sally stepped forward and gave her dejected looking husband an awkward side hug. Nick stood up straight, he robotically returned Sally's hug then turned and opened the fridge in the slim hope of finding anything with an alcohol content in it.

The rest of the evening passed uneventfully.

Jenny telephoned at 6.30pm and arranged with Sally to visit with Polly on Saturday morning so they could have an informal chat and a cup of tea.

After washing up Sally and Nick collapsed on the sofa to watch the Great British Bake off, relaxing and easy viewing, just perfect for a Tuesday evening.

That night, Sally and Nick both collapsed into bed feeling a little less anxious about money and the immediate future, but neither looking forward to the pressure and tension that the impending Ofsted visit would inevitably create.

Celeste sipped her wine as she watched her daughter's elegant frame disappear gracefully into the ladies cloakroom of the wine bar, they both favoured for their monthly mother and daughter catch up.

She noted men and women following Phoebe with their eyes. She had such an easy grace about her.

An older version of her daughter, Celeste was an only child of parents who had owned a small, individual, but highly profitable restaurant serving westernised Chinese cuisine.

They had met at catering college and three months into the course were planning their future together. Whilst their fellow students would socialise and relax after a day's study at college, or after their work placements, the two of them would take on extra shifts to learn their craft in more depth and save as much of their earnings as they could for their joint future.

After graduating, they lived together for two years in one room, in a house share, which was cheaper than renting a one bedroom flat, working and saving until they had enough to purchase a flagging, down trodden restaurant in Stentbridge. After much hard work and a complete renovation they opened their sleek, modern restaurant to rave reviews.

Ten years later along came Celeste, who was included in all aspects of running the restaurant as she grew up. She'd loved the buzz of the process of running a restaurant but her favourite place was the kitchen. At weekends, during the day, she would spend precious time with her father, watching his skill and speed with a knife in awe and wonder, wanting one day to emulate him and to make him proud of her.

Whilst away at university she'd met her husband, Paul. They were both studying Business Management and both came from a background which promised hard work reaped rewards. Paul, a tall, broad, muscular man, was a polished rough diamond from a simple but loving upbringing, he was a family man in the making and the moment he spotted Celeste in the university cafeteria he set about respectably courting her. He wanted to build a life with her. The year after they left university, they got married and moved in with her parents at the restaurant.

Celeste continued working for her father, gradually taking over the front of house from her mother, whilst Paul started investing in property up for auction to develop.

The couple never took their eye off the ball. They worked, saved and invested. It paid off.

They now had a substantial portfolio of properties and through these had been able to privately educate their only daughter, Phoebe, who had finally come along after years of waiting when Celeste was forty one.

Now both of her beloved parents were deceased, Celeste and Paul were very wealthy pensioners, although Paul would never stop working entirely, it just wasn't in his nature. They had sold the restaurant for a substantial amount of money and were quietly watching the housing market for another property.

A home for Phoebe and Portia.

Their daughter didn't know it yet but she was going to need it one day.

Phoebe came hurrying back from the cloakroom; Celeste smiled warmly at her only child. Celeste's blood boiled when she considered that Phoebe's bastard of a husband may still be hurting her. She hadn't shared her fears with Paul as the consequences would be unsalvageable. She had just hinted that their characters were at odds and maybe purchasing a bolt hole for their daughter and grandchild might be prudent.

Celeste had no solid proof that Phoebe was being assaulted but her body language when she was in the company of Sebastian definitely gave cause for concern. Fear constantly crossed her eyes. She checked, tidied, wiped and straightened objects and soft furnishings around the house. Over the past three years, Celeste had observed her daughter gradually metamorphosise from an outgoing, confident, gregarious, relaxed young woman to an anxious, watchful shell of her former self.

The subject of abuse was touched on a few weeks after Portia had been born. Celeste had lovingly thrown an arm around Phoebe's waist to give her an impromptu cuddle causing Phoebe to wince in pain. She pulled away from her mother and wouldn't meet her mother's puzzled gaze. Without saying a word Celeste had pulled up Phoebe's jumper and had drawn a gasp at the blurry edges of the fist shaped bruise that unapologetically spread over Phoebe's rib cage.

Phoebe lamely protested that she had fallen but Celeste wasn't fooled. Post pregnancy hormones still playing host, Phoebe had burst into tears and begged her mother not to say anything. It had been an accident, he hadn't meant to, he'd been so tired with the arrival of Portia; he really was a wonderful husband.

Celeste, against her better judgement, but mindful of keeping the lines of communication open with her only child, bit her tongue and said nothing but vowed to herself to keep a watchful eye over her daughter.

"That jacket looks gorgeous on you, darling," admired Celeste as Phoebe sat down and took a sip of her sparkling water. Phoebe looked down at it.

"Sebastian bought it for me; he thought my khaki one made me look washed out."

Celeste bristled.

"How thoughtful of him."

"Mmmm.." Phoebe replied, giving her mother a small smile, not really wanting to enter into a Sebastian bashing conversation after recent events at home. She may just crumble if her mother pressed too much.

'How is Sebastian, darling?' Celeste asked casually, piercing an olive with a cocktail stick, imagining it was Sebastian's eye.

"He's fine," nodded Phoebe, a practised, bright smile, fixed into place, on her face. "He thinks it time to have another baby."

She tore a piece of ciabatta bread, dipped it into the accompanying oil and bit into it. She looked up at her mother with eyes that betrayed her demeanour; they held the same look a deer has when it looks into headlights.

Celeste used all her powers of restraint not to raise her eyebrows in astonishment. Sebastian's input into Portia's baby years had been nonexistent as far as Celeste could make out.

A month before Portia had arrived; Sebastian had personally vetted, and then employed, two Norland nannies, one for the daytime and one for the night time. Phoebe had protested initially at this huge expense and invasion into her time with her firstborn, but quickly realised it was futile. What she hadn't foreseen was that Sebastian still expected her to keep up with her appearance, keep her figure maintained and to be available for all of Sebastian's work and social engagements, not to mention moral obligations, baby or no baby.

The bruise on her ribcage had been a reminder to Phoebe that the aroma of baby sick, unnoticed by Phoebe, coming from her Nicole Fahri sweater would not be tolerated.

The unexpected upside of having the nannies was that they soon caught on to the state of affairs within the Whitehall marriage and took it upon themselves to support and protect Phoebe throughout those early baby months.

When the daily email came through the daytime nanny would do the daily shopping and run Sebastian's errands whilst Phoebe spent precious time with her baby. Two hours before Sebastian was due home she would gently remind Phoebe of the time so she could shower and change. Phoebe would kiss her baby goodbye and get herself ready to present to her husband.

In the morning, before the night time nanny went off duty, instead of feeding and bathing Portia, she would hand the grateful Phoebe her baby and do the bathroom checks herself.

Blind hung at fourth tile, towels measured to a 40cm width, bath room cabinets double checked.

That first Christmas, a grateful Phoebe had bought them both a Chanel handbag as a thank you for their care, discretion and loyalty towards her and her daughter those first few months.

Celeste pierced another olive; obviously Sebastian was after promotion thought Celeste cannily.

"Well dear," she paused for a moment, then, "the daughter of a friend of mine has just returned to work and has had one of those contraceptive hormone releasing gadgets, inserted under her skin, on her arm." Celeste pierced yet another olive, "you know, to prevent any surprises."

She bit into the olive and waited to let that piece of information sink in.

Phoebe stared at the olives whilst she absorbed that coded message. Her mother was obviously aware how controlling Sebastian was and intuitively sensed that taking the Pill orally would not be an option as could easily be stumbled across by him.

She sat back in her chair whilst the waiter served them their starters. She picked up her napkin and smoothed it over her toned thighs. Eventually, Phoebe replied,

"Something to look into maybe."

She picked up her knife and fork.

Time to change the subject.

"So how's Dad? Has he bought any more property lately?"

The 'state of marriage' conversation dealt with, mother and daughter gossiped their way through lunch. Celeste listened and laughed at her daughter's conversation about her granddaughter, basking in her glow, as Phoebe's face lit up and lost its tight, pinched look as she recalled to her mother Portia's antics.

One day soon, thought Celeste, as her daughter ordered figs for pudding, one day soon, the fog will clear, and when that day comes, Celeste and Paul would be there to steer and support their daughter onto a clear and brighter future, far, far away from Sebastian.

Later that evening, Portia was tucked up in bed; her nanny relaxing on the third floor in her studio flat with the baby monitor, just in case Portia woke. The night time nanny had handed her notice in after two years as she had been offered a once in a life time position with a famous actor and his family, which would involve jetting off all over the world. Phoebe had written her a glowing reference and tearfully waved her goodbye. It was Gabrielle who had made Sebastian realise that one nanny was adequate to look after Portia, now she was a little older. She went to Sally's one day a week and would soon be starting pre-school. She was rarely unwell during the night so Gabrielle had offered to have the monitor in her room just in case she woke. Sebastian had surprisingly agreed to it on a trial basis and had insisted on increasing Gabrielle's salary by five thousand pounds. Sebastian had many faults, but being miserly was not one of them.

Phoebe was in the kitchen cooking Sebastian's duck breast, which he'd requested, when the phone rang. It was her mother.

"Hi mum, is everything ok?" Phoebe questioned anxiously. She rarely phoned in the evening as she knew they had a hectic social life.

Celeste nodded into the phone.

"Yes, yes, darling, I just...I just wanted to say how lovely it was to see you today, I had a really lovely time and...and I just wanted to phone and say thank you darling."

Phoebe smiled into the phone,

"Oh mum, you're so kind, it was lovely to see you..." she broke off, "Oh no!! Mum, I've got to go....oh no! The duck!"

Phoebe hung up the phone and dashed over to the griddle where the duck was smoking furiously, a layer of carbon continuing to burn underneath the meat.

Celeste hung up the phone, worried. She'd phoned because she'd just wanted to hear Phoebe's voice again, to check she really was ok. Phoebe had sounded panicked as she'd hung up the phone, not annoyed she'd burnt the duck, panicked!

Celeste walked through to the sitting room and poured herself a sherry. A cold dark sense of foreboding crept through her body.

Had she just made things worse?

Phoebe quickly turned the extractor fan on above the hob, in an attempt to rid the kitchen of the acrid smell of burnt duck, and scraped the charred remains down the food disposal. She grabbed another duck breast out of the fridge and hastily began to marinade it.

Her heart missed a beat. Sebastian's key turned in the lock. Her heart now sank. Maybe, just maybe, he would overlook her misdemeanour this one time.

The front door opened, and then closed.

"Hello darling, good day?"

Phoebe called through to the hallway. She heard Sebastian enter the kitchen and turned to greet him, her lips forced into a warm smile. Sebastian walked over to the sink to wash his hands. His back was facing her.

"You've burnt the duck." he said in a low voice, hunched over the sink, thoroughly soaping and rinsing his hands four times.

Phoebe winced as steam rose from the hot tap, Sebastian's hands barely visible under the pressured jet of hot water.

He rinsed his hands for a further fifteen seconds, took a clean hand towel from the drawer and dried his hands with quiet, deliberate precision.

Phoebe's smile began to fade.

"I'm so sorry Sebastian, my mother phoned, to say thank you for today, we had a really lovely lunch and I bought everything you asked for," she finished quietly.

She knew it was futile, but tried anyway.

"There's a fresh piece grilling as we speak."

112

Sebastian carefully hung up the hand towel on the rail, folded, bending to check both ends were hanging in equal length, and then walked towards Phoebe.

"That doesn't help the smell that is now permeating my nostrils, my hair, my clothes....now does it?"

Phoebe felt the slap before she saw his hand.

Her head swung around forty five degrees causing her forehead to swing round and catch the corner of the glass hood of the low hanging extractor fan.

The pain was instant and intense. She cried out.

"I'm sorry Sebastian, please don't..." she cowered, anticipating a follow up blow the other side of her face.

Tears sprung in her eyes which she furiously tried to blink away.

She lifted a hand to her forehead, it was wet.

Sebastian calmly walked over and fetched some kitchen towel, without hurrying, or an apology, he handed it to her.

"You're bleeding."

It was a statement.

"Please remember, next time the telephone rings, when you are cooking, to turn the heat off. This is the fourth time since Portia was born that I have had to remind you."

He glanced at the glass corner of the hood.

"Remember to thoroughly disinfect that hood when you clean it. I'm going to shower. I will be down in twelve minutes."

Sebastian climbed the three flights of stairs of their townhouse to their bedroom. He was unhappy with Phoebe. Why had she made that error and forced him to correct her? Before he stepped into the shower he sent an email to his personal assistant.

"Send a dozen red roses to my wife tomorrow with an appropriate message. Sebastian"

The incident, to him, was now forgotten.

He stepped into the threads of steaming water and closed the door.

Eyes closed, he lifted his face upwards to greet the cleansing spray of water.

Sebastian frowned, he grimaced in to the spray.

A vision.

He gave his head a slight shake to rid the presence of it.

The vision was stubborn.

An uninvited, distant memory now accompanied the vision.

Unwillingly, he was transported back twenty five years to boyhood.

"Sebastian? Come upstairs."

His mother's voice was calling him from upstairs.

The tone was accusing.

In the kitchen, Sebastian froze.

The bathroom.

He had checked and double checked.

"SEBASTIAN! COME IMMEDIATELY!"

Quickly wiping the crumbs away from his sandwich and carefully hanging the dishcloth evenly over the taps, he ran upstairs.

Breathless, he arrived at the top of the stairs.

Without warning, his head was whipped round to the left by a seemingly invisible force.

Searing pain immediately reverberated through the right side of his head, causing an instant, deafening ringing in his ear.

Stars began to form, unapologetically, in front of his eyes, blurring his vision.

His left knee unconsciously buckled at the intensity of the pain.

Unleashed, it whirled around the circumference of his skull, gaining intensity as it gathered an unforgiving momentum, commanding him, with its power, into a prayer position of submission.

There he stayed until it began its merciful descent.

His mother slowly lowered her arm, her left hand holding one of his table tennis bats.

"A reward for your sloppiness."

She stepped over the nine year old she had bore and made her way down stairs.

She addressed her son without turning or pausing her descent.

"We measure the towels on the drying rail Sebastian. A sloppy house equals a sloppy mind. Failure is then, just around the corner."

Downstairs, Phoebe took the duck breast off the griddle and placed it to rest on a wooden ridged board. That was the third correction this month, Phoebe noted to herself. The cut was small, but deep. She had placed two steri-strips over the cut and checked that her fringe covered it.

No one would notice.

She robotically washed the salad, carefully checking each leaf for grit, her mind processing the evening's events, so far.

Sebastian didn't love her.

The realisation of the sham of their relationship brought fresh tears to her eyes.

She was just a show horse to him to be trained, corrected and rewarded, all to sustain Sebastian's image of perfection and success.

How blind and naive she had been.

Two arms slid around her waist. Phoebe jumped, startled.

"I feel we missed out on our proper greeting,"

Sebastian turned Phoebe around in his embrace and gently kissed her on the lips.

"How was your day, darling?"

His voice was full of lust.

She forced herself to lean in to his chest and closed her eyes.

Bile began to rise in her throat.

"Lovely, thank you."

His hands slid down her hips, over the tautness of her buttocks.

"Hmmm...Well done Phoebe. Stepping those lunges up from fifty to one hundred has certainly paid off." he murmured into her ear.

"You were right as usual, Sebastian." She replied. The physical contact, the compliments, made the contents of her stomach curdle.

Before her stunned brain could process what was happening, Sebastian had undone and pulled down her trousers and panties and spun her around. He bent Phoebe forward with one arm, hand firmly in the middle of her back, the other arm pulled her hips towards him. Brutally, without love or tenderness, he penetrated her.

The act was aggressive, controlled, and possessive.

A release.

Twenty seconds later, Sebastian pulled up Phoebe's panties and trousers' and whispered into her neck,

"That was wonderful, shall we eat?"

Spontaneous, thought Phoebe as she speared a piece of lettuce. She lifted the fork to her mouth and glanced at Sebastian methodically chewing his duck. She used to think their sex life had always been spontaneous.

That was the word she used to use.

Now?

Now, how did it make her feel?

Violated.

Four weeks after their first date, on their fourth date, Sebastian had taken her back to his car, after an exquisite meal of oysters, lobster and champagne. He had parked on the top floor of a multi story car park.

It was virtually empty.

He had whispered as they approached the car that he had to have her.

Right now.

And he did, over the bonnet of his car, her cheek resting on the cool metal of the bonnet.

Shocked, but thrilled at her apparent desirability, Phoebe had fallen intensely and passionately in love with Sebastian.

An older, more experienced woman might have questioned why Sebastian felt the need to do this at the beginning of a new relationship with a young, beautiful woman, who hopefully, one day, would become the mother to his children. Why, the first time they made love, he hadn't wanted to privately explore her, cherish her, and respect her.

Phoebe took a sip of wine.

Looking back, she realised their sex life had always been about possession and domination.

They finished their meal in silence.

Sebastian's mind processed the day's events at work. Phoebe sat, numb, her head throbbing, as she slowly came to the realisation that her marriage wasn't what she'd thought it was as an inexperienced year old twenty one year old.

A shift had occurred in her mindset but she wasn't quite sure where this would take her.

Yet.

After life had calmed down following their fairytale wedding, Millie had continued to work at the estate agent. Karen, the female negotiator whose job she had covered, came back from maternity leave but only wanted to do a three day week. This meant that Millie's role in the office became less intense and more varied. She was now enjoying it. She did two days a week job share with Karen as a negotiator, two days in a secretarial role and the fifth day tidying up any loose ends in the office, be it taking photos of houses, uploading Rightmove with new properties, assisting viewings and, occasionally, she had the opportunity to go out on a valuation, which Millie loved. She thoroughly enjoyed looking around people's homes and was rapidly developing a keen eye for accurately valuing properties.

Darius still had dreams of branching out by himself as an interior designer but wasn't quite ready yet to take the leap into self-employment.

Two years after they married they bought a new three bedroom detached faux period house, in the village, on an upmarket small development that had just been completed. It was perfect for bringing up a family in. It had been built to a very high specification with a solid oak kitchen, utility room, double garage and landscaped garden. As with the wedding, Darius inspired Millie with his suggestions on decor and furnishings.

They both had traditional taste; neutral walls, leather sofas, (very child friendly), lamps, throws and cushions but Darius had suggested a few contemporary pieces to help keep the interior cosy but modern.

Millie had to admit that the sitting room looked great with an unusual bureau, a 1970's occasional chair and stool, and an antique lamp. Darius, who had a penchant for collecting glass, came home one day with an exquisite candelabrum for the mantelpiece.

It did look good.

A year after they had moved in Millie found out she was pregnant. They were both over the moon at how quickly it had happened after deciding they were ready to start trying.

Darius insisted Millie give up work immediately to enable her to focus on their growing baby and prepare for the birth of their child. Millie had been touched but insisted she gave a month's notice, with promises of returning at some point on a part time basis after the birth of the baby.

Darius had been promoted six months previously and was now responsible for overseeing a number of design projects at any given time. His salary had increased considerably and now they were embarking on a new life as a family all thoughts of becoming self-employed were shelved.

He read the baby books with Millie, massaged her back and legs and as the pregnancy progressed he did all he could to support his wife through the unchartered waters of pregnancy and the forthcoming birth. Millie was deliriously happy and content and knew she was incredibly lucky to have a husband like Darius.

One Friday, eight months pregnant, Millie had arranged to meet Karen from work, for lunch.

Having ordered their lunch, the two women proceeded to a long overdue catch up.

"So Millie, you're looking fab, how are you feeling?" asked Karen, taking a sip of her drink.

"FAT! in a word!" Millie groaned, "you think at six months, that's it, your stomach can't possibly get any bigger but I looked in the mirror this morning and it seems to have taken on a life of its own," Millie paused and thought about what she had just said, "which of course it has I suppose." She shrugged and they both laughed.

"How's Darius doing? Is he looking after you?"

"God, yes! He can't do enough for me," Millie rolled her eyes, "I remember what some of my friends have said in the past, how their husbands just don't seem to appreciate how tiring and uncomfortable it is being pregnant. I know I'm really lucky, Karen." Millie looked thoughtful and sipped her organic orange juice.

Karen humped and leaned back in her chair.

"Well, you can add me to that list of friends," she said grimly. She leant to one side so the waitress could place their food down.

"Thank you," smiled Karen at the waitress, "that looks great. Seriously, Millie, when the midwife handed Paul the baby he went into complete shock! I don't think he had ever come to terms with the fact that I had been carrying an actual real life baby inside of me all those months. Don't get me wrong, he's a great dad now Cameron's coming up for four but he certainly wasn't a natural!"

Karen picked up her knife and fork and surveyed her plate.

"Well, you're a great mum, Karen, I'm sure I'm going to be on the phone to you all the time for tips," Millie paused, reflecting, "I'm a bit scared to be honest, what if I do something wrong? How will I know what the baby needs when it's crying?"

Millie frowned and cut into her duck breast. She'd meant what she'd said about Karen. She juggled motherhood with work, housework and running a family. Millie knew Paul wasn't a natural around the house and the majority of it was left to Karen.

Karen chewed and swallowed her stuffed mushroom.

"You'll just know, Millie. There will be times when the baby just won't stop crying but between the two of you, you'll get through. One thing I have learnt about being a parent is that when I've been at the end of my tether and feel I can't cope anymore, Paul has stepped in and taken over, and vice versa. You never both hit the wall at the same time. I suppose that's why it's best to have two of you to bring up a baby. Do you think you'll come back to work?"

Karen tilted her head to the side, with a soft smile on her face. She already knew the answer to her question. Millie shook her head slowly.

"Darius is dead set against it, which is lovely in one way. I know, again, I'm very lucky, but," Millie trailed off, not wanting to say anything negative about Darius. She continued, "I will, eventually, you know, Two days a week or something. This time off had been great, but I do miss the adult company a bit."

Karen nodded, completely understanding Millie's situation.

"We'll see," Millie said, "I think because Darius's mum was always there for him and his brothers, he just thinks that's the norm."

"Well that's lovely you've got his support Millie, I have to work three days a week for the family pot, but even if I didn't I still think I'd do a couple of days. I'm Karen then, not Cameron's mum or Paul's wife..."

Karen looked at Millie, trying to weigh up her situation. All their friends and colleagues knew the great Millie and Darius love story. They were a great couple and Darius still obviously worshipped Millie, but Karen knew only too well how mind-numbing being a mum could be. The endless washing, changing of nappies, sleepless nights and child hood illnesses could be utterly overwhelming and exhausting and your identity as a woman can easily become swallowed and suffocated. Millie nodded,

"I can see that see that definitely, I'll just play it by ear I think.....ooo, the baby just kicked," Millie sat up straight to give the baby as much room as she could in the restricted space it had.

"You ok?" Karen looked concerned, "sure it's not a contraction?"

"No, no..NO! Good lord! Don't wish that on me yet!" Millie's eyes widened and she shook her head. "I'm in no hurry to get to that stage at all!"

The women both laughed and spent the rest of their lunch gossiping about office politics and life in general.

When Darius returned home from work that night with an organic mushroom risotto from the deli opposite his office, Millie told him about her lunch with Karen and the possibility of her returning to some form of work, eventually.

Darius picked up their forks from the work tops, smiled and said,

"Well thankfully darling that is something you don't need to worry about. I earn enough money for you not to, so you can focus fully on our little one." He patted her tummy and leant over and kissed her on the lips. "Love you, darling." He picked up their plates and carried their risottos over to the dining room table.

Millie stared at his retreating back and felt only the tiniest twinge of concern. Well, we'll just see what the future brings, she thought to herself joining Darius at the table. No need to rock the boat now. Millie sat down adjacent to Darius and covered his hand with hers.

"I love you too, Darius, I'm very lucky to have you."

Millie smiled at Darius, she meant it.

If this was going to be the only hiccup in their life, she really was very lucky. Darius smiled back at her, his eyes full of love.

"Millie, I'm lucky to have found you too. You fully deserve me, this lifestyle, you're very special."

He leant in and kissed her again. Their lips held and Millie's mind was taken back to the first night they had met when he had uttered those very words.

Her heart ached with love and gratitude for her wonderful husband and their life together.

Maggie let herself into the flat after her day of cleaning. She thoroughly washed her hands in the bathroom then went through to the kitchen, filled the kettle and switched it on. Her mobile phone rang, she picked it up.

It was Dean.

Her heart sank.

What now?

"Hi Dean, everything ok?" she asked, opening a cupboard and reaching for a mug.

"Maggie, I'm five minutes away, how long before you have to pick Adele up from school?" Dean's voice crackled, the village's reception was unreliable at the best of times.

Maggie glanced at the kitchen clock.

"Um, about thirty minutes, thirty five tops, why, what's wrong?" Maggie frowned to herself, he sounded strange.

"I'll see you in a minute." He hung up.

Well, that was odd. He should be teaching a lesson now, Maggie shrugged to herself. It had probably been cancelled. Great, it didn't bode well for his mood.

She poured the boiling water into her mug and reached into the cupboard for another mug for Dean. She really wanted to talk to him tonight about their future, maybe suggest a trial separation. Maggie knew he wasn't happy.

Whilst cleaning today, it had suddenly all seemed so simple. She wasn't happy, Dean wasn't happy, why not go their separate ways, remain amicable and share joint custody of Adele?

She heard Dean's key in the lock and poured milk in to both their mugs.

Twenty minutes later, Dean was gone.

He'd left her.

Maggie stood in their narrow hallway, staring at the front door that Dean had just closed quietly behind him.

Left.

Without drama.

Without shouting.

Without looking back.

Dean had come home to tell her he was leaving. He'd found a room to rent outside of Stentbridge and had suggested that they put the flat on the market and split the small profit that they would make from the sale.

Maggie had stood in the kitchen, holding her mug of coffee, slightly stunned that Dean had been thinking upon the same lines about their relationship and was being proactive about dealing with it.

He explained he felt as though he couldn't provide for them, the stress of the uncertainty of their future regarding the ever pending mortgage application, the stress of the unreliability of his work. He felt he was at the bottom of a well, with no means of climbing out.

Dean had looked worn and beaten, how Maggie had felt, for quite a while. He'd had his hands on his hips, waiting for an outburst from Maggie.

There was none.

Realising Maggie wasn't going to put up a fight to save their marriage; he had exhaled deeply and hung his head, strangely deflated. He had done it. Instead of feeling relived and free he'd just felt terribly sad.

It felt so very final.

Maggie had taken a step towards him, put her arms around him and hugged him. Dean, hesitantly, had hugged her back.

Young adults, defeated in their struggle, to create and sustain a life together, in the twenty first century.

Rosie arrived home from work Friday afternoon.

The hallway to her cottage was cool and dark, the house silent.

Glorious.

Rosie kicked off her shoes and laid her briefcase on the decorative half table that stood to the left of the hallway. She shrugged her long overcoat off and hung it up on a hanger in the built in cupboard, under the stairs. She closed the cupboard door and dropped the black latch in place.

Rosie paused and ran her hand down the old wooden panels of the door. John had made the door out of floorboards from their bedroom. Most were rotten and beyond saving, but John had lovingly sanded, treated, then stained the few boards that could be salvaged and over a couple of evenings, made the door.

Together they had made so many memories, renovating and restoring the cottage. There was so much of them as a couple wherever you looked. The kitchen table had been purchased on a Saturday afternoon trawl through second hand shops. The outing had started out as an exercise to get out in the fresh air and walk off a hangover after an evening with friends and too much wine, but it had rewarded them with an old, heavy oak table with eight matching chairs for £150.

It was a complete steal and John had decided that as his hangover was worse than Rosie's he had despatched her to the nearest cash point whilst he stood guard over their find.

Rosie turned around from the cupboard and stood still. She closed her eyes and breathed in deeply, exhaling she dropped her shoulders, letting the calmness of her home work its soothing magic. She felt the stress of the weeks teaching seep away.

Luke had been picked up from school by John's mother; he was going to spend the weekend with his Grandmother, having every whim pandered to

127

and being spoilt rotten. John had left just after lunch to go on an old school friend's stag weekend.

The weekend was all Rosie's.

Saturday would be a quick clean through, a spot of marking, (she'd managed to get most of it done at lunchtime,) then an amble around the shops in the afternoon. That evening she had the girls coming over for wine and nibbles around eight. Sunday, she would relax with the papers, go over her planning for the week, then pop a joint of beef into the oven and prepare the menfolk of her family a welcome home roast dinner. Wonderful!

She couldn't remember the last time she'd had a whole weekend to herself.

What mother could?

Rosie only had Luke to look after and worry about.

They hadn't meant him to be an only child but Rosie just hadn't fallen pregnant again. It had bothered her initially as she herself had been one of three children; they had all been close in age and got on really well. She had loved her childhood and had dearly wanted a sibling for Luke, but as the months, then years went by and she witnessed her friends having two or three children and often struggled with tiredness, stretched finances and juggling childcare, she had come to terms with the reality that there were some benefits to having just one child.

She walked through the downstairs turning on lamps and closing curtains, shutting out the cold, dark, January night. She went into the kitchen and filled the kettle for a mug of tea and turned it on. She turned to get the milk from the fridge when something caught her eye on the kitchen table.

A bottle opener was holding down a piece of paper.

It was from John.

'Hey, Rosie, hope you've had a good day! Enjoy your girlie evening and don't drink too much! See you Sunday, John xxx'

Rosie smiled to herself; it was rather a case of the pot calling the kettle black, considering his leisure pursuit this weekend!

Her wine evenings were always good fun with plenty of gossip, laughter, whispered confessions and 80's music.

Rosie went over in her mind who was coming. Firstly, there was Millie, who now had two children; Jane who was nine and Drew, who was six and in Luke's class at school. Rosie had bought the cottage through Millie and they had bumped into each other again at the Ladybird's toddler group. They had clicked right away and talked houses, renovations and sleepless nights and remained firm friends to this day.

Secondly, there was Sally, Rosie's childminder, both were middle children, both no nonsense and direct but sensitive to each other's positions as a working mum and a childminder. Rosie always appreciated and never took for granted Sally's kindness and flexibility over unexpected delays or overrun meetings. Sally always reassured her it was never a problem. Being a childminder meant you had to be prepared for these situations, it was inevitable, but Rosie was very aware that Sally had her own family with their own timetable and took great pains to give Sally plenty of notice if she could of any change to her usual routine.

Then there was Sharon, whose son was in Luke and Drew's class and she lived just up the road from Sally. Rosie smiled to herself, what a woman! Dry as a bone, great fun and lived life to the full. She both worshipped and loathed her husband and children with equal measure, like most women, and kept the girls entertained with her take on family life.

Lastly, there was Phoebe.

The girls had also met Phoebe at the Ladybird's toddler group. She has walked in one Monday morning, eight months pregnant, to find out dates and times of the group. She had stood behind Rosie, in the queue to pay, who had turned and smiled at the simply understated, but stunning young, pregnant woman behind her and introduced herself. Although Luke, Freddie and Drew were four and would be soon going to school, Rosie, Millie, Sally and Sharon all clicked with this new mum to be and took her under their wing.

All independent, strong minded women, who were discreet and confidential, but knew how to let their hair down and have a good time.

Rosie, being a teacher, had to be careful about school issues and she'd noticed Sally would go quiet and potter about refilling wine glasses and nibbles if the conversation turned to a family of a child she minded. The other women quietly respected this and never tried to press her for information. It was a good group and Rosie knew she was lucky to have these women in her life.

She poured the boiling water onto the teabag and two minutes later made her way upstairs for a leisurely soak in the bath.

John had packed his bag carefully for his weekend away. He was really looking forward to catching up with everyone and their lives, having one too many drinks and just relaxing with old friends. He loved being a husband to Rosie and a dad to Luke and wouldn't want his life to be any other way, but this weekend he could just be John.

In the bottom of his wash bag in a small, black, cloth bag, he had packed a pair of plain, black, silk panties. He would put them on just before he went out, but underneath his normal black boxers. He couldn't risk the other blokes seeing them, they'd verbally rip him to shreds, although, given the nature of the weekend, he could probably get away with it. John stopped and thought, no, better be safe than sorry, they'd never understand.

Millie answered the door.

More packages!

She could hardly contain her excitement. She thanked the postman and shut the door.

All week parcels had been arriving. New silk curtains for the dining room, bamboo framed prints of Chinese writing, so the children would be inspired, (or so Millie thought), Kimonos for the whole family to relax in, in the evening, Chinese music to listen to, whilst they relaxed in their Kimonos and the most important package of all, 'Battle Hymn of the Tiger Mother' by Amy Chua, which now lay in prime position on the coffee table in the sitting room.

It had arrived Tuesday afternoon, as Millie had paid the extra for the one day delivery.

Millie had broached the subject sensitively with Darius last night, after a night of passion inspired by one of her new purchases from Ann Summers.

"Darius, do you think we do enough for Jane and Drew academically?" She nuzzled into his neck and gave it a kiss. Darius, fighting sleep after the surprise, midweek antics from his wife, rolled onto his side and kissed her forehead.

"Of course we do darling, we make sure they do their homework, get enough sleep and get to school on time."

Millie, not wanting to upset the equilibrium in the bedroom too much, ventured with,

"You're right, I just think maybe a little extra something might not be a bad thing, maybe learning an instrument or discussing a cultural issue over supper, y'know? Anyway, let's not worry about it now," and she gave him another kiss and a cuddle.

"Night Millie, love you," murmured Darius, and was gently snoring before Millie had rolled over and turned the lamp off.

Millie laid back on her pillow and thought about the timetable she had drawn up earlier that day for Jane and Drew. They would need to get up earlier to allow time to do their Tai Chi exercises, rote learn a bank of words and their meanings then leave enough time to get to school without driving. She had read in one of the broadsheet weekend magazines a few months earlier of a mother who had been very inventive in this department.

Power walking, skipping, rollerblading and, Millie wasn't so sure on this one, a space hopper!

It all sounded very impressive; apparently it helped improve cognitive development, increased lung capacity and oxygen levels conducive to empowered learning.

Millie rolled over on to her side, surely that would result in a lot of perspiring therefore requiring another shower and re applying of make up? She frowned to herself; hmmm...she'd have to think that one through. She closed her eyes and drifted off to sleep; looking forward to the new project she and her family were going to embark upon together.

Darius got up early Friday morning and kissed Millie on the nose.

"Five more minutes," she murmured, Darius smiled,

"It's alright darling, it's 5am, I'm going to London, remember?"

"Oh that's right," Millie rolled onto her back, stretched and yawned, "will you be late home tonight?"

"No,no, probably about 5ish, shall I bring home supper, give you a night off?" he suggested, fishing a shirt out of the wardrobe. Although Millie was a 'stay at home mum', Darius was well aware of the monotony of having to produce a meal seven nights a week, so once a week he'd bring home supper to give Millie a night off from the kitchen.

Millie was now wide awake, leaning up on her elbows.

"Oooo..... that would be lovely Darius, what about some Chinese dishes from Waitrose, they stock Chinese wine now too?"

Darius twinkled at her,

"Chinese eh, well that's a surprise," Millie looked bashful and tried to hide a smile.

"Ok, no problem, Chinese it is."

He shrugged on his jacket and picked up his keys. "Shall I see if I can get some chopsticks as well?" he teased, leaning over and kissing her, caressing her corseted breast, still aroused from last night.

"That would be great," Millie murmured, returning her husband's kiss. Millie was thrilled; she would research the correct usage of chopsticks today so she could guide the children throughout supper. "Darius....you're going to miss your train," she whispered in his ear, Darius groaned,

"The only day I have to catch a train...." he got off Millie and picked up his briefcase, reaching the bedroom door he turned and said, "so that's corn beef hash and baked beans I'm buying for tea, is it?" He grinned,

"Oh ha, ha," Millie laughed, throwing a pillow at the rapidly closing door. She knew he was teasing her and letting her know he would support whatever she was planning, just like he always did.

Millie lay back on her pillow and smiled to herself.

It was meant to be.

Darius shut the front door and got into his car.

He wasn't stupid.

He knew the signs.

He and the children both did.

He had noted the book on the coffee table, the Chinese themed packages arriving and the extra lovemaking sessions.

133

He was an experienced husband who had witnessed his wife take on projects before. As long as it made Millie happy and kept her mentally stimulated, it was fine by him.

Darius was genuinely impressed with Millie's mothering skills and the time and effort she put into raising Jane and Drew.

They were her success and he respected how valuable she felt the role of motherhood was.

He did feel a slightly different frission in the air though, he'd not experienced before, as though this project might be a little more intense than the previous ones.

He reversed the car out of the drive and thought about Millie's corset last night. He'd not seen that one before, but it had been much appreciated.

Very much appreciated indeed.

Later on that day, after school, Jane, Millie's nine year old daughter, came into the kitchen to hunt for her book.

"Hi Mum, what's for tea?" Jane asked, looking from the work surfaces to the oven and not seeing much activity. Her face suddenly lit up. "Oooo...is Dad bringing home something?" Jane was suddenly excited, "Pizza?.....hotdogs?...." She guessed hopefully,

"No," answered Millie smiling, she was sitting at the table putting the final finishing touches to the timetable.

Jane's face dropped,

"Not mushroom risotto from the deli," she groaned, "Uh! I hate that! It's Friday, it should be fun!...." she lamely trailed off as she caught her mother's stern eye.

"Jane Matthews! You are sounding like a petulant, spoilt young lady! You are jolly lucky you have a takeout once a week, a lot of people can't afford it!"

Jane looked suitably chastened and murmured,

"Sorry Mum."

"Ok, well, we're not having pizza, or hotdogs, Dad is going to bring home a selection of Chinese dishes and we're all going to try and use chopsticks to eat it with, won't that be fun!"

Millie's face was alight with enthusiasm as she beamed at Jane. Jane, an astute girl, sensed change in the air.

"What's that you're doing Mum?" She picked up her book from beside the toaster where she'd left it that morning and pulled out a chair to sit next to mum.

Millie decided to seize the moment.

"Well Jane, I don't know if your father and I are doing our absolute best to help you with your schooling," Millie began, "to help you realise your full potential."

Jane's heart sank.

Another project.

She quickly scanned the timetable her mother was working on and her brain registered, Tai chi, rote learning, piano practice... Millie continued,

"I've been reading this particular book and it's given me some ideas about how I, sorry, your father and I, could help us do that." Millie leant across and put her arm around Jane's shoulder and gave it a squeeze. "You'll thank me, I promise!"

Jane pulled away from her mother,

"But I don't even play the piano!" she exclaimed indignantly, pointing at the 'Piano Practice' box on the timetable every day at 5pm.

"You are from tomorrow afternoon, Jane, it will help you with your maths," Millie nodded decisively.

"Muuuuummm..!' protested Jane.

She absolutely did not want to learn the piano.

She stood up and faced her mother.

"Mum, I haven't got a musical bone in my body, I can't sing, I'm useless at music at school, everybody knows it, even my teacher knows it, she lets me change the words on the overhead projector because I can't even play the tambourine. I have no rhythm. Please don't make me do it! Please!" Jane begged.

Millie wouldn't budge an inch.

"You're being childish Jane, I'm sure you'll discover you're very good once you've practised for an hour or two a night," Millie finished quickly, not meeting Jane's glare,

"An hour or two every night!" Jane exclaimed, shocked, "when am I meant to see my friends?"

"At school" Millie offered, she didn't think now was the time to point out that play dates weren't on the time table. Enough had been covered tonight. Millie's mobile rang; Jane seized the opportunity and fled to her room.

"Oh, hi, Sally, are you still on for tomorrow tonight?"

Jane had been expecting some new project from her mother as it had all been quiet at home for the past month or so until this week.

The macrobiotic diet had been shelved after Millie had inadvertedly released fermented bean and pulse gas during a Pilates class. She had never gone back. The whole family had been relieved, as had their bowels, when meal times returned to family favourites of fish fingers, shepherd's pie and chicken and pasta.

Thanks to the literacy project, Jane and Drew could name and give a brief synopsis of Shakespeare's plays and Charles Dickens's better known novels. They could cook five well balanced meals in case Millie and Darius should ever be in hospital at the same time and their grandparents were on holiday!

"Because that happens all the time!" Jane had whispered to Drew as the two of them made a jolly good attempt at mashing out the lumps in the potato for the shepherd's pie.

They had learnt to waltz, fox trot and cha cha, but not tango.

Millie hadn't been comfortable with the amount of passion and emotion in it.

"It will look good on your CV!" Millie had said at the time.

"We're only eight and five!" Jane had yelled in reply, utterly loathing the pink chiffon, sequins and hairspray in her hair.

Drew, although only five at the time, knew his best bet was to appeal to the testosterone in his father. He looked down at his purple, sparkling outfit his mother had made him wear.

"Daaaad!" Drew had turned to his father despairingly. "Dad! Tell Mum I'm going to be picked on at school! Please!"

Darius knew better than to jeopardise the married life sporadic bedtime treats his wife offered, especially when Millie had started a new project. Sporadic, but interesting, and always appreciated, he picked up his newspaper and nodded in the direction of Millie,

"Your Mother knows what's best for you and Jane, Drew," and with that infinite piece of wisdom handed down to his five year old, Darius walked out of the kitchen, tying to ignore the pressure of his son's eyes boring into his back and the long drawn out,'

"Daaaaad"

Darius knew Millie wouldn't make them do it forever, just until they could do it competently.

"Tea time!" Millie called up the stairs.

Jane walked sullenly down the stairs feeling like a big black cloud was hovering over her head. Drew was already in the kitchen looking at the array of food on the table that Darius was efficiently unpacking. He looked up when Jane came into the kitchen.

"Hey Jane, good day, darling?" Drew extended one arm and enveloped Jane with a one- armed bear hug and gave her a kiss on top of her head.

"Well, I did until Mum told me I've got to learn the piano!" Jane looked at Millie's back accusingly, "AND practise two hours a day!" she finished dramatically.

Darius shot a look at Millie, who was not going to rise to the bait during tea. Realising this, he turned back to finish unpacking their Chinese and proceeded to pour oil on troubled waters,

"I'm sure your Mother has got your best interests at heart, Jane. You can both come to an agreement over the amount of time you practise, I'm sure. Drew, do you want to help Jane unwrap the chopsticks?"

"Yes please, thanks Dad, how are we going to eat with these?" Drew looked puzzled, turning them around and upside down, "there are no prongs!" Darius laughed,

"You'll see," Darius handed Jane a packet and what looked like a timetable caught his eye on the work top.

"Wine, Millie?" he asked Millie, reaching for the glasses in the cupboard above the worktop where it lay, reading as he reached up.

"Lovely Darius, thank you." Millie was getting out the paper napkins to deal with the inevitable spillages.

Darius handed Millie her wine and leant back faux-casually against the marble top.

He chose his words carefully.

"Crikey darling," he said, picking up the timetable, "this looks very organised!" He smiled at his wife as she looked up.

"It's meant to be Mr Matthews! I mean to get the best out of our children."
She smiled back and clicked some chopsticks at him. "The piano's being
delivered tomorrow morning around eight." Millie finished, opening a
cupboard, for the soy sauce.

Darius raised his eyebrows at her.

"How much did that cost?" Darius enquired gently,

"It's second hand darling, I'm not that ridiculous. It will be fine for Jane to
begin on."

Darius put the timetable down on the work top.

"Don't forget to let them let off steam now and then Millie, ok?" he leant
over and kissed her cheek.

Tea passed off with great hilarity. Millie, to Jane's delight, was completely
inept at using the chopsticks and the first one to resort to using a fork.
Millie decided that now wasn't the time to go over the finer points of
Chinese etiquette after the intensity of the piano discussion and let the
children enjoy the different tastes and textures of the food.

It was a lovely mealtime.

The last for quite a while.

Music pumped through the club, the beat matching John's pulse, or was it the other way around?

The atmosphere was electric, an air of opportunity and illicitness hung in the air. The club's website had promised a night that wouldn't disappoint, and so far, it was delivering.

John had always felt he was fairly experienced in the ways of the world but on entering the club it was all he could do not to stand and stare, mouth agape in awe and wonder at the sights his brain was struggling to process. Places like this really existed then!

He shot a look at his mates and could see that they were thinking the same thing.

One hundred or so dancers of every nationality, colouring, height and frame seemed to adorn every bar stool on the floor. They were everywhere, incredibly beautiful, pert, scantily clad and available......at a price.

John had done his homework and knew that intoxicated males were easy prey for these astute ladies. Ten pounds a drink for a dancer, £20 for a private dance; if you weren't careful you could end up being fleeced.

A podium was home to girls who danced and gyrated in pairs, Beyonce being the track of the moment. 'Ring on it' seemed a rather contradictory song in a gentlemen's club as if your wife knew you frequented them, you probably wouldn't have a ring on your finger for long, John thought to himself.

The group had stopped at one of the two bars that were situated at either end of the floor, grasping a drink each they made their way down some stairs. The atmosphere descending the stairs changed, it seemed brittle, more charged. It soon became apparent why.

The focal point, situated in the middle of the floor, was a catwalk, where a never ending succession of mesmerising women entertained male clientele in barely there lingerie, or in the nude.

John and his mates had clubbed together to reserve five faux leopard-skin covered seats next to the catwalk and had pre-charged their credit cards in exchange for the clubs heavenly money. This money could then be used to tuck into a dancer's garter or pay for a lap dance.

The five men took their seats, sat back and grinned expectantly at each other. Five boys in a sweet shop whose mothers had told them to eat whatever they wanted.

Mr Young

'Till death do us part'

James Young drove the ten miles home on Friday evening slowly, telling himself it was because of the winding country lanes. There could be a cyclist around the next bend, or a dog walker, stretching his pets legs before the long night began to descend.

It wasn't though.

He pulled into the gravel driveway and brought the car to a stop. He turned off the engine and sat back in the driver's seat, staring at his house.

His wife would be waiting.

Tanya.

She had phoned him at work today, during lunch time and told him they needed to talk this evening when he got home.

His heart had sunk. He knew what she wanted to talk about.

James simply could not condone what his stubborn, brave, beautiful wife was contemplating.

Had already decided.

Her condition was worsening.

He knew.

Tanya had drawn the short straw. From diagnosis to the present day had been eighteen months. Some people's decline was sporadic. There would be months of living on a fairly even keel before the disease reared its ugly head again, but Tanya's poor weary body seemed to have had no respite from the cruelness of the disease.

He thought back to their summer holiday two years ago when the first sign that something was amiss with Tanya became apparent to him.

They had spent a gorgeous day sightseeing in the old town of Marbella and were ending their day enjoying an evening walk, hand in hand, after having eaten an early light supper of sardines and salad, with warm crusty bread and a glass of white wine.

Life was perfect.

They'd stopped to look in a jeweller's shop window. Tanya had admired a ring on display and James had made a mental note to pop back before the end of the holiday and buy it. He would surprise her with it on the flight home.

They'd started to walk back towards their hotel when Tanya's left leg had given way beneath her, causing her to lurch sideways. James had almost been pulled over too but had managed to regain his footing and twisted in front of Tanya to catch her.

Unable to weight-bear on her left leg they had both stood standing together, Tanya leaning into James, his arms clasped tight around his wife's body, cradling her into his chest.

He could sense the shock and fear radiating out of her tense and frightened body. He tilted his head sideways to look into her eyes and tried to lighten the incident with humour.

"One too many love?"

Panic blazed out of Tanya's cornflower blue coloured eyes. She quickly shook her head. James frowned and kissed the top of her head.

"Can you try standing now?" he questioned gently.

"I'm not sure" Tanya replied hesitantly.

She lowered her foot flat on the ground gingerly and leaned onto it, still holding tightly on to James.

"It just feels sort of crampy now....I think I can hobble if you walk on my left side so I can lean into you."

Once back at the hotel, Tanya explained over coffee to a bewildered James, that over the past six months she had been experiencing muscle cramps and intermittent pain in her lower left leg and had been using Ibuleve to try and alleviate them. She had also noticed she had been dropping things more frequently as unable to maintain a firm grasp, mainly with pens and her car keys. She'd also had to stop her beloved embroidery as could no longer hold a needle.

James sat in stunned silence as he listened to his wife's concerns and worries and wondered how he could have been so blind to his wife's physical struggles with everyday tasks.

A sudden memory resurfaced. A close friend of his father's. Dropping things, leg spasms....wheelchair.

A cold chill spread throughout James's body.

How cruel life was.

James's worst fears had been confirmed. After a series of tests and through a process of elimination, Tanya had been diagnosed with Amyotrophic Lateral Sclerosis.

The most common type of Motor Neurone disease.

James and Tanya had sat like frightened children, holding hands, whilst they listened to how their lives were now going to travel on an unscheduled, different path.

The doctor had explained how the disease could progress, although there were variables. Starting gradually with a general feeling of tiredness, a weak grip and lax fine motor skills in general would give the first clues of muscle problems along with cramping and muscle weakness in the arms and legs, making everyday tasks more difficult, as Tanya had experienced. Throat muscles may be affected and lead to difficulties swallowing and speech, along with the chest wall muscles affecting the patient's ability to breathe.

There was no cure.

It all sounded very desperate and bleak.

The prognosis given to the shell-shocked couple was grim.

Three to five years from the start of the symptoms, given how unpredictable the disease was. Tanya could have more or less time. Tanya had turned her head slowly to look at James, her eyes full of tears.

James had never felt more helpless and desolate. His beautiful, erethral Tanya, his soul mate. So good, so giving....... so unlucky.

That first night, after the diagnosis, they had curled up on the sofa together, with a large brandy each. Tanya had told James that when she felt the situation was intolerable, she was going to travel to Switzerland to an organisation called Dignitas.

James had turned his head in horror to Tanya and slowly, mechanically shook his head. Over my dead body, he'd vowed, his voice shaking with raw emotion. But Tanya had been resolute. She was not going to end her days in total body paralysis, unable to talk or breath unaided.

Dignitas was an assisted dying group that helps people with terminal or severe physical illnesses to die, assisted by qualified doctors and nurses. Unlike the UK, Swiss law dictates that assistance to suicide is only illegal if it is motivated by self-interest.

With a trembling hand, Tanya slowly lowered her arm from her ear.

Willing her left arm to cross her imprisoned body she pressed the end call button against the knuckle of her right hand.

She succeeded on the third attempt.

Tanya exhaled deeply and slumped back in her wheelchair.

She knew that James thought her plan to travel to Dignitas and end her life was selfish.

He simply couldn't understand why she wouldn't fight more to live.

No one could understand why she wanted this outcome for herself.

Your being, your identity, your soul, slowly, but surely, being diminished, then little by little, extinguished.

Month by month, week by week, and now, day by day.

The physical vessel that was meant to transport her through the wonder of life's journey, now had a different captain to navigate it.

No one else could even begin to imagine the sense of loss she felt.

Loss for her relationships.

As a daughter, sister, cousin, friend.

As a woman, wife.....lover.

She was glad no one could understand.

She wouldn't wish this living hell on anyone.

She closed her eyes.

She would need all the strength she could muster for the evening ahead.

Tanya watched her husband of thirty years from the sitting room window.

Her eyes filled with tears for the pain she knew that he was in.

She ached for him.

He looked so vulnerable, so childlike, floundering and lost, at his inability to take control of her disease and give it extra homework, or a lunchtime period in support club.

She wiped her eyes clumsily and took a shuddering breath.

She had to stay strong.

For both of them.

Robotic, numb, he moved his body forward.

He was in the house.

Movement.....

Whirring........

His wife's motorised chair......his wife.

"Hello darling..." Tanya spoke slowly, with effort, "pour yourself a brandy, me too...please."

They adjourned to the study, James's favourite room in the house.

They faced each other.

James in his favourite second-hand leather wing backed chair and Tanya in her motorised prison.

"It's time."

Tanya spoke quietly and calmly.

James shook his head, he'd been expecting this.

"No!"

"James....It's TIME."

She spoke firmly.

It was non-negotiable.

James stared down into his brandy glass, trying to control the rising panic that was welling up inside him, threatening to overwhelm him.

"Tanya....please...don't." he whispered

Tanya continued.

"Four months ago, I became a member of the Dignitas Association, I've provided all the medical evidence necessary and I've met all their criteria," she paused, "I've told them I'm ready to go ahead with the assisted suicide."

James's head snapped up, his eyes blazed, his face aghast. Out loud, they were harsh words.

"ASSISTED SUICIDE!"

James was now on his feet

"ASSISTED SUICIDE!" he yelled,

"Have you gone MAD? Have you lost your mind? Do you know what that means? DO YOU?"

James was now towering over Tanya, verbal rage, despair and hatred, for the complete lack of control he had over this utterly torturous and hopeless situation, spilling out of him.

Tanya let him rant.

When he drew breath, she uttered,

"You're being bloody selfish James, pull yourself together."

Tanya hated herself for being so tough, but one of them had to be.

James sank back in his chair, elbows on his knees, his head in his hands.

He tried again,

"Tanya darling, please don't....." he fell down onto his knees, at her feet, threw his arms around her waist and laid his head on her lap, "please don't darling. I will do anything.... anything...let me take care of you.." James was now sobbing like a little boy, "Please rethink this....it's just so.....just so..... barbaric!"

James was struggling to verbalise his revulsion and the finality of what she was planning to undertake.

Tanya stroked his hair. She had to bring this conversation to a close, for both of them.

'I fly Monday.'

Silence.

James lifted his head and his eyes met Tanya's.

He retched. Bile rose up in his throat.

Half an hour later, stomach contents expelled, James sat on the cold hard cloakroom floor, back against the door, staring at the porcelain cistern.

He was beyond coping, beyond comprehending.

Unable to process or digest the events that were going to take place over the next week, James broke down once more. Helpless, uncontrollable, animal bellows.

Movement....

Whirring......Tanya

She reached out and stroked the cloakroom door, James torturous despair, enveloping them both.

She dropped her hand.

She couldn't reach him.

Not now.

Her motorised servant took her down the hall to the dining room, now their bedroom.

She had her own, one-way journey to navigate.

John slammed his now empty pint glass down on the table,

"Right boy's! Who's for another?"

This question was greeted with good natured,

"Too right!"

"I'm in!" and,

"What took you so long?"

John grinned and got up out of his chair. He was on the wrong side of merry, but didn't care. He was having a cracking night, as was the groom to be, if the dreamy, slightly drunken smile on Alan's face was anything to go by.

Alan was now dressed in an outfit of condoms, plastic handcuffs and balls and chains, all attached to his waist coat and trousers. On his head perched a pair of blow up plastic antlers on his head to represent his stag status.

Two dancers, who could smell money waiting to be spent, wrapped themselves around Alan in a seductive way and faux-adoring manner, purring compliments and innuendos into his ears.

They were doing their job well.

An aura of pure boyish happiness exuded from every pore of Alan's twenty eight year old body, in his alcohol, blurred eyes, the girls were thoroughly earning the Heavenly Dollar notes that were secured in their thongs.

John milled through the throng of men and girls on his way to the bar. He inadvertedly made eye contact with a Brazilian looking girl.

Tall, voluptuous, stunning.

John tore his eyes away and swallowed.

He was slightly overcome with the expanse of female flesh that he was privy to tonight. What with the female pheromones and heady perfume that hung in the air he could easily see how men became victims of the 'one night stand' scenario on stag nights.

Better take it a bit slower from now on. John looked back at Alan again; better keep an eye on him too!

Ten minutes later he arrived back at the table with the fresh drinks.

"Here we go, lads! Everyone having a good time?" A rhetorical question, of course.

John sat back with his drink and looked at his mates. Life had certainly done what it does best to them all. Dishes out tickets to ride its rollercoaster of life experiences; some good, some not so good and some just bloody awful.

They'd all been at the same school together. John and Gabe had gone to a different Sixth Form to the others but they had still met up for Fifa nights on the XBox and boys nights out. Then the university years arrived, they'd kept in touch via social networking sites but generally life was kept busy with girls, partying and studying, in that order!

John had trained to become an accountant, had met Rosie and had Luke. Life had been kind to them, so far, he knew. Rosie had been unable to have any more children after Luke, but they were all healthy and financially stable, so he couldn't complain really, and didn't.

Bill though, poor chap, was now divorced because of his wife's infidelity, living back at home with his parents whilst his wife and two children lived in the marital home, the mortgage paid for by Bill.

Alan was finally getting married after a ten year engagement, Graham, a GP, was happily married with three children but his wife had been diagnosed with bone cancer ten months ago and the prognosis wasn't good.

Then there was Paul.

John was struggling mentally to get to grips with his friend's bombshell, the friend from who he had lived up the road from since he was three years old. They'd attended the same nursery, primary and secondary school and John hadn't had a clue.

Paul was gay.

Unfortunately he'd been married with a sixth month old baby when he decided he couldn't live a lie any more. He had come out to his poor wife who, quite understandably, had been devastated at the realisation that her life to date with Paul had been built on a lie. She had thrown him a well-aimed right hook, broken his nose and cracked a cheekbone in the process, then fled with their daughter to her parents' house.

It was a mess, but Paul had tried to explain to his friends that he had woken up one morning, unable to carry on living a lie anymore.

John took a sip of his beer.

It certainly put into perspective his little quirk.

Maybe Rosie would understand after all if he broached the subject carefully. He hated having a secret from her. They were happily married; he was a loving, caring husband, most of the time, and a hands on father to Luke. He had never been unfaithful and didn't intend to be.

Bolstered by male logic and a fair amount of alcohol, he vowed to himself that within the next few weeks he would come clean with Rosie.

He was sure she would understand.

Saturday morning arrived. Millie had got up early as she had a lot to get done before the children's first music lesson that afternoon.

She hung the new purple and red silk curtains in the dining room along with the prints of Chinese writing.

She stood back to admire the effect. She chewed her bottom lip. Millie didn't know if the curtains were calming, they were more, well, stimulating, not a bad thing perhaps.

Millie had decided the dining room would be the 'education room', where the children did their music practice, Tai Chi and homework. It would be minimalistic and free of clutter, conducive to effective learning, Millie reasoned. The second hand piano which Millie had bought for the ridiculously cheap price of £110 from the Bits and Bobs leaflet, had been dropped off and now stood against the wall, almost apologetically, as though it knew it was going to be the cause of arguments and tears in the coming weeks ahead.

Millie was now a third of the way through 'Battle Hymn of the Tiger Mother' and marvelled at the similar traits in character between the author's daughter, Lulu, and Jane, her daughter; single minded, stubborn, obstinate but infectious and beguiling. She would have her work cut out for her with Jane, she would have to be strong, be tough and, according to Amy Chua, not afraid to be hated.

She completely agreed with her viewpoint that most children naturally want to give up something if it becomes hard to do and requires effort, apparently it was Millie's role, as Jane and Drew's parent, to pick up the slack and make them keep repeating the said task until they succeeded at it. They would then experience success and achievement and therefore want to keep doing the activity.

Millie was also intrigued with the Chinese view point regarding children's self esteem. Western parents tend to be anxious that they will damage their child's self esteem if they express disappointment at a low test mark, whereas Chinese parents have no qualms in showing disapproval at anything less than an A grade. They will ask what went wrong and tell the child that they have brought shame on their family and themselves, inspiring the child to work harder.

Millie was hooked.

She was inspired and captivated by this woman's wisdom and knowledge on successful child rearing and the possibility of high achieving children excelling at playing their instruments and all aspects of the curriculum...except P.E and Drama of course.

She had been a shocked when she had realised she was going to have to allow up to three hours for piano and violin practice. This was what Amy Chua aimed for. Millie would maybe have to rethink the Tai Chi in the morning and just stick with the walk to and from school to stimulate their cognitive development, to allow for an hour's music practice in the morning.

Millie had been online and researched SUZUKI music teachers. This was the method used by the author's daughters and Millie, out of interest, wanted to know if there were any teachers using this method, in the UK. After a few investigative clicks, she found there was a teacher for both the violin and piano, in Stentbridge.

Stentbridge.

It was doable; it was only an hour away.

Millie had booked an hour's tuition each for Jane and Drew. They would then have a group lesson once a week which would benefit them socially playing with other children and learning from playing with children of different abilities.

Millie was thrilled, especially as the tutor had informed her that she didn't usually start tutoring children over the age of five, except in exceptional circumstances. She agreed to see Jane and Drew and take it from there.

The SUZUKI method of teaching a musical instrument is based on the philosophy of teaching methods developed by a Japanese violinist called Dr. Shinichi Suzuki.

He believed that parents should have an active role in their child's learning of their instrument. The parents are expected to attend lessons, take notes and to practise with their children.

Millie couldn't wait. The lessons weren't cheap but if they cut back on meals from the deli and eating out as much, they could manage. After all, thought Millie to herself, as she picked up the violin she had ordered from Amazon, you couldn't put a price on the value of a child's education, could you?

If Millie had read the entire award winning book before she embarked on her version of Chinese parenting, she may have saved herself, Darius, Jane and Drew a period of arguments, screaming and tears......but she didn't.

At 11.45am on the dot, Millie, Jane and Drew were fastening their seat belts ready to drive the hour to Stentbridge for their lessons.

Millie could hardly contain hardly contain herself. She had absolutely no doubt that this was the start of a new positive way of life for her and her family. She had opted to take the children to their lessons, the first week, by herself. They were both disgruntled at having what Drew called 'more school' on a Saturday and Millie felt it would be easier for her to be new, tough Millie without Darius sitting next to her, raising his eyebrows or questioning her motives at such an early stage of her project and the children would be unable to play off one parent against the other.

Darius had waved them off.

'Have a good time, make sure you make the most of this opportunity, you're very fortunate your mother cares so much to do this for you.'

He hoped he sounded convincing. He was now more than a little concerned about this new venture of Millie's.

He'd started to read Battle Hymn of the Tiger Mother without telling Millie. The book was indeed about the benefits of Chinese parenting and how Chinese children are often such high achievers through being brought up this way, but it was written to undertake this form of parenting with caution. No two children are the same and one learning style does not fit every child, which the author found out to her cost. She was then inspired to put her experiences down on paper.

As a cautionary tale.

He tried to smile positively to his scowling children in the back of the car. He just couldn't, or didn't want to believe, that Millie was seriously going to put the same restrictions on Jane and Drew's lives that the authors parents had put on hers.

He dropped his arm as the car disappeared from view and the smile left his face.

He felt uneasy.

How far was Millie going to take this?

Millie had started the journey filled with such optimism and enthusiasm but by the time they had all arrived at the tutor's house she felt utterly drained. Jane had given one word answers to all of Millie's questions, as had Drew, eager to side with his sister.

Things continued to go steadily downhill. Jane's lesson had gone appallingly.

The first part of the lesson Jane watched and listened to another child play. When she was asked by the tutor if she would like to sit on the stool and play some keys, just to get the feel of the piano, she refused.

Millie was mortified.

"Jane! Don't be so silly, please have a go," Millie said quietly but firmly.

"What are you worried about?" gently probed the teacher.

"I'm not worried about anything!" declared Jane, defiantly, "I just don't want to learn the piano! My mum wants me to, it's her latest project!"

Millie nearly died on the spot and could feel herself turning a deep shade of red.

"Jane! Don't be so rude! I just think it would be beneficial for you."

The tutor looked witheringly at Millie.

"Mrs Matthews," she began, "Jane is NOT an exceptional case I'm afraid. This is a waste of my time and your money. I suggest that the two of you sit down, have a chat and try to find some common ground regarding which instrument Jane might deem herself to attempt."

Millie slunk out of the house, utterly humiliated. She had cut her losses and cancelled Drew's lesson which the tutor, taking pity on Millie, didn't charge her for. They all climbed in the car and started the drive home in silence, Millie so incensed she didn't trust herself to speak to her children.

Half an hour into the journey Drew piped up,

"Can we get a McDonald's?"

"Not a chance!" snapped back Millie, struggling to control the rising anger that threatened to erupt from her being.

"But I was good!" protested Drew, "I didn't even get to play!"

"Well you can blame Jane!" replied Millie

Drew glanced sideways at Jane and frowned to himself, questioning his earlier loyalty towards her.

Jane sat and wisely said nothing. She was ashamed of herself. She knew her mum was furious with her. She'd just felt trapped in a corner. She thought of her Dad back home. He wouldn't shout or punish her; he'd just look at her with disappointment and quietly turn away.

She felt as small as small could be.

Why couldn't mum just leave things as they were? She always did her reading, spellings and homework without being asked, she was near the top of her class, why wasn't her mum happy with that?

On arriving home, Millie had thrown her keys on the work top and let rip,

"How dare you, Jane! How DARE you! Who do you think you are to behave SO atrociously? Do you not realise how lucky you are to have the opportunity to learn an instrument? Do you not realise how lucky you are that I care enough and am interested enough in your education to want to learn with you?"

Millie stopped for breath, giving Drew the opportunity to escape to his bedroom, upset, hungry and scared.

Jane burst into tears,

"I JUST DON'T WANT TO LEARN THE PIANO! ....OK!" she yelled and ran up to her room, sobbing.

The atmosphere was as tense as the strings on Drew's unplayed violin.

Darius appeared quietly in the kitchen doorway and leaned, arms folded, against the door frame.

"Is this how you want your weekends to be, Millie?" he asked gently, "a war zone."

Millie put her hands on her hips, temporarily beaten but defiant.

"Darius, she's just a child. She cannot and more importantly, will not, dictate what she will and will not do! I will pay for someone to come to the house and teach her. She can choose the piano or the violin and if she doesn't, there will be consequences. I will not give in!" finished Millie, eyes blazing, staring at Darius, daring him to object.

Silence.

"Just make sure you're doing this for the right reasons, Millie." He held her gaze, then unfolded his arms and walked out of the kitchen and up the stairs to see his children and suggest they apologise to their mum.

Millie stood alone in the kitchen.

Monday morning she'd begin the time table in earnest.

She would buy a piano and violin book for beginners which the children could read and have a tentative attempt at playing, with Millie's help, until she found a replacement tutor.

She just hoped the children didn't get any play date invites next week.

Her heart sank, Amy Chua had a backbone of steel to enforce that one.

She pushed the thought from her mind.

We'll cross that bridge when we come to it, she thought to herself, hoping the bridge wouldn't appear for a few more weeks.

Millie reached over for the kettle and started to fill it for a much needed cup of tea.

Sally was adhering to her usual Saturday morning, strict routine of self indulgence. She had been mentally exhausted after her first week back and even the thought of the pending Ofsted visit couldn't keep her awake and she had slept soundly all night.

The boys all slept in, catching up on much needed teenage rest and sleep and Nick brought her the only cup of morning tea he made her all week before he left for work at 6.30 am, purely because she was always up first during the week.

Every morning, like clockwork, Sally's alarm on her phone would go off at 5.30am. She would press the ten minute snooze button and when that went off she would swing her legs over the side of the bed and search for her bed socks that she always kicked off during the night. She would then get up, shower, and get ready for the first child of the day at 6.20am. Twelve hours of minding children later, she would shut the door on the last child.

 On Saturdays, the routine changed. Around eight, Sally would get up, make another cup of tea, put the washing machine on, grab the laptop and head back to bed to read the news online, check her emails and then visit the Rightmove website just to check if there was the perfect, magical house with four bedrooms that the vendor would only sell to them at a ridiculously cheap price.

This morning was going to Sally's usual, Saturday morning routine. Jenny and Polly were coming at eleven, so she had plenty of time. She leant over, popped the electric blanket on to eco and leant against the pillows with a sigh of pure pleasure, refusing to let her mind worry about next week's Ofsted visit.

She was fortunate that her boys were eighteen, sixteen and twelve. She knew many childminders with young children whose week of entertaining and looking after them didn't stop on Friday evening at 6.30pm. Without a doubt, childminding could be tough on family life. Children who had to share their mums all week with other children, quite rightly, expected their mum's full attention at the weekend, but after a fifty or sixty hour week, mums sometimes just wanted to recharge their batteries. It was a struggle, Sally knew.

Ten thirty arrived.

Sally was up and showered and had half an hour before Jenny was due to arrive. Although it would be an informal chat, Sally had contracts, child record forms, permission forms, a leaflet detailing her childminding history, qualifications and fees, and a copy of all her policies for Jenny to take home and read at her leisure.

At eleven o clock, on the dot, there was a knock on the door.

"Hello Jenny, hello Polly," greeted Sally, "How lovely to see you both, come on in."

Sally led the way into her cosy little house, through to the conservatory. She turned to Polly, "Well now, Polly, this is where the children spend a lot of their time." She opened a cupboard, "I've got games and puzzles in here," Sally then turned to her dining table, "and lots of craft bits and pieces, colouring pens, painting, beads and threads for jewellery making....what sort of thing do you like to do?"

Sally smiled at a bright eyed, expectant Polly. She eyed the mountains of stickers, pom poms, card, glitter and glue that Sally had set out on the table.

It was just like Maisie had promised, thought Polly in wonderment.

"Craft please!"came her definite and clear reply.

"Great!" replied Sally "Would you like to do some craft whilst mummy and I have a chat and a cup of tea?" Polly nodded and sat down at the groaning table.

"Can I use the glue, paper and pom poms please?" Polly asked, eyes shining wide, her brain whirring with the possibilities she could create.

"You can use whatever you like, Polly." Sally smiled at her and then turned to Jenny. "Tea or coffee, Jenny?" Sally asked,

"Tea would be lovely please," replied Jenny, taking in the well-stocked conservatory. "Goodness me, Sally, don't you get fed up having all those toys out in your home? I think I'd go crazy!"

Sally laughed,

"Well I put most of them away at night, the baskets , well, just pop away into the wall units, and a lot goes into the blanket box, but....well, I really don't mind, at least everything is in the conservatory and at night you can shut the door and forget about toys for the evening." They both laughed.

"Right," said Sally, "I'll pop the kettle on and show you the downstairs......it won't take long, it's a very small house!"

"Well, it's got a lovely, homely feel," complimented Jenny, "really cosy."

"Thank you," said Sally, genuinely pleased. Sally was very conscious her home was filled with second hand furniture which didn't match and the throws and cushions could really do with being replaced, but it was home to Sally and her family and she was glad that Jenny felt that way.

Five minutes later, Sally had given Jenny a tour of the downstairs and they were now sitting at the table in the conservatory with their tea. Polly was now thoroughly absorbed in creating a colourful picture with the large selection of craft resources that lay on the table.

"That's a wonderful picture you've done Polly," praised Sally. Polly smiled but didn't lift her eyes from her creation, completely focused on her handiwork.

Sally and Jenny discussed Sally's hourly rate and what was included in that rate. Each childminder was different but Sally offered a pick up service from school at no extra charge, a healthy snack and refreshments and a safe, warm, stimulating environment for children to be in.

The sitting room was known to the children as 'the quiet room' where children could unwind, watch television or a film, or look at books on the sofas if they wanted to, but it was a 'noisy play' free zone. The conservatory was food, crafts, role play and games. It worked well and all the children enjoyed the routine that this offered.

165

Sally went through all her policies with Jenny, bringing her attention to the sickness policy, which required Polly to be free of sickness for forty eight hours before Sally could continue minding her; they then discussed Polly's likes and dislikes.

"Well, that seems to be everything Jenny. You can now go away and digest everything, have a chat with Polly and then see what she thinks," said Sally.

"Oh no, no," Jenny said quickly, "I'm very happy and I know Polly will be absolutely fine, she's told me all about you. She sometimes sits next to....is it...Maisie? The girl you have in Year 4."

"Yes, Maisie and Hannah, her younger sister from Reception," Sally replied.

"Well, she sits next to her sometimes at lunchtimes and Maisie is always talking about what she gets up to here, I know she'll be just fine," finished Jenny, who was eager to get Polly's childcare arrangements sorted out as soon as possible. She knew that before and after school childcare places were hard to come by and had been surprised, but relieved, when Sally had said she had a space.

Sally felt elated.

"Well, that's lovely to hear Jenny, thank you, would you like to take all the paper work away with you today then?" Sally offered.

"Lovely, yes please. I'll fill them in tonight and return them tomorrow. Would Polly be able to start on Monday with you?" Jenny asked hopefully.

Relief flooded Sally's body.

"Yes of course Jenny, that's no problem at all."

The pair finished their tea whilst chatting about juggling work and family life and when Polly had finished her picture, Jenny got up to leave.

"Thank you so much Sally, I just know Polly is going to be very happy," said Jenny, looking from a beaming Polly, who was clutching her masterpiece, to Sally.

"Well, thank you Jenny, I'm sure Polly will be fine, but just let me know if any issues arise and I'll do my best to solve them."

Sally waved them goodbye and shut the door with a huge smile on her face. I always worry, she thought, but something always turns up, and she walked back into the sitting room to phone Nick to tell him the good news.

Not even the thought of Ofsted coming next week could dampen her optimism.

She was going to relax, enjoy herself, and have a few glasses of wine at Rosie's tonight. She couldn't wait!

The Girls night

Sebastian pulled up at Rosie's period cottage and eyed it with a critical eye.

The thatched roof, the reclaimed front door, he imagined it had those loathsome beams inside that provided dwellings for mites and other such microscopic organisms that ensured the house was never completely dust free.

Its decor was probably typical for that style of house, filled with Laura Ashley or Liberty furniture and soft furnishings, which Sebastian detested.

He gave an involuntary shiver at the thought.

Phoebe bent down to pick up her bag and reached for the door handle to open the door.

"No kiss goodbye, Phoebe?" Sebastian asked petulantly.

Phoebe turned the corners of her mouth into a small smile and leant forward and kissed her husband lightly on the mouth.

Sebastian looked deep into her eyes,

"Not too much wine tonight, Phoebe......you've worked so hard to rid your legs of cellulite it would be a shame to undo your good work."

The smile never left Phoebe's lips,

"I'll be drinking sparkling water tonight, Sebastian," and she turned to open the car door.

"I'll pick you up at 10pm, don't keep me waiting like last time." Phoebe held the car door and the smile now left her lips.

"I was in the toilet, Sebastian. It wasn't intentional to keep you waiting," and with that she shut the car door.

Sebastian frowned at her back as she made her way up Rosie's path to the front door.

A retort.

Phoebe had answered him back.

Sebastian reversed his car into Rosie's drive, and then pulled away in the direction of his house.

If she did it again, there would have to be consequences.

Phoebe knocked on Rosie's front door wondering if the other mums in the village were encouraged to put so much effort into their appearance and figure. Her question was answered when Rosie answered the door without a scrap of make up on, her hair still damp from a bath and wearing a soft jersey tracksuit. In her hand, a half empty glass of wine.

"Phoebe! Great to see you! Oooo....you look stunning!" Rosie gave a laugh and looked down at her casual attire,

"I, on the other hand, am in my usual Friday night uniform of loose clothing so I can drink and stuff myself with crisps and dips and not give a monkey's about my waistline! Come on through and let's get you some wine!"

Phoebe followed Rosie down her warm, cosy hallway, she loved Rosie's house. Hers felt sterile compared to Rosie's, which had a friendly, welcoming feel. "White or red?" asked Rosie, waving a bottle of each.

"Do you have any sparkling water by any chance?" Rosie opened her mouth to protest but stopped herself. A look of embarrassment flashed across Phoebe's eyes and she dropped her gaze.

"Coming right up! Why don't you go through love, Sharon and Sally are already here." Wanting Phoebe to feel relaxed and welcomed, she gestured through to the sitting room. Rosie opened the fridge to retrieve a bottle of sparkling water. That was alright, you don't have to drink to have a good time, she told herself. But it jolly well helps! With that thought, Rosie topped her glass up and carried it through on a tray laden with bottles of wine, sparkling water and nibbles.

Later on that evening, Rosie's sitting room floor was the evidence of a good night had by all. Various 80's CD cases were open on the floor, wine bottles littered the marble topped coffee table, bowls of nibbles were scattered on every surface and on the floor, where the women had ended up, sitting crossed legged, as the gossip intensified.

Millie had mused that they were reducing the distance that they would fall, and therefore limit the likelihood of injury, in their lubricated state of mind. They had all agreed that this was a very good point. Phoebe listened with intent at her friends' lively gossip about their lives; they each regaled various mishaps that seemed to happen on a daily basis at home, with laughter and self depreciation.

Not fear.

The gossip and laughter was punctuated by a loud knock on the door. Rosie, heading for the wrong side of tipsy looked round the room at everyone.

"Have I invited someone I've forgotten about?"

For the second time that evening Phoebe looked embarrassed and she jumped up out of her chair.

"That will be Sebastian"

Four pairs of eyes swung round to Phoebe, who, without meeting anyone's stare, ran to the front door.

Rosie, hastily remembering her role as hostess, got to her feet and followed Phoebe, with only the slightest of a wobble, to the front door.

Phoebe had already opened it and was expertly doing up the straps on her high heeled shoes with one hand.

"Sebastian! How lovely to meet you again, early start tomorrow?" Rosie called over Phoebe's shoulder.

Sebastian smiled back at Rosie with a smile that didn't quite reach his eyes.

"No, no," Sebastian replied smoothly, "we don't want Phoebe getting premature wrinkles through not enough sleep now do we?" and guiding Phoebe firmly by her upper arm, steered her down Rosie's path to the direction of his car.

"Bye Rosie...." called Phoebe over her shoulder, "....and thank you."

Rosie stood rooted to the spot as she watched Sebastian and Phoebe drive away. Had Sebastian really said what she thought he'd said?

She closed her front door and went back to the girls; something was definitely not right within their marriage.

She walked thoughtfully back into the sitting room and was met by three sets of questioning eyes.

"Everything alright with Mr Control Freak?" Sharon asked sarcastically, taking a sip of wine and raising her eyebrows as she did so.

Rosie shook her head slowly, thinking back over the years they had known Phoebe.

"Something's not right with that man....I can't put my finger on it..." Millie nodded in agreement.

"Do you remember how vivacious and open she was when she first started coming to Toddlers when she was pregnant? She was just a breath of fresh air....but now...."

Sally said nothing but picked up a bottle of red wine and topped her and Millie's glass up. The girls were just echoing what she had thought for some time.

There was a coldness to Sebastian that had made Sally feel anxious about Phoebe for some time.

Rosie's telephone rang; it was someone wanting John. Putting the phone back Sharon asked where John was that evening and the gossip returned to lighter subjects such as do the girls at lap dancing clubs wear any clothes at all?

Later that evening

"Christ! It's not one o'clock is it?"

A bleary eyed Sharon was trying to focus on Rosie's clock on the mantelpiece. The three other women stopped talking and all tried to focus on the clock as well.

"No, no, surely not, I think it says eleven o clock," giggled Sally, winking at Rosie.

"It can't be! I haven't even started to tell you what John's mum said to me about working mums and delinquent children!" said Rosie, half full wine glass held up in mock indignation.

"Well, whatever she said it will be complete rubbish!" declared Sally, "I'm all for working mums......they pay my mortgage!"

All four women collapsed with wine-fuelled laughter.

Millie managed to get to her feet and put her nose right up to the clock.

"Ladies," she said slowly, "we have done it again! It is indeed one o'clock in the morning and I think we can all agree we have successfully put the world to rights."

"Hear, hear!" seconded Sharon,

"It's always over too soon," moaned Millie, bending to pick up a bowl of peanuts off a CD case. The other women all agreed. They had all been looking forward to it as it was always a great stress release, now it was over it meant Monday morning was just around the corner, waiting to greet them.

Half an hour later, the four women were congregated in Rosie's hallway.

"Bye, Sally, thanks so much for coming. It's been long overdue, now you're walking with Sharon?"

Rosie gave Sally a hug and a nod towards Sharon who was hugging Millie in a 'I've had one too many' way, saying,

"I've had SUCH a good time, we should do this more often!"

"Yep! We're going to stagger home together and finish putting the world to rights," grinned Sally, who too, had had a great evening offloading about the trials and tribulations of life in general. She linked arms with a slightly unsteady Sharon and said,

"Come on missy! Let's get you home, although in those heels it might take us a while!" she teased.

Sharon tried to look down at her four inch stilettos and nearly fell over.

"Hmmm....." She looked a little bashful, "I didn't really think through the 'walking home' bit when I put them on, did I."

She burst out laughing.

Sally, Rosie and Millie rolled their eyes at each other in a good natured way at their friend who had obviously had a great time and they bustled round her making sure her coat was done up and she had her key with her.

"Right, are we ready?" Sally asked

"Oooo, you sound just like a childminder," giggled Sharon, as they staggered down Rosie's path and down the country lane. Sally laughed,

"Sharon, you sound like you've had a really good time tonight,"

"Bloody brilliant!" declared Sharon, "What with work, Duncan and the kids you forget who you are sometimes. I really needed tonight." She squeezed Sally's arm in thanks.

"Me too," smiled Sally, and she returned the squeeze. "Isn't it funny how we've lived ten houses apart, for eight years, and only found out eighteen months ago?"

Sally was ten years older than Sharon and Eddie had been in year 6 when Sharon's oldest child, Freddie, had started reception. They had met through one of Rosie's wine evenings and got on brilliantly.

She worked for the probation service, an incredibly stressful job. She listened to and appeased irate and sometimes abusive people, all day at work. She listened to her husband's woes of how he hated his job but wouldn't try and change it and to top it all, she had two children.

She deserved a night out once in a while getting merry.

"Ten houses?" Sharon stopped and thought, struggling at one o'clock in the morning and ever so slightly intoxicated, with the conundrum that Sally had just thrown at her.

"But you live at 180 and I live at 160, so that's twenty houses!" she finished, with a puzzled look on her face. Sally snorted with laughter at her friend's logic.

"Yes but Sharon, the houses are odd and even numbered, and we're on the even side so that's ten houses apart," she explained patiently.

Sharon looked at Sally as though she was a little backward.

"No, no, no....Sally...!" she stopped and belched, "God, sorry about that, too many olives me thinks.....ANYWAY.." Sharon paused for dramatic effect then spoke in a slow, loud voice,

"YOU LIVE AT 180 SWAN BELL STREET AND I LIVE AT 160 BELL STREET......THAT'S 20 HOUSES...S.I.L.L.Y.." Sharon was nodding slowly as she talked to Sally to emphasise her point.

Sally, trying not to laugh out loud as she didn't want to disturb the quiet street, gave up.

"Oh right, got it! Silly me...." and they both collapsed into giggles.

Ten minutes later, Sharon, on the third attempt, placed her key in the door and with a smile on her face, she fell into her house with a

"Byee..." and shut her door. Sally walked the ten houses back to her front door and let herself in.

"Alright love?" Nick called from the bedroom.

174

"All good love, boys ok?" Sally answered softly

"All good....night."

"Night love, I'm just going to pop the kettle on and I'll be through."

Sally went to bed that night with cheek muscles that ached from laughing so much and woke the next morning with just the tiniest headache which she didn't mind at all.

It was a reminder of a great night had with good friends.

Rosie opened the door to check the beef. It was John's favourite. She drained off the juices into a jug ready to make the gravy and popped the joint back into the oven.

The house smelt like a home. The roast dinner aroma filled the downstairs, ready to welcome her boys home. Rosie looked at the kitchen clock and poured two half glasses of red wine. John would be back any minute now. Luke was arriving home around six so Rosie was looking forward to a leisurely late lunch with John, hearing all about his boys' weekend.

He had phoned her twenty minutes ago from the station and she had grinned into the phone as she heard several subdued,

'Hi Rosie,' from the young stags, obviously weary, hung over and carrying much lighter wallets than they went with.

John had pressed 'end call' on his phone after speaking to Rosie and hailed a taxi.

Closing the door, he sank back in his seat in the taxi.

He felt rough.

His mouth was like sandpaper, refusing to release a drop of saliva as his dehydrated body needed every drop of fluid to function after its punishing weekend.

His head throbbed and unusually, so did his eyes; the backs of them seeming to pound rhythmically in his head.

He closed his eyes and thought of his four friends collapsed in their seats, worse for wear, on the train home, and he mentally smiled. They had looked how he felt. He definitely couldn't hold his alcohol as well as he could ten years ago.

He looked down at the phone in his hand.

He was looking forward to seeing Rosie.

He took a deep breath and exhaled deeply.

He was going to tell Rosie at the next appropriate moment.

He leant his head back and closed his eyes.

How would she react?

Would she be repulsed, sickened, hurt?

He opened his eyes, turned his head slowly and looked out of the window of the taxi.

God his eyes hurt, everything outside was moving far too fast.

Perhaps he'd leave his confession another week or two?

Twenty minutes later, John arrived home.

After Rosie had finished laughing at his sorry state, he downed two pints of water and gratefully climbed into a steaming hot bubble bath. Instead of the glass of red wine Rosie had poured for him earlier, he sipped a huge mug of strong coffee with two sugars, whilst feeling sorry for himself, in the bath.

Rosie popped her head round the bathroom door,

"Dinner's in forty minutes. Do you think you'll be up for it?" She enquired, smiling at his fragile state.

"God, yes," John said, reaching for his coffee, "I need something to rebalance the alcohol content in my body!" He leant forward to take a sip of coffee and winced, "God, I'm too old for this weekend drinking malarkey! My head!" he groaned, and gingerly lay back against the bath.

Rosie snorted with laughter,

"Well, if the smell of your clothes I've just put in the washing machine, is anything to go by, it was worth it!" and left John to it.

Johns grip on his coffee mug slipped a little.

His washing!

The silk pants!

Dear God, no! Not today, he couldn't deal with this today.

But Rosie hadn't said anything, he realised. Maybe she hadn't seen them.

John sat up in the bath.

He'd have to be on the ball and empty the washing machine before Rosie did. It wouldn't look suspicious; he often put a load of washing on when Rosie was working.

He slowly lay back down again.

He had to come clean with Rosie sooner or later, it just didn't bear thinking about if she found out accidentally like she very nearly just did.

"Bye, have a good day." Sally called after Rosie and closed the door.

"Oh, well done Luke," Sally smiled to herself as she watched Luke line up his shoes perfectly and put his gloves safely in his coat pockets before picking up his motorbikes and running into the sitting room. None of her boys had ever done that, she thought to herself ruefully.

Sally followed Luke into the sitting room.

"Children, can we all say good morning to Luke please," said Sally

"Hello Luke," chorused Jimmy, Adele, Pippa and Peter.

Pippa and Peter were brother and sister and attended the primary school in the next village. As there weren't any childminders in their village their parents had an arrangement with the school that Sally could drop the children at 8.30am where the children read a book in the office with the friendly office staff, enabling Sally to be back at St Michael's in time for the 8.40am bell.

It made for a busy morning and usually Sally managed to deliver all the children to the right schools in time.

Usually.

Sally glanced at the sitting room clock.

It was Wednesday, Eve would arrive soon.

Eve was two, bright as a button, mischievous and very entertaining.

She often had Sally and the children in fits of laughter at her take on the world. However, today Sally was planning a quiet day as Eve was getting over a chest infection, Play-doh and sticking with cotton wool balls to make a snowy scene, which would give Sally the opportunity to cover some winter weather vocabulary, stories and generally just go with the flow. She only had Eve today between nine o clock and three o clock so when Eve had a nap later on in the day, she would triple check she had everything in place for Ofsted.

When Ofsted had telephoned to inform Sally they would be visiting the following week she had told them she worked every weekday, all day, but attended toddler groups on a Monday and Tuesday am and would still like to do so, so as not to unsettle the children's routine.

Thankfully, the inspector was very down to earth and had told Sally that it would probably be the latter part of the week, so to go ahead with the groups.

Sally felt strangely calm this time around.

Walking through the conservatory to get out Eve's favourite shopping game, she remembered with shame, three years ago, her first Ofsted inspection.

Sally had waited in, every day of the week, only leaving the house to do the school and nursery runs, so when Thursday evening had arrived and the last child had been picked up, it was obvious the inspection was to be Friday.

Sally was at fever pitch.

She was a nervous and emotional wreck. Nick and the boys felt as though they were living on a knife's edge as the tension in the house grew with every passing day that Ofsted didn't arrive.

Sally felt vulnerable, exposed and full of self doubt.

Rationality had left her body by Wednesday lunchtime. They were going to come, judge her, find something hideously wrong and strike her immediately off the Early Years register.

She had even contemplated re-painting the sitting room ceiling Thursday evening and failed to see why Nick didn't think it was necessary.

"Sally, love, you're being ridiculous. It will be fine. You will be fine. Now go and have a hot bath and relax. Please."

Sally just looked at Nick and sighed,

"It's going to be on the internet Nick. Everyone will be able to read it." Sally's bottom lip wobbled.

Nick stepped forward and hugged his fraught, wrung out wife.

"I know, love, but look around, you've risk assessed the house, garden, outings, the car. You assess, observe and plan; you are great with the kids, now stop."

Nick leant back and kissed her on the forehead. He then physically turned her around on the spot and gave her a gentle push in the direction of the door.

"Bath, now," and he gently swatted her behind with a tea towel. Sally didn't react with her usual giggle. She was numb.

She walked through the door and started to climb up the stairs to the bathroom.

"I'll cook tea," Nick called after her retreating back, "Just relax."

"Thanks, love," Sally called absentmindedly over her shoulder.

It was Nick's turn to sigh.

Roll on tomorrow evening, bloody Ofsted!

They had no idea of the day to day life of a childminder.

He had seen Sally, when she had had three under the age of two, start changing nappies and when she'd finished the third; the first child had done a number two and needed changing again! It took half an hour; he didn't know how she and other childminders did it!

The caring, planning of activities, meal times, snack times, school runs, nursery pick ups.

It was full on, nonstop work, from dawn to dusk and then, to write it all down and evidence everything seemed a little over the top to Nick.

181

Surely the parents should be the judge of how their children were looked after?

Every parent Nick had spoken to had said they just wanted someone to care for their child as they would if they were at home and didn't have to work.

Nick went into the kitchen and reached into the cupboard for the matches and the vegetable oil.

Spaghetti Bolognese. No problem.

Nick poured the oil into the frying pan, lit the gas ring to let the oil heat up and started chopping an onion.

Upstairs in his bedroom, Chris was working on a college assignment whilst listening to some music on iTunes. It was a fairly local band. Dad and Mum had been friends with the bass guitarist and his girlfriend, now his wife, before they had him and his brothers. He also worked for Fedex.

It was a small world, thought Chris, putting down his pen and turning around to look at his bedroom door.

Two minutes later, Chris appeared in the kitchen.

"What's burning Dad?" he asked, walking through to the conservatory to open the windows.

Nick looked up in surprise from the onions and carrots he was stirring,

"Nothing Chris, I'm just cooking tea, look, it's not burnt!" he offered, walking through to the conservatory with the frying pan to make his point.

Chris frowned. Dad had overheated the oil again.

It was Sally's biggest bug bear. It made the house smell and lingered for hours.

Nick really struggled with the timing of a meal.

He just had no concept of timings; it was a bit of a family joke. He would put the spaghetti on to cook before he'd even started to brown the mince for the Bolognese resulting in it resembling long, water filled soggy worms rather than al dente spaghetti and when in charge of sausage, chips and beans, he put the sausages and chips in the oven to cook and would then turn the beans on.

Not usually a problem.

Tonight was different.

Nick walked back through to their galley kitchen. The door to the sitting room flung open with such force it banged on to the chair behind it.

"NICK!"

Nick jumped and turned around. Sally was standing with a towel wrapped around her, soaking wet with mascara smeared down one cheek.

"YOU'VE OVER HEATED THE FUCKING OIL AGAIN!!"

Sally was screaming, completely beyond herself, a ragged, emotionally fraught mess.

"FOR FUCKS'S SAKE! HOW MANY TIMES HAVE I GOT TO TELL YOU!"

Nick stood rooted to the spot, his face ashen.

Chris stepped back into the shadows of the conservatory and held his breath.

He'd seen it coming.

Sally, hands on hips, continued relentlessly.

"DID YOU NOT HEAR ME WHEN I SAID THEY ARE GOING TO PUT MY INSPECTION ON THE INTERNET? DID YOU? IT DOESN'T TAKE A FUCKING GENIUS TO WORK OUT IT'S ME!!"

183

Sally took a breath and held out an outstretched hand and counted off her fingers, still shouting,

"SHE LIVES IN PENTCROFT, HAS A HUSBAND AND THREE KIDS AND LIVES IN A HOUSE THAT SMELLS LIKE A FUCKING GREASY CAFE!!"

Nick looked as though he had been punched.

Upstairs, Jack texted Eddie, in the adjacent bedroom.

'Don't go downstairs for a bit, Mum's a bit stressed'

Eddie leant over and texted back,

'K', then turned the volume on his speakers up and went back to blasting zombies.

He wished Ofsted would hurry up and visit so he could get his normal mum back.

Sally, fury spent, slapped both hands to her face, wailed and ran from the sitting room, sobbing as she ran. She was mortified by her complete lack of control. She ran into their bedroom, slammed the door and threw herself onto the bed, hating every fibre in her body. She lay and sobbed and sobbed; the tension and mental exhaustion of the build up to her first Ofsted inspection pouring out of her.

The sobbing eventually ceased.

What have I become? What a complete and utter bitch I am. Sally closed her eyes in shame.

Nick, her loving, loyal Nick, who only ever tried to help when things were getting too much.

Her boys!

Chris...Jack.... Oh God! Eddie! Sally started crying again. Eddie was far too young to have to hear his mum completely lose control and verbally abuse his dad like that.

Half an hour later, Sally sat up and swung her legs over the side of the bed. She hunched over with her elbows on her knees and her head in her hands.

She had crossed a line.

She heard Nick's footsteps stop outside their bedroom door.

"I'm just going up the Co op to buy some Febreze."

Without waiting for a reply he left the house and drove off in his car.

Tears of shame started to fall once again.

She didn't deserve Nick or her boys.

Self-loathing well and truly in place, Sally got up off the bed in a fashion not unlike one of the zombies her youngest son was shooting upstairs and walked out of their bedroom and up the stairs to the bathroom.

She washed her face, got dressed and knocked on Eddie's door.

Time to start rebuilding the cracked, fragile bridges that currently stood between her and her family.

A knock at the door jolted Sally from a walk down memory lane she would dearly love to erase.

"Eve, hello my love, how are you?" Sally said gently,

A slight little girl with big blue eyes looked at Sally with bleary eyes. Her dad didn't look much better.

"She's really tired Sally, the antibiotics have really taken it out of her, and she's only had a cup of milk for breakfast,"

"Ok Graham, we're going to have a quiet day so I'll just go with the flow," reassured Sally.

"Thanks Sally, do ring though if she's not coping," offered Graham,

"Will do Graham, don't worry, I'm sure she'll be fine, antibiotics do tend to scour their little tummies."

She reached up to take Eve from Graham. Eve just flopped into her arms. Sally frowned a little. Well, we'll just see how it goes, she thought to herself. She knew how quickly children could pick up and the sight of other children could be a great tonic for convalescing children.

Sally carried Eve into the sitting room and sat down on the sofa to give her a cuddle and let her come to. Eve's eyes kept shutting. She did seem tired, which was unusual for busy two year old, antibiotics, or no antibiotics.

The door bell rang. That will be Jenny and Polly, Sally thought to herself, and got up, lying Eve down on the sofa and covering her with a blanket. She welcomed Jenny and Polly, who was settling in beautifully, exchanged pleasantries, and then hurried back to check Eve.

Eve had fallen asleep in the same position that Sally had put her down in; she definitely wasn't right.

Sally's mobile rang; it was Eve's mum asking after her. She'd had to leave at 6.30am for work and wanted to know how Eve was.

"I don't think she's right actually Sarah, she's just fallen asleep on the settee, I'm going to have to put her in the car in ten minutes to do the school run."

"Listen Sally, Dad's at home around the corner from you. I'll get him to come and get her shall I?" Sarah suggested, she knew it was unfair to ask Sally to look after an unwell child.

"Sarah, that's really kind but she may just need another nap as she's been unwell. I'm happy to see how she goes this morning." Sally offered.

"Well, if you're sure Sally, that's great! Thank you so much!" Sarah said, relieved. She relied on her mum and dad a lot anyway, so was grateful that Sally was happy to see how Eve got on.

"No problem, Sarah, I'll call you if there are any problems, try not to worry." Sally put her mobile down and started bustling the children into hats, coats, scarves and shoes. She gently scooped up the sleeping Eve, blanket as well and walked through to the hallway where the five children, all wrapped up against the January cold, stood waiting, apprehensively, their eyes wide and expectant.

Eve usually came in and picked up toys or games, they were playing with, demanded their attention, as two year olds do, and made them laugh with her beguiling two year old smile and personality.

They had not seen Eve as unresponsive as she was today and they found it unsettling.

"Ok, children," said Sally, reaching for the front door keys from the hook, "I'm going to put Eve in the car then call you one by one as usual, alright?"

"Yes Sally," they all chorused, clutching their book bags and lunch boxes.

Sally lived on a busy main road so getting the children into her people carrier safely was a military operation. No-one moved past the front door unless Sally called their name. When Sally had babies and very young children, she used the travel cot that was permanently erected in her bedroom, which was situated next to the hallway, to keep the little ones safe and secure whilst the front door was open.

"Thank you, children, won't be a minute!'"

Sally opened the rear car door and placed the sleeping Eve gently into the car seat. It was Sally's newest car seat with extra thick padding. Eve looked really comfortable, thought Sally, as she lifted the blanket to negotiate Eve's arm through the strap.

Eve's eyes opened and shut, roused by the cold air.

"Sshh....it's ok Eve, I'm just putting you in your car seat my love.....go back to sleep..," Sally cooed.

Sally reached for the second arm to put through the strap when Eve gagged in her sleep.

Her eyes opened.

Then shut.

Sally froze... No!

She looked back at the children, waiting so patiently.

"Children, I'm so proud of you, I've nearly finished," Sally forced a smile at the worried looking children. She turned back to Eve, all seemed well.

Then Eve gagged again.

A small amount of liquid milk dribbled out of mouth.

Sally quickly wiped up the liquid with the blanket, while experience told her that that was just the start.

She put her right hand behind Eve's back to get her upright and with her left hand, quickly unstrapped Eve's right arm.

Eve then retched and partially digested milk, projectile vomited from Eve's mouth.

"OH NO!!" exclaimed Sally, involuntary, lifting her hand up and grabbing the blanket to catch what she could of the fountain of foul smelling liquid.

Stomach ejaculation over, Eve started to cry.

Sally had a five second mind blank.

She looked at Eve, covered in vomit.

She looked down at her five year old faded brown Puffa gillet, covered in vomit.

The whole of her left arm, covered in vomit.

It was 8.25am. She had two school drops to do, which was a six mile round trip, before St Michael's registration at 8.55am. She did not want to be responsible for any unauthorised absences if she could help it.

Sally looked back at the children standing on the door step. All five had their jaws dropped in horror at what they had just partially witnessed.

"Ok children, everyone back inside and go back into the sitting room, Eve has been sick, I need to clean her up and phone her mum."

The children dutifully turned around and plodded back to the sitting room in silence.

Sally turned back to Eve just in time to miss raising the blanket to catch the second torrent of vomit that Eve wanted to share with Sally and her car that morning.

Sally looked at the vomit in horror.

Dear God! She was never going to get them to school at this rate. She had to get Eve indoors.

Scooping up for the second time that morning a vomit covered Eve and blanket, Sally stood up, cuddling her as best she could and partially shut the car door, so at least some of the smell could escape from the car.

She took a step towards the house when a silver Renault pulled up on the drive beside Sally.

Sally stood puzzling. She looked towards the house where she mentally named and counted all the children and checked, yes, it was Wednesday, six children, seven, including her. That was a full car. She hadn't overbooked as apart from Polly, who had filled Simon's place, they were regular minded children.

A blonde woman was getting out of the car.

Sally's heart skipped a beat.

She recognised her from three years ago.

Her mouth went dry. You have got to be kidding me? She thought, now!

The woman turned and smiled at Sally, then shut the door and locked it.

Sally had quite literally frozen to the spot.

The woman walked around to the front of Sally's car and introduced herself.

"Hello Sally, I thought I recognised the address. I'm Sandra Peckham, I'm from Ofsted." Sally opened and shut her mouth like a goldfish. Sandra continued, "Now I know you've got to do to the school run, is it alright if I wait here and make a start on your paperwork?"

Sandra's smile began to fade, something was amiss. Her eyes dropped to the now grizzling Eve at the same time, catching a whiff of cooling vomit.

"Oh my, goodness me!" Sandra stammered,

Sally snapped into childminding auto pilot.

"Yes indeed!" she replied, now in no mood to pander to an Ofsted inspector, "This way, I need to sort this little one out!"

Sally marched purposefully indoors with a now slightly reluctant inspector following her.

The children were sitting like robots on the three old settees. Sally twisted her head in the direction of the inspector.

"You can sit at that table through there," Sally said, nodding towards the conservatory, "the folders are all there, Children, this lady is called Sandra, could you say hello please."

"Hello Sandra," chorused the children in unison.

"Adele love," Sally said, hurrying through the sitting room, "could you fetch me Eve's changing bag and bring it through to the bathroom please."

Adele jumped up. Sally carried on through to the kitchen and turned left through the small lobby in to the bath room.

Sally threw the blanket into the bath and sat down on the toilet with Eve on her lap. Sally shrugged herself out of her vomit covered gillet and dropped that into the bath as well.

Sandra, to her credit, followed Sally into the bathroom.

190

"May I help at all?" She offered as she watched Sally ease Eve out of her vomit soaked wool coat and drop that too, into the bath.

"I've got Eve's bag for you Sally," came a small voice from behind Sandra. It was Adele.

"Well done Adele! Thank you love, I'm so proud of you. Now, don't worry, go back in to the sitting room and ask everyone to choose a book from the bookcase to look at and I'll be with you in a minute, ok," reassured Sally.

Sally now eased Eve's long sleeved top over her head. She did her best to roll it up and peel it gently over Eve's head. That, too, joined the ever growing, foul smelling washing in the bath.

Sally was suddenly aware that she hadn't got on any disposable gloves; a bit late for that now, she thought grimly, copious amounts of antibacterial hand wash would have to do!

"Could you open that bag and get the spare clothes bag out please; they will be in a carrier bag."

Sandra quickly located the bag, unknotted it, and passed Sally a clean vest and top.

"Thank you," said Sally, "alright Eve my love, let's get you cleaned up a bit and get you into some nice clean clothes."

"THICK!" said Eve, looking at Sally with her big blue eyes. She was now shivering and looked frightened and bewildered at what had just happened.

"You were, you were so brave, Mummy and Daddy would be so proud of you!" Sally gave Eve a quick cuddle and finished dressing her. Sally stood up with Eve, then sat on the edge of the bath and washed her hands with antibacterial hand wash then followed Sandra back through to the sitting room.

"Children, thank you for being so grown up and helpful, Eve's fine now but she needs to go home so I'm just going to ring her Mummy, so just carry on reading your books, ok?"

191

"Are we going to be late for school?" asked Jenny worriedly.

Sally looked at the clock. 8.40am.

"I think we might just make it, but don't worry, no-one will be getting into trouble if you are," Sally reassured the five anxious faces on the sofas.

Sally phoned Eve's mum, who immediately dispatched Eve's grandfather from around the corner to pick up Eve, then phoned St Michael's to inform them that three children might be slightly delayed.

Five minutes later Eve's granddad picked up Eve. Sally quickly pulled on disposable gloves and pulled the car seat and floor mat from the car and surveyed the inside. Not too bad considering, thank God for the blanket! She wiped down the back of the car seat and called to the children.

"Ok children, let's go! Let's pretend we're soldiers. Quick march! Quick march!" Sally smiled, big eyes, forced smile, desperately trying to take the edge off their upsetting start to the day. Double checking they had all their lunch boxes and book bags she called into the house to Sandra,

"See you soon; I'll be about half an hour. Help yourself to tea and coffee," and shut the door. After checking seat belts were safely in place and windows were ajar, they finally pulled off Sally's drive to start their days.

Sally was so charged with adrenaline she couldn't have cared less about the Ofsted inspector sitting in her house.

What had happened this morning was the reality of her job! If it wasn't vomit it was dirty nappies, runny noses, bumps and scrapes, giving love, care, nurturing, routine, being a taxi driver, school runs, nursery runs, chef, negotiator, and pacifier.

Sally felt invincible.

Ofsted.

Bring it on!

After delivering the remaining five children safely, and on time, (just!), Sally headed home.

"Hello again," Sally said breezily, Sandra was sitting at the table, laptop open along with Sally's folders.

"Hello Sally, what a start to your morning," she smiled sympathetically, "are you alright?"

"I'm fine," replied Sally with a grimace, "Would it be alright if I just change my clothes and put the washing in the bath on a rinse wash, then I promise I'll make you a coffee or tea?"

Ofsted inspectors usually come first but Sally kept getting a whiff of vomit every time she moved.

Thankfully, Sandra was human.

"Good lord yes! Take all the time you need, your files are very user friendly so I've plenty to keep me busy for now. I'll have a white coffee with one sugar please when you get to it." She returned to her laptop and resumed typing.

Fifteen minutes later, clothes changed, washing machine on and coffee with sugar for two made, Sally joined Sandra at the table.

As expected, Sandra grilled Sally on the EYFS and how she was delivering it. She was impressed with the five week play plan that Sally was using, as this was evidence that Sally was observing the child's interests, planning to meet their interests and recording the next steps at the bottom of the plan. These next steps could then be rolled over to the next month's five week plan and Sally's planning would incorporate these.

It was fairly foolproof.

Thank goodness for the childminding website she had downloaded them from, Sally thought to herself.

Sandra did pull Sally up on the lack of parental feedback.

She understood that parents were busy but Sally must try harder to get them on board in writing their comments down. Sally had not completed a two year old progress check yet as Eve was just two, but she explained that she knew what she had to do and would be completing one in the next two or three months.

Three hours later, Sandra got ready to leave.

"If I could give Outstanding for efficiency, care, empathy, common sense and multi tasking skills I would award it to you, Sally," Sandra said warmly.

She awarded Sally an overall Good which equated a strong childminding setting.

Sally worked more than fifty hours a week, her parents were happy and the children were happy.

She ran a home and a family.

Sally was pleased.

She could live with a Good.

The first day of the rest of your life.

Thursday morning dawned; James sat in his study, a brandy in hand.

Through the French windows the sun streamed in, warming his still body.

Time seemed to pass at the same pace as usual.

Not slowing down to respect the enormity of the forthcoming day's events.

Over the weekend he had phoned his deputy head and informed him that he would be working from home on Monday and to phone him only if absolutely necessary.

Tania's alarm had gone off at 4.15am Monday morning. Her flight to Zurich was at 7.15am. Her sister would be arriving at 4.50am, ready for them to at leave at 5 am.

Swiss law dictates that a patient has to be in Switzerland for four days to allow for a cooling off period, a chance for them to change their mind.

James would not allow himself to think past this morning.

Tanya's carer, Kath, had helped her wash and dress. She'd agreed to visit earlier than normal this morning to help Tanya for the last time.

James had got up to make tea for everyone, strong and sweet, especially for poor Kath, who'd looked after Tanya for the past six months. She knew of today's and the coming week's schedule and was just barely holding it together.

Donna arrived and hovered by the car, checking the windscreen wiper blades and that there was enough water in the bottle under the bonnet to clean the windscreen.

All was completely unnecessary in practice, but necessary to allow her to keep her distance to allow the tragic couple the inevitable, final, goodbyes.

She knew James was desperately struggling to deal with Tanya's decision. She herself had tried to talk Tanya out of it but then when her condition deteriorated and her quality of life was rapidly declining with no hope of a miracle cure, she got on board with her brave younger sister's wishes.

Inside, Tanya had looked up at James, her blue eyes soft, full of love.

One more time, James fell to his knees, hugging her for the last time, smelling her for the last time.

What if he forgot how it felt to hold her?

His heart could surely not survive the physical pain of this planned, permanent separation.

He quite simply worshipped her.

He still couldn't accept he was about to lose her.

He'd tried one last time.

"Darling, please don't do it, please...."

He knew it was futile. She had seemed so calm and at peace the last few days.

She gently pushed him away.

"Thank you for loving me, James, I got so lucky with you my darling man."

She pulled his face towards her and kissed him for the last time.

Tanya sat back in her chair, waiting to move forward. James, realising there was no going back, mechanically stood up.

It all suddenly seemed very surreal, as though he were floating up, out of his body, watching himself and Tanya act out a scene in a play.

Was this really the last time he was going to see Tanya?

He hadn't slept at all last night.

He had simply stared at Tanya's sleeping face, trying to memorise every line, every feature, every expression.

Tanya gently negotiated her chair past James and travelled down the hall towards the front door. She turned her chair slightly.

"I'll say goodbye here, James," she nodded to him, "is that alright?"

James feared he was going to pass out from the pain, his throat dry and tight. He managed to reply.

"Yes love, of course...anything you want...." he trailed off.

"I love you," she smiled.

"I love you too darling," the words were simply not enough to convey how much.

Tanya straightened her chair.

For the last time, she travelled through the front door and down the ramp.

James was conscious of Kath bustling past him, closing the front door, coming back towards him and gently turning him 180 degrees on the spot.

"Now Mr Young, I just need you to come this way," she steered him into the study and guided him down into his chair.

She handed him the brandy that Tanya had instructed her to give him after she'd left and put a blanket over his legs.

"For the shock," she said gently, "I'll let myself out."

Kath walked briskly out of the study, picked up her handbag and hurried out of the house, quietly closing the front door behind her.

She climbed into her old green Micra and started the engine.

She drew out of the drive, turned left and parked fifty yards up the road where she gave in to the huge wracking sobs that confined had made her ribs spasm in their struggle to contain them.

On Tuesday and Wednesday, James had gone into school for 7am and stayed until late. He'd shut himself in his office, cleaning his shelves, sorting and reorganising school policies and procedures, anything to prevent his mind thinking about what was happening in Switzerland.

On returning home around 10pm, he had poured himself a large brandy and fitfully slept in his chair in his study.

He was in no man's land.

Thursday; 10.30am:

The requested text arrived on James's phone.

Kinder to Donna.

More bearable for James.

She's gone, not a moments falter. Will email you tomorrow. Donna x

James poured himself a brandy, picked up the bottle, went into his study and closed the door.

Later that day, James reached over and refilled his brandy glass.

The sun had now moved around away from the French windows.

Outside, the day was thinking about going to bed.

What now? He thought to himself, what now?

The week started out fairly well considering the shaky start to Millie's new way of parenting, but it started to steadily go downhill on Wednesday.

Sunday had been spent with Millie and Darius tiptoeing around each other and the children keeping a low profile.

Prompted by Darius, Jane said sorry to Millie. Millie scooped Jane into a bear hug and explained again that she just wanted her to have the best start in life, to focus and to make the most of the short, brief, education-filled years and not waste them.

Like she had.

Jane had looked up at her Mum; Millie was looking wistfully over the top of Jane's head.

"What did you want to be Mum? y'know, when you were my age?"

Millie had stepped back and leaned against the fridge.

"Do you know darling, I had no idea and to be honest, I didn't give it much thought at school, I just sort of drifted through secondary school. Mum and Dad never asked me, or advised me," Millie paused and thought, "not that I am criticising them. I could have joined the circus for all they cared, as long as I was happy."

Millie shrugged and smiled,

"They struggled to conceive me, you see, so when I finally arrived I was loved and spoilt and absolutely no pressure was put on me whatsoever."

"That sounds great!" exclaimed Jane, raising her eyebrows and pulling a face. Millie smiled at her daughter, at her childlike view of what seemed cool parenting.

"I can see why you think that Jane, but an adult placing an idea, or suggestion, or even insistence that I carried on with a language at school or an instrument would have meant that I was skilled in two things that I'm not now." Millie finished and looked at her daughter in a 'do you see where I'm coming from?' way.

Jane felt brave enough to tackle her mum about the timetable.

"Mum, y'know the time table?" she ventured.

"Yes Jane," Millie knew what was coming,

"Well, on it right, you've got music practice on Wednesday nights after school when I normally do netball practice, and on Friday, well that's normally play date night...." Jane stopped, faltering, not wanting to ruin the moment and also aware, after her dad's little chat Saturday afternoon, not to overstep the mark. She needed to go carefully with her mum.

Millie too, chose her words carefully.

"Jane, give me until half term, ok? I just want to invest some time and effort into you and Drew without diluting the effects with activities that aren't important."

"But netball is important!" exclaimed Jane, unable to contain herself, "it's a great sport and I'm good at it! Next year I might even make the team!" she finished, arms spread out to maximise her point.

Millie kept her voice calm and even.

"You do P.E in school twice a week, you have a morning play and an hour during lunch to do sport or socialise with your friends. By the time you take out assemblies, playtimes, lunchtimes and P.E there's really not that much lesson time left."

Millie could feel herself rising to her cause but checked herself, not wanting another argument this weekend, which this could quickly become.

"Look darling, the term's just started; let's see how we go, ok?" She stepped forward and gave Jane an olive branch cuddle, "Pizza for tea?" Jane's favourite, Jane wasn't fooled but wisely played along.

"Great mum, thanks, may I watch Mamma Mia before tea?"

Perfect Sunday afternoon viewing, in Jane's view.

"Yes of course, I might even come and have a sing along with you," answered Millie.

She was a poor Amy Chua substitute, she thought to herself.

She would have said no to such triviality, or maybe agreed, but after ninety minutes of piano practice.

Hmmm..... the niggling flicker of doubt about Millie's new venture just wouldn't go away.

Before bedtime, Millie had let Jane and Drew choose which way they wanted to travel to school the following morning, except by car.

Power walking? Bike riding? Space hopping had all drawn looks of horror from Jane and Darius. Drew, on the other hand, thought it sounded great fun at the tender age of seven.

"No way!" Jane had declared, "The school day isn't long enough for the laughing to stop!"

Darius had walked past Millie and said under his breath,

"Millie, if I have to I will back Jane on this one!"

Power walking it was.

The following morning Millie rose at 5.30am and made herself a cup of green tea and sat down at the kitchen table, scanning the children's timetable as she went over that morning's activities.

The children were to rise at 6.30am and gently come to with some Thai Chi exercises until 7am. They would then wash, dress and breakfast until 7.30am then rote learn ten spellings.

Today's spellings were British Prime Ministers, working backwards from the present day.

Millie looked at the clock. It was time for her shower, then, once dressed, she would wake the children.

Millie was in the process of pulling on her tracksuit trousers when Jane appeared in her bedroom doorway, rubbing sleep from her eyes.

"Mum, have I really got to power walk to school today?"

Millie really didn't want to get into a confrontational conversation so early in the morning.

"Jane, don't think of it as power walking darling, think of it as walking briskly to school," replied Millie, now pulling on her socks. Jane dropped her hand from her face, she looked worn out before her busy nine year old school day started.

"What about if I meet Chloe and Hannah, can I walk with them?" Jane tried one more time to negotiate with her mother.

"Why don't you see if they'd like to power walk with us?" Millie answered in a bright voice.

Jane gave up.

She turned wordlessly around and made her way to the bathroom. Had her mum really forgotten how cruel children could be if their friends were seen to be doing something even remotely weird?

After breakfast, Millie handed the children an exercise book and pencil each.

"Ok, Jane, Drew," Millie began, "this week we are going to be learning to spell the names of past Prime Ministers, we'll start with the current Prime minister, David Cameron."

Drew sat at the table and screwed up his nose in thought.

"What's a Prime Minister, is it like a prime number?" Millie turned and looked at Luke and frowned,

"No, no, darling, a Prime Minister is a person who is head of the political party that is elect........ I mean chosen to run the country."

Drew looked blankly at his mother.

"What, so like a marathon?" Millie stared at her son as he struggled with his parallel analysis of what a Prime minister was.

A growing feeling of panic crept over her at his apparent lack of working knowledge of how their country was governed; completely overlooking the fact he was only just seven.

Millie reached for her own exercise book and hastily wrote down in it under 'Topics to cover' the words 'Government and Politics'.

Forty five minutes later, spellings practised, teeth cleaned and relevant bags for the day allocated, Millie shut the door to her house firmly, feeling positive and empowered.

The morning had gone like clockwork. Although the children had tackled their tasks without, it could be said, enthusiasm, they had performed their Thai Chi exercises and practised their spellings without any moaning.

"Now," said Millie smiling, walking briskly on the spot to warm up, "are we ready?"

Jane could feel her face turning red with embarrassment at the sight of her mother exuberantly lifting her knees up high as she warmed up.

"Seriously mum! Please stop! Please can we just walk normally to school, please?"

Millie thought it best to ignore Jane's last ditched attempts to appeal to her better judgement and turned to Drew and said,

"Ready, Drew?"

Jane dramatically exhaled, adjusted her back pack higher up her back and flounced ahead quickly, to put as much distance between her mother and herself as possible.

Drew followed happily alongside his mother, still young enough to think that what his mother was suggesting was fun.

"Well done Jane, that's a great pace," called Millie trying one last time to get Jane on board with this morning's method of transport to school. She was rewarded with a look of pure loathing from her nine year old daughter, who, having glanced back over her shoulder and having seen her mother and brother closing the gap on her, had picked up her pace to create as greater distance between them as possible.

"Hi Millie, hi Drew," smiled Sally at the speeding duo as they overtook her and her minded children. She had had a rather dejected 'hello' from Jane, seconds earlier.

Not having to do a school run to Chudley that morning, due to a non pupil day, Sally was enjoying a rare opportunity to walk to school.

"Are we late Millie, have I forgotten a school trip?" she called, suddenly concerned and she started to increase her walking pace.

"No,no," Millie called back over her shoulder, "Just ensuring the old cognitive juices start flowing....." and purposefully carried on with her power walk, oblivious to the puzzled stares and raised eyebrows from the other children and parents.

Sally smiled to herself, ah yes, the Chinese parenting phase.

Well under way obviously. Sally was used to Millie's phases and refused to judge her. They never harmed anyone and were always done with good intent.

"Does Drew need the toilet?" asked Luke, staring at Drew's bottom as he was concentrating on copying his mother's exaggerated walk.

Sally swallowed a laugh with difficulty.

"I don't think so Luke, I think he's doing a special type of walk, called a power walk to warm up his muscles." Luke looked excited,

"Maybe we're doing P.E this morning!" he said excitedly. Sally decided a diversion tactic was the best conclusion to this no win conversation. She knew it would be Maths and Literacy, as usual, first thing this morning.

"Goodness me! Look at that digger in Dillon's garden!" she exclaimed in a drama laden voice and pointed to a mini digger looking out of place on a neat, semi detached house's front lawn.

"Whoa, cool!" replied Luke, "do you think it's going to knock down his house?"

Mission accomplished, with Millie, Jane and Drew far ahead of them, Sally and Luke leisurely discussed the probability of Dillon's house being demolished over whether Dillon's parents were going to have a new drive laid.

Luke favoured the former whilst Sally, who had it on sound authority, favoured the latter.

"Bye, Jane," Millie called to her daughter's back as she made her way to her classroom.

Jane didn't even bother turning her head; she just raised her hand in a curt wave then disappeared into school.

Millie felt a pang of guilt. Would Jane spend the next six hours of school hating her mother and dreading tomorrow's walk to school?

Had Millie created a positive learning experience for Jane this morning or had she created a situation whereby Jane would find it impossible to concentrate because of the embarrassment and stress she had experienced this morning? Millie kissed Drew, who was suffering no obvious repercussions from the means he travelled to school that day, and started to make her way home, deep in thought, at a more leisurely pace.

After school there was a decompressing period in the dining room; green tea for Millie, hot chocolate and carrot cake for the children before music practice began.

The children's proper lessons began the following week so they read through the first pages of their respective books and got used to their instruments.

"My arm aches," complained Drew, holding his violin up with one arm, the other hung down by his side holding the bow.

"Ah! Now," enthused Millie, "Amy Chua says you don't hold the violin up by your arm, but you clasp it between your chin and your shoulder."

"Who's Amy Chua?" asked Drew, "is she my new violin teacher?"

"No, she's an author of a book mum's reading. Mum is learning how to make us super intelligent children," piped up Jane, clonking dutifully on the piano. "Has it been ninety minutes yet mum?" she asked hopefully.

"No Jane, it hasn't, it's been fifteen and I don't want to turn you into 'super intelligent children'" Millie replied exasperatedly, "I just want you to fulfil your potential!"

"I know...." Jane replied woefully and found middle C again.

Wednesday had proven a stumbling block, not with the children but, once again, with Darius.

He arrived home, unexpectedly early.

He'd found his family in the dining room having their afternoon snack.

He had to avert his eyes from the Chinese inspired curtains; they gave him a headache, so bright and brash. They clashed dreadfully with the rest of the house.

"Hey guys, no netball practice tonight Jane?" he asked innocently.

Darius had arrived home early on purpose.

He'd read the timetable properly when Millie and Jane had been singing and dancing Sunday afternoon and knew he had to make a stand with his wife.

"No Dad, I'm going to miss practice for a while. I do P.E at school and have dinner time and playtime to play. I don't mind, honestly." Jane bit into her carrot cake, glancing from her mum, to her dad, sensing an atmosphere in the room.

"Millie, can I speak to you in the kitchen please?" Darius turned and left the room.

"Oooo, sound's serious...." Millie smiled at the children, "when you've finished children, start on your homework and then we'll go through the newspaper and find a story that's happened in another country and find it on the map, ok?"

Millie stood up and joined Darius in the kitchen.

"What's up, darling?" Millie was genuinely puzzled; he seemed cross with her, it couldn't be the timetable, she'd gone over with him what she wanted to do, granted, she hadn't gone through the timetable hour by hour.

"Millie, you can't, just can't, stop Jane taking part in competitive sports." Darius had his power stance on.

Straight back, legs astride, arms crossed in front of him, direct stare.

"Look Darius, she does P.E twice a week, she doesn't need to do it, and it's time out of our schedule."

Millie was solid in her defence. She really thought Jane did enough sport.

"Have you read the whole of that damn book yet?" Darius asked her coldly. Millie flushed red.

"Don't talk to me like that Darius, it's a great book. I believe in a lot of what she says, I........" she broke off;

Darius was looking at her with what looked like contempt.

"Do you? Do you really? " Darius spat, "We don't live in China, neither of us is Chinese and I certainly don't want to produce mechanic, robotic, parent-serving children, thank you very much!"

Millie tried again, sensing, quite rightly, she was on shaky ground.

"I just want them to achieve their full potential Darius, because I didn't, ok?" She looked at him, set faced.

Darius stood firm.

"Finish the book Millie and re read the prologue. Jane IS going to netball practice next week. I'm sorry you feel you didn't fulfil your potential but you are not going to relive your lost educational years through our children."

He bent down and picked up his brief case.

"I'm going to have a shower then I'll go through the newspaper with the children."

His turn now to offer a small olive branch.

He left the kitchen.

Millie stood alone, humiliated. Was she really getting it so wrong? Was she really trying to relive her education through her children? She went through to the dining room where the children were diligently doing their homework.

She drew the curtains.

God, the colours were harsh.

"Let me take your plates children, Dad will be down in a minute. He's going to go through the papers with you tonight, so I'll start tea."

She picked up their plates and cups.

"Thank mum," chorused Jane and Drew.

"Love you mum," said Jane, she felt a bit sorry for her mum.

She got her, she wasn't like her but in her nine year old way, she got why she was doing this for them. She had overheard her Dad's words and thought he'd been a bit hard on her mum. It was great he thought Jane should take part in netball practice after school but mum hadn't been horrible about it, she'd just asked her to give her until half term which Jane had thought was fair.

Jane went back to her poem.

Home felt funny at the moment. She looked forward to going to school tomorrow.

Friday

Friday evening, Darius arrived home and went straight to the dining room.

"No play dates tonight?" he asked his children, working at the table.

Drew replied in his seven year old little voice,

"Callum asked me, Daddy, but I was busy tonight."

"I see!" replied Darius.

Jane, sensing her Dad getting tense, tried to pour oil on troubled waters.

"It's ok Dad, we see our friends at school,"

Darius inhaled sharply and held his breath, trying to control his rising anger.

"Dad!" Jane said urgently, "It's really ok, OK?"

Jane felt on edge, she hoped her mum and dad weren't going to argue again. Darius turned and went to find Millie in the kitchen.

Half an hour later, the yelling stopped. Darius came back to the dining room.

"Come on kids, we're going to Pizza Hut for tea then how about the cinema?" he said with forced brightness.

Darius felt weary.

He needed to get as far away as possible from this new Millie.

A Millie he didn't recognise anymore.

The children quickly packed away their homework and got their coats.

"Is Mummy coming?" asked Drew, trying to do up his zip.

Jane already knew the answer.

"No pet," replied Darius quietly, "Mummy's going to do some reading."

Millie heard them go.

She sat at the kitchen table and broke down.

The house had never felt so horrible.

The tension, the hostility, the screaming.

Had it only been a week?

The music lessons hadn't even started yet!

She couldn't remember a time when Darius had disagreed so strongly with her or when they had argued so much.

And the way he had looked at her! As though he didn't know her!

Millie felt scared.

She could feel her family slipping away from her.

She stood up from the table and poured herself a glass of Chinese red wine from Waitrose......£9.99 a bottle!

It was okay, nothing special.

She took a deep breath.......it was underwear time!

She needed to dig deep and tonight she would dig deep in her lingerie drawer.

The contents never failed to smooth troubled waters between her and Darius.

Darius and the children arrived home just after ten pm.

He shooed them quickly to bed, full of pizza and popcorn and, without going to see Millie, headed for the shower.

That evening, Darius hadn't tasted the pizza or watched the film.

His mouth chewed and swallowed and his eyes stared at the pictures on the screen but his brain whirred and raced, going over the events of the past week or so.

Things were very wrong at home.

Millie was being brainwashed by that book. He hoped she was reading it tonight.

For the first time in his marriage to Millie he was questioning it.

Tonight, he couldn't reach Millie. He'd lost his temper with her, he'd tried reasoning with her, but Millie wasn't budging.

Deadlock.

Darius stepped out of the shower, dried off and wrapped a towel around his waist. He leant on the sink with both hands and stared at his reflection in the mirror.

He looked old, tired and beaten.

He sighed, opened the door and went across the landing to their bedroom.

He really didn't want to be in the same room as Millie tonight. He planned on fetching his pyjamas and robe and spending the night downstairs on the sofa watching car crash TV and having a couple of glasses of wine. Hopefully, the pair of them would be ready to face their problems in the morning, after putting some distance between them.

He opened the door to their bedroom and was immediately greeted with a pungent, exotic perfume that hung densely in the air.

Soft lighting lit the room, and there, surrounded by candles and new Chinese style influenced cushions, lay Millie, looking like a model, straight out of a La Senza brochure.

She was provocative and beckoning in an oriental inspired corset with a tied ribbon front bravely restraining her chest, which threatened to jump out of its finery, matching suspenders which gallantly held on to the satin trimmed silk stockings that clad Millie's toned thighs, finishing in four inch peep toe stilettos, Darius's favourites.

The whole outfit was accessorised with a diamond choker and elbow high red and black satin gloves.

Millie had pulled out all the stops.

Darius felt as though he had been punched.

He stopped, motionless, hand still on the door knob, struggling to process the all the information his senses were firing at him.

Perfume....arousing,

Soft lighting....enticing,

Millie....ravishing.

She was quite simply stunning.

Her dark smoky make-up, her sexual appeal, her desire and availability, mixed with the scent of the perfume was a heady scent.

She just seemed....what was it?

She just appeared....lower?

Lower?

Darius was puzzled.

Lower!

He blinked.

His peripheral vision kicked in.

Where was his solid oak antique headboard?

Darius's heart skipped a beat.

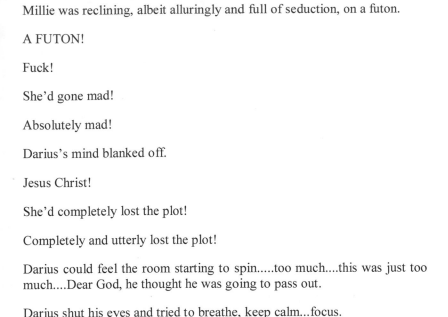

Millie was reclining, albeit alluringly and full of seduction, on a futon.

A FUTON!

Fuck!

She'd gone mad!

Absolutely mad!

Darius's mind blanked off.

Jesus Christ!

She'd completely lost the plot!

Completely and utterly lost the plot!

Darius could feel the room starting to spin.....too much....this was just too much....Dear God, he thought he was going to pass out.

Darius shut his eyes and tried to breathe, keep calm...focus.

Darius opened his eyes again and stared at the futon, rooted to the spot.

He was staggered by the lengths that Millie had gone to in her pursuit of her version of Chinese parenting.

Millie, sensing her ensemble wasn't creating quite the effect she was hoping for, propped herself up on both elbows.

"Darius? Are you ok? You've gone grey, look I just wanted to say..."

Darius cut her off, barely able to contain himself.

"I'm sleeping downstairs tonight Millie."

He stepped backwards and quietly closed the bedroom door.

Millie's jaw dropped at the closed door.

Rejected!

She sat up on the futon, stunned.

She felt utterly ridiculous!

Never, ever, ever had Darius failed to be aroused by her efforts in the past.

He had never, not made love to her when she instigated it.

Ever!

She swung her legs over the side of the futon, her knees nearly touching her nose with all heels on. She looked to her right.

The futon.

A step too far?

She kicked off her shoes, unclipped her suspenders and wriggled out of her corset.

After having changed into some fleecy pyjamas, Millie sat down.

Things were bad.

Very bad.

Millie felt tears of shame, inadequacy and fear rise up in her.

After half an hour had passed, Millie got up and crept out of the bedroom.

She decided she would beg forgiveness from Darius and see if they could find some common ground to work from.

She didn't ever want to anger him or see that look of contempt in his eyes again.

Millie found Darius in the sitting room, lit only by a lamp.

He was holding a near empty glass of brandy.

She walked hesitantly into the room and dropped to her knees, kneeling on the floor opposite her husband, the coffee table a buffer between them.

Darius met her tentative look with dead eyes.

Millie dropped her gaze.

The room suddenly felt very cold.

"Did you read the rest of the book?"

His tone was accusing.

Without looking up, Millie shook her head slowly and tears welled up in her eyes again.

She'd been too busy trying, and failing, to win Darius over with sex.

Darius leant over and picked up the book from the coffee table, with the other hand he tossed Millie a blanket.

"Right, go and sit over there and I'll read it to you,"

Millie looked up at him questioningly.

He continued, "Millie I don't believe in divorce, but from where we are at the moment, if things don't change, if YOU don't change, I don't see what other road we can go down."

Darius looked at Millie with the same brown eyes that were once filled with love and respect for her.

She couldn't remember the last time she had seen it in them.

She slowly stood up and carried the blanket over to the adjacent sofa. She curled up under it, feeling like a stranger in her own home which, to her husband and her children, she was.

Darius opened the book.

He read from Chapter 24 titled 'Rebellion'.

He read the next sixty two pages until the end of the book.

Millie sat in silence, humbled.

Darius stopped momentarily after chapter 31 and their fateful family trip to Russia. He left the sitting room and returned a moment later with a glass of Wolf Blass....now that was worth the £9 upwards price tag, and handed it to Millie.

She reached and took it gratefully with a shy, watery smile of thanks.

Darius bent over and gently kissed her damp cheek, went back to his seat and continued reading.

In the early hours of the morning, Darius closed the book.

He placed it on the floor.

The symbolic new place for it wasn't lost on Millie.

"What do you think Millie?" he spoke softly and got up and poured himself another measure of brandy.

Millie had sat in growing horror as she listened to how Amy Chua described how she had nearly got it so wrong with her second daughter Lulu.....so like Jane.

Battle Hymn of the Tiger Mother was written by the author to inform the reader of her comeuppance in trying to educate and mould her second daughter to conform using traditional Chinese parenting methods, not as guide to producing successful, exam passing, children.

She was thunderstruck and shaken to her very core. She hung her head in shame and sobbed again, struggling to speak.

"Darius, I'm so, so, very sorry. I just....I just..." and Millie once again, broke down and gave way to a torrent of emotion that had built up over the past few weeks.

Inadequacy, frustration, hope, love, humiliation, anger, rejection and fear.

Darius sat and waited until Millie was spent.

When she'd reached the snivelling stage and taking shuddering breaths, he got up and moved over to the settee where Millie sat, looking broken and tiny.

He wrapped the blanket around both of them and pulled her towards him and wrapped his arms around his wife.

Millie gratefully leant into his body, inhaling her husband's presence.

Steady, strong.....forgiving?

They stayed that way for ten minutes or so, then, hesitantly, Millie tried to explain again.

"Darius," She started falteringly, "Darius, deep down, I think I've thought, all of our marriage that one day......one day, you were going to wake up from the haze you were in, that Friday night, when you first met me and realise that I'm not that special, there's not that much to me and I'm actually not worthy of your love. I flunked at school, flip flopped around jobs and apart from the children, have achieved nothing in life."

Darius listened at his wife's raw admission and felt shocked.

Did she really think that?

Millie continued, she had nothing to lose now, she was so close to losing it all anyway.

"I think, in some way, I just felt if I was the best mother I could be, made it my job, you would be proud of me," she finished pensively;

"God that sounds pathetic, doesn't it?" she grimaced, nervously glancing up at her husband.

Darius shook his head slowly, as he stared ahead.

He was literally stunned.

He'd had no idea Millie felt so inadequate, or unsure of herself.

He'd been so proud of himself, that he was able to provide for his wife and children, to enable them to have a good quality of life; he had failed to see he had robbed Millie of that opportunity too.

To achieve, contribute and provide on equal terms for their family.

This Chinese parenting phase of Millie's was the result of his selfishness, he felt as though a cold bucket of reality had been thrown over him.

He bent his head and kissed Millie on the top of her beautifully styled hair which now, looked faintly ridiculous, offset by her puffy eyes, red nose and fleecy pyjamas.

"Millie my love, I think I've been an incredibly selfish husband," he said softly.

Millie, not expecting this in a way of a reply at all, pulled away from Darius's arms and turned to look at him in astonishment.

"What!" she exclaimed, "Selfish? You! Whatever makes you say that?"

"I think I've suffocated you," he nodded as he spoke, as if he was just realising it as he said it.

"It was me that insisted you gave up work when you fell pregnant, me that wouldn't hear of you returning to work because I earned enough for you not to......" Darius paused and took a deep breath,

"I thought I was being a good husband, the right sort of husband, like my father."

He turned to face Millie,

"Do you remember saying that after Jane was born you suggested maybe going back to work two days a week and I wouldn't hear of it?"

Millie nodded and blew her nose in a tissue.

"Well, why don't you ring Peter at the estate agent, or...." now it was Darius's turn to grimace,

"God, I'm doing it again...organising you!" he rolled his eyes at Millie, who, for the first time, in a long time, gave a small smile, feeling a shift in their relationship. "What I mean to say is I think it would be a great idea if you wanted to work for a couple of days a week so you can be Millie, and not Jane and Drew's mum, or Darius's husband.....if you want to...."

He trailed off, uncertainly.

Millie felt a little lift inside of her.

"Do you know, I think that's a great idea?" She looked up at Darius and kissed him warmly on the mouth, once again, so grateful for her understanding, patient husband.

Darius returned her kiss with a small hint of passion.

She pulled back.

There it was.

That look of love, back in his beautiful brown eyes.

She never wanted not to see it, ever again.

She wanted to reassure Darius that she knew she overstepped the mark and would never do anything, ever again, to risk losing their marriage.

She shifted around in her seat and sat crossed legged, facing Darius.

"Darius, I'm so very sorry for the past couple of weeks. I really, nearly lost the plot, didn't I?"

She was so embarrassed at how far she'd gone.

Darius, ever the diplomat and somewhat relieved to have his old Millie back, patted her feet, grinned and replied.

"I was getting a little worried, to say the least, however, now we have survived what I hope is going to be the worst thing you're ever going to do to me....."

Millie pulled a face, so ashamed and nodded her head,

"I'm so sorry, darling......" Darius interrupted her,

"Oh no! I'm not talking about the whole Chinese Mothering scenario, I'm talking about making me live in a house with those bloody awful curtains, bamboo prints and where, oh where, has my antique bed gone?"

Darius stopped with a big grin on his face.

Millie's eyes widened and she clamped her hand to her mouth which failed to hide her shout of laughter,

"Christ! I went MAD didn't I?"

Darius held his hand's up in mock resignation and said,

"Your words sweetie....your words.." and they both collapsed into each other laughing and wrestling, the tension of the past two weeks, gone.

The wrestling turned to kissing, turned to caressing, turned to........ just to check to see if the other was still really there.

They were.

Dean drove away from the flat, numb.

Maggie hadn't argued, shouted, or hurled abuse at him.

Her eyes had just mirrored what he was feeling.

When he had explained how inadequate he felt she had just gently nodded, understanding, with a sad smile on her lips.

It had completely thrown him when she had hugged him goodbye.

It suddenly dawned on him.

She was at the same dead end he was at.

Their lives were like a monopoly board.

Do not pass go.

Do not collect £200.

Pay the Inland Revenue, buildings insurance, bill, bill, bill.....

Dean drove on to the next stage of his life wishing he felt what he was doing was the right thing and not wondering if he had just made the biggest mistake of his life.

Maggie stared at the closed front door of their flat for a full two minutes before taking a deep breath, turning and walking back into the lounge area and stopping by the sofa bed.

This is what she had wanted.

She folded her arms and shivered and surveyed the small square footage that had twenty minutes ago been a family home.

It felt lifeless.

Empty.

Guilty.

As though it knew its walls had failed them.

Maggie dropped to the sofa bed, put her head in her hands and sobbed.

Fifty minutes after driving away from the flat, Dean drew up outside a large, imposing Victorian terrace. It was situated in a village on the outskirts of Stentbridge and was owned by a woman whose husband had suddenly died and left her a sizeable amount of money.

An avid 'Homes under the Hammer' viewer, Catherine Tyler had decided to invest in a 'buy to let' property which would enable her to draw an income from her investment.

Catherine had chosen this Victorian terraced house as not only was it set out over three floors and had six bedrooms, it was situated on the side of Stentbridge which was home to Barley Heath hospital, a constant source of income in the shape of student doctors and nurses.

It had been a wise decision.

The day the advert had been placed in the local newspaper, Catherine had received three phone calls enquiring about the rooms available and by the end of the week, all six rooms were filled.

An attractive, well preserved and sociable, forty something woman, Catherine enjoyed meeting new people and hearing about their lives.

To date, she had not had a bad experience with her tenants.

She had heard the horror stories on the grapevine and chose not to use a management company. She preferred to meet all her perspective tenants at a coffee shop in Stentbridge to find out their background, whether they were employed, what their long term plans were and just generally get a feel for them.

The new tenant she had just taken on had struck a chord with her. Sipping her coffee, and she listening to his honest, no holds barred, account of his

223

life to date had made her throw her 'must be employed' rule out of the window.

He had told her his plans, how he hated being a driving instructor and wanted to retrain as a carpenter. He knew being in an apprentice position would be poorly paid but it was his dream to make, and to create and he planned to enrol on a carpentry course to gain a qualification. He wanted to support his daughter properly and hoped she would be proud of him.

He had offered to pay six months' rent in advance as security and Catherine found herself putting down her coffee and offering to drive him to the property straight away.

Catherine stood in the kitchen of her business venture and heard the keys go in the lock. She didn't normally greet each new tenant at the property on moving in day but there was something about him.....

Dean closed the door and walked through the hallway and into the kitchen. He stopped on seeing Catherine.

"Oh, hello," he stuttered.

He was a bit thrown.

He'd been expecting to see one of the tenants and make introductory conversation with them, but not the owner of the house.

He was concerned.

"Did the bank transfer go through ok? The money's left my account...." he trailed off.

"Oh yes, yes, absolutely fine, no problem at all!" Catherine was flustering and knew it.

"I was just checking the fridge, one of the tenants reported the light didn't work anymore so I just thought I'd check it."

She opened the fridge door and light beamed out,

"Seems fine to me..." She coughed nervously, and an awkward ten seconds passed.

"Well I'll be off then and let you get settled in."

She walked past Dean, then turned and smiled, holding his gaze a little too long for comfort.

"Do let me know if the light plays up again, won't you?"

Then she was gone.

Dean absorbed what had just happened and made a mental note to himself to be careful there.

He had a new life to build and didn't need any distractions.

Sally was cleaning her teeth, getting ready for bed when Nick knocked and called through the bathroom door.

"Your phone's gone off, love."

Nick didn't question the lateness of the hour, Sally never turned her phone off.

The nature of her business meant she felt she had to be available to parents at all times because life demanded it, especially from the parents that used her daily.

Children got sick, parents got sick, had accidents. Grandparents went to hospital, sometimes died. Cars broke down, parents split up, lost jobs, got promotion.

All these episodes and more had been texted to Sally at all hours of the day as parents had wanted to keep Sally in the loop of their lives as it happened as she, as their childminder, was a vital curve in that loop.

Sally popped the toothbrush back.

"Thanks love, be out in a minute."

Five minutes later, Sally checked her phone.

It was Maggie.

"I'll take Adele to school tomorrow; can I pop round for a coffee tomorrow after the school run?"

Sally frowned, puzzled.

This usually meant a parent's situation had changed and they either wanted to give notice or increase/change their hours.

"Of course, see you tomorrow," she replied

Sally snuggled up to Nick's back in bed.

"Everything alright love?" he murmured,

"Not sure, I'll know more tomorrow." Sally replied and closed her eyes.

"Bye love, have a good day at school, don't forget Daddy's picking you up tonight, alright?"

Adele nodded and Maggie gave her a hug and a kiss on top of her head.

Adele slipped into class, completely oblivious to the changes that were taking place in her parent's life.

Dean often worked in the evening so she hadn't missed him last night and he'd telephoned that morning before school to say good morning, that he loved her and would see her at 3.15pm.

The previous evening had been a blur for Maggie.

She had functioned on autopilot.

She'd picked Adele up from school and fielded her daughter's questions on Dean's whereabouts with the answer of having to work late.

Once Adele was tucked up in bed, Maggie had caught up with the ironing.

She'd opened the cupboard door in the hallway, which she'd used for their clothes, and realised his clothes were gone.

His holdall was gone.

She hadn't noticed.

He must have packed whilst she had been at work that morning.

She felt betrayed.

Unreasonably so she realised.

It had been what she had wanted.

She closed the doors to the cupboard, firmly.

Tomorrow she would start the ball rolling, her end. She'd let Sally know and in the morning she'd contact a couple of agents and get the flat on the market as soon as possible and lastly, she'd enrol herself on the AAT level 1 book keeping and accounting course she'd been meaning to for the past year.

Time to be proactive.

Sally shut the door behind Maggie.

How very sad, she thought as she watched the young woman stride purposefully down her drive, turn right and continue down the hill to phone the estate agent.

They really were a lovely couple and it was clear they both thought the world of Adele.

Sally knew Dean could be hot-headed but in a way she understood his frustration. Things were so hard for young couples these days. She knew how frustrating Nick felt sometimes about his salary and had questioned whether he should have travelled further to secure higher managerial positions when he was younger instead of staying local to see more of the boys.

They certainly wouldn't have been able to get on the property ladder now, if they had their time again.

Sally carried on with the rest of her day, feeling grateful for her family and home.

By Friday, Maggie had the flat on the market and her distance learning bookkeeping course was on its way.

When Dean had rung to speak to Adele, Maggie had asked Adele to pass her the phone when she had finished talking to her dad.

'Hello Dean, how are you?' Maggie enquired politely, watching Adele go into her bedroom.

"Fine, thank you, Adele sounds ok, have you said anything to her yet?" Dean asked, dreading that conversation himself.

Maggie was determined not to be childish.

"Not as yet, but I will broach it if you like?"

Dean felt relieved and grateful to Maggie for how she was behaving.

"Yes, yes, that would be fine, you'll be far better at it than me, I'm sure," he replied quietly.

"If it's ok with you Dean, I'd rather go down the road of we're living apart due to the nature of your work, y'know, it being mainly Stentbridge based, rather than 'Mummy and Daddy don't love each other anymore. I just think that's a bit harsh for a six year old to hear....what do you think?"

Dean was momentarily taken aback.... 'didn't love each other any more...' it did sound harsh...was it really true?

He still hadn't answered Maggie.

"Absolutely! God, yes, that's fine, no problem."

He was floundering, he knew,

"Great, also, the flat's going on the market tomorrow, so as soon as we hopefully, get a viewing, I'll let you know, ok?" Maggie waited patiently for Dean to answer.

Again, he was taken aback.

Wow! Maggie wasn't wasting any time. He nodded into the phone.

"That's great Maggie, thanks for that, yeah...thanks" he finished lamely.

"That's fine Dean, it's got to be done and the sooner the flats sold the sooner we can move on with our lives is the way I look at it," she replied, matter of factly.

Ouch! Why did THAT hurt so much? Dean stared hard at a mark on the wall next to the memo board.

"You're right, well, thanks again.....um, the room's looking ok, do you think it's too soon for Adele to stay tomorrow night if I pick her up after school?"

Maggie swallowed.

Yes it was too soon.

Far too soon for her.

"That's fine Dean, are you thinking Saturday night too?" her heart sank.

This was hard. She continued quickly,

"Which is fine but we need to make sure she gets her homework done at some point and her reading and times tables."

Maggie finished, mentally scanning Adele's homework diary.

"Can we say Friday night and Saturday for the day?" suggested Dean,

"I'd like to spend Sunday looking through the local papers and in newsagents windows for some carpentry work.....if that's alright?"

Maggie's eyes filled with tears.

Once again she swallowed.

He really had been so unhappy, so restricted, so frustrated.

She completely understood why he had felt so trapped.

"Of course it is Dean, of course it is," she said quietly, her throat aching through trying not to cry.

"Listen, I'll see you tomorrow when you pop by for Adele's overnight bag, ok?"

"Ok Maggie, and thanks again," he paused,

"I really mean that." He finished quietly.

So much unspoken, unsaid, but understood by both.

"I know Dean, I know. Goodbye."

Maggie hung up and leaned heavily against the wall, shattered and emotionally spent.

After Sally's stressful start to the term, things started to jog along nicely.

The weeks flowed seamlessly along, one after the other, eating up the term at a pace.

Their finances were stable for the foreseeable future and Sally and Nick both crossed their fingers it would stay that way for a while at least.

The only cloud over the village had been the horrible news that Mr Young's wife had passed away early on in the term.

The children had been informed in assembly one afternoon by the Deputy Head teacher. When school had finished that day, the younger, children all jostled to be the first to tell Sally the sad news in loud voices, whereas Maisie and Jimmy came out quietly, processing the news at their own pace that their head teacher, strong, invincible and dependable Mr Young had now taken on a more human persona.

He had lost someone he loved and was sad.

Mr Young had rarely been seen during the past few weeks in the playground, at the beginning and end of the day, which Sally had thought was unusual.

He was usually a hands-on head teacher who liked to touch base with parents regularly, enabling him to deal with any issues quickly and efficiently, preventing grievances from festering and escalating.

Now it was clear why he had not been seen for a while.

Sally had listened sadly to the children's news.

Life was cruel and senseless sometimes.

She put a comforting arm around Maisie whose eyes were full of tears, bottom lip wobbling and gave her a squeeze.

"Come on love," Sally said quietly to Maisie, "I think we all need a chocolate biscuit with our fruit snack tonight, what do you think?" and was rewarded with a nod and a watery smile from Maisie.

Mrs Young's memorial service was attended by everyone in the village and the overflowing church stood to mark the wealth of feeling towards the Youngs and their union which had been tragically cut short.

One Sunday evening, with Easter just around the corner, Sally started to give some thought to the following term.

She really wanted to start growing some vegetables and involve the children.

She remembered a conversation she'd had earlier on in the year with Sue.

She was having Fin in the morning; she'd ask Julia if she could pass her number on to Sue to see if she was still willing to give Sally some growing tips.

Monday morning arrived, cold but bright and sunny.

A perfect spring day.

After feeding five children, preparing four lunch boxes and doing two school drop offs, Sally was on her way to Julia's farm with Fin.

Julia was without a car today so Sally had offered to pick up Fin. Sue was doing her grandmother duties and dropping her grandchildren to their various schools.

"Where are we going?" frowned Spencer, looking suspiciously out of the window, "Dis isn't the way to Thally's house?"

"We're going to pick up Fin from his house today, because his mummy's car isn't working," smiled Sally, glancing in her rear view mirror to reassure Spencer, she continued, "Fin lives on a farm!"

Spencer looked suitably impressed.

233

"Does Fin's farm have a tractor?" asked Spencer,

"Yes, two I think," replied Sally

"Does it have a sheep?"

Sally knew how this conversation was going to continue so tried a different tact,

"Well, let me see, Fin has lots of sheep, two pigs and four dogs on his farm and his daddy grows wheat to make bread."

Sally once again glanced hopefully in the rear view mirror at Spencer, who was now frowning.

"Does he have a snake?"

Sally smiled to herself.

 Point to Spencer.

They drew into Julia's farm yard,

"Here we are, Spencer," said Sally, changing the subject, "this is Fin's farm."

"Why is Fin's car broken?" Spencer was now looking left and right out of the window as much as the straps on his car seat would allow, taking in all the sights of the farmyard. Barns, tractors, a sheep trailer, hay......it was a yard full of questions.

The farmhouse door opened and out bounded four dogs followed by Julia with Fin in her arms, followed by Sue.

"Sally! Thank you so much for driving out of your way, I insist on paying you some petrol money," smiled Julia gratefully.

"Goodness Julia!" exclaimed Sally, embarrassed, "there's no need for that! This little impromptu run out is going to keep Spencer absorbed for the rest of the day, and me too, for that matter," laughed Sally ruefully, thinking of how this little visit would inspire Spencer to paint farm animals, sing

234

animal nursery rhymes and find all Sally's animal books on her book shelf for her to read to him.

The women all laughed again as Spencer did his best to do a 360 degree head swivel at all the exciting new sights in the farm yard.

Sally turned to Sue,

"Sue, I'm so glad I've seen you, I was thinking about you last night and your kind offer to help me with my tomato plants at some point."

Sue nodded quickly,

"Ah yes Sally, more than happy to! You can start planting the seeds now, just pop them in some soil in small pots and pop them on your window sill, then in two or three weeks when you see some leaves, give me a call and we'll take it from there," Sue finished helpfully,

"That's great Sue! I really appreciate it, would it be alright if I took your mobile number?" Sally asked,

"Yes of course!" Sue whipped out her phone out of her back pocket.

Five minutes later, with numbers exchanged and Fin strapped safely into Sally's car next to Spencer, Sally drove out of the farm yard, inspired with the knowledge that hopefully this year's tomatoes would fare better than previous year's attempts.

Julia and Sue both turned and made their way back into Julia's cosy kitchen. Julia filled the kettle with water and turned to Sue.

"Another coffee before we tackle the end of year books?"

Sue grimaced,

"As long as there's a slice of cake to go with it!"

Julia laughed,

"Now that sounds like a plan!"

One hour later, Sally, Spencer and Fin were completely engrossed in painting. Once home, whilst the boys familiarised themselves with Sally's toys after the weekend break, Sally filled the table with A3 paper, paints, cotton wool, glue, kitchen towel and baby wipes.

Baby wipes!

How did childminders get through the day before baby wipes were invented!

They were a childminder's best friend.

The trio were using cotton wool and white paint for sheep.

Sally counted the legs on the sheep as she drew an outline then asked the boys to count their legs with Sally's support.

 One, two.

"How many legs have you got Sally?" asked Fin, seriously,

"Well, let me see," Sally looked down and carefully counted her legs, "one, two, just like you and Spencer, Fin,' Sally smiled at Fin, who nodded, content that he was the same as Sally and Spencer.

After lots of toddler chat about animals, where they live and what they eat, the painting activity came to an end. Hand washing, snack time, then it was time for a walk into the village to buy tomato seeds, flower pots and a small bag of compost for some seed planting that afternoon.

Manoeuvring her tandem through the side gate, Sally saw Nick washing his car on the drive.

"Oh hello love, I forgot you were off!"

"Hello Nick, can I help you wash your car?"

Spencer's blue eyes shone with adoration for Nick.

He absolutely worshipped all the male figures in his life and as Sally had looked after Spencer from four months old, three days a week, Nick fell into that category too. He ran to his dad before his mum, his Grandads before his Grannies and would happily entertain Nick with a toddler question and answer time on anything that interested Spencer at that moment in time.

"Well, hello young Spencer, hello Fin, have you been keeping Sally busy this morning?" smiled Nick, noting the white paint on Sally's cheek and streaked through some of her hair. He didn't point it out to her; her appearance was way down her list of priorities when she was working.

"Yes!" they replied in unison,

"We've been painting," declared Fin,

"Me too!" shouted Spencer, not wanting to be left out.

Nick feigned shock,

"Really! Well, when I've finished cleaning the cars I'll come and see them," he turned to Sally, "buying anything interesting love?"

"Fraid not, just some tomato seeds and compost." Sally replied

"I'll pop up and get the compost love, do you need it now?" asked Nick, thoughtfully,

"No, we're not gardening until after lunch, are you sure?"

It was one of Nick's star qualities, he was the kindest person Sally had ever met.

"No problem, I'll pop up and get you a big bag, should keep you and the mini troops going for a while!" he grinned.

Sally leant forward and gave him a kiss on the cheek,

"You're the best!"

"You're not wrong there!" Nick winked and went back to washing his fifteen year old car.

After a detour to the park, Spencer and Fin played in the garden whilst Sally prepared lunch.

Her kitchen overlooked the garden, which was ideal for observing little ones whilst she worked.

Sally smiled to herself as she noted Fin, as usual, was immersed in his play in the large muddy area, set within wooden sleepers to one side of the garden.

He was digging spadefuls of mud and filling a pull along trolley.

Sally knew the filling and emptying of the trolley would easily take Fin up to lunchtime.

Sally picked up an apple to wash it and stopped.

Spencer was standing halfway up the garden looking so cute in his all in one weather suit which already had muddy knees and water dripping from the front. He was looking intently at the six foot side gate that led around to the front of the house.

Sally lowered the apple and pondered Spencer.

He was planning something.

Sally watched him survey the garden then toddle down to the bottom of the garden to where the three old Little Tikes ride on cars were.

Spencer grabbed the steering wheel of one and started to pull it up the garden.

He decided this was taking too long.

He then hurried around to the back of the car and with both of his pudgy arms locked straight; he started to push the car up the garden. The front wheels refused to stay in a straight line but Spencer persevered.

Sally, intrigued, was now on full alert, watching from the doorway of the kitchen which opened into the conservatory.

She didn't want to unnecessarily interrupt him, as he might just want to ride the car down the garden, but experience and instinct told her that Spencer had something else planned.

With great effort, Spencer negotiated the protesting car around the corner of the conservatory and was now parking it against the side gate.

Frowning, Sally walked through the conservatory and slipped on her old garden shoes, never once taking her eyes off of Spencer.

She now knew what he was going to do!

Quick as a flash, in one effortless two arm pull, Spencer was now kneeling on the roof of the car, his eyes fixed on the top of the gate. He reached up with both his chubby little hands, determination written all over his two year old face.

Sally was now at the corner of the conservatory having cleared the area of ground from the back door of the conservatory in two huge leaps, not wanting to call Spencer's name and startle him, but once again, aghast at his feat.

Would she never learn?

There were preschool children and the normal realms of development and then there was Spencer!

"Nick? NICK! Can you SEE me?" Spencer called, feet flailing against the gate.

He had now pulled himself up, his head clear of the gate, car forgotten, as he was fully prepared and able to heave and climb up and over the gate without a care, or thought, of the six foot drop on the other side.

Two firm hands reached up and scooped him down to safety.

Spencer tried to cling to the gate and gave a shout of protest.

"No! Nick! He clean my car!" he wriggled and squirmed with all his might in Sally's arms. "Nick, Nick!!"

Sally kissed his cheek and held him close, waiting for the struggle to finish, relief flooding her body.

"Come on, my love, its lunch time now, it's your favourite; ham sandwiches with apple slices,"

Sally could feel Spencer's little body start to relax a little as he contemplated Sally's words.

Sally popped him down on the gravel and bent down so she was eye level with Spencer.

"Spencer, Nick's not cleaning cars now; he's gone to buy some compost so we can plant our tomato seeds after lunch."

Spencer looked at Sally, processing what she had just said.

It did the trick.

World domination and car cleaning could wait.

He turned around and shouted to Fin, who was completely oblivious to the Herculean events which had just taken place.

"FIN!! Its lunchtime!" and off Spencer ran, up the conservatory steps, to wash his hands.

Sally stood up and sighed. I wonder how much climbing walls are, she thought to herself and followed Spencer into the house.

After lunch and the planting tomato seeds, Nick got the hose out in the back garden, whilst Sally produced sponges and washing up liquid and they spent the rest of the afternoon, much to Spencer and Fin's delight, washing the three old Little Tikes cars.

Later that evening, purely out of interest and not desperation, Sally told herself, she searched the internet to find out the price of climbing walls. After ten minutes of surfing the internet and noting the out of their price range prices, Sally decided that parks and play centres would have to do!

She put the laptop down and got up off the sofa and went through to the kitchen where Nick was pouring her a glass of red wine.

"Crikey Nick, it's only Monday! I'm trying to leave the wine until at least Wednesday evening," Sally mildly protested, taking the glass from him.

"Don't worry love, it's only eleven per cent, we'll lay off the fourteen per cent until Thursday...deal?" he smiled and kissed her cheek, "There's only a glass each left so relax."

Sally took a sip of her wine and reflected on her day,

"Spencer definitely had an extra Duracell battery in today!" she said, following Nick back into the sitting room,

"I think I'm on the ball with him, I think I've got every eventuality covered then he goes and does something like that!"

Sally shook her head,

"His upper body strength is incredible!" she finished, her eyes following the flicking channels as Nick scanned that night's viewing for something tranquil.

Countryfile!

That would do.

He patted Sally's leg.

"Tomorrow's another day love, you've survived this one and.....," he raised his glass, "there's always wine!"

Sally laughed and rested her head on his shoulder.

Five minutes later, she was gently snoring.

Nick took her glass of wine and gently negotiated his arm around her.

He settled back in their old threadbare, comfy sofa to find out more about the countryside and the world of lambing.

"Come here darling, stay close to Mummy and Gaby, there's lots of people around and we don't want to lose you."

Portia was running between the trolleys laden with bags and suitcases, excitement radiating from her big blue eyes.

"We're going on a plane! We're going on a plane! Daddy, are you coming on the plane?"

Portia was now doing star jumps between Phoebe and Gabrielle; she was finding it impossible to keep still.

"Yes, Portia."

Sebastian stood in the speedy boarding queue at Gatwick airport, trying to ignore his daughter's exuberance.

"Portia darling, just pop into your buggy whilst the baggage gets checked in, there's a good girl."

Phoebe glanced nervously at Sebastian.

There appeared to be no reaction from him.

No clenching of the jaw, no tightening of the facial muscles. Phoebe dared herself to relax a little.

As if he had read her mind, Sebastian turned to Phoebe and gave her a warm smile then turned back to show their passports.

These past few weeks since the last correction, Sebastian had noticed that Phoebe seemed a little distant.

He couldn't quite put his finger on it, she was still as subservient as always, still ensured his life, his meals and that she and the home was kept to his liking.

There was just something else within her, that hadn't been there before.

He sensed a shift between them so; as work had been fairly quiet he had booked a week's holiday in Marbella.

A colleague's villa, complete with an in house cook and maid, to ensure Phoebe truly relaxed.

Maybe this would be the week the necessary brother or sister for Portia would be conceived.

Sebastian sensed he needed to make the same effort he'd made when courting Phoebe for conception to take place.

Questions at work fuelled him on.

"So Seb, when can we expect the news that Phoebe's expecting again?" was the jocular, lunchtime banter of the moment.

"Whoa hoa! I'm working on it!"

Sebastian had smirked, inwardly cringing at the abbreviation of his name and the roars of approval from his Neanderthal colleagues.

He just needed to apply the same mental strategies he used at work to deal with maintaining relationships with colleagues and apply them to holidaying with Phoebe and Portia this coming week.

One hour into the flight, Portia was being entertained by Gabrielle in economy, whilst Sebastian and Phoebe sipped champagne in first class.

Phoebe had initially been mortified that her nanny and child were not flying in luxury with them but Gaby had reassured her that Sebastian had spoken with her and apologised but he really wanted this week to be a second honeymoon for them and had paid Gaby a handsome bonus for coming on the holiday to look after Portia, and for keeping Portia entertained on the plane.

It was only a two and a half hour flight after all, Gaby had quite rightly said.

"I'm looking forward to this holiday, Phoebe," murmured Sebastian, stroking the back of her hand as he spoke.

"Me too." Phoebe replied, taking another sip of her Moet.

She was still feeling a little wary and cautious.

Sebastian had something planned.

This impromptu holiday was completely out of character.

They never went away as a family together.

Sebastian and Phoebe would go for weekend breaks to Paris, Rome or Prague, or Phoebe would take Portia to Center Parcs, or travel to France, with her parents, to stay in their house in the Dordogne for a summer break, but never away as a family on holiday.

There were just too many negative variables that could arise with a toddler that would enrage Sebastian, so it was an unspoken rule that family holidays were off the table.

Until now, apparently.

The past few weeks for Phoebe had been spent in quiet reflection and deliberation of her marriage to Sebastian and for her and Portia's future.

Could she leave Sebastian?

What would she do?

Would he agree to it?

Phoebe's mind would never let her play through that scenario.

The fallout from her requesting a divorce didn't bear thinking about, that would mean admitting defeat for Sebastian, which was in his world, not an option.

She did have a trump card to play if she absolutely had to but she wasn't there yet, and hopefully it wouldn't come to that.

She closed her eyes.

Let's see what unfolds this week, she thought to herself.

Phoebe woke the morning of their last day, stretched her limbs, yawned, and rolled over in bed.

She listened as she watched the sun's rays pour through the open French doors that led out to the pool.

She could hear Portia's squeals of delight whilst she played with Gaby, still enjoying the novelty of being able to get up out of bed and straight into a swimming pool.

Sebastian's side of the bed was empty; he was obviously still out jogging.

Phoebe wondered whether he had decided to enter a marathon, he had definitely upped his daily mileage this holiday; well the weather was certainly lovely to jog in, early in the mornings.

She looked at the clock on the bedside table; she'd better get up and pack their final bits and pieces ready for the flight home later that day.

She sat up slowly and winced.

She was feeling a bit chaffed and bruised down below, Sebastian had certainly used this holiday as an opportunity to, if not emotionally, then physically, get reconnected to Phoebe again.

Morning and evening, they had had sex in every room, over various pieces of furniture, in various positions.

Not one time could it be called love making.

Phoebe turned the shower on and stepped in to its refreshing spray.

Their flight was at 4pm so they'd have to make sure they arrived at Malaga airport by 3pm at the latest.

Phoebe started to wash herself briskly; it would be good to get home.

She felt no nearer to a decision about her marriage to Sebastian.

If she was honest with herself she couldn't see a long term future for them. She now knew that Sebastian didn't love her in the way she wanted to be loved, or deserved to be loved, but how to broach this with him?

He just wasn't rational enough to have a mature conversation with.

Phoebe sighed and reached up to turn the shower off.

Something would happen, she was sure, to force her hand.

Life had a funny way of intervening, well, she would just bide her time and wait a little longer.

"Well, hello sleepyhead."

Sebastian stepped into the shower to join her.

Phoebe's heart sank.

"How was your jog?" she asked, desperately hoping that Sebastian didn't want sex.

"Good, good," Sebastian murmured, kissing the side of her neck and running his hand over her tummy.

"I wonder if we've managed to make a sibling for Portia this week."

His lips travelled to her collar bone.

Phoebe closed her eyes, so that was it!

That was the reason for this holiday, the fervent sex sessions and the uncharacteristic softness towards herself and Portia.

Sebastian's relationship with Portia was distant at best.

He viewed Portia as a trophy to be brought out of its display cabinet when necessary, when he needed to be perceived as a loving family man.

The rest of the time he rarely saw her through choice.

He worked long hours and used this as an excuse to cover up for his complete lack of interest in her.

Why he wanted another child was beyond Phoebe.

"We'll have to see."

She said quietly and pulled away gently from his embrace.

"Sebastian, I'm feeling a little sore, could we perhaps postpone sex for a couple of days?"

Sebastian's eyes glinted fleetingly with anger at being thwarted, but stepped aside to let Phoebe reach for a towel.

"Of course."

"Thank you darling." then, for good measure she offered, "It really has been a special week," and left the bathroom.

Once in the bedroom she exhaled.

Thank goodness.

She hurriedly dried herself and slipped a sleeveless silk wrap, around herself and tied it at the waist then went outside to enjoy the last morning of the holiday with her daughter.

Sebastian carried on with his shower, vigorously soaping, rubbing and rinsing himself.

He was almost at his maximum, mental capacity with the stress that this holiday was causing him.

He had had to run an extra five miles that morning to try and rid the rising tension from his body, the increased sessions of sexual intercourse with Phoebe hadn't nearly helped to dispel it.

He was almost out of his mind with frustration at the relaxed timetable that being on holiday required.

He had accepted the invitation to use this particular villa because of the hired help included but even he knew he couldn't expect them to pander to his exacting standards like Phoebe did.

The flight home couldn't come fast enough.

He could not fathom how it didn't bother others that the tea towels in the kitchen and the beach towels on the veranda were not hung so they were level.

Tins and packets of food were just put away in cupboards with no thought to alphabetical or size order, and surely it was just common sense that the labels all faced the front, so one could see at a glance what was in the tin or packet?

Sebastian actually groaned, closed his eyes and leant his forehead on the hard, cool tiles as the mental vision of the vibrant, asymmetric beach towels taunted his tense and fraught mind.

The chaos, the mismatched patterns, not to mention Portia's wet footprints on the tiled floor as she scampered in and out of the villa.

Thank God this will all be over soon!

Phoebe had better be pregnant, Sebastian thought to himself, reaching for a towel.

Maybe he could initiate one more session of intercourse if he suggested a massage first, not something he usually instigated as it prolonged physical contact, which he thought unnecessary.

He preferred a quick, intense act, no fuss, minimal contact, allowing him to, as quickly as possible, continue with his planned, daily schedule.

After a light brunch, Phoebe gathered up the last of her toiletries from the bathroom and packed them into their suitcase.

She scanned the bedroom for anything she had missed, no, that was everything now.

The bedroom door opened and Sebastian appeared in the doorway.

"Gaby's taken Portia to buy an ice cream, why don't you lie down and I'll give you a relaxing back rub before the journey home?"

Phoebe opened her mouth to protest.

They had to leave in two hours but Sebastian was already undoing the tie of her sundress and slipping it from her shoulders.

He led her to the bed and gestured for her to lie down on her front.

"Sebastian! We have to leave in two hours and Portia could be home any minute!"

Sebastian acted as though he hadn't heard Phoebe and squeezed some lotion into his palm in preparation.

Defeated, Phoebe laid down.

Sebastian massaged Phoebe as he lived his life.

Meticulously, conscientiously and thoroughly.

Her back, buttocks, thighs, calves, feet and toes. He let his hand rest at the top of her inner thighs for a moment.

Phoebe tensed.

God, he was selfish!

He knew she was sore.

Sebastian, however, hadn't finished his massage.

Ever the perfectionist, he moved to Phoebe's shoulders, her arms, wrists, hands, fingers, back up to the upper, inner arm area, out to sides, then back to the soft skin on the inside of her arm.

He stopped.

Phoebe froze.

Sebastian moved a finger over the area above her elbow on the inside of her left arm.

He got off her.

Phoebe rolled over quickly and tried to get up, her hair falling over her face, temporarily hampering her vision.

The next sensation she was aware of was being dragged up of the bed, then flying, weightlessly across the room, only stopping when her body made contact with the bedroom wall on the opposite side of the room.

She didn't cry out.

Momentarily stunned and disorientated, Phoebe groaned and tried to get up.

"HOW DARE YOU! HOW DARE YOU!! Sebastian roared, 'YOU LYING, CONIVING, TWO FACED WHORE!!"

Sebastian, a week of pent-up frustration now being given an excuse to vent itself, leapt across the bed to Phoebe's crumpled form.

"No!" Phoebe cried out, making a futile attempt to curl her naked form into a ball.

Sebastian leaned over, grabbed her hair and pulled her across the floor, incandescent with rage.

"Sebastian! Please! No!" screamed Phoebe, her pleas fell on deaf ears.

 Sebastian swung back his arm, as though he was going to throw a ball, winding his hand viciously into Phoebe's hair as he did so, paused, then yanked Phoebe's head forward violently smashing her face into the corner of the wall leading to the ensuite.

Blood spurted from her nose and splattered the wall, herself and Sebastian.

Her top lip split, blood filling her mouth.

Fury partially expelled, Sebastian released his grip on her hair.

Phoebe slumped to the floor, floating in and out of consciousness, he was going to kill her, of that she had no doubt.

She heard him step over her.

Two, well aimed, violent kicks were delivered to her bare, blood splattered stomach.

Phoebe groaned, then threw up.

"DADDY! STOP!"

Sebastian spun round, his face white with fury, eyes unseeing, a fog of rage blurring his vision.

Portia was now in the room, desperately trying to get to her mummy, but being held back by the vice-like grip of Gabrielle, her nanny.

Stunned by the violence that was taking place in such a beautiful setting, Gabrielle stood rooted to the spot, mouth wide open in horror at what the pair had unwittingly walked in on.

"GET OUT!!" Sebastian bellowed, "GET OUT!"

He sprang over Phoebe's broken form towards Portia and Gaby, raising his arm across his body as though to deliver a backhand to the shocked pair as though to physically expel them from the room.

"NO!"

Horrified, Gaby scooped up Portia and ran from the bedroom and out to the poolside, shouting for Paulina, the maid.

Mind racing, she did her upmost to soothe a distraught Portia as she ran past the pool, through a low gate that led down a path and on to beach.

They stood, partially hidden by three orange trees, their branches heavy with the nearly ripe fruit.

Sebastian had been about to strike Portia, of that Gaby had no doubt, but Phoebe, Phoebe had to get to a hospital, and soon.

Gaby had been Portia's nanny since her birth and knew the restrictions that Phoebe lived her life by.

She had often seen suspicious bruises over the years on Phoebe's arms, and more recently her head, but she had witnessed nothing like this before.

Sebastian had seemed crazed, like a mad man!

Five minutes later, Sebastian emerged from the villa in his running gear.

"I'm going for a run," he announced to no one in particular, as though nothing out of the ordinary had happened.

Gaby waited until she saw Sebastian's figure disappear down the rough Spanish road, then quickly spoke to Portia in her arms.

"Portia my love, Paulina is going to take you into your bedroom to put the last of your toys in your suitcase, while I go and look after mummy, alright?"

Portia nodded, quietly crying.

"Gaby, is mummy going to die?"

Fresh tears welled up in her three year old eyes.

"No, no, darling, but I need to go and help her, ok, so go with Paulina and I'll be back as quick as I can."

Gaby gently placed a trembling Portia into Paulina's arms who she clung to like a limpet.

"Come, Bella, I think I saw your teddy under your bed. You don't want to forget him, now, do you?"

Gaby hurried into the villa ahead of Paulina and Portia just in earshot to hear,

"Why did Daddy kick Mummy, P'lina?"

Because he's a monster, thought Gaby to herself as she hurried into the villa.

A monster.

Gaby knocked gently on Phoebe's bedroom door and stepped inside.

"Phoebe?....Phoebe?...it's Gaby....Sebastian's gone for a run, can I......Oh Phoebe, stop, please stop....I'll do that!"

The broken form of Phoebe was on her hands and knees, feebly attempting to clear up her vomit and blood from the floor.

She didn't answer Gaby, or show any sign that she had heard her.

She was obviously in shock.

Phoebe had managed to pull on her t-shirt dress that she wore to bed and was now slowly and painfully wiping the floors with the bath towels.

Gaby rushed over to her and gently placed her hands on Phoebe's wrists.

"Phoebe, stop, just stop." Gaby urged gently.

Phoebe lifted her head as though she had only just realised someone else was in the room with her and looked at Gaby.

Gaby took a sharp intake of breath.

Her face.

"Dear God Phoebe, we have got to get you to a hospital!"

Phoebe's left eye was had doubled in size and swollen shut.

Her left cheek, still bleeding, had a gash along it and was already black and blue.

Her nose was a bloody mess and her top lip had a gash that threatened to join the base of her nose.

Phoebe's right eye filled with tears as she fell into Gaby.

"I thought he was going to kill me!" she whispered, trembling and shaking in Gaby's arms.

So did I, thought Gaby to herself, thanking God that they had arrived back from their walk when they did, so did I.

"Phoebe, listen, we have to get you to a hospital. Your face needs looking at, you're probably concussed and I think they should check your tummy."

Phoebe's eyes widened with fear, terrified, she shook her head, then retched when a searing pain shot across the back of her eyes.

"I can't......Sebastian....flight....Portia!" her eyes widened with panic.

"Portia's with Paulina"

Gaby refrained from mentioning Sebastian,

"And you need to get to a hospital; you're not flying anywhere today. Now, let's get you into the car."

Ten minutes later, Phoebe was in the car clutching a bowl, with her seat reclined back and a pillow either side of her head to prevent too much movement.

Gaby hurried back into the villa where Paulina was zipping up Portia's suitcase, Portia was sitting crossed legged on top, cuddling her rescued Teddy.

"Paulina! I need you to drive Mrs Whitehall to the nearest hospital, bring Portia's suitcase please."

Gaby picked up Portia and ran through to her room.

She grabbed her holdall, purse and key's, and called over her shoulder,

"Let's go Paulina!"

She reached the car at the end of the drive and scanned the road both ways.

Sebastian was nowhere to be seen.

He'd be back shortly though.

She shut Portia's car door and glanced at Phoebe in the front seat.

Phoebe had been sick again in the bowl. She frowned and pulled some tissues from her bag and placed them on top of the vomit.

There was no time to empty the bowl now.

Paulina came hurrying up the drive, Gaby ran round to the front of the car, handed her the keys and quickly climbed in beside Portia.

"Ok Paulina, as quick as you can but mind the pot holes if you can, and thank you."

Gaby placed a reassuring hand on the young Spanish girl's shoulder.

"Si," Paulina nodded, shocked and unsurprisingly more than a little panicked by the day's turns of events.

She gingerly started to reverse out of the drive.

Content they were finally on their way, Gaby leant forward to check Phoebe, who, probably sensing she was now safe, appeared to be dozing, although clutching her seat tightly, groaning gently when the car went round a bend.

Gaby looked sideways at Portia who too, looked shocked, sucking her thumb and staring out of the car window.

Her three year old little eyes had seen what no three year old should, her father attacking her mother in such a frenzied and abandoned manner.

Gaby sat back to gather her thoughts.

The car rounded another bend down the mountain.

Phoebe groaned loudly and leant forward, vomiting again into the bowl.

Gaby leant forward, wiped her mouth and put more tissues over the vomit.

She made Phoebe as comfortable as possible then leant down and rummaged in her bag.

With Sebastian now out of the picture she couldn't look after Portia and Phoebe.

Phoebe needed someone with her here in Spain as Gaby was sure her injuries would involve at least a few days in hospital.

She found her phone and dialled a number.

Celeste put down her coffee and walked over to her mobile. She didn't recognise the number, maybe Phoebe was phoning from Spain on a 'pay as you' go phone.

"Hello?"

"Hello, is that Celeste, Phoebe's mother?" a familiar voice asked,

Celeste couldn't place the voice, puzzled, she replied,

"Yes, who is this please?"

"Celeste, its Gaby....Portia's nanny, please listen carefully, I don't have much time." Gaby paused; there was no easy way to say it.

"Phoebe has had an accident."

Celeste gasped and brought a hand to her mouth,

"No! Is she alright, how bad, oh my god, Portia! Is Portia alright?"

Gaby cut in.

"Portia's fine Celeste, now listen. You need to fly out to Malaga airport as soon as possible and ask to be taken to the Hospital Costa del sol. I'm taking Phoebe there now and will phone you again as soon as I know more....and Celeste..... Sebastian's not with us."

Gaby finished, not wanting to say too much in front of Portia.

She didn't need reminding of what her dad had done to her mummy.

Celeste's blood ran cold.

Sebastian.

The bastard.

Was he behind the accident?

"Right Gaby," replied Celeste pulling herself together,

"I'm going to put the phone down, phone Paul and we will be on the next available flight out. Will you stay with her Gaby?" she asked, and immediately regretted it.

Of course she would!

"Yes, I'm not going to leave her. I have an emergency credit card that I can use for food and necessities, so Portia will be fine."

"Gaby, thank you, thank you so much," replied a grateful Celeste. "We'll be there as quick as we can."

Celeste ended the call and immediately phoned Paul.

"Everything alright love?" Paul's customary answer.

"No darling, it's not. Gaby's phoned; Phoebe's been in an accident. We need to fly to Malaga tonight!"

Her voice was shaking.

She waited for Paul's response.

It took four seconds.

"I'm on my way home now. Get online now and book the next available flight, I don't care how much it costs!" He ended the call.

Gaby manoeuvred herself around the reclined front seat to check Phoebe. She appeared to be sleeping but kept giving intermittent groans. Her face looked worse than it had when they stared the journey and now Phoebe's fringe was parted Gaby saw an angry gash along Phoebe's hairline.

Gaby felt sick.

Sebastian was nothing more than an animal.

Her eyes were then caught by something moving lower down Phoebe's slip.

Blood.

Phoebe was bleeding from between her legs.

"How much longer?"

Gaby asked Paulina quietly.

"Five minutes."

Half an hour later, Phoebe had been examined and was immediately taken down to surgery to repair a suspected ruptured uterus.

Gaby, trying to retain some normality, was trying, and failing, to persuade Portia to eat a roll with some grapes when her phone rang.

Sebastian.

Gaby took a deep breath and answered her phone.

"Yes Sebastian?" Gabrielle answered coolly.

"Where are you? Where's Phoebe? We need to hurry if we are going to catch our flight."

Sebastian's voice betrayed nothing of the events that had taken place earlier that day.

Gaby used her last remnants of professionalism and remained calm.

"Sebastian, Phoebe won't be flying anywhere today. She is in hospital having surgery as we speak to see how extensive the injuries she has suffered are."

Silence.

Gaby waited.

Eventually.

"Well, that seems a trifle unnecessary. It was a minor correction compared to the unforgivable action that my wife has carried out."

Gaby's eyes widened and her jaw dropped in astonishment at the extent of Sebastian's delusional mind.

She tried to inject some reality into the conversation.

"Sebastian, Phoebe's parents are flying out this evening to be with Phoebe and Portia. You should be aware that the doctors are asking questions as to how Phoebe came to receive her injuries....."

Sebastian interrupted Gaby impatiently,

"This is utterly ridiculous! I don't have time to pander to my wife's amateur dramatics! I will be catching the scheduled flight home today as I have to work tomorrow. Phoebe can book a flight for herself, you and Portia when she comes to her senses. I will await Phoebe's explanation and apology when she returns home."

The line went dead.

Gaby stared at the now silent phone and blinked in disbelief.

Phoebe and Portia could never go back to him, of that she had no doubt.

Hours later, tired and emotionally wrung out, Paul and Celeste stood at their daughter's bedside in muted horror at their only child's bandaged, bruised and bloodied form.

Tears poured down Celeste's face as she held Phoebe's hand and gently stroked a small, unbruised part of her face.

Paul, in his later years but still a formidable man standing at six feet three inches tall, was struggling to maintain his composure.

He wanted to kill.

He didn't care if he spent the rest of his days in prison. The person who did this was going to pay for it and he had a very good idea who that person was.

He left his wife and daughter and went to find Gaby.

He found her, in the visitors' lounge, slumped in an armchair with a sleeping Portia sprawled over her.

"It was Sebastian, yes?"

Paul answered his own question.

Gaby nodded, tears welling up in her eyes.

She finally allowed her emotions to give way, emotional and practical back up had now arrived in the form of Phoebe's parents and she was slowly starting to feel the toll, emotionally and physically, of the enormity of the day's events.

She quietly cried, delayed shock kicking in.

"He went crazy! He was going to attack me and Portia when he saw we'd seen him!"

Paul inhaled sharply through his nose.

God help him if that bastard was still in Spain.

Gaby shook her head vehemently as her mind ran through the sickening events of that afternoon.

"They can never go back to him, he's a monster!"

Paul moved over to Gaby and his sleeping granddaughter.

"Gabrielle, thank you so much for saving Phoebe and keeping Portia safe. You have coped magnificently and I hope, when all this is over, that we can find some way to repay you."

He then tried to make light of the situation for Gaby's sake.

"I bet they didn't put this scenario on the job description at that Norland College of yours, did they?"

He was rewarded with a watery smile from Gaby.

"Do you know if Sebastian has flown home?" Paul probed gently.

Gaby nodded as she tried to quietly blow her nose so as not to wake Portia.

Paul pursed his lips and shook his head.

"A coward as well as a thug!" he said under his breath.

Gaby gently shifted her position.

"Do you know, I don't think he flew back because he was scared? In his eyes he's done nothing wrong. He really thought we were making a fuss about nothing and he is waiting for Phoebe to apologise to him when she's ready!"

Pauls eyes widened in disbelief.

"Sebastian will never be seeing Phoebe again. I'll make sure of that!"

Paul said in a low voice and stood up.

"Now then, let's see about booking you and Portia into a hotel."

In the early hours of Monday morning, Phoebe started to arouse from her anaesthetic-induced sleep.

She tried to open both eyes but only one eye would obey.

She was in a bed.

It smelt like a hospital.

Portia!

Phoebe tried to turn her head to the right but had to stop.

Her head felt like it was ten times its normal size.

Every inch of her body complained in unison at the abuse it had suffered the previous day.

She felt a hand next to hers and reached for it.

"Phoebe"

Celeste eagerly sat forward in her visitors chair to reassure her daughter.

"Mum?"

"Oh darling!" smiled Celeste, thrilled to hear her daughter's voice, "yes it's me, Mum. Dad and I are here, Portia's tucked up safely in a lovely hotel nearby with Gaby, fast asleep. Everything is going to be just fine."

Phoebe had never been so grateful to her hear her beloved mother's voice. Everything would be alright now.

There would be no more secrets.

No more lies.

She and Portia were now safe; she instinctively knew that as she lay in her hospital bed, they were lucky to still be alive.

Celeste leaned over her fragile daughter and kissed her gently on her right cheek.

"Are you in pain my love?" Celeste asked

"It's ok, not too bad," lied Phoebe.

She carefully turned her head to face her mother.

Celeste took hold of Phoebe's hand and looked into her daughter's one eye.

"Do you want to talk about it?" she coaxed.

Phoebe's good eye filled with tears, but she nodded slowly.

No more secrets.

"He found the implants."

Celeste stared at her daughter's battered face and froze at the horror of her daughter's words.

A coldness slowly but stealthily crept through her body, paralysing her, threatening to suffocate her as it rose upwards, asphyxiating every muscle.

Contraceptive implants.

It had been her idea to have the implants.

To prevent further anxiety in Phoebe's life, or so she'd thought.

She'd interfered and now Phoebe was suffering the consequences.

Celeste bowed her head in failed parental shame.

"Oh Phoebe, my darling, I'm so very sorry." Celeste started to cry, it was completely her fault.

She stood and tried to gently cuddle her daughter, without hurting her.

"Can you ever forgive me?"

"Shhh, Mum, it's not your fault..... in any way."

Phoebe put an arm around her poor mother and gave her a slight, painful, squeeze.

"Husbands aren't meant to beat their wives for doing something they don't agree with; most couples talk these things through, yes?"

Phoebe tried to cock an eyebrow at her mother to lighten the mood but winced with the pain.

"Ow!' she moaned, trying to lighten the mood for her shocked mother, "too soon for comic expressions!"

Celeste let go of her daughter and gave a small smile,

"Well, yes, usually, I suppose,"

Phoebe tried to smother a yawn, her left cheek felt on fire.

Celeste stroked her daughter's hair.

"Try and get some sleep darling, your body needs to rest."

Phoebe gave a small smile, and closed her eyes.

Ten minutes later, Paul, functioning on adrenaline and little else, arrived back from organising two rooms at a nearby five star hotel. One for Gaby and Portia, one for himself and Celeste.

"How is she, love?"

Celeste led Paul to just outside the bay where Phoebe was sleeping and relayed the earlier conversation she'd shared with her daughter.

Rage and fury, once again, flooded Paul's body.

Celeste, reading her husband's thoughts, took a step forward and placed a calming hand on his arm.

"I'm with you darling, regarding Sebastian, but he can wait. Phoebe needs us now. Let's focus on her, Portia and Gaby."

Celeste straightened her stiff, aching back and squared her shoulders.

"We'll sleep on it, and then we'll deal with Sebastian."

Paul opened his arms for his beloved wife to fall into. He folded his arms around this woman whom he had loved almost a life time and rested his cheek on the top of her head.

"You're right as usual, my love. All in good time."

James woke up on the first Saturday of the Easter Holidays feeling like he had done every morning since Tanya had gone.

Emotionally rung out, after another, tortuous dream filled night.

There was little respite from their content.

Only when he was exhausted, after having spent a week or so of nights where he dreamt of Tanya and the past few months, did he have a blissful night's sleep of nothing.

Nothing that he could recall, the following morning, anyway.

Those mornings he would wake up in the same position he had fallen asleep in, stiff, aching and utterly exhausted from the emotional turmoil that reigned throughout his being.

The dreams would differ in time span.

Sometimes they would be when he and Tanya were at university together.

Carefree days of studying together, long lie ins and evenings filled with friends, cheap wine and earnest conversations on how they were going to change the world.

Other nights it would be of their wedding day, the start of a whole new chapter in their young lives, with so much to plan for, and look forward to.

The future seemed to stretch out endlessly.

The most painful nights were when James dreamt of their last, fateful holiday together, when their lives as they knew it, had slowly, but steadily started to unravel.

Sometimes James would dream that they were sitting in the doctor's surgery and the doctor would tell them that there was hope, a new treatment that would keep the disease at bay.

James and Tanya would look at each other, a ray of hope filling the room.

Most often though, and more cruelly, his mind would play over and over their last morning together.

Tanya would decide she couldn't go through with the assisted suicide and James would fall sobbing with joy and relief into Tanya's lap, overjoyed at the extra time he had been given with her.

James would wake from this particular dream feeling momentarily elated, only for the fog of sleep to lift and the devastating reality to dawn that Tanya had indeed gone to Switzerland, and died there.

He lay there, this particular Saturday morning, on his left side, staring across Tanya's empty half of the bed at the facing wall.

He was purely existing, an empty shell, barely functioning and had been doing so since the day that Tanya had left.

Tanya's sister had helped him plan the memorial service which had come and gone.

A blur.

He had gone back to school and went through the motions of his role as head teacher. The strict routine of the primary school day brought welcome, temporary relief to his hollow existence.

Assemblies, playground duty, although not first and last duties of the day; he wasn't yet ready for the sea of sympathetic eyes that would scan his face with concern.

Lunchtime clubs, staff meetings and teaching; the school day filled a large chunk of the day.

James taught Art to Key Stage 2 and found the times when he was teaching to be the most therapeutic.

Nurturing, encouraging and enabling the young.

He dreaded the finality, when it inevitability came, of the end of the school day.

The cheery goodbyes from his staff.

The cleaning cupboard being locked after the ritual clean through by Mrs Jenkins, the school cleaner. The lights being turned off by the caretaker and the jangling of the keys outside his office accompanied by the daily,

'I'll leave the main door for you to lock Mr Young, shall I?'

There was no prolonging it.

Locking the main door to the school behind him, he would cross the playground to the staff car park and make his way home.

Except it wasn't a home.

It had been a home when Tanya had been alive.

They had made a home together, lived a life together.

Husband and wife.

Now Tanya was gone, James felt rudderless, unable to define himself anymore.

He was no longer a husband. His job was a head teacher, but who was James?

He heaved himself out of bed.

An effort.

He felt as though his chest was filled with bricks, so heavy was the weight of the physicality of his grief.

Two weeks.

Two weeks!

The longest amount of time he would have to fill since Tanya had left.

Died.

She hadn't changed her mind.

Gone.

Forever.

Weekends came and went, easily filled with the myriad of tasks a headteacher was responsible for.

The spring term was over before it had started and if he were honest with himself, he had simply been going through the motions of work and life.

His emotions had understandably shut down.

He had been functioning on autopilot as he dealt with the aftermath of Tanya.

Now, however, James was living the reality of being a widower.

Life moved on.

People's lives moved on.

Something had to change.

He was being suffocated by his grief.

He made his way through to the kitchen, filled the kettle and switched it on.

He looked up out of the kitchen window.

It was a beautiful day.

He walked in the direction of his study to turn his computer on, opened the door and stopped.

Light flooded through the French doors, shining directly onto his favourite chair.

There was a light frost, but the sun, although still low, promised a bright, sunny, cloudless day.

Having made his coffee, he returned to his study and sank into the leather of his chair now warm, soft and soothing after being bathed in the early April sun.

Forty five minutes later, after a second coffee and a hot shower, James Young was striding down the lane from his house with a vigour he hadn't felt for a very long time.

He climbed a stile into a nearby field and strode purposefully across it.

He emptied his mind and focused on the activity of walking.

Arms swinging, long strides, his arms in rhythm with his step, their motion gradually releasing the load in his chest.

His head was beginning to clear.

Outside in the open, away from the house, away from work, the distance provided a breathing space for his grief weary body.

He turned around and looked back in the direction of his house.

He took a deep cleansing breath and surveyed the fields.

At this moment in time he felt he could be the only person in the world.

He felt tranquil, calm.....peace.

For the first time in a very long time, James was beginning to feel a little like the old James again.

Not wanting to question or examine this feeling, just relish it, he continued with his walk.

Sue filled the kettle to make a mug of tea.

A freshly baked and iced cake sat on her glass cake stand decorated, with good reason, a little childishly, with Smarties, Maltesers and hundreds and thousands.

The weekends could always promise a visit from one or all of her five grandchildren from her son Gabe and daughter in law Julia and a glass of milk or mug of hot chocolate, if it was cold, and a slice of cake, was always on offer, without fail.

Sue pushed open a door that had been kept ajar with an old knitted owl doorstop to fetch some milk from the fridge.

It was a walk-in pantry which measured five feet square and it housed the fridge and numerous shelves filled with all Sue's dried goods plus umpteen jars of homemade jams, pickles and chutneys, perfect for a light lunch with homemade bread and a wedge of cheese.

Under the lowest shelf, on top of an old homemade duvet in an oversized basket, lay a very pregnant golden Labrador.

Bella was one of Julia and Gabe's many dogs, and she was in pup for the third and last time.

For reasons that no one could fathom, although Sue privately thought it was for the peace and quiet, though would never say so, Bella would take up residence in Sue's pantry in the later stages of her pregnancy and stay there until all the pups had been weaned.

When the pups were born Sue would extend their living area using an extending baby gate and section off a third of her kitchen so they had plenty of room to safely explore and exercise.

The large quarry tiles were perfect for cleaning up the frequent deposits left by half a dozen or so puppies.

"Alright my love," cooed Sue to a snoozing Bella.

She did look uncomfortable bless her. Sue, along with the majority of women she was sure, had never forgotten that stretched, oversized feeling she'd had at eight months pregnant.

You think it's not possible to get any bigger, and then you do!

Sue fetched the milk, made a mug of tea and left the bottle on the side. She'd be back for a top up at some point that morning and didn't want to disturb Bella unnecessarily.

She took the mug over to the window sill by the back door and pulled on John's old gardening gillet and her gardening boots. Picking up her mug of tea, she opened the old stable door and walked out into the garden.

She was greeted by a cloudless bright April morning.

She stood for a moment and tilted her face towards the sun and let its warmth soak into her.

Well, it felt good to be alive. She took a sip of tea and made her way down to the old potting shed.

Her aim that morning was to have a good sort out and see if she could gather together some unwanted trays and pots for Sally.

A good two hours later, Sue had swept and tidied the shed and put aside several trays, plastic pots of various sizes, some plastic labels and a selection of child friendly vegetable seeds that Sue thought would quickly produce some results for the children.

She took everything out on to the gardening table next to the shed and reached back in to rescue her now empty mug.

She could certainly do with another one after all that hard work.

She stretched her back and scanned her garden.

The signs of spring were well under way she thought with pleasure and she walked to the end of the garden where a small gate led to the fields which her son, Gabe, now owned.

It really was a beautiful day.

She let her eyes roam across the field where they idly took in the space and stillness.

It would be so easy to take all this for granted.

Her eyes fixed on something moving, along the edge of the field.

It was a person, a dog walker probably, making the most of the lovely day.

It was such a pleasure walking a dog, Sue thought to herself.

She ambled to the gate, keen to see what breed of dog was lucky enough to be exploring the fields on a day like today.

A dog failed to make an appearance, but the walker, a man, came closer.

Sue squinted, he looked familiar.

He looked like the headteacher, Mr Young, wasn't it? Although her grandchildren went to the school in the next village they always attended the summer fair at St Michaels as it was open to the general public and always very well organised.

He had served Sue strawberries and cream and she had joked to go steady with the Pimms otherwise she'd be rolling up the lane to her house.

Mr Young had laughed and reassured her that he was sure she wouldn't be the only one.

The man drew closer and having spotted Sue, waved as thought to get her attention.

Sue opened the gate and walked through it into the field and she saw a look of relief flooded the man's face.

"Hello! Hello there!" he panted, approaching Sue with an out-stretched hand, a little out of breath.

"Good morning!" smiled Sue walking to greet him.

"It's Mr Young isn't it, headteacher of St Michael's?"

James took Sue's hand and warmly shook it, covering their hands with his other hand.

"Yes, yes, that's right," he frowned, "Now you're Mrs Hancock, aren't you, Gabe's mother. I remember he's a good man to have on you your team at a quiz night." Sue laughed,

"That's right, though do call me Sue."

"Well, in that case, you must call me James. I must say it's a bit of a relief to finally come across a person. I've been walking for hours, got a bit carried away, I think, and I've completely lost my bearings."

He had let go of Sue's hand and was now standing with his hands on his hips catching his breath.

"Would you be so kind as to point me in the direction of Stockling and I'll be on my way."

Sue laughed and exclaimed,

"Of course I will but not till you've come inside and had a drink and a slice of some unsophisticated but delicious cake."

James slumped his shoulders and replied gratefully,

"Do you know, I'm not even going to try and attempt to say no, that sounds wonderful!" Then, worried he may be forgetting his manners,

"You're sure I won't be holding you up?"

Sue held up her empty mug.

"I promise you I was just on my way for a refill,"

She tilted her head towards the farmhouse,

"This way,"

A tired and thirsty James followed Sue into the farmhouse.

Fifteen minutes later, James was devouring a huge slice of cake and just finishing a large, steaming mug of coffee.

He surveyed the half eaten cake on his plate and commented,

"Do you know, I think the Smarties are my favourite part, absolutely love them!"

He took another big forkful and sat back in his chair, thoroughly enjoying the variety of toppings on his piece of cake.

Sue laughed,

"It's a firm favourite with the grandchildren as you can imagine. Now, are you ready for a top up?"

"Good gracious, I can't hold you up any longer!" James exclaimed putting down his empty mug, he looked appreciatively round Sue's large, informal kitchen,

"You have a lovely cosy home, Sue," he commented,

"Thank you James, it's been a very happy home....." she stopped and listened, frowned then turned to James,

"Excuse me James, I'm just going to check....." and she hurried into the walk in pantry,

"Oh Bella! You clever girl! Oh my goodness, my love, hang on, I'll just grab a towel," and she hurried back out of the pantry.

"James! Bella's in labour! There's five already! Will you help me rub them down and check them over?"

She was now yanking open her tea towel drawer and grabbed a handful.

A little stunned, had Sue just said puppies? James was on his feet and seconds later he and Sue were on their knees in the warm, cosy pantry murmuring quiet encouragement at Bella whilst tenderly picking up, rubbing and checking the new born puppies.

"So far so good," said Sue relieved, rubbing the seventh puppy and placing it gently back next to its mother,

"You're doing so well Bella, what a good mum you are!" she encouraged and stroked Bella lovingly.

James, much to his embarrassment, was struggling to keep his emotions in check.

The still fresh rawness, of his loss, coupled with the reality of birth and new life that was now wriggling in his hands, so desperate to live, to survive, was overwhelming.

Their energetic rooting, searching for their mum.

It was the most moving and unexpectedly emotional sight he had witnessed, and been part of, in a very long time.

One of the puppies returned repeatedly to try and root James's knee.

"Wrong way little one," James gently laughed and resettled it nest to Bella's tummy.

"She seems to like you, that one," said Sue, in a low voice.

She took a sideways look at James,

'They'll be sold, you know, apart from one......would you be interested James?"

Once again, the determined little pup, eyes closed, rooted around towards James.

He scooped it up and let it nuzzle his face.

He could no longer hold back the tears that began to fill his eyes.

Unable to stop the flow, they silently fell in abandonment.

Sensing more was needed from it, the little pup snuggled further into Jame's neck.

"Well, I don't think you've got a choice in the matter," smiled Sue, gently, handing James a tea towel,

"It's clean," and through his tears James gave a little chuckle and wiped his face.

"Sorry Sue, life's a bit of an emotional roller coaster at the moment," he bent and kissed the puppy on its head.

Sue nodded in experienced agreement.

"You're not wrong there, it gets me when I'm least expecting it."

James remembered the passing of Mr Hancock.

"I'm so sorry for your loss, Sue," he replied gently.

Sue simply shrugged her shoulders,

"It's been over a year now and it can be the silliest of things."

She deftly turned a stray pup back around to a spare nipple to suckle.

James stroked the now sleeping puppy and a comfortable quiet fell between the two of them as they both momentarily reminisced.

James took a deep breath.

"Deep down, I think I'm cross with her....Tanya,"

James paused.

He felt he was betraying her, saying it out loud.

But the simple fact of the matter was, deep down, beneath the loving her, the missing her, he was cross.

Bloody cross.

Sue sensed, correctly, that James hadn't off-loaded his grief to anyone before and just nodded her head slowly in encouragement as she oversaw the puppies and stroked Bella during the lull of labour.

James continued,

"I wish she'd fought harder......I wish she'd tried harder......I feel angry she didn't try harder for......for us."

He shook his head as he heard what he had just said.

"I know that sounds unreasonable, childish and selfish, but that's how I feel."

He continued stroking the sleeping puppy.

Sue said nothing for a while, allowing the silence to be filled by the mewing and rustling of the tiny puppies.

Eventually, she spoke,

"If you don't mind me saying James, it seems to me maybe, that you feel robbed of the mourning period that happens when someone is caring for a terminally ill loved one,"

She paused and glanced at James.

He was listening, very slowly nodding his head, she continued,

"When you are caring for them, nursing them, little by little you are preparing yourself for the final goodbye. You watch them grow weaker. As the illness progresses and takes hold, death, when it comes, although terrible, in some ways is a merciful release."

Sue stopped again, and then finished,

"I think Tanya making the choice, she did, which was right for her and I think she was incredibly brave to do it, you feel it has robbed you of the ending you feel the two of you, as a couple, should have had."

James closed his eyes and bowed his head,

"That's it," he whispered, "that's it, exactly."

Sue felt she had to speak for Tanya, she hadn't known her, but as a woman, she guessed why Tanya had chosen the exit from life that she had.

"James, Tanya was a woman, and women are used to thinking of everyone but themselves. When Tanya made the decision she did, I bet you all the Smartie covered cake in the world it was to spare you the wretchedness of what she knew the end would probably be like. She didn't want to be a burden. She had no control over the disease so she took control of what part of it she could, for the two of you. You know that deep down."

Silence fell once more.

James took a deep cleansing breath and stared unseeing at Bella.

Sue had summed it up perfectly. He did feel robbed but then he hadn't had Motor Neurone disease. What had Tanya said, that he was being selfish, acting the way he had done, and here he still was, acting like a victim.

Shame flooded his body. He turned to Sue.

"Sue, thank you, you have just verbalised what I have been, for months, struggling to comprehend." He looked down at the sleeping puppy and made a decision, "if this little one is really for sale, I think I'm ready to start a less selfish chapter in my life." He looked across at Sue, who smiled back and nodded her agreement.

"Granny?.......Granny are you in here?" called a little boy's voice.

"In here darling, in the pantry," Fin appeared in the doorway of the pantry, with his older brother, Giles. He stopped in his tracks on seeing James there as well.

'Hello Fin, hello Giles, Bella's got a surprise for you both,' smiled Sue and leaned sideways so they could see Bella's basket.

279

Their faces were a picture. James momentarily forgotten, both the boys rushed forward and eagerly squeezed between their Granny and the strange man.

"She's had her puppies!" exclaimed Fin in wonder, eyes like saucers.

"Shall I get Mum, Granny?" questioned Giles, eager to find out which one they would be keeping.

"That would be very helpful Giles, thank you." replied Sue, giving her grandson a hug. Feeling he was now intruding, James gently placed the sleeping puppy back with its mum and whispered to Sue,

"I'm going to make a move Sue, thank you so much for our chat." He carefully got to his feet and gingerly stretched his legs. Sue got up to and spoke quietly to her youngest grandson.

"Fin, will you look after Bella and her puppies for a minute for me please?" Fin nodded solemnly.

"I will be very careful and grown up!" he declared.

"I know you will my love, thank you," praised Sue. Fin, a farmer's son, knew how to behave around newborn animals and took his temporary position of being in sole charge of Bella and her puppies very seriously.

Sue went into the kitchen to speak to James, who was now pulling on his boots.

"James, let me run you home, Julia will be......oh here she is! Hello Julia darling, Bella's been absolutely wonderful!" she said, on seeing her daughter in law hurry through the door.

"God, so sorry Sue!" exclaimed Julia, "I've just got back from Tesco's, the girls are just shoving the frozen stuff in the freezer and then we can give you a break." Julia spotted James and stretched her hand and greeted him warmly,

'Well, hello there, Mr Young. Were you dragged in from a walk to help my poor, put upon mother-in-law deliver our puppies, by any chance?" James held his hands up in mock protest,

"No, no, no....the exact opposite actually! Your very kind mother in law rescued me from a walk that I got lost on and fed me coffee and cake, and well........ If it's alright with you, I would very much like to buy one, when they're ready to be sold of course." he finished with a smile.

"Good Lord!" replied Julia, looking from James to Sue and back again in amazement, "that's the quickest sale I think we've ever had!" she held out her hand to James, "It's a deal!" Laughing, James shook Julia's hand. Sue quickly interjected,

"I think he had his eye on a particular pup, Julia," she said while talking to Julia with her eyes. Julia didn't miss a beat. Walking towards the pantry she said,

"Right, have you got the nail varnish handy, Sue and we'll dab it straight away."

"Daddy, Daddy, the puppies have been born!" Fin ran into Gabe's arms. He had come in from the fields and heard the news from the girls.

"I know Fin, I've come to see how Bella's getting on," he shifted Fin over to his other arm so he could shake James outstretched hand.

"James, good to see you, how are things?"

"I'm very well, Gabe, and you?"

"Keeping busy," Gabe nodded pointedly at the boys and the pantry. Everyone laughed, "organised chaos is the term I think," he finished diplomatically. "Do you have time for a coffee?"

"I've had one thank you Gabe, and have already overstayed my welcome," replied James, now trying to zip his coat up.

"Well it's no problem, I've finished for the day and it'd be good to catch up," Gabe encouraged, Julia and Sue both nodded in agreement.

Half an hour later, Gabe, James, Julia, Sue and four of Julia's five children were seated in various chairs around the kitchen table, eating cake, homemade bread, cheese, cold quiche and Sue's homemade pickles. In between checking Bella and her puppies, they caught up on each other's lives, swapping stories, in the cosy surroundings of Sue's farmhouse. Three hours later, Gabe drove James home with an invite from the family for lunch next Saturday.

A perfect opportunity to check on his puppy, Gabe had pointed out.

James sat in his study that evening with a glass of red wine and looked out over the garden. He reflected on his first day of the Easter holidays. A completely unexpected, wonderful, turn of events had taken place and he felt truly grateful to the Hancocks and their generosity of spirit.

What a lovely family they were.

He turned his chair around to face the computer and typed into Google, 'Tips on raising a puppy' He surveyed his study whilst the computer thought about his request. A basket would fit nicely by his desk he thought to himself and feeling more positive about the future than he had in a long time, he turned back to Google's results and started reading about the dos and don'ts of puppy ownership.

Millie walked briskly back home after doing the school run.

It was the last day of term and since the ill fated 'Chinese Parenting' episode, harmony had fallen over the household.

Jane and Drew were far more happy and relaxed now they had their old mum back, whilst Darius, suitably humbled by Millie's frank and honest outpouring, was also thankful to have his old Millie back but now viewed her and their marriage through new eyes.

Marriage really was a work in progress. Darius had thought to himself as he had mulled over this subject as Millie slept at the end of the catalytic evening all those weeks ago. He'd looked down at his exhausted sleeping wife and felt more deeply in love with her, more connected, than ever before in their marriage. If someone had asked him ten hours ago he probably would have said he had never disliked Millie as much, that day, as he had during his marriage to date.

The Chinese parenting episode had been a real test of strength of their relationship. They had survived it and come through the other side, stronger and with a deeper understanding and respect for each other.

Darius vowed to himself that night that he would never let Millie feel as worthless as she had been feeling, ever again. She was his wife, the mother of his children, which made her his entire world. She had to know she was everything to him.

The following evening, after a day spent reinstalling his bed, changing the curtains and throwing away the bamboo prints amid much teasing and humbled laughter from Millie, Darius had taken Millie out for dinner.

Earlier that day he had gone into town to buy a gift for Millie which he hoped would ensure that she never, ever, had to question his love, or more importantly, his respect for her and the importance of her being there, with him, on their journey through life together, as one.

Carol, Darius's mum, had arrived at 6.30 pm that evening and bustled around the kitchen, fussing over Jane and Drew. She produced from a bag a comic for them each, a bag of their favourite sweets and an assortment of DVDs she had rented from the library for them.

"Mum, thanks for coming over at such short notice, I really appreciate it." Darius gave his mum a squeeze and kissed her cheek.

"Not at all my love, any time," Carol smiled, her eyes concerned, Darius looked emotionally drained, although seemed relaxed.

Millie came into the kitchen.

"Oh Carol, you're here! Thank you so much for babysitting," it was Millie's turn to hug her mother-in-law. "We really appreciate it, really," she repeated, echoing Darius's words.

Millie looked at Darius and smiled hesitantly. Darius smiled lovingly back. Carol didn't miss a trick.

This was a makeup date.

Well, good, as long as they were making up there was no need for her to worry. Marriage was tough and she'd babysit every night of the week if she had to for her children to ensure the rocky road of marriage was as smooth as she could make it for her offspring.

"You look lovely darling, darling, very classy," Darius commented.

Millie blushed.

After the previous night's failed attempt at a no holds barred oriental vixen, she had chosen a high necked, long sleeved black tailored dress with a small slit at the back with black, high heeled sling back shoes and a black shimmering shrug to complete the outfit.

"Thank you darling," she replied, still feeling emotionally raw and exposed. She could see that Darius did too. They needed to reconnect and tonight would be a good starting point.

One hour later they were in an intimate restaurant in a quiet village ten miles away in the countryside. Darius had ordered champagne and there they sat, on the sumptuous chesterfield sofa, sipping their champagne, making small talk about Darius's job, the children and holiday destinations, just enjoying being.

Together.

Darius and Millie.

"Your starters are ready sir."

The waiter smiled and led them to their table.

Quiet music and unobtrusive staff. They could both feel the stress and the strains of the past few weeks start to fade.

One and a half hours later, the waiter served them coffee.

He smiled to himself at the couple holding hands across the table.

They seemed to glow; you didn't see it often, the air of being united, of being one.

He excused himself, one day I will find that, the waiter promised himself.

Darius stirred some cream into his coffee.

"Darling, do you remember the night we met, at the wine bar?" He asked Millie,

"Remember! It's burned on my brain Darius! I passed out!" They both laughed.

"No seriously," Darius continued, "do you remember how sure I was of us, sure enough to ask you to marry me that first evening?" Millie nodded and smiled shyly,

"Yes Darius, I do, you completely swept me off my feet, literally."

"Well, my love," Darius reached into his pocket, "I want to give you something that will remind you, which you can look at every day, of your worth to me and the children and how lucky I feel that you said yes to being my wife and the mother of my children." Reaching over he placed a velvet box next to Millie's coffee cup. Millie looked at the box, then at Darius, unable to stop the tears from welling up in her eyes. Darius moved to the chair next to Millie, put his arm around her shoulder, pulled her gently towards him and kissed her cheek.

"Let me help you," he said softly, as Millie's hand shook with emotion, he opened the lid of the box.

There, nestled in red velvet was a platinum, diamond, eternity ring.

Millie gasped at the sight such a stunning piece of jewellery.

Words failed her.

It was quite simply breathtaking.

"It's an eternity ring my love," Darius faltered, "if it's ok with you, if you can bear it, that's how long I intend to be with you...."

He stopped talking and waited.

Millie turned to Darius, completely overwhelmed.

She leant forward and gently kissed him. Darius could tell she was struggling not to cry, he held his breath and then Millie finally felt composed enough to speak.

"Eternity eh?...... Well now, I'll just have to check my diary......" she smiled, the emotional tension broken. Darius laughed and replied,

"Oh will you now!" and kissed his wife on the tip of her nose, he then reached for the ring, "Now let's see if this fits."

It was perfect.

They finished their coffee, admiring Millie's new ring, a symbol of their continued, promised love for each other and gently arguing over what type of omelette Darius had made for Millie, the first night they had met at the wine bar.

It was ham and tomato.

Millie let herself into the house, filled the kettle and switched it on, moving a recorder book off the worktop and onto the kitchen table.

The recorder had been the agreed choice of musical instrument by both Jane and Drew, Darius oversaw the practice sessions to show his support for Millie and to let the children know this was a compromise to the 'Chinese parenting' episode.

Millie walked over to the fridge to fetch the milk; she had a lot of last minute errands to do. They were flying to Tenerife early Saturday morning for a week relaxing by a pool, the second week would be filled with playdates, swimming, visits to the cinema and shopping for new school clothes for the children, as they were both shooting up, and work clothes for her.

She shut the fridge door and walked back to the kettle.

The timing couldn't have been better.

A week after Darius had given Millie her eternity ring, she had telephoned Peter, her old boss at the estate agents, to enquire if he had any vacancies, and if not now, would he consider her for any that may arise. Millie was in luck. Karen, her old work colleague, was going on maternity leave at Easter with baby number four and he was looking to cover the three days that she worked. It would be similar to her old role, a mixture of secretarial work, negotiating and valuing properties.

Millie had telephoned Sally to see if she had any availability after Easter, before and after school, but she was full. Sally had reassured her that if any sessions came available she would let her know as soon as possible then gave her Anna's number to try. As luck would have it, Anna had two siblings leaving the village at the end of term and she would be pleased to fill their spaces.

Millie met Peter for lunch, feeling confident that she would be able to cover all of Karen's hours.

On returning home after seeing Peter, Millie could hardly contain her excitement. It had been great seeing Peter and catching up, Karen had joined them and filled her in on all the other staff and their foibles. Her hours of employment would be 9.30-4pm leaving Millie to have to only organise after school care. Both Anna and Sally had said they cover the holidays between them so Millie had driven home feeling upbeat and positive about returning to paid work after nine years at home.

Millie stirred her tea, the holiday would be lovely, she knew, but now she had a job she just wanted to get started. Darius had been so pleased for her, Jane and Drew, on the other hand, had been a little more sceptical.

"Will we come home alone?" Drew had asked worriedly,

"We haven't got to go to a childminder's EVERY night, have we?" demanded Jane, hands on hips. Millie and Darius answered all their worries as well as they could and reassured them that little would change to their daily routine.

Millie knew there were bound to be some teething problems to start with but her hours were near to perfect as they could be, and she had her in laws on standby to help out if she really needed them. She was more fortunate than a lot of parents, she knew.

Adele flopped down on the futon chair in her Dad's room which he rented and let out a deep sigh.

She wished her Dad would move.

She hated coming here.

She wanted to see her Dad but she hated this room.

The kitchen.

The bathroom.

The house.

It had strange people in it and it smelt weird.

Her Dad opened the door and came into the room carrying a tray.

"Here you are love, beans on toast with grated cheese on top and your favourite strawberry yoghurt for dessert."

Dean smiled brightly, willing Adele to feel comfortable and at home.

"Shall I pop CBBC on for you?"

"Thanks, Dad and yes please."

Dean switched on CBBC and Adele started to eat her tea.

That was another thing she hated, she thought, as she forked a mouthful of baked beans into her mouth.

The forced, happy way in which both her Mum and Dad acted around her now they had split up.

They weren't normal any more with her.

Whatever she suggested, the park, the cinema, McDonalds, everything was 'Ok love' or 'Wow! That's a great idea, let's do it!'

Adele cut a piece of her toast.

She preferred it when they had all lived together and Mum and Dad had argued sometimes, or if Dad had shouted if a lesson had been cancelled.

She felt cross if a programme she wanted to watch wasn't on.

That was normal wasn't it?

It was better than this, anyway.

"What do you fancy doing tomorrow, Adele?" Dean asked, dipping his bread into his soup.

"Swimming?" offered Adele

"Great idea!" nodded Dean smiling and picked up another piece of bread.

Adele rolled her eyes as she bent her head and opened her yoghurt.

"Bugger!" thought Dean as he chewed his bread and watched some medieval kids programme.

Swimming!

Maggie used to take Adele swimming; he absolutely loathed getting into a germ-filled soup with strangers.

He dipped his bread again and bit into it.

Bugger!

The next morning, after a mind numbing, freezing visit to the local pool, Dean and Adele walked across the road to the McDonalds. As they waited in line, Dean sneezed. Great! He thought to himself, caught a cold already! Bloody swimming pool!

At their table, they sat and hungrily tucked into their meals.

"Have you got any homework to do love?" Dean asked Adele as she dipped a chicken nugget into a too small pot of tomato sauce.

"No, just reading," she bit into a nugget and chewed, "Mum and I do our homework together in the week."

Dean raised his eyebrows,

"What homework does Mum do?"

"Um..I think it's number work or something," Adele screwed up her nose and thought.

"Bookkeeping?" she nodded as she said it, "Yeah, I think it's bookkeeping, she wants to get a proper job, y'know, not cleaning,"

Adele picked up another nugget.

"Are you still making a kitchen?"

Bookkeeping.

Dean took another bite of his wrap. Maggie had often spoke of studying the AAT Level 1 course but had never had the time as she was too busy cleaning to help Dean try and save enough money for a large enough deposit.

He was pleased for her.

He swallowed his mouthful of wrap.

"Yes I am love; you know I'm training to be a carpenter? Well, I go to a college on a Monday, which is like school for grownups, and I do homework too, just like you and Mum." He smiled at his daughter,

"Do you think they'll have a 'Children's evening' where children can go and talk to their parents' teachers and see if they've been working hard and behaving themselves?"

Adele laughed out loud.

291

"Daaaad! You're so funny!" and then she put on a mock, stern face and said, "now, have you been doing your homework and behaving in class, Dad?"

Dean pretended to think hard

"Hmmm.. I think so, I never talk in class and I always put my hand up if I want to go the toilet."

Adele laughed; she loved her Dad being silly. Dean laughed too; it was a funny mental picture.

"Come on love, do you fancy a Mcflurry, I think I'm going to have the Crunchie one?"

Adele's eyes widened and she nodded her head frantically.

"Oooo yes, please! A smartie one, thanks Dad!"

Half an hour later the pair left McDonalds with full tummies and smiles on their faces.

Adele looked up at her Dad as they walked back to the car.

He seemed happy enough, but still a little bit sad. They reached the car and Adele grabbed her Dad around his waist for a hug she hadn't known she'd wanted.

"Love you, Dad."

"I love you too, Adele, very much!" said Dean and kissed the top of her head.

She'd had to deal with a lot these past couple of months.

"Let's get back in the warm and do your reading, shall we?"

Dean drew up at their flat later that evening to drop off Adele back to Maggie. They had come to the mutual agreement that it would be better for Adele if she had a sleepover with Dean one night of the weekend, every weekend, rather than all weekend every other week. Dean was still working on a part time basis as a driving instructor on a Sunday and week day evenings and it meant that Maggie got to spend a weekend day with Adele as well every week.

"Hi love, Hi Dean," greeted Maggie with a big smile.

She gave Adele a hug, "Good time love?"

"Great Mum, I just need the bathroom!" Adele pulled a funny face and rushed down the hall to the bathroom.

"Everything ok?" Maggie asked Dean, making conversation.

She did look younger; thought Dean, fresher faced.....less worry?

Maybe that was it.

Maggie's eyes followed Adele into the bathroom then when the door had shut she quickly turned back to Dean, eyes shining.

"We've had an offer on the flat! For the full asking price!" she whispered excitedly.

Dean was shocked then instantly relieved; he hadn't thought it would happen that quickly. He knew of properties taking a year or more to sell.

"Great, great! Are they first time buyers?" he asked hopefully,

"Yes, mortgage all arranged, so....fingers crossed..." Maggie nodded smiling broadly.

It would help them both on their new paths of personal and professional growth.

Maggie was going to stay with her parents in the village so she could study and look for work in an office, fairly local, and Dean would have a bit of a breathing space whilst he concentrated on retraining as a carpenter.

There was a lull whilst they both stood and absorbed what the sale of their home together would mean for both of them.

Dean came back to the present first,

"How's your course going?" he asked a surprised Maggie. How did he know?

"Good thanks, I'm really enjoying it. How about your carpentry course?"

"Yeah, it's great! This bloke I've managed to get a couple of days work a week with, is building a kitchen for this chap who's doing a barn conversion. Oak, it's a beautiful wood to work with."

He trailed off, a little embarrassed at himself, expressing himself in such an open way.

Maggie smiled warmly at him.

"That's great Dean."

"All done!" Adele said, running back up the hall, from the bathroom.

"Well, bye love," Dean gave Adele a big bear hug and a kiss. He looked at Maggie, over the top of Adele's head, "Bye Maggie, have a good week." He said.

"Will do Dean, you too, and I'll keep you posted about the offer, ok?" Goodbyes over, Dean walked back to his car.

He felt he was in a transitional stage.

He had to go through this stage to get to where he needed, no, wanted to be.

Maggie closed the door on Dean. He looked well. She turned to Adele,

"Do you fancy watching Enchanted with some pop corn love?"

Fifteen minutes later, Maggie's mind wandered. With the flat hopefully sold, a few months at her parents enabling her to save some money, and her course well under way, Maggie felt as though things were finally headed in the right direction.

Rosie woke up one morning, the week before the end of term feeling odd.

She got up to go to work and the bedroom spun. Whoa! She thought she was going to pass out.

She steadied herself on the nearby chest of drawers and walked gingerly through to the bathroom.

She felt floaty, surreal.....nauseous?

A few moments later Rosie knelt back from the toilet bowl.

You have got to be kidding me, she thought to herself, staring at the raised toilet seat.

Slowly rising into a standing position she rinsed her mouth, cleaned her teeth and gingerly made her way downstairs to the kitchen.

Rosie opened a cupboard door and reached up for the peppermint teabags, thinking back, as she did, to the last time she had had her period.

Life had been so hectic lately, what with the school trip, exams, and Luke and John, the weeks had just flown by.

Leaning back against the worktop she waited for the kettle to boil.

She had definitely finished a period the week before John had come back from his stag do because after a hot bath, paracetamol and a full stomach of roast beef, they had enjoyed a romantic night enjoying each other after their weekend apart.

Rosie frowned as she poured in the boiling water, stirring the bag as she did so.

Had she had a period since then?

She'd always been fairly erratic and since nothing had happened since Luke had arrived they never bothered using contraception. Rosie walked through to the hallway to fetch her diary from her briefcase and started to flick through the weeks, trying to pinpoint an event in her diary that which would tie in with her period happening.

Nothing.

Rosie caught sight of herself in the mirror in the hallway.

Forty.

Pregnancy wasn't really in her plan for the future and she was pretty sure it wasn't in John's.

It had been for many years, but now?

Rosie sat in the doctor's surgery three and a half hours later, after having phoned in sick at school, in controlled shock.

She was trying to keep a check on her emotions which were now rollercoastering inside of her.

"Well, your urine test confirms the pregnancy test you did at home this morning. Congratulations! Judging from your last known period I'd put you at around 8 to 9 weeks pregnant," beamed the doctor.

"You're sure?" questioned Rosie, feeling stupid as soon as she had said it.

"Yes, yes, quite sure. Was this a planned pregnancy?" the doctor questioned, gently, sensing, quite rightly, probably not.

Rosie sat in her car in the doctor's surgery car park.

What was John going to say?

How would Luke react when he was eventually told?

She sat in the car park for half an hour.

It was a neutral place.

She tried to absorb the news.

Pregnant.

Four hours ago she had been a mother of one, married, with a job she loved. She had mourned a second baby for five years and had eventually made her peace with the fact that it was never going to happen.

She needed to talk to John.

Not as a husband, as her best friend.

She needed to hear his voice.

She dialled his number and waited.

Dean put his key in the lock of his front door and let himself into the house.

He closed the front door and started to make his way up the stairs.

The door down the hall to the kitchen, opened.

"Oh, hi there!"

Caroline, Dean's landlady stood in the doorway to the kitchen. Her makeup was heavy and seductive, ready for a Saturday evening out on the town she wore a black, clingy number with heels to match.

"Hello," replied Dean, desperate to be alone, so he could check his emails and prepare for tomorrow's lessons,

"Is everything ok?"

"Yes, yes, I'm just restocking the utility cupboard with cleaning bits," answered Caroline, smoothing down her dress as she spoke.

Dean looked puzzled, restocking the cleaning cupboard on a Saturday night, whilst being dressed up to the nines.

Caroline laughed at his very readable expression and looked down at her attire.

"I admit I look a bit overdressed to do the landlady role but it's enroute to my friend's house so I thought I'd kill two birds with one stone."

She explained, giving Dean her best kilowatt smile.

It was a plausible reason, she told herself. She didn't want to admit to herself the real reason.

The possibility of bumping into Dean.

Dean gave a raised eyebrow acknowledgement and restarted climbing the stairs. Caroline watched his disappearing legs go up the stairs.

"Of course, you're welcome to join us...y'know...if you're at a loose end...and ... and want to get out.." She blurted out.

Caroline cringed inside.

What WAS she doing?

The legs stopped climbing.

"I'm good thanks, got a lot of work on."

The legs continued their climb then disappeared from view.

Caroline heard Dean's door open, close and lock.

Great move girl, great move!

Caroline was beyond mortified.

She'd managed to frighten a grown man into locking his own bedroom door!

She sighed and went back into the kitchen, closed the utility room door and left the house to entertain her friend with the fallout from the midlife crisis she was obviously going through.

"Thanks Shelia, can you set up a meeting for next week? I'm off out now for the Threadball's appointment so if you can take any messages that would be great. I'll be a couple of hours I imagine."

John put the phone down to his secretary and got up to leave.

His phone beeped.

Rosie.

John frowned and glanced up at the wall clock.

Five minutes to eleven.

Rosie should be teaching now.

He answered his phone, more than a little concerned.

"Rosie? Is everything ok?"

"John? John, I don't know? I...I'm at the doctor's....in the car park....I'm really sorry....I can't believe it...I've just found out...."

John was now on full alert, he cut Rosie short.

"Rosie, what's happened? Are you ill? You're not making sense....what's wrong love?"

John was now pacing up and down in front of his desk.

Rosie closed her eyes and with an elbow on the steering wheel she rested her head in her free hand. She took a deep breath.

"I'm pregnant."

The words hung there.

John stopped pacing.

Pregnant!

He blinked.

They hadn't used contraception for six years!

"John?....are you there? I'm so sorry! I feel so stupid....I'm 40. You're 42......I just didn't think...."

Once again, John interrupted his fraught wife, quickly gathering his thoughts, desperate to say the right thing as Rosie was obviously in shock.

"Rosie, love, stop! Pregnant! Wow! Life's certainly not boring is it?" he heard himself say, thinking on his feet.

He thought he heard a chuckle from the other end of the phone,

"Now, listen, can you drive?"

"Yes, yes, I've just been sitting here, trying to take it all in but, I'm fine.....it's just...." she trailed off, still reeling from the news.

"Right, now listen, I have to meet this guy in fifteen minutes but then I'm coming straight home, ok?"

John really wanted to go home straight away but it was too late to cancel this appointment.

Rosie nodded, staring at a mother pushing a pushchair. "Rosie?" Rosie came back to the present.

"That would be great John, thanks, and I'm so sorry again."

"Darling stop saying sorry.....we both thought it wouldn't happen didn't we? Well, it has and we will deal with it. Now, when you feel ready, drive home, make some peppermint tea, put the heating on and I'll be there as quick as I can, ok?"

John was saying all the right things and Rosie loved him even more for it.

"Alright love....I love you." She murmured gratefully.

"I love you too, now drive carefully and I'll see you soon."

John ended the call and sat down on the end of his desk and stared at the wall.

Pregnant!

Christ!

Well, what can you do about it? John thought to himself, pragmatically.

They could afford it; they had the room so they were more fortunate than a lot of people.

He turned and looked at a photo of Rosie and Luke on her desk.

Better get to that meeting!

Rosie hung up the phone from John and slumped back in her seat.

They were a team.

As John said they would deal with it.

She took a deep breath and started the car.

Just over an hour later, John was on his way home.

He had carried the customer through the meeting at break neck speed and agreed to a follow up meeting at a time to be arranged the following week.

He swung his car into their drive, next to Rosie's, got out and hurried into the house.

Sally

The first week of the Easter holidays had flown by in Sally's house.

She now only worked Tuesdays, Wednesdays and Thursdays during the school holidays, as last year, her fifth year of childminding, she had hit a metaphoric wall at the end of week four during the summer holidays.

She had spent the Saturday afternoon, after vacuuming, dusting and washing all the sofa covers, sobbing on the sofa.

Chris, her eldest, came into the sitting room and carefully observed his Mum wiping her eyes from the doorway and pondered the best way to communicate with his obviously upset Mum.

She never, usually cried.

If overtired or angry, she would give the boys fair warning to tread carefully as she wasn't in the mood for their teenage reasoning and banter.

Crying though, that was a different matter.

Chris tried the obvious, he looked at the clock.

Too early for wine.

"Cup of tea Mum.....with two sugars?" he offered hopefully.

Sally wiped her nose with a now useless tissue and nodded gratefully.

"Thanks love, sorry, I'm just knackered in a word."

Sally leant forward and yanked another tissue from the nearly empty box on the blanket box in front of her.

"I just don't know how much longer I can go on at this pace, it's like being on a rollercoaster!"

Sally was grabbing at words to try to get over to Chris what her life felt like.

303

"Do you know how many times a day the children say 'Sally'? Hundreds! I sit down to eat and someone wants something! I sit down on the toilet and someone wants something, I ache, physically ache. My head is numb; I fall into bed, shattered after a twelve hour day, only to start all over again ten hours later. I spend Saturday trying to catch up on washing, cleaning and ironing, Sunday is spent visiting Granddad, then it's Monday again, and it starts all over again! It's suffocating!"

Fresh, hot tears erupted from Sally, she felt bad for Chris, bless him. He'd probably only come down for a teenage snack and was now listening to his self-pitying Mum moan about how much work she had, when plenty of families struggled to get by.

Chris came back around the corner from the kitchen having turned the kettle on and got the mug ready.

Two and a half teaspoons of sugar, just to be on the safe side.

He leant against the wall, the solution seemed simple to him.

"Look Mum, you just need to do fewer hours during the holidays. 7 till 6 every day with 6 or more children is a bit much for anyone to do. Can't you take Mondays off.....or Fridays? At least you'd have a long weekend then."

Sally took a deep breath and looked at Chris. So like her in appearance, but being a man, saw things in black and white.

She nodded slowly as she processed what her eldest had suggested.

"You know what, love, that sounds like a plan; I just know I can't go on like this anymore."

She used to worry that she'd lose business if she didn't offer full time care, fifty weeks of the year, but as the years progressed she had come across childminders who only worked term time, or just did before and after school children, and some only cared for the under fives. She'd be no good to anyone if she ran herself into the ground and her boys didn't want her being short and snappy with them in the evenings because she was exhausted.

Two cups of sugary tea later and half of Chris's Yorkie bar later, Sally started to feel a little bit more positive about her work-life situation.

Chris kept her company whilst she off-loaded ideas and work patterns for the autumn term and after an hour or so and a grateful hug from Sally, he disappeared back upstairs to the teenage sanctuary of his room.

Sally's work-life balance was now more even.

She worked a short day on a Monday, finishing at 3pm, and during the holidays she had Mondays and Fridays off, giving her a four day weekend which enabled her to do all her housework, washing and ironing. It also gave her two extra days where she could run her children and their friends to the pictures or swimming.

Her parents had all understood when Sally had broached the subject, much to her relief, so now, thanks to Chris, a calmer, more relaxed atmosphere resided over the Slater household during the school holidays.

At six o'clock on Thursday evening, Sally closed the art drawer, after putting the last of the craft bits away.

She mentally ticked off the list of jobs she wanted to do that evening.

Sweep the conservatory, take the car seats out the car, wash the sofa covers and lastly, vacuum through the downstairs. Maybe I'll get Jack to vacuum, Sally thought to herself.

Jack vacuumed in the same way he tackled his school work, meticulously and thoroughly.

Inch by inch, in straight lines, the carpets would be vacuumed. Jack never hurried the task; his six foot frame bent over the vacuum, eyes intent on the floor, no speck of fluff was safe.

Right on cue, Jack jogged down the stairs and through to the sitting room on his way to the kitchen.

"Yo, Mother! Wassup?"

Sally grinned at her lanky, blonde-haired, blue-eyed middle son, so young and full of life.

"Perfect timing, Jack! The vacuum cleaner is waiting for a dance with you, my lovely!"

She waited.

Jack moon walked backwards to the conservatory and surveyed the carpet with mock interest.

"I don't answer to Jack anymore, its God now please, and I honestly don't think the carpet needs vacuuming. Your house keeping skills are so wonderful it looks like it been vacuumed already!"

He smiled innocently at Sally, widening his eyes for effect.

Sally laughed at her son's attempt at being obnoxious,

"Nice try, smoothie, now, vacuum please. You don't have to do it now, just this evening. I want to leave the house tidy, as we won't be back until Monday lunchtime and I don't want to be cleaning Monday evening before work."

"Fine, fine," said Jack in dramatic surrender, "If I fail all my GCSEs you'll have no one to blame except yourself!" and with that parting comment he went back to the fridge in his constant search for food.

Their weekend away had been a last minute, but very welcome affair.

Nick's cousin, Susie, owned a holiday cottage outside Bath. It had been left to her in her mother's will and rather than sell it, Susie and her husband saw a business opportunity.

Using her flair and attention to detail Susie turned her childhood home into a luxury three bedroom holiday let.

It was set in glorious countryside, near a well served village, perfect for a weekend away.

Not one to shy away from hard work, Susie, with the help of two ladies from the village and her teenage daughter, Poppy, would clean the cottage. It was a frantic time. Cleaning two bathrooms and one en suite, changing the beds, vacuuming, re-stocking the welcome basket, checking for breakages or damaged items, be it light bulbs, cracked crockery or loose toilet seats, all these jobs had to be completed after the guests had left at 10am and before the new ones arrived at 4pm.

It was always a rush, made more stressful if the next guests arrived early! Susie, ever the diplomat, would invite the early birds to drop off their luggage and suggest they find their bearings and explore the neighbouring village with its gourmet pub, delicatessen and grocery store until 4pm, allowing Susie to finish off whatever last minute jobs needed doing. Usually the cottage was fully booked but Susie had had a last minute cancellation due to illness and had phoned Nick to see if he wanted a short break away. Sally had jumped at the chance at an unexpected weekend away and the boys, once they'd clarified there was wifi and the connection was sufficient to run three x boxes, tablets, phones and laptops, had begrudgingly agreed to be separated from their bedrooms for three nights.

One hour later, Nick arrived home,

"Alright love, how's it going?"

He called through the house, pulling his boots off as he did. He'd had a trying day at work and was looking forward to a weekend away too, far away from work and its problems.

"I'll just get changed then give me your list."

Sally was hanging the sofa covers on the airing stands in the conservatory. They would be dry by the time they got back.

"Ha ha!" Sally called through to her husband. It was a standing joke between them that if Nick had a day or week off, Sally would have a list of jobs for him to do. To be fair, she always had a list for herself and she was right, it was very satisfying to look at a list of jobs or errands, all crossed through, at the end of the day.

307

Nick came through to the conservatory, tucking his t shirt into his jeans. He quickly kissed Sally on the cheek, looked at the table then stepped back to check the kitchen worktop.

"Right, where's my list then?" he said, looking back at Sally, frowning.

"Very funny, Nick, you make me sound like a slave driver!" Sally smiled, carrying the airing stand over to the corner of the conservatory. Nick gave her a, 'Well, if the shoe fits!' look.

"Nick!" Sally exclaimed, putting her hands on her hips,

"Only teasing, love, seriously though, what can I do to help?"

"Nothing, I'm all done, we've just got to pack for three nights away and that's it! So ha! No list for you, take your time saying, sorry Sally," she finished, leaning on a chair and raising an eyebrow expectedly.

Nick looked impressed and relieved at the same time.

"Well shall I do tea then?" he offered, a bit at a loss now as he'd psyched himself up for an evening of jobs before their weekend away.

"No need! Fish fingers and chips are in the oven!"

Sally stepped forward and kissed her husband,

"Just relax love; we are now on our mini holiday!"

Nick returned Sally's kiss warmly, feeling the tension of the day slipping away. He then had a thought,

"What about the salad?" he questioned knowingly, he knew Sally hated making a salad. All that peeling and chopping.

"Ah, yes, now THAT you can do!" Sally grimaced gratefully, and whilst Nick went to raid the salad drawer, Sally took the car seats down the shed.

Sally's family weekend was just what the doctor ordered.

It was spent doing nothing more strenuous than walking into the village for supplies, or to the gourmet pub for their evening meals, reading the papers and playing Articulate.

The boys usually moaned when forced to play a board game but Articulate was a fast-paced, knowledge based, team game set against a timer; noisy and great fun.

Sunday night arrived all too soon.

The boys were holed up in their substitute bedrooms, whilst Sally and Nick relaxed on the sofa together, a glass of wine apiece, enjoying each other's company.

"How are you feeling love?" Nick asked his lounging wife,

"Great! In a word, our life seems a million miles away. What a great bolthole this place is." She snuggled into Nick's chest, "What about you?"

"I could certainly do with a weekend away here, a couple of times a year," he said, taking a sip of wine, "the old batteries are certainly recharged."

"Well, maybe we could ask Susie about the October half term?" Sally suggested, "I'm sure we'll both need a break before the craziness of Christmas starts."

Nick nodded in agreement, thinking of the workload Christmas created at the depot.

"You're not wrong there love, I'll ring Susie when we get back and see what's available around that time."

They finished off their evening eating pizza and playing Articulate with their three mildly protesting sons.

Sally looked around the table at her husband and her boys, all healthy, laughing, teasing and jostling, and gave a deep sigh of contentment.

She felt very blessed.

Early the following morning, after Phoebe's emergency surgery, her consultant appeared to check on her condition.

He spoke in a low voice to her parents whilst Phoebe dozed and asked Celeste and Paul how long they were thinking of staying in Spain as they might want to consider visiting the Estepona hospital.

The Estepona hospital was a private hospital which was highly regarded in the field of plastic surgery.

The consultant went on to say he had operated on Phoebe's nose and her facial injuries to the best of his ability, but when the swelling had subsided there might be scaring and irregularities which Phoebe may want to consider cosmetic surgery for.

Phoebe laid in her bed listening to the low voices, not caring if her face was scared and her nose crooked.

She was alive.

She closed her eyes and gave in to the residue of anaesthesia that was left in her body.

Ten minutes later, Celeste left to relieve Gaby and spend some time with Portia, leaving Paul to watch over Phoebe.

Checking Phoebe was asleep; Paul settled back in the visitor's chair and took out his phone to double-check his flight details for later that evening.

Phoebe's phone punctuated the silence.

Not wanting Phoebe to be disturbed, he quickly leant over to her bedside unit to silence it, the screen catching his eye.

Sebastian.

Without thinking he pressed the button to receive the call and waited.

"Phoebe?........Phoebe?......are you there?"

Without waiting for a reply Sebastian vented his frustration down the line.

"Phoebe, I am coming to the end of my patience with your playacting and ridiculous behaviour. I insist you come home immediately!"

"Or you'll do what Sebastian?"

Paul's voice was cool and monotone,

"Kill her next time."

Silence.

"Disappear off the face of my daughter and granddaughter's world, Sebastian, otherwise I'll make sure you do."

Paul pressed end call on his daughter's phone and picked up his own and dialled a number.

Hand shaking, Sebastian placed his phone carefully on his desk.

Beads of perspiration began to form on his forehead.

His mouth was dry and his insides threatened to expel themselves.

His world as he knew it was slowly, but steadily, unravelling.

Two corners of his triangle life were not in place and he was struggling to perform.....to function.

He wasn't in complete control anymore of the pieces that made up his egg shell existence.

If Phoebe's father thought he was just going to fade away from the life he had carefully, painstakingly and at great cost to himself, created, he was a fool.

Divorce was unthinkable.

It signalled failure, and failure wasn't a word that existed in Sebastian's vocabulary.

Just before lunch, Celeste came to relieve Paul.

"All set, darling?" she asked as she approached Phoebe's bed. Paul was standing, waiting for his wife to arrive.

"All set love; she's slept really well, woke for some water then drifted off again."

"That's good...good....come here, my love."

Celeste pulled her strong, capable husband towards her and hugged him close. She pulled back slightly and looked into the eyes she knew so well and said,

"Hurt him, Paul, but don't kill him."

"Don't worry love, don't worry. I'll just make him wish we had."

They kissed tenderly and embraced one last time before Paul made his way to Malaga Airport to catch his flight.

Several hours later, Paul pulled into the car park of a rundown pub on the outskirts of Clemsford.

A set of headlights flashed him.

He flashed his lights in response.

Four doors opened and three heavy set men, all wearing baseball caps, got out and walked towards Paul's car.

They stopped at the driver's door.

Paul pressed a button to open his window.

"All set?" he questioned, in a low voice.

"All set, Boss."

Paul nodded, pressed the button to raise the window, and drove out of the car park.

2am the following morning, a bloodied form lay on a kitchen floor.

Eyes swollen shut, so tightly they wouldn't obey the brain's command to open.

Nose smashed to a mash of broken bone and flesh, forcing the form to breathe through its mouth, which was agony, as several of its teeth were chipped and displaced.

The cool night air from the front door, that had been left open, was drawn into the mouth over the exposed nerves with every shuddering breath.

Abdominal swelling, cracked ribs and a fractured radius completed the injuries sustained to the form, and as it laid there, the air gradually filled with a pungent smell and the humiliation of knowing that it had soiled itself.

Taped to one of its bloodied hands was a photo of a face.

The sex of the person was unknown because of the severity of the beating they had suffered.

On the reverse of the photo, a simple quote from King Hammurabi, the sixth king of the Amorite dynasty of Babylon,

'An eye for an eye'.

Five minutes later, a tentative knock on the gently swinging front door,

"Hello?......hello?...did somebody call an ambulance?"

James negotiated the last tight bend of the country lane slowly and cautiously, then after a further five hundred yards or so, swung into Sue's driveway.

The first week of the Easter holidays had sped by.

With the arrival of a new puppy imminent, James had spent the past week changing the layout of the study and the kitchen.

On advice from one of the many dog rearing internet sites he had visited he had started to look at these rooms from a puppy's point of view. He checked the perimeter of the garden for gaps that an inquisitive little puppy could squeeze through and bought two kennels for when it was a little older.

He intended to take the puppy to school with him as his office opened out onto a twenty foot square courtyard area that was big enough to accommodate the second kennel. It was separate from the rest of the school, allowing the puppy to get some fresh air and stretch his legs.

James had it all planned.

A walk first thing in the morning, then at lunchtime in the neighbouring fields so they could both get some much needed exercise and hopefully ensure that the puppy slept most of the afternoon before home time, dinner and another walk before bed.

James climbed out of the car with the eagerness of a young boy. He couldn't remember the last time he had felt this child-like enthusiasm for something.

The farmhouse door swung open and there stood Sue, beaming, with a wriggling puppy in her arms.

"Good morning, James! How lovely to see you again, come in. Come in and take this little one whilst I pop the kettle on."

James waved and hurried towards Sue, eagerly taking hold of the excited warm bundle and pulled it close to him. The puppy instantly calmed down and snuggled into his jumper, nose buried in the crook of his arm.

Peace flooded James's body.

"Good Lord, Sue, they should bottle this." he said quietly, stepping into the warm sunny kitchen, gingerly trying to remove his boots, just using his feet.

"Oh don't worry about your boots, James. These quarry tiles are easily swept." Looking at the sleeping puppy, she smiled, "I know what you mean, dogs bring us so much comfort and love."

She filled the kettle and switched it on.

"When John died, obviously I was upset fairly often...." she grimaced and reached for two mugs, "Bella would just come and sit by me, or lay at my feet, just to let me know she was there for me."

Sue spooned coffee into the mugs,

"They're very instinctive, you know, I would never be without a dog now, I think they just complete a family."

Sue poured boiling water and milk into the mugs and carried them over to the large kitchen table.

The door flung open.

"Granny! Granny!"

Giles appeared in the kitchen, out of breath, and stopped short when he saw James.

James looked up and smiled at Giles.

"Are you going to keep that puppy?" asked Giles suspiciously.

James laughed. He loved the directness of children.

316

"I am going to buy one of your puppies, if that's alright Giles, but I don't know if this one is mine," he looked questioningly at Sue.

"Yes, yes, that's your one, see the red nail varnish on his tail."

James was relieved.

This one felt right, he felt connected to it in some unexplained way.

It was so calm in his arms; it would be hard to leave it today.

"Is Mummy ready for us soon, Giles?" asked Sue, smiling at her protective grandson.

Giles tore his gaze from the puppy James was holding.

"Mummy said lunch is in half an hour......is it a boy or a girl?"

Giles turned his attention back to James, once again James came unstuck.

"Do you know, I really don't know! Sue, do you know?"

He felt stupid not even knowing what sex of dog he was buying.

It hadn't been important.

"It's a girl James, is that alright?" Sue answered, scanning James's face for a flicker of disappointment or regret.

James nodded, smiling down at the now sleeping puppy, gently stroking the back of its tiny head.

"That's perfect....just perfect!"

Half an hour later, the sleeping puppy returned to Bella, Sue and James were seated in Julia's equally cosy kitchen, her large table positively groaning with food.

Gabe, Julia, their five children, Sue and James tucked into roast beef with all the trimmings. A huge dish of sticky toffee pudding waited patiently to be demolished on the worktop.

317

The room was filled with lively conversation centred on puppy rearing, hilarious dog anecdotes and how everyone was spending their Easter break.

Julia rose from the table to top up the gravy boat.

"Sue, I've found some more flower pots if you need any more to take to Sally's."

Sue swallowed her piece of Yorkshire pudding, nodding gratefully.

"Lovely Julia, thank you, I sorted out some bits last weekend but I'm sure they won't go to waste."

Sue took a sip of water,

"I wonder how her tomato plants are getting on?" she said thoughtfully.

"Is Granny going to help Sally with our tomato plants?" piped up Fin, his mouth full of roast beef.

"Fin! Can you empty your mouth before you speak please?" said Julia, rolling her eyes at her youngest son, as she sat back down with a refilled jug of gravy.

"Yes Fin, I am. I'm going to help Sally and her minded children grow some vegetables, is that alright?"

Sue was mindful of little children and their territories.

Fin frowned and said nothing, then,

"Will you go into her house......and use her toilet?"

He tilted his head to the side as he tried to imagine his granny in Sally's house.

He had only seen her in his house and her own.

Sue laughed.

"Yes I will, my love, and if I have to use her toilet I'm sure that will be fine."

Fin processed this carefully and then reached his decision.

"You can see how high me and Spencer's plants have grew, Granny!"

Everyone laughed at Fin's final acceptance of his Granny at Sally's, and his grammar.

James interrupted the subsiding laughter,

"Do you have green fingers then Sue?" James asked hopefully.

"Green fingers!" exclaimed Julia, "my mother in law has green fingers and green toes! If she can't grow it, it can't be grown!"

Julia reached for the roast potatoes.

Sue laughed self-consciously, embarrassed by Julia's glowing accolade,

"Well, I do enjoy growing things; of course I don't do it on the scale I used to when the children were younger."

"Really," said James thoughtfully, a plan beginning to form in his head.

He put down his knife and fork.

"Sue, don't answer me now, I want you to think about it, as I'm sure you're a very busy woman, but would you consider running a gardening club at school, say, maybe one lunchtime a week. With help of course," he added quickly, seeing a look of panic cross Sue's face.

A gardening club was one club the school didn't have organised; it would be such a benefit to the children, especially the practically minded ones.

Sue cut a piece of beef and potato and slowly put it into her mouth, staring intently at her plate.

Good Lord!

She couldn't possibly run a club in a school.....a school!

319

Helping Sally was one thing but organising a gardening club, well, she wouldn't know where to begin!

She finished chewing and opened her mouth to explain this.

Julia looked from Sue to James, and then back again, she knew exactly what her mother in law was thinking.

She quickly cut in.

"I think you'd be great, Sue!"

Julia stopped Sue in her tracks.

Sue shook her head wordlessly at Julia who in turn gave her a 'yes you can,' look and turned to James.

"What were you thinking James, cress, tomatoes, beans, things like that?"

Julia desperately wanted Sue to think before she said no.

This would be a great venture for her, to get out and about properly, give her a purpose, a focus. She'd been flailing slightly since John had passed away.

"Yes, yes, Julia," replied James quickly, sensing an ally, "just really basic gardening."

He turned to Sue,

"I could help you Sue, with the planning of each week; I know a bit.....Tanya used to grow vegetables. It wouldn't be anything complicated or time consuming as the children have to eat their lunch as well."

James sat back in his chair and wiped his mouth with his napkin as he thought.

"One week could be spent washing the flower pots, talking about the soil, playing with it; week two could be planting the seeds and so on. We could even buy some ready grown plants so the children can visualise what they're growing and plant them in a vegetable plot in week three..."

James trailed off looking hopefully between Julia and Sue.

Gabe, who had been quiet up until this point, lifted his wine glass to take a sip. He took a sideways look at his mother and casually put his glass down.

"It doesn't sound like anything you couldn't handle Mum, you could do it with your eyes shut."

Sue shot Gabe a look of surprise.

He rarely gave his opinion on anything she did.

Gabe shrugged his shoulders at his mother's quizzical expression,

"You've done the very same thing with this lot over the years,"

Gabe waved his arm around the table at his children,

"What's a few more?"

Gabe nodded encouragingly at her, willing her gently with his eyes, you can do it.

Do it.

Sue felt very uncomfortable with so many pairs of eyes focused on her. She cleared her throat and stood up.

"Well I'll definitely give it some thought, now, are we all finished? Yes? Right, I'll start clearing away this lot. That sticky toffee pudding isn't going to eat itself."

Taking cue from the matriarch of the family, the adults changed the subject and finished the rest of their meal in genial conversation.

Later on that day, dusk now falling, Sue sat alone in her kitchen in John's favourite old chair.

She'd lit a small fire and was now warming her toes whilst drinking a cup of tea.

Staring into the fire she let her thoughts mull over the lunch time conversation.

A gardening club.

It really wouldn't be so hard to organise.

She sensibly realised her biggest challenge would be getting a task completed in the relatively short period of time she would have over the lunch time period.

Excited children, eager and full of questions, all wanting to share the experiences of gardening they'd already had.

Gabe was right; she had dealt with that with her many grandchildren.

She took a sip of tea.

It felt good to be wanted, to still be thought of as useful, with something to offer.

She felt a little lift inside of her. She sat upright in the chair and swung her feet off the stool onto the floor.

'I'm going to do it!' she declared out loud to the fire.

She stood up to reach for her mobile phone off the kitchen table.

She wasn't going to let this opportunity pass her by.

She was going to grab it with both hands.

Dialling James's number she suddenly felt excited. It dawned on her that it had been a long time, since the last time, she had felt this way.

James answered his phone.

"Hello James, it's Sue, if you're serious about the gardening club, I'd love to be involved...."

Half an hour later, James put down his phone and reached for a notepad and pen with the intention of drawing up a list of things he thought would be needed to run a gardening club.

Tomorrow morning he would go through the shed and greenhouse to see what could be safely used by children.

Sue had already done hers so he had suggested picking her up after lunch and bringing her back to his house so she could see what James had uncovered. They could then draw up a shopping list of what they still needed to buy, and then sketch an outline of the first half terms sessions.

Goodness me, thought James to himself, where is the holiday going?

They only had a week to get organised!

He started to jot down some ideas.

Julia answered the phone on the eighth ring.

She had five children and a husband in the house somewhere but she seemed to be the only one capable of answering the phone.

"Hello, Drake's Farm, how can I help?"

"Julia darling, sorry to bother you, you must be sick of the sound of me after today." apologised Sue,

"Don't be silly Sue," replied Julia, slightly concerned, "is everything ok?"

"Yes, yes, everything's fine darling, I was just wondering if one of the girls were free tomorrow afternoon to check in on Bella? It's just that I've told James I'll help with this gardening club thing and he's picking me up tomorrow afternoon so we can discuss the ins and outs of it...." Sue paused, "Would that be alright?"

Julia listened to Sue with a growing feeling of relief spreading through her.

This was a start, a new start for her loving, generous mother in law; she smiled into the phone and replied,

"Of course Sue, absolutely no problem at all, just text us when you're leaving." Julia hung up the phone and gave a 'whoop!' and a little jump on the spot and called through the house excitedly.

"Gabe?.....GABE?"

The summer term was well under way and Millie had quickly settled in and was enjoying her new job. She loved the variety of it although on one of her days she had discovered she was actually running the office to cover Paul's day off,

"You'll be fine," Peter had reassured her breezily, "nothing will happen that you haven't dealt with before."

Millie had nodded at Peter nervously, wondering if he had forgotten it had been nine years since she had last worked for him.

The first week had been a shock to the system.

Everything had to be ready the night before. Millie checked and double checked whether it was swimming, football, netball or cookery club the following day. There was no room for error.

When she hadn't worked she had been able to pop home if the children had forgotten something, but not now. It was all about lists and being organised, that was the key!

Millie dropped the children at 8.45am, which gave her plenty of time to travel the twenty minutes to work, park behind the office and fetch a coffee before she started her day.

The children had settled into Anna's quickly as they knew everyone Anna minded as they all went to their school. They went to Anna's on a Wednesday and Thursday whilst Darius finished work early on a Friday and picked them up from school himself.

This was a time that Darius and the children both looked forward to.

Darius would take them bowling, swimming, or for a bike ride, whilst Millie would pick up a takeaway on her way back from work. Then they would all meet up at home to start the weekend together. It usually worked well......

"Mum.....I don't feel so good..."

Millie looked up from sorting her briefcase.

She was going straight from the school run to a valuation in a neighbouring village.

Jane was standing in the doorway to the kitchen, dressed for school, but clearly unwell.

Her face was flushed and her eyes were bright with dark circles under them.

 Millie's heart sank and melted at the same time.

Jane had obviously tried to get to school; she'd even dampened down her cowlick in an attempt to tame it.

"Oh love, you really don't look too good." Millie said, feeling her head. "Hmmm.....you are warm, how do you feel?' She reached up into the cupboard where the vitamins and Calpol were kept.

"My throat's sore, my head hurts and I feel sort of, um...floaty." Jane finished. Millie dished out 2 spoonfuls of Calpol while mentally running through her diary for the day.

Apart from the valuation, she was just doing admin today, which could easily be done at home. She turned to Jane. "Jane love, do you think you'd be okay sitting in the car whilst I do a quick valuation, then I'll just pop to the office to pick up some work, to do at home, what do you think?"

"That's fine Mum...." she turned to go back upstairs to get changed, then stopped and looked back at her Mum who was now going through her list of contact numbers. She first needed to phone the school, then Anna, to see if she could drop Drew straight home after school, then the office, to explain the situation.

"Sorry, Mum," Jane said woefully.

Millie stopped scanning the list.

Bullseye!

A verbal dart loaded with guilt, aimed, fired, and delivered on target.

She spun round and rushed towards Jane, scooping her into the biggest bear hug she could give.

"My darling child, it's not your fault, and please don't say you're sorry! It's just one of those things."

She took a step back and held Jane by the shoulders.

"Listen Jane, you and Drew are far more important than any job. If I had a really busy day, I would ask Granny to come over but if she couldn't, and Dad couldn't, I would cancel everything. Houses can always be valued another day. Now, if you really don't feel up to it I'll cancel the valuation.....ok?"

Jane gave a watery smile and fell into her mother's arms.

"I'll be ok, Mum, I'll just doze in the car then change into my onesie and go to bed when we get back."

Millie frowned to herself over the top of Jane's head, her conscience was pricking her.

How would she react if another mother told her she'd left her unwell daughter in the car, albeit safely on a drive on a small housing estate, whilst she carried out a house valuation.

It was a no brainer.

"Jane, let's forget about work. Go and change into your onsie and snuggle back down into bed. I'll phone Anna and see if Drew can join her walking crocodile to school."

Jane's face immediately relaxed,

"Are you sure, Mum?"

"Absolutely!"

Millie reassured her daughter, with conviction, her mothering instinct was now fully in force.

"Now upstairs, my lovely, and I'll bring you up some orange juice and throat lozenges."

Watching her daughters disappearing figure go up the stairs, Millie leant back against the work top and sighed.

How did parents who worked full time without back-up manage?

She picked up the phone to see if Darius's Mum was free at all that day before she phoned work; Darius was in London so he was out of the equation.

Whilst Millie waited for Carol to answer her phone, Drew appeared in the kitchen having spent an unusually long time in the downstairs cloakroom.

"Mummy, I don't feel very well, my bottom's runny and I feel sick."

With that, Drew threw up all over the kitchen floor, tiny specks of vomit decorating Millie's shoes.

Millie just stared, stunned at what this morning was literally throwing at her.

"Hello?.....hello?..is anybody there?" Carol had answered her phone.

Millie was brought back to reality by the sound of her mother in law's voice.

"Carol, it's Millie, so sorry, got to go, Drew's just been sick!" and she quickly hung up on a bemused Carol.

"Oh Drew, you poor thing....!" Millie grabbed for the washing up bowl and hopping over the creative artwork of sick that now adorned the floor, ushered her poor, shivering, retching son, back into the confines of the cloakroom.

"S....s...sorry Mum," gasped Drew, throwing up a slightly smaller amount of his stomach contents. "I don't think I'll be able to go to school today."

Millie gave a little laugh as she saw pragmatically saw the comedy element of her morning so far.

She wiped Drew's mouth and kissed the top of her son's head,

"I think you're probably right my love, I think you're probably right."

An hour later, work phoned, kitchen floor cleaned and bottoms and tummies temporarily behaving themselves, Millie stood at the kitchen sink inspecting her shoes.

Washing machine for them, Millie thought to herself then jumped at a knocking on her back door, which then opened slightly.

"Is it safe to come in?"

Carol popped her head round the corner and grinned at her daughter in law.

Millie laughed and said,

"Yes, of course Carol, but I warn you, we may all come down with whatever they've both got, so if you'd rather not...."

Carol humphed, loftily.

"I'm far too old for bugs to bother me. Now, do you need to have another shower or did the little man miss you. I've got nothing on today so if the children don't mind it being me and not you, you could scoot off to work?"

Carol bustled in and started to fill the kettle.

Millie's eyes filled with tears at her generous, unselfish mother in law.

Carol turned and saw Millie struggling to keep her composure and she put down the kettle.

"Oh Millie, come here,"

She opened her arms to give Millie a hug.

"Being a Mum is tough, being a working Mum is tougher still. If I can help you, I will. Now, shall we go and see what those grandchildren of mine think?"

Thirty minutes later, Millie was off to work, valuation rescheduled and two children snuggled under duvets on squashy sofas with Calpol, sick bowls and a doting Granny looking after them.

Millie knew she was damn lucky and made a mental note to send a bouquet of flowers to Carol the following day.

She really was a star.

John had found Rosie sitting by the patio doors that looked out over the garden in their low ceiling sitting room.

"Hey love, how'y doin?" he humoured gently.

Rosie appreciated his attempt at lightening the mood and stood up for a hug.

John held her close, chest to chest, hip to hip, thigh to thigh.

They just stood, being.

"I'm scared." she whispered,

"I know, love, I know."

He did know.

He knew how desperately she'd wanted another baby.

How withdrawn she became every time her period arrived.

How practical she became when nothing happened after two years.

She didn't mope.

She counted her blessings.

One healthy child, a healthy husband, educated with a good job. Dust yourself down and get on with it, had been her approach.

He loved her all the more for it.

Now?

Rosie pulled back from John's embrace,

"Thanks for coming home love, let me make you a coffee. Have you eaten?"

John took her hand,

"No, let's go through to the kitchen, sit down and I'll make us a drink whilst we have a chat, alright?"

John took the lead.

He knew Rosie would want to talk through the practicalities of their unexpected situation.

The end result would still be the same but she needed to air her worries.

He pulled out a dining chair, pushed Rosie gently down by the shoulders and turned to pop the kettle on.

He then turned back to Rosie and said,

"Right, I'm ready, go for it....." and started bustling around the kitchen making a sandwich for them both, not bothering to ask Rosie if she wanted one. He was pretty sure food would have been the last thing on her mind that morning. Whilst gentle domesticity took place in her kitchen, Rosie took a deep breath and started to offload all her fears and her worries.

"Well, from a practical point of view I'm forty, I'm not a young slip of a thing anymore. There could be something wrong with the baby as we speak. I'm more prone to having a baby with Down's syndrome, early miscarriage and placenta praevia as Luke was a caesaerean. My diet's been crap lately. I didn't plan to get pregnant so I'm probably low on folic acid which means the baby is more likely to develop spina bifida......."

Rosie trailed off realising she sounded a tad dramatic.

John sat down and put a chicken sandwich in front of both of them.

She looked helplessly at John,

"I just don't want to get used to the idea of being a mum to a new baby, and all the lovely feelings that brings, for it to be all......"

Rosie couldn't continue.

She brought her hands up to her face and started to cry.

John sat and let his wife give way to the inevitable tears.

He leant forward and hugged her and finished the that she hadn't wanted to finish,

"For it all to be snatched away.....I know, love, I know."

Rosie dropped her hands, let her tears fall, and nodded,

"I just don't think I'm strong enough."

They sat there, together, in silence for a while.

Rosie blew her nose, took a deep breath, gave a small smile and shrugged at John.

John nodded, understanding completely.

It was his turn now.

"Love, why don't we take one step at a time? All we know now is you're pregnant. You have just as much chance as anyone of going full term and delivering a healthy baby. There are risks at any age and it doesn't change the fact that you are pregnant and we are just going to have to get used to the idea. It's not going to go away and if there are any problems we will deal with them together, ok?" He smiled at Rosie and took both her hands in his and continued, "Life is a rollercoaster love, you know that, you take what good you can when it comes your way and when the bad comes.....if it does.....then we'll wait till it passes, because it always does."

Rosie's eyes looked uncertain and she clasped his hands.

John pulled her on to his lap and cuddled her.

"You ARE strong enough Rosie, WE are strong enough. Together we are strong enough to deal with anything life throws at us, I promise."

Rosie leaned into John's strong, warm embrace and laid her head on his shoulder, they sat there for some time then Rosie said quietly,

"You know, we're going to be in our sixties with a teenager in the house."

John grinned and gave a low laugh,

"No worries, it's just what I'd planned for my retirement!"

They both laughed at the rollercoaster ride ahead of them.

The afternoon spent with James during the holidays had been very productive.

They had sorted out what equipment they had, what they thought parents might be willing to donate and what they may need to buy.

They had decided to start the club a week after the start of term.

The children would be told about the club Monday morning in assembly and a letter would go home in the children's book bags on Monday evening asking for donations of inexpensive items such as seed packets, plastic flower pots, old aprons and a couple of trowels of compost secured in a plastic bag from those that had any to spare; to be delivered to the school by Friday afternoon.

Mr Parkins, the owner of the local hardware store in the village, had already offered to donate some hand held trowels and forks when he found out about the school's plans from Sue, and a permission slip, allowing the child to take part, would be included at the bottom of the letter.

Friday, after school had finished, James and Sue could tick off from their list what had been donated and buy the shortfall that weekend.

After numerous cups of coffee they had pencilled out five week's worth of gardening clubs that would take them up to the half term.

Both knowing that children love to get their hands dirty, especially the young ones, digging and exploring the soil would be available every session. Sue had thought back to something she used to do with her children and grandchildren,

"What about a 'Can you find?' area, which involves a large plastic tray filled with soil and the children have to dig and discover various plastic mini beasts, vegetables and fruits and match them to a corresponding picture chart? A different year five or six pupil could volunteer each week to oversee this area and help the child identify the object and encourage them to say what they know about their find and add any other information?"

"Brilliant!" commented James, scribbling down Sue's ideas as she spoke nineteen to the dozen as ideas kept popping into her head.

Sue dipped a chocolate biscuit into her coffee and bit into it, thinking as she chewed.

"I don't know if Tanya's vegetables suffered like ours used to but the hours we spent trying to rid our vegetable patch of slugs," she said ruefully, taking another, rather harsh bite of her biscuit, at the memory, "What do you think James, kids love creepy crawlies. A session touching, feeling and holding, if the children want to, some slugs, snails and worms. The bad and good of the animal kingdom, we may need extra help with that session?" she grinned.

James was thrilled and couldn't help but think how Sue's face lit up as she spoke. She had a ready smile that reached her eyes and James was finding her manner quite infectious. He loved her idea and thought about how they could build on it.

"That's great! We could tie that in with Art and science. We could let the children use magnifying glasses to observe them, then they could sketch them, or make models using clay, and then they could research their lifestyle and habitats!" James held up his pencil for effect, like a eureka moment.

Sue smiled at him. Once a teacher, always a teacher, she thought to herself.

He was slowly coming out of the fog, little by little.

Sue took a sip of her coffee and then with a start realised that they both were.

James and Sue had finished their productive afternoon with a walk across the fields to clear their heads and stretch their legs, pleased with the progress made in their new project.

Sue woke up the first Monday after the Easter holidays with a new zest for life. Quickly making the bed, Sue had a quick shower, got dressed and went downstairs. After the school run that morning, Sue and Julia were paying a visit to the vets to buy worming tablets and puppy food, then doing the monthly grocery shop at Tesco. On the way back they had planned to pop into Sally's, drop off some pots and trays and see how her tomato plants were getting on.

Catching sight of herself in the hallway mirror, she stopped and stared.

Her skin had a rosy glow to it; the grey pallor that had seemed the norm since John had passed away had gone.

She gave her reflection a nod, pulled back her shoulders, took a deep breath, then released it and said to the mirror, 'You know the trick now. Keep busy and don't wallow in self pity as life usually has a way of catching you when you fall.'

With that positive thought firmly in place she walked purposefully into the kitchen to have a quick breakfast before starting her day.

Dean and Maggie

Dean leaned against the brick wall that surrounded the playground and checked his watch. A couple more minutes and the bell would sound.

Once he'd picked up Adele they would stop by the flat and collect her overnight bag, then, as a treat, they were going to the cinema and then to Pizza Hut for tea.

His Dad had sent him some money for his twenty fifth birthday so he thought it would be a nice change to do something different with Adele.

Ten minutes later, Dean turned the key in the front door to the flat and opened it.

Adele ran through to her bedroom calling over her shoulder,

"Won't be a mo, Dad, I forgot to put in my colouring pens."

"No worries love,"

Dean shut the door behind him.

Maggie appeared from the bathroom wearing rubber gloves.

"Hi Dean, everything ok?" she held up her hands and waved them,

"Just giving the bathroom and kitchen a deep clean, the people buying are coming tomorrow to measure up so I just thought I'd give them a once over."

"Good idea," agreed Dean, "Have we got an exchange date yet?"

"Well, the solicitor thinks everything should be ready in a couple of weeks then a further two until completion. It's quite quick as it's only them and us in the chain." Maggie smiled,

"Have you got time for a cuppa?"

Dean took a deep breath,

"I have, yes, but I was going to ask if you fancied coming to the cinema with me and Adele, then Pizza Hut afterwards?"

Maggie looked a little awkward but Dean carried on,

"It's just that my dad has sent me a little extra for my birthday as I'm twenty five, bless him, and I thought it would be nice if we could socialise together once in a while for Adele's sake."

He finished talking and casually leant against the hall wall.

That was a stroke of genius, he congratulated himself. Maggie had been mature throughout their whole separation; he knew she wouldn't say no.

Maggie briskly whipped off her rubber gloves.

"That sounds lovely Dean, thank you. I'll finish off the cleaning when I get back."

Ten minutes later the later, the trio set off for their treat together.

Adele sat in the back with a big smile on her face listening to her Mum and Dad.

Dad was offering to help Mum move their things to her parents when they moved and Mum was saying that would be very helpful as her Dad's back was playing up.

Adele turned and looked out of the window, still smiling.

Grown ups were so funny sometimes.

They couldn't see what was right in front of them.

It didn't matter.

Adele had a feeling it would work out for them all in the end.

She just had to be patient.

"John, are you coming?" Rosie called up the stairs, "I don't want to be late!"

"Coming love,"

He'd put on a security pair of pants, as he now called them to himself, under his boxers.

He immediately felt calmer.

He couldn't let on to Rosie that he was worried about this scan.

What if they couldn't find a heartbeat, or if they could, what if they found an abnormality?

He'd had a few weeks to get used to the idea and was secretly looking forward to a new addition to their family.

He picked up his keys and bounded down the stairs.

"Right love, let's go!"

He kissed Rosie on her frowning forehead, and said, "Stop worrying!"

Rosie just nodded, turned around and quickly walked out the open front door.

She got into her car whilst John hurried past and climbed into his.

His car needed an MOT so the idea that morning was to drop John's car at the garage in Huntsdon, then drive on in Rosie's car to Barley Heath in Stentbridge.

Driving through Huntsdon, the small town before Stentbridge, was tedious at the best of times.

Mini roundabout followed mini roundabout, not to mention the traffic lights.

Rosie was in a slow moving queue, approaching one of the many mini roundabouts, changing down a gear and braking, preparing to stop.

Except she didn't stop.

Her mind on the looming scan that could brighten or shatter their future, she pressed hard on the accelerator, instead of the brake and drove straight at the car in front.

Rosie yelled out at the force of the impact.

She hadn't been going fast but it was enough of an impact to deploy the airbag.

Rosie, her nerves ragged and raw, screamed and burst into tears, it just all too much.

On an unexpected morning off, Sally was on her way to Argos to buy a paddling pool, when she heard the unmistakable sound of two cars colliding.

She turned and looked back.

Was that Rosie's car?

She turned around and hurried back along the path.

It was.

An irate man from the car in front was getting out of his car, and was that John, Rosie's husband getting out of the car behind Rosie?

She hurried over to the car and opened the passenger front door.

Rosie was hysterical.

"The baby! The baby!" she sobbed,

Sally hid her shock at Rosie's words.

She, like everyone else, had thought Rosie couldn't have any more children.

"Rosie. It's ok, we'll get you to a hospital and get you checked out. If John's car can't get you there, I will, ok? Now take some deep breaths."

Sally held Rosie's hand and saw John, ever the peacemaker, approach the driver who was storming towards Rosie's car.

"God mate! I'm so sorry! Completely my wife's fault, she's just found out she's pregnant, hormones are all over the place, we'll pay for the damage, whatever the cost. Again, we're so sorry."

The driver, completely disarmed by this wholehearted apology and acceptance of the blame, held up his arms in mock surrender and took a sharp breath in.

"Ok, well, now then.....you can't argue with those pregnancy hormones now, can you?" catching sight of a sobbing Rosie behind the driver's wheel.

John stepped forward to gratefully shake the now appeased driver's hand.

"Thanks mate, shall we pull over and exchange phone numbers?"

Sally got out the car and gently coaxed Rosie over to the passenger seat.

She walked around the front of the car. No serious damage done, as far as Sally could see, just a couple of dented bumpers.

She climbed into the driver's seat and drove Rosie's car off the main road, down a side street.

Sally turned the engine off and turned to Rosie, who had now stopped crying and was just quietly sniffing.

"We're late for the scan now!" sniffed Rosie, trying not to give way to tears once more.

"Have you got your appointment letter with you?" Sally asked, reaching into her gillet for her phone.

"I think so.... I don't know," replied Rosie, not moving.

Sally leant across for Rosie's handbag.

"Is it ok if I look through your handbag Rosie?" Rosie just nodded.

Retrieving the letter from Rosie's bag, Sally quickly located a phone number and dialled.

Two minutes later, after explaining the situation, she hung up.

"Ok Rosie, they said just turn up any time this afternoon and they will fit you in, so just relax and..."

John opened Rosie's door.

"Hey Sally, thanks so much for staying with Rosie. Rosie, are you alright love?" he asked gently.

Rosie just nodded, her bottom lip trembling.

This was not how this day was meant to unfold.

Sally quickly filled John in with what the antenatal clinic had said.

"Right," said John decisively, "Sally, have you got to get going?"

"No, no. I've got until 2.45pm" replied Sally

"Would you stay with Rosie, maybe get a coffee somewhere? I've cancelled my MOT and the guys are on their way to pick up Rosie's car to check it over. Then when they've picked it up, we can make our way at a leisurely pace to Stentbridge."

"Yes, yes, of course, how does that sound Rosie?" asked Sally in a bright voice, keen to do anything to help in the situation.

Rosie, again, just nodded.

Five minutes later, Sally and Rosie were sat in a nearby cafe, killing time.

"Do you want to talk about it love?" Sally gently asked.

Rosie quietly started to cry again.

"I've been bloody stupid these past few weeks, wondering if I wanted another baby, wondering if was right for us as a family, worrying if there was something wrong with it and now......,"

Rosie broke off as a fresh flood of tears flowed.

"It will be alright, Rosie, I'm sure of it, it really was a tiny prang."

Sally tried to offer some words of comfort but she knew they sounded empty.

Rosie took a deep breath in between her sobs.

"I want this baby more than anything, and now, because of me, something might have happened to it!" she finished the sentence with an anguished wail. The other customers in the cafe were wonderful in pretending not to notice the emotional scene happening at the table in corner at the back and dutifully drank their coffee and commented on the weather to each other.

Sally waited; words seemed futile compared to the torrent of emotions that poor Rosie was going through.

Once again, the sobbing eventually ceased.

At that moment, thankfully, John arrived which meant that hopefully, within a short time, Rosie would soon have her mind put to rest.

Sally excused herself, waving off the thank yous and grateful hug from an emotionally rung-out but now calm Rosie and made her way to Argos.

She hadn't said congratulations, it just hadn't seemed appropriate in the situation.

Time for that after the results of the scan.

1.40pm. Barley Heath hospital

Rosie lay back on the blue tissue sheeting that covered the bed and subconsciously held her breath.

John held her hand tightly, he wasn't sure if it was for Rosie's benefit or his.

Rosie's bladder ached as it struggled to hold its liquid contents but Rosie didn't care. She could put up with anything if it helped her hear the news she so desperately wanted.

"Now Rosie, it will feel a bit cold," said the sonographer as she squirted a small amount of lubricating gel onto Rosie's tummy.

She picked up the probe, pulled the monitor towards her then gently placed the probe on to the gel. She moved the probe round in a widening circle until the lower part of the abdomen was completely covered in gel, she then kept the probe in one place and stared at the monitor.

The silence weighed heavily in the room.

The probe was moved again; then, a second of silence, followed by the unmistakeable sound of an echoing heart beat filling the room.

The sonographer's face broke into a broad smile.

"Ah ha! The little one was playing hide and seek with me," she turned to Rosie and John,
"Sounds lovely and strong to me, I'll just do some measurements."

Tears streamed unashamedly down the relieved couple's faces.

Measurements taken, the sonographer finished she said,

345

"Well, everything looks fine from the scan, do you want to see?" She turned the monitor so the two forty somethings could say hello to the new addition to their family who was going to turn their worlds upside down.

Ecstatic, John grinned at the image on the screen and bent down to kiss Rosie's cheek, who was staring at the monitor, transfixed by the movement on the screen.

"Now will you stop worrying?" he whispered.

Rosie smiled and turned to kiss her husband on the lips.

"Maybe," she replied, deliriously happy at the sight and sound of her baby.

All the drama and worry of that morning rapidly faded away to be relegated to the depths of their memories, only to be revisited amongst friends, years later, over wine, as the, 'Do you remember?' story.

James sat in his office at school, dialled Sue's number and waited.

It was Friday afternoon, the end of the first week of the summer term.

"Hello Sue, it's James, is there any chance you could pop by the school this afternoon instead of tomorrow morning, the donations are all in and I feel I want to sort through everything sooner rather than later. The parents have been incredibly generous!"

"Yes of course James, I'll just sort out the puppies then I'll pop along, how exciting!"

Sue hung up the phone and checked on the puppies, which were now three weeks old and just starting to wean.

She picked up her keys, locked the front door and climbed into her old Land Rover and drove the five minute journey to school.

James met her at the main gate, brimming with enthusiasm, smiling from ear to ear.

"Thank you, Sue, for coming at such short notice, come this way and I'll show you why."

Sue stood with James in the school hall, astonished at the amount and variety of gardening donations that filled the stage at one end of the hall.

There were bags of compost, pebbles, seed packets, trays, umpteen children's forks and spades, gloves, aprons, plastic labels, bamboo sticks and watering cans. One of the dads, who was a landscape gardener, had donated eight sleepers which he had offered to cut down to size and build some raised beds for the vegetable plot.

"Goodness me, James!" exclaimed Sue, finally, "Haven't people been generous?"

"Wonderfully so, Sue, and look how many children want to take part," he said, opening a large envelope and pulling out a thick wad of reply slips. "Seventy children want to take part in the gardening club, seventy!" James repeated, "Now obviously it's going to be a novelty for some, but it's an amazing uptake! I don't think any other club has attracted so much interest. We need to seize the moment and build on this interest. It will be a great way to build a sense of community within the school."

"Seventy children!" Sue tried not to sound alarmed and waited for James to explain how he expected Sue to organise seventy children over one lunch time.

James looked at Sue's face and smiled broadly,

"Come into the staff room, Sue and we'll have a coffee and I'll run through how I think the club should best be run and don't worry, I've got lots of volunteers!" A relieved and intrigued Sue followed James into the staff room.

How WAS it going to work? Sue thought to herself.

Having made two cups of coffee for them both, James started to talk Sue through the logistics of running the club.

Due to the large number of children who wanted to take part he thought that running the club twice a week would be the most sensible thing to do, but Sue certainly didn't have to commit to helping at both sessions.

He didn't want to disappoint some children by saying it was oversubscribed and it was only going to be run for Key Stage 2 children, which he had considered.

The club was only going to run in the summer term this year and several of the teaching assistants had already volunteered to help, so two sessions a week should be manageable.

Each session would have approximately thirty five children attending which sounded a lot but James reasoned that about half of that number had school dinners and went into the hall first leaving the children who had a packed lunch to go to the club first, do the planned activity, explore the soil tray with the hidden plastic creatures, touch and feel the worms, slugs and snails or colour in some gardening pictures until it was their turn for lunch and the school dinner children could then have their turn.

James took a sip of his coffee,

"What do you think so far, Sue?" asked James smiling,

"Well, it all sounds very well organised James. Where are we going to hold the club?" asked Sue, extremely relieved that there was going to be plenty of help.

"Ah yes," answered James, "I thought behind Class 1 under the gazebos we use for the children to sit under on Sports Day. It's a sun trap there and sheltered from the wind, does that sound suitable? There's an outside tap there and Mr Spencer has kindly offered to build the raised beds round there."

Sue smiled, "That sounds perfect; I was a bit worried about how we were going to deal with the inevitable soil falling on a classroom floor and getting it tidied up before the end of lunch!"

"Yes, well that was Mrs Turrett's idea, she's a teaching assistant in Class 2 and I think you'll get along with her very well. She normally only works in the afternoons but is an avid gardener too and on the two club days she has offered to come in early before lunch and help you set up the awnings with all the equipment and tools you'll need, and if I can help I will too."

"Jean Turrett?" questioned Sue, "Oh I've known Jean for years! How wonderful! Now she IS a good gardener and makes wonderful cakes!"

"You'll definitely have a lot in common then," replied James, remembering how delicious Sue's cake had tasted after a morning striding, somewhat lost, through the fields three weeks ago.

Several staff came into the staff room to fetch their belongings before they made their home and introduced themselves to Sue.

Everyone enthused about the gardening club and Sue now felt far more relaxed than when she had arrived that afternoon.

Eventually the staff made their way home and Sue stood up to leave.

"How's Lottie, Sue?" James asked, rinsing his coffee cup out.

Sue's face lit up,

"Oh, is that what you're going to call her, how lovely! I used to have a dog called Lottie," reminisced Sue, looking wistful, "Anyway, she's absolutely fine. We're going to start weaning them at the weekend." James nodded and smiled,

"I can't wait to bring her home. My house badly needs some chaos in it." He picked up a tea towel, briskly dried his mug and popped it away in a cupboard.

Sue understood completely,

"Not long now James, another five weeks and you can take her home." Sue picked up her bag and as an afterthought said, "I'm not going out Sunday, James, so if you're passing, feel free to pop in for a coffee and a cuddle with Lottie."

James opened the door to the staffroom,

"I may well take you up on that offer, Sue, thank you."

Sue arrived at St Michael's at 11.30, as prearranged with James.

Jean Turrett met Sue at the office with a broad smile.

"Good morning Sue, how ARE you, I haven't see you for ages?"

"Jean! I'm so glad to have a familiar face to work with, I'm a little nervous to say the least!" smiled Sue ruefully.

Jean gave her arm a friendly squeeze,

"It's going to be a blast, Sue! Our feet won't touch the ground for an hour or so and they'll be plenty of laughs along the way! Are you ready!" she grinned at Sue.

Sue laughed at Jean's enthusiasm, it was quite infectious and she replied, "Come on then Jean, lead the way!"

Jean had taken Sue round to the awnings where all the equipment had been set out on garden benches.

It certainly looked inspiring.

The children were going to have a wonderful time and hopefully learn something too.

The large, deep investigating tray looked inviting with brightly coloured trowels sticking in and the two glass tanks, one with soil and worms and the other with snails and slugs, would be sure to produce lots of squeamish squeals from the little ones.

It was just perfect.

The bell signalling lunch time soon rang and the club was off.

"Mrs Hancock, I've dropped my tomato seed....."

"Mrs Hancock, Matthew's taken my trowel....."

"Mrs Hancock, do worms lay eggs?....."

"Mrs Turrett, I've dropped a worm....."

An hour and a half later, the club was over.

It had passed in a flash and now Sue, Jean and James were recovering from the whirlwind of activity with a much needed cup of tea.

"Well, THAT was fun!" exclaimed Jean, clearly a person who thrived on action,

"What do you think, Sue?"

Sue was feeling exhilarated.

What an hour!

Children were such a tonic, their enthusiasm and their questions!

Sue had never felt so alive!

"I completely agree with you, Jean, the children seemed to really enjoy it, what do you think James?"

James nodded enthusiastically,

"I think the proof of the success of it is in the pudding. The only word I heard all lunch time was 'gardening'. The whole school was so interested. Tia in year four had a good idea; she suggested we could sell what we grow at the summer fete to raise some money for next year's club."

The two women nodded in agreement and then started to discuss what could be done to improve the club, if anything.

Photographs, to make a scrapbook of the club, word searches and quizzes?

The suggestions came thick and fast.

Ten minutes later, Jean looked at the clock in the staff room and made her excuses.

She had some photocopying to do.

"Bye Sue, great working with you, see you soon," smiled Jean

"Bye Jean, thanks for all your help today. I'll say goodbye to you too, James" replied Sue, "I must be off; those puppies will be wanting their third meal of the day soon."

"Absolutely Sue, thanks again for today and we'll see you next week," said James.

Sue drove off down the lane to her farm, not quite believing how her life had changed in the past month or so. She felt so grateful for this new, second lease of life.

Millie

Millie arrived back in the office after lunch, one Friday afternoon.

All was quiet. It had been a beautiful hot, summer's day which promised to carry on through the weekend. Potential buyers had postponed their search for a new home and were getting ready for a weekend of barbeques, trips to the seaside or a forty eight hour DIY makeover. Millie herself was looking forward to a weekend at her mother's in Bath.

The children were going to be spoilt rotten whilst Millie and Darius took in the sights.

It would be an opportunity to recharge their batteries.

She put her bag down behind her desk and turned to the office junior who was trying to text her Friday night arrangements to a friend without being seen.

"Would you like a coffee or tea, Chloe?" asked Millie, as she made her way through to the kitchenette off to the left of the office.

"Thanks Millie, but I've got a diet coke thanks," replied Chloe, casually dropping her hand down by her side.

"Peter, can I get you anything?" Millie asked her boss as he came through into the front office.

"Nothing for me, thank you Millie, have you got a moment?" he gestured to Millie to go through to his office, at the rear of the building.

"Yes of course," replied Millie, suddenly anxious.

Had she done something wrong?

Had all her sales suddenly fallen through over lunch and he was calling her in to say he was going to have to let her go?

"Can you hold the fort for half an hour, Chloe? Phone through if something crops up you're not sure of." Peter asked his office junior.

"Ok Boss, no worries!" replied Chloe her phone dropping out of her hand, on to the floor.

She did at least have the grace to blush.

Peter turned and rolled his eyes at Millie as they walked through the narrow hallway to his office.

He closed the door behind Millie.

"Her days are numbered; she is blatantly ignoring our 'no phones on the shop floor' policy." Millie said nothing; she was more concerned with the reason for this impromptu meeting.

"Right Millie, I'll come straight to the point," began Peter, "I'm opening up another branch of Markham and Son's, with my father, in Folkstead and want to be based there for the foreseeable future. I would like you to take on the role of manager, here. What are your thoughts?"

He paused, waiting whilst Millie attempted to digest this piece of information.

Millie was quite simply thunderstruck.

She blurted out,

"Sorry, Peter, what did you just say?" Peter calmly repeated,

"I would like to offer you the position of branch manager, here, at this office."

Millie shook her head, trying to process his words.

355

"Peter, I don't know what to say, I wasn't expecting that at all! I thought you were going to tell me my target had been increased.....or....you wanted to reduce my hours but manager? .....I really don't know what to say?" Millie gave a short, nervous laugh, "I mean we both know I'm not the greatest salesperson!"

She stopped and just looked at Peter,

"I'm sorry Peter, I'm rambling I know, but you've completely thrown me," Millie said truthfully.

Peter took up where he had left off.

"Here's my thinking Millie. You may not be the top salesperson in the office, but that isn't what managing is all about, you know that. You are diligent, meticulous, you dot the 'i's and cross the 't's . You chase leads, you leave no stone unturned and you're excellent at communicating these skills to the staff. In my eyes, without meaning to sound sexist in any way, being a woman is a bonus. Women are used to multi-tasking and managing is just that. Keeping everyone on task, ensuring the house sales keep going through and motivating the staff to keep focused when the phones stop ringing."

Peter sat back in his chair.

Millie looked Peter straight in the eye, there was no point beating about the bush.

"It would mean I would have to work full time, yes?" Peter leant forward in his chair,

"Full time ish!" He teased, his eyes twinkling.

He wanted Millie to run the office for him.

He trusted her completely, but he knew her family would be the rub.

He'd expected it and respected her for it.

"I was thinking four and a half days with two 9.30am starts and one early finish."

Millie gave a half smile.

He was offering hours that most working mothers would kill for.

"Listen Millie, I've given you a lot to think about. Go home now; it will be dead this afternoon with the weather forecast predicting a mini heat wave. Talk to Darius about it and we'll meet again, ten o'clock next Tuesday, how does that sound? Oh, one more thing, the manager's salary is a generous basic with a percentage of all house sales as commission."

Millie drove home in a state of shock.

Had Peter really offered her the role of manager?

Her, Millie?

Was she really capable of managing the office?

She pulled up at some traffic lights.

As Peter had said, she was involved in every aspect of running the office. She stepped into any role when it was required, that of secretary, negotiator, carrying out valuations and, in Peter's absence, she ran the office.

She mediated between vendors and buyers and grumbles within the office. The traffic lights changed to amber, Millie put the car into first gear and released the handbrake.

It was just the hours.....she needed to talk to Darius.

357

Maggie drove down the bypass.

She was picking Adele up today and she was running late.

Dean had phoned her and said he was running late on a job and he would pick Adele up from the flat at six.

The hotel where she worked after she'd finished at the school was preparing for a large party of wedding guests and everyone had felt the stress of the extra work load this had created.

Twenty minutes later, Maggie pulled up at Sally's. She'd phoned ahead to apologise and let Sally know she'd be late so she wouldn't worry.

"Hi Maggie," smiled Sally, as she opened the front door, "she's out in the garden, come on through," and shut and locked the door behind Maggie. "Adele, Mummy's here!" called Sally, from the conservatory.

Adele was at the bottom of the garden, engrossed in making a snail garden, complete with clumps of mud, twigs and stones.

She looked up and beamed.

"Mummy!" and bounded up to Maggie, snail garden forgotten momentarily. She reached the steps of the conservatory and bounded up them, giving Maggie a kiss and an open armed hug.

"I won't cuddle you properly Mummy, my hands are all snaily!" and she pulled a face.

"Well, thank you for not Adele," laughed Maggie, "off you go and wash your hands, missy!" and with a flick of her long, brown plait, Adele disappeared through the kitchen to the bathroom.

Sally turned to Maggie,

"How are things Maggie, alright?"

"Yes, good, good, thanks Sally, the flat completes in a couple of weeks, which will be great, and then I'll be able to focus on changing my job." Maggie grimaced, "I've just about had enough of cleaning!"

"What sort of job are you looking for, if you don't mind me asking?" said Sally,

"Something in an office ideally, I've nearly finished a bookkeeping course and would like to go on and do the next level, but anything in admin would be great, just to get my foot in the door," finished Maggie

"Good for you, Maggie, well I wish you luck in your search. I'm sure something will come up," smiled Sally

"I hope so," said Maggie, "I seem to spend a large amount of my waking hours with my head down a toilet!"

They both laughed when Adele appeared,

"I'm ready, Mum!"

"Come on then love, you've just got time to get changed then Dad should be here."

Mother and daughter said their goodbyes and made their way home to start their weekend.

Millie, Darius and her parents sat around her parents' dining table having ordered a Chinese takeaway and opened a couple of bottles of wine.

The topic of conservation was of course, Millie's surprise job offer.

Darius was thrilled for his wife.

This job would boost Millie's confidence and career. She was more than capable of managing the office, of that Darius had no doubts.

He refilled their wine glasses whilst Millie talked through her worries regarding the logistics of working full time.

"It's just the children; three days is completely different to four and a half. What about when they're ill, and the school holidays?" she quite rightly pointed out.

"Well, I know I'm too far away to help out at short notice," answered her Mother, "but I'm more than happy to have the children during the school holidays," she kindly offered, not wanting Millie to miss out on this unexpected opportunity. She knew she'd regret it if she didn't.

Darius added,

"I'm sure Mum would help out too, and don't forget you're going to get six weeks holiday, as do I, so I'm sure we will figure it out." Millie's father joined in the debate, adding his words of wisdom.

"Millie darling, as with any job, there will be a probationary period of an agreed period of time for you to test the waters, so to speak. Try it for a month and see how you get on."

Millie continued staring at her father after he had finished speaking. He made complete sense.

She put down her wine glass decisively.

"Well that's decided then! I will accept the job on a month's probation!"

She looked around at the grinning trio and smiled widely.

"I want this job, and I think I can do the job, so I'm going to give it a go!"

She raised her glass and said, "Cheers!"

Her father rose from his seat and pushed his chair back.

"Oh I think we can find something a little more celebratory to drink than this plonk!"

Moments later Millie's father returned with a chilled bottle of Moet and four champagne glasses.

"Now let's really celebrate your new job, Millie," and he popped the cork without spilling a drop.

The following Friday it was Millie's turn to host their termly girls' night out, but the numbers were dwindling fast. Sharon had cried off as both her children were unwell and she felt it was a little unfair to leave both of them for her husband to look after, and Rosie was definitely feeling her age with this pregnancy.

She'd phoned Millie to cancel and apologise.

"I can now see why they call it a 'geriatric pregnancy at my age! I certainly feel like a geriatric! I'm just so tired all the time. God, listen to me, moan, moan, moan, sorry Millie, how are you?' Millie laughed and replied,

"I'm good Rosie, listen, no worries at all. Drag yourself up those stairs and go to sleep. Listen to your body, you're growing a baby!"

"It's all I'm doing lately. Well, I'm so sorry I'm missing your evening but I will just end up moaning, bore everyone to death and probably fall asleep over the nibbles!" Rosie gave a deep sigh,

"Listen, how about we meet for a coffee or peppermint tea soon, more chance of you staying awake then," Millie teased,

"Sounds perfect! Have a good night Millie and congratulations again on your job."

No sooner had Millie put the phone down and it rang again, it was Sally.

"Hey Millie, what time do you want me?" said Sally brightly,

"Anytime after seven suits me Sally, but it's just going to be just you and me, I'm afraid, as Rosie and Sharon can't make it," replied Millie,

"Oh that's a shame, do you want to reschedule the evening, Millie, I really don't mind," offered Sally,

"No, no, I could really do with a chat this evening. I promise I won't monopolise the conversation with work talk but I really would like to

362

offload with someone who is pleased for me, but who can also be objective."

"Got it! I completely understand," replied Sally, which she did.

Millie knew she'd be honest with her and check she'd thought about the ins and outs of her new position, unlike her proud parents or Darius as although he had been so supportive, it wasn't the same as sitting down with a close friend, who knew what it was like to work and have a family, and go over the day to day logistics over a glass of wine.

"I'll come round just after seven; do you need me to bring anything other than wine?" Sally offered,

"No thanks, Sally, I've got plenty of nibbles so just you will be great," replied Millie.

After putting the phone down she glanced at the clock.

Darius wouldn't be back until late with the children. He had taken them to Nando's for tea, then the cinema so she had time for a long soak in the bath.

It had been quite a week.

Millie had met with Peter on Tuesday morning and agreed to the job in principle, but requested that she got back to him on what days she would start late and finish early if possible. Peter had shaken her hand and congratulated her on her decision. He was happy to be flexible on her hours and leave that to her to organise. If her days changed from one week to the next, it was fine with him. He wanted Millie to start her new position in two weeks' time.

Her first job would be to give Chloe her notice.

Her second job would be to interview for her replacement.

Later that evening, Millie and Sally were feeling mellow and relaxed, sipping their second glass of red wine.

Millie had confided in Sally that she felt guilty as not so long ago she was a stay at home mum who just wanted to work a couple of days a week and now, she was going to be working nearly full time hours. She was worried about the impact this would have on Jane and Drew.

Sally had put down her glass of wine and given Millie her opinion.

"The thing is, Millie, there is no perfect life/work balance, there just isn't. Life's a bitch. No sooner have you got your life sorted it goes and throws a spanner in the works!"

Sally paused and grinned,

"Except your spanner is promotion, more money and fairly flexible hours,"

Millie looked shamefaced,

"Sorry Sally, I know it's a great opportunity and I am looking forward to it but I just need to hear another mum say I'm not being selfish."

She stopped talking and put her wine glass down.

"Am I......am I being selfish Sally?"

"Of course you're not! Look at me, you could say my children are compromised by having other children in the house five days a week but the alternative would be, I go out to work and they go to a childminder five days a week. Life's messy and there are no guarantees, Millie, but as your Dad said, you've got to at least give it a go."

Sally smiled at Millie encouragingly.

"The children can still have play dates on your half day, you can take them to school two, maybe three times a week if you do a ten till two on your half day instead of going in for eight thirty and finishing at twelve thirty. It's flexible, you can fit your days pretty much around the children's needs AND it's Monday to Friday!"

Sally leant over and topped up Millie's glass and continued,

"It's in our nature as women to feel guilty, Millie, we just have to grin and bear it!"

She topped up her own wine glass, raised it and said,

"Cheers Millie and congratulations! You'll be just fine."

Millie chinked Sally's glass and grimaced.

"I've got my first 'management' job to do already. I've got to sack the office junior!"

Sally grimaced back,

"God, I don't envy you that job! Why?"

Millie sat back and filled Sally in on the office junior's failings according to Peter.

Ten minutes later, Millie's character assignation of Chloe came to a close.

"So, I've got to take on someone who can work full time to cover my old three days which just involved some admin, filing, photocopying, manning the phones when the negotiators are out, taking messages and sending out property details. Karen's not returning from her maternity leave so Peter really wants me to employ someone with experience, y'know, not a school leaver who's on facebook every time they get a minute!"

Sally's ears pricked up,

"I might just know someone, Millie," Sally said slowly, thinking as she spoke.

Millie looked interested,

"Go on,"

"Well you know Adele that I child mind?" said Sally,

"Oh yes, Drew told me that her Dad doesn't live with them anymore, such a shame," commented Millie,

"Well," continued Sally, "her mum, Maggie, is just finishing a book keeping course and is looking for an office job. I think she'd be great,"

Sally genuinely did think Maggie would be perfect.

"She's a great time keeper, organised, plans ahead, she religiously pays my bill on time, and yes, they have separated, which is common knowledge, but they are managing it brilliantly. They are on amicable terms and in fact I think they still socialise together occasionally, as a family, which shows she's someone with a level of maturity."

Millie was mulling over Sally's glowing character reference of Maggie when the sitting room door opened.

Darius, Jane and Drew popped their heads round the door.

"Hello Ladies, putting the world to rights are we?"

"As always," grinned Sally,

"Absolutely," agreed Millie, "I think Sally has just solved my admin conundrum,"

"Oh well done Sally," exclaimed Darius, "horrible first job she's got to do, isn't it? Anyway, I'll just pop these two to bed then I'll come down and join you two for a glass of wine, if I may."

Fifteen minutes later, Millie filled Darius in with what Sally had told her about Maggie.

"Well, you can't get better than a personal reference," said Darius, "What does her husband do, if you're allowed to say, Sally?"

"Yes, it's not confidential; he's retraining as a carpenter. He's working on a kitchen in a barn conversion near Stentbridge at the moment I think. Apparently, he's really quite talented."

Darius sat up in his chair.

"My company has the interior design job for that barn conversion, if it's the one I'm thinking of, in Claverly?"

"Yes that name rings a bell." replied Sally, nodding, "He had to work late last Friday for some reason or another, was it the customer changed their mind and they wanted an island in the centre of their kitchen?"

"What the customer wants, the customer gets.....if it's at all possible." Darius said wryly, "and you're right, for someone that has only just come into carpentry, he's very skilled, a real natural, talented and very conscientious. It sounds like they both are," commented Darius, raising his eyebrows at Millie.

"Do you want me to tell Maggie that I know of a possible vacancy and to phone your office," offered Sally

"Definitely," said Millie, "Tell her to ask for me so we can arrange a suitable time for an interview, but to be honest, she sounds ideal."

Maggie

The following morning, Maggie hurried home after her morning cleaning.

She was shattered.

It was the second Monday in a row the hotel had been fully booked at the weekend with wedding guests and the workload this created was back-breaking.

However, the prospect of the possibility of a job change on the horizon filled Maggie with suppressed excitement.

Sally had telephoned Maggie on Saturday and told her about the possibility of a job opening in an estate agents in their neighbouring town.

If she was interested she was to contact the Branch Manager, Millie, as soon as possible to arrange an interview.

Interested! Maggie had thought to herself as she ended the call to Sally, she didn't know how she was going to get through the weekend.

Time seemed to stand still from that moment on.

Poor Adele was taken from one outing to another on Sunday.

Unable to sleep, Maggie had risen early and found Adele, used to her weekday early morning starts, already colouring in bed.

She had to get out the flat, it was suffocating her.

Wherever you looked there were boxes piled high, ready for the following Friday's completion day.

"Morning love, do you fancy going to a car boot sale today?" Adele's eyes lit up.

"Oooo, yes please Mummy, can we look for some more dresses for my dolls?"

"Yes love, make sure you bring a cardigan, it may be a bit chilly first thing."

Adele quickly popped the lid back on her pen and flung back the duvet.

Walking slowly around the rows of various wallpaper pasting tables filled with the general public's unwanted personal belongings, Maggie's mind began to wander as she dared to think of how securing this job could drastically change their lifestyle.

Well paid, regular income, paid holidays, sick pay and most importantly of all, work experience.

She forced herself to try and stop thinking about it, it was torturing her.

She checked her watch; it was only ten forty five. Maggie turned to Adele,

"Would you like to go to Mc Donald's next and then to Cineworld?"

Adele's eyes rounded like saucers,

"Wow! Yes please Mum," replied Adele jumping up and down on the spot, "and it's not even my birthday!"

Maggie laughed,

"Well, next week and the following weekend are going to be really hectic with us packing everything up and moving to Granny and Granddad's, so I thought we'd have a fun day today," explained Maggie.

It wasn't quite the truth but it fitted in with Maggie's schedule and made sense to Adele.

Monday morning arrived.

Maggie dropped Adele at Sally's and drove to the school to start the first of her two cleaning jobs that day.

Her nerves were in shreds.

The first available time she'd have to telephone the estate agents would be her morning break at the hotel.

Once at the hotel, she cleaned toilets, bathrooms, stripped beds and remade them; she dusted, polished and vacuumed. Every five minutes or so she would check her watch to see if it was time for her break.

Eventually, her break time arrived. Maggie hurried to her car, feeling jittery and nauseous, to phone Millie about the job.

Ten minutes later, after briefly chatting to Millie about her work experience and qualifications to date, Maggie ended the call.

She could feel the adrenaline pumping through her veins.

She had an interview that afternoon at four o'clock.

She looked at herself in the rear view mirror and gave a little smile at her reflection.

It was really going to happen.

She had the opportunity and had to grasp it with both hands. It was down to her now.

She quickly texted Sally.

Sally, sensing quite rightly that Millie would want to fill the post quickly, had offered to pick up Adele from school if Maggie were to be offered an interview that day, even though she didn't usually work Mondays.

Once home, Maggie showered, washed her hair and dressed in a pair of simple black trousers, a white blouse and low heeled pair of black shoes.

She tied her hair back into a low ponytail and applied a sweep of black mascara and nude lip gloss to complete the look of understated but smart, interviewee.

She met her gaze in the bathroom mirror.

"You can do this; you ARE going to get this job." Maggie told herself firmly.

She turned around purposefully and left the bathroom.

She picked up her handbag and keys, and opened the front door of the flat.

Closing it behind her, Maggie made her way to what was hopefully, a doorway to a new career.

One hour and fifteen minutes later, Maggie arrived at Sally's to pick up Adele.

Sally opened the door, dearly hoping that Millie had liked Maggie.

Maggie stood on Sally's doorstep with a big grin on her face.

"I got the job! I GOT THE JOB!" Maggie threw her arms around Sally and hugged her, "I can't believe it! Thank you so much!" she said through her tears.

Sally was thrilled for Maggie and hugged her back.

"Maggie, I'm so pleased for you, but I didn't do anything, YOU did it. Well done you!"

"Mummy, why are you laughing and crying at the same time?" Adele came through to the hallway looking puzzled.

"Mummy's got a new job, Adele," Maggie said, bending down to hug her daughter, wiping her tears at the time,

"I only have to clean for one more week then no more toilet cleaning for me!"

She laughed, she was on cloud nine, she'd got the job.

"I can't wait to tell Daddy, Adele."

Sally smiled to herself.

"What about our toilet Mummy?" asked Adele, frowning as she pulled the straps of her shoes tightly across her foot and velcroed it firmly down.

"Well, maybe you could clean it for Mummy, Adele," teased Sally.

Adele's face told them both exactly what she thought of that suggestion, and everyone laughed.

"Well it was worth a try, Sally," smiled Maggie, "and thank you so much for minding Adele on your afternoon off, I really appreciate it."

"No problem at all, Maggie, happy to help out," replied Sally, and she was.

She knew this job would change their lives for the better.

Things were finally looking up for them.

Sebastian returned home two weeks later from one his unplanned stay in hospital to find all trace of Phoebe and Portia erased from the house. Photographs, ornaments, clothes, shoes, make up, jewellery, toys...... gone.

To an outsider, it would appear it was occupied by a single male.

Mechanically, Sebastian descended the stairs and walked stiffly through to the kitchen.

There, lying ominously, on the central island was a large brown padded envelope.

Sebastian walked slowly over to the package and stared at it.

Reaching over with one hand, he carefully pealed open the flap and lifted the envelope just enough to see a glimpse of what its contents were.

He frowned; it appeared to be an album.

He reached inside and pulled out an exquisite leather bound photograph album, on the front cover, the word 'Phoebe' had been printed in gold lettering.

Puzzled, Sebastian opened the front cover.

His blood ran cold, his skin felt brittle.

He could feel bile rising up in his throat.

He retched.

He turned the page.....and the next, and then quickly flicked through the album.

It held the final nail in the coffin of his existence.

Inside the album were twenty five pages of photocopied photographs of every injury Phoebe had ever suffered at the hands of Sebastian, along with a description of the incident, the correction issued by Sebastian, and the date.

Attached to the inside back cover of the catalogue of abuse were a set of divorce and custody papers awaiting Sebastian's signature.

The custody papers requested that Sebastian give up all paternal rights to Portia.

Something else caught Sebastian's eye.

Lying half out of the brown envelope was a cream envelope.

Numb, Sebastian opened the envelope.

A letter.

> Please sign, Sebastian. A copy of the photograph album's contents are waiting to be sent to the Police and your place of work if you choose not to.
>
> Phoebe

Phoebe had played her trump card.

The room spun.

Sebastian closed his eyes, he inhaled then exhaled.

Failure was winning the race.

He opened his eyes, picked up the album, papers and letter and placed them carefully back into the brown padded envelope.

He picked it up and walked over to the tall, metal waste bin.

He took the lid off and placed it on the floor.

Walking over to the utensil drawer, he selected a hand-held gas lighter; he turned back to the bin, bent over it and lit the contents.

It took a while to catch.

Satisfied it was well and truly alight, he picked up his keys and briefcase and left the house.

Two hours later, Sebastian rode the elevator to the top floor of the investment bank where hc worked.

He acknowledged no one.

Opening the alarmed fire door to the roof, he strode to the roof's edge. There was nothing to keep him company except an empty, disused, crisp packet, swirling aimlessly around the barren roof top like tumbleweed across an anonymous plain.

No one cared where it was going, or where it would land.

Forty seconds later, Sebastian Whitehall's life was extinguished.

Failure had won the race.

On hearing the news from the two policemen that sat in her parent's drawing room, Phoebe felt nothing.

No, that was a lie.

Truthfully, there was a tiny flicker of relief.

It was over, finally over.

Paul and Celeste showed the policemen out and thanked them for delivering such awful news with compassion and understanding.

Paul closed the door behind them.

They both smiled broadly and hugged each other.

"Well played my darling," Paul whispered, "well played."

"I knew the photo album would be the checkmate for the bastard. Thank God Phoebe had the foresight to take the pictures," Celeste replied quietly,

"Good riddance to him, and may he rot in hell."

A month later, Maggie and Adele had moved into her parents' house and had spent three weeks in her new job.

Her parents were being so accommodating. Although Maggie still had to use Sally for childcare as both her parents worked full time; they refused to take any rent money.

"We want you to save as much as you can, my dear," explained her mother, who was thrilled her daughter's life was turning around for the better.

Maggie had hugged them both, she was very grateful to have their support.

It was a Saturday evening and Dean, Maggie and Adele were having their monthly night out as a family. Maggie had realised with a start as she got dressed to leave that she was looking forward to it.

The trio sat in Nando's eating and chatting, the easy conversation of a close family.

"Maggie, how's your new job?" asked Dean, trickling Peri Peri sauce all over his chicken.

Maggie replied, her eyes lit up as she spoke,

"It's brilliant Dean, just brilliant, I love it! There's always something to do, the time just flies by, and......" Maggie paused for effect, "they haven't asked me to clean a toilet....yet!" and they all burst out laughing.

Dean watched Maggie as she told him about her job and was reminded of the young, zestful Maggie he had first met, all those years ago.

Her eyes shone with laughter as she spoke.

She was quite beautiful.

Dean tore his eyes away from Maggie, aware he was probably now staring and took a long sip of his lemonade.

"How about you?" asked Maggie. Dean put down his glass and cleared his throat.

"Well, I don't know if you're aware, but your boss is married to the guy running the interior design gig over at the barn conversion I'm working on and she's been singing your praises."

Maggie was surprised but thrilled,

"Really, well that's a coincidence, isn't it?" she commented, blushing.

"Isn't it? It came out over a coffee break. We were all talking about how funny life was, I mentioned how much my life had changed over the past few months and happened to say that my wife was now on a new career path hopefully, as a secretary in an estate agents. This bloke, Darius, then said his wife had just taken on a secretary at her office, Markham and Son's and was a real asset, was my wife's name Maggie? So there you go!" Dean finished, raising his eyebrows, "It sure is a small world isn't it?"

Adele looked from one parent to another as they spoke.

She cut her chicken breast thoughtfully and quietly dipped her chips in tomato sauce and ate them.

She felt no need to be the centre of attention.

She was content to just be, in the company of her mum and dad, to listen and absorb their presence and conversation.

It felt like home.

Maggie nodded at Dean, her mind reeling.

She pierced a chip.

Had Dean just said 'his wife'?

Maggie listened to Adele and Dean bantering about his college work and glanced sideways at her estranged husband.

He looked so much younger than she remembered when they were living together.

Now?

Now he seemed so relaxed.

So motivated.

His life had a new purpose, as did hers.

They both had futures.

Neither of them was just working to live.

The meal continued in genial conversation amongst the three of them. Dean started to explain how the barn conversion he was working on had been purchased at an auction.

"It was a wreck, don't get me wrong I've seen the photos, but it's the way nowadays to get on the property ladder if you don't mind a bit of hard work,"

Maggie nodded in agreement.

"You're not wrong there. I've been watching that 'Homes under the Hammer' programme first thing in the morning, it's on at seven, while I do my hair and as long as you do your homework and read the legal pack thoroughly, it's definitely an option for first time buyers. Oh, before I forget, it's Adele's parents evening in two week's time. I'll let you know what the teachers say."

Dean took another, casual sip of his lemonade.

"I'll come with you if that's alright?" Maggie looked at Dean, he held her gaze.

His eyes were steadfast, confident, in their unspoken conversation.

Maggie felt herself being drawn into Deans eyes, she heard herself answer.

"Of course you can, great. Adele, did you hear that? Now we're both going to hear what mischief you've been up to at school."

They all laughed and the tension was broken.

Finishing their meal, they made their way to the car park.

Maggie unlocked her car and opened the passenger door for Adele.

"Well bye, Dean, see you next week," said Maggie.

She had butterflies in her stomach; there was a tension between them.

Dean stepped forward and gently kissed Maggie on the cheek.

"Bye Maggie, have a good week."

He waved at Adele in the car, turned, and walked back to his car.

Maggie just stood there, watching his disappearing figure.

She didn't want him to go.

One Saturday, eight weeks after the arrival of Lottie and her brothers and sisters, James was on his way to Sue's to finally bring her home to live with him.

He bombed along the country lanes as fast as the speed restrictions would allow him and he drew up outside Sue's at ten o clock on the dot.

In the back of the Land rover was one of three dog crates he had bought from Pets at Home for Lottie.

One was in housed in the kitchen and the other in his bedroom, just in case Lottie, or he, needed company.

"Good morning James, bright and early I see," grinned Sue, she hadn't expected anything else. "Would you like a coffee whilst we go over her immunisations and feeds?"

"Lovely Sue, thank you," smiled James, and followed Sue inside the farmhouse.

There, in the kitchen, wagging her tail so hard it was barely visible, was Lottie.

"I'm positive she knew something was happening today!" said Sue, "She's been under my feet ever since I came downstairs and when she heard your vehicle she sat by the door. Dogs are so intuitive, they really are!"

As if to prove Sue's point, Lottie bounded over to James, her paws looking far too big for her but adding to her cuteness factor.

Excitement filled the air.

James bent down to scoop her up into his arms and was rewarded with a barrage of licks.

"Hello, my Lottie," James said quietly into her fur,

"I'm never going to leave you...ever again."

Sue had to turn away as tears filled her eyes.

The depth of emotion in the kitchen was tangible.

Without doubt, Lottie was the key to Jame's emotional recovery following the death of Tanya.

Having made their coffee, Sue produced a piece of paper.

"James, I've just jotted down the vaccinations Lottie has had and when she needs her boosters. Also, her feeding schedule, when to cut down her meals from four times a day, to three, to two meals," she paused and frowned at the piece of paper. "I do hope you can read my writing." she apologised.

"That's super Sue, thank you so much for everything. While I'm here, I didn't manage to catch you before you left on Tuesday, was everything alright during gardening club?" James knew it was a full on, busy club and he hoped Sue was enjoying it, despite the hard work.

He'd heard wonderful things about Sue from the children and Mrs Turrett.

"Yes, yes, everything's growing beautifully and the children are being so responsible and caring towards their plants. Mrs Turrett tells me they line up every lunch time to dutifully water their plants, and the wonderful thing is, if a child is unwell and not in school, there is always someone offering to take care of their plant for them, isn't that lovely?"

James was pleased to hear that Sue was enjoying the club as much as the school was grateful to have her time and expertise.

"I think I'm going to make a move now Sue, if that's alright, so Lottie can get used to her new surroundings as soon as possible."

Sue smiled at James.

He looked ten years younger than the first time she had met him.

"You're very welcome, James; feel free to phone any time if you're worried about anything."

Driving home, Lottie stated to whimper in her crate.

James immediately stopped his Land Rover, opened the back door, and then lifted the latch on the crate.

He scooped Lottie up in her new sheepskin blanket he had bought her, lifted her out and carried her around to the driver's side, got in, shut the door and started the engine.

Lottie immediately snuggled down on James's lap and settled down to sleep.

He put the vehicle into gear and carefully continued his journey home.

'Oh dear, Mr Young, breaking the rules already. What would the governors say?' James said to himself, 'What would they say?'

With a sigh of pure contentment, he drove home to start the next phase of his life.

With Lottie.

"I'm getting up now," groaned Rosie, "I promise."

"You've been saying that for the past half an hour!" replied John good naturedly, entering their bedroom with a second cup of peppermint tea for Rosie.

"I know, I know, it's hard work though, the logistics of getting out of bed when you're this fat!"

Rosie rolled on to her side and swung her legs over the side of the bed and pushed herself up into a sitting position on the side of the bed.

"Ta da!" she grinned, "Success!"

John put her mug down on the bedside table,

"I don't want to alarm you love, but if you think you're fat now......well, you're only half way there, that tummy is going to become enormous!"

He nodded as he spoke, "remember Luke?"

Rosie pulled a face at the memory,

"God, I know, I was huge!" she held out her arms in front of her, "Give me a pull up love, will you?"

John dutifully took both his wife's hands and pulled her to a standing position, moaning and groaning as he did so, hamming it up to make Rosie laugh, which she did,

"Oh shut up you!" she giggled.

John leant forward and kissed her,

"Only teasing, my little whale! Now hurry up as fast as that load will let you, scan number two awaits us."

And with that, John disappeared to put a load of washing on and make Rosie some breakfast.

An hour later, they were on their way.

"Feeling alright love?" John asked, eyes on the road ahead,

"Yes I'm fine," said Rosie, thoughtfully, "obviously a bit nervous as at the twenty week scan they are checking for physical disabilities, but I'm trying to be logical about it. The baby is always on the move and apart from being so large, I feel really well, so fingers crossed." She sat back and looked out of the window concentrating on the hedgerow whizzing past.

They had both decided against having the blood tests to determine whether the baby had any abnormalities. Rightly or wrongly, they both felt they were blessed to be having this baby and had agreed that what will be will be.

Forty minutes later, Rosie lay back on the bed with a feeling of de ja vu. As usual, the baby was wriggling and stretching. John paced up and down the little room. His silky security pants weren't helping as much as they usually did. He wanted this son or daughter very much; he hadn't shared his fears with Rosie but one couldn't escape the fact that due to her age, there was more chance of something being wrong with the baby or difficulties during the labour.

The sonographer walked briskly into the room.

"Sorry to keep you waiting, my name is Holly," she smiled at the nervous duo and quickly walked over to the hand wash basin. Drying her hands, she popped the paper towel into the bin and made her way to Rosie's bedside.

"How have you been feeling, Rosie?" asked Holly as she rolled back Rosie's top and squirted the clear gel onto Rosie's tummy.

"Good, good, thank you. I feel huge this time, but the baby is very active, honestly, it never seems to sleep, which is very reassuring I know......." Rosie stopped talking, she was rambling, she knew, nerves were taking over.

"That all sounds great, Rosie, ok, let's see how this little one's doing." Holly placed the probe on Rosie's stomach and started to spread the gel around. A minute or so passed, and then Holly put the probe down. She turned to John and Rosie and said, "Everything looks fine, I just want a second opinion on something, I won't keep you a moment," and she hurried out of the room.

The pair looked at each other in alarm. John took Rosie's hand; he knew he had to be strong for both of them.

"She said everything looked fine, Rosie, don't panic, just be patient,"

Rosie nodded, closed her eyes and started to count to herself, 1, 2, 3, 4, 5, 6....... thinking only of the next number.

John looked at the monitor that was turned away from them.

He'd sounded calmer than he felt.

If everything was alright, why did she need a second opinion?

The door opened.

Rosie opened her eyes.

Holly walked in with another woman. She introduced herself,

"Hello there, my name is Kate; I work as part of the antenatal team. I'm just going to double check something for my colleague."

With that she made her way over to Rosie.

"We'll just pop a little more gel on you Rosie," then she picked up the probe and ran it over Rosie's tummy, eyes focused on the monitor.

After a very thorough scan, Holly put down the probe, looked up at her colleague and nodded. She got up from her chair, smiled at Rosie and John and left the room. Perplexed, Rosie and John stared at the disappearing back of the second sonographer, watched the door close, looked at each other then back at Holly who was now facing them with a deadpan expression.

"Ok Rosie, John, I have something to tell you. Everything looks fine as I said before, I do need to take a few more measurements but for now, you need to know you are carrying twins, Rosie."

Dumbfounded silence filled the room.

Rosie and John just stared at Holly, muted, by her words.

Rosie found her voice first.

"Twins?" she questioned,

"Twins?" repeated John,

"Twins" confirmed Holly.

Rosie and John looked helplessly at each other, too shocked to offer any appropriate words to the other and burst out laughing.

This rollercoaster they were on certainly had a few twists in it.

"Would you like to see?" and she turned the monitor to face the completely unprepared parents.

There, as clear as day, were two tiny babies.

"I just don't believe it!" said Rosie, stunned, and she turned to John who was openly crying. "Oh John, come here, it will be fine.....crazy, but fine."

She suddenly felt empowered.

Twins.

She had to get her act together now.

There were plans to make.

Life changing plans and they only had approximately seventeen weeks to get ready.

John wiped his tears.

"Darling I'm fine," he promised, grinning like a Cheshire cat. "I just feel, with this pregnancy, that for years we were told there were no desserts, then suddenly after years, we are offered a bowl of ice cream, and we end up with a huge bowl covered in chocolate sauce and sprinkles!"

He blew his nose,

"Twins! That's perfect, just perfect." And he enveloped Rosie and his babies in a grateful bear hug.

Holly waited for the moment to pass then started to talk about the practicalities of a twin pregnancy.

"Rosie, your twins share an amniotic sac which generally means they will be identical. Now by the looks of things they are sharing a placenta, although it is large so it could be two fused together. We will need to keep an eye on the babies' growth, as if there is only one placenta it can affect the growth of one or both of the babies later on in the pregnancy, so from now on Rosie, you will be having scans every two weeks."

Holly paused and smiled reassuringly,

"Try not to worry, you've both had a bit of a shock this morning I know, but we will take really good care of you Rosie, and if you are worried about anything, day or night, then phone the clinic, alright?"

She handed them some leaflets,

"Now, do either of you have any questions?"

Later, the couple made their way back to their car, arms wrapped round each other, still coming to terms with the fact that in about four months the amount of children they had was going to triple.

"Twins!"

"I know! It's unbelievable, isn't it?"

"Well they say it never rains but it pours!"

"Hmmm....well a monsoon's coming our way then!"

They both burst out laughing for the second time that day.

Well, what else could you do?

Arriving home, the pair went straight upstairs and looked critically at the upstairs space.

Eventually, they would have to extend, but for now, the main bedroom was large enough to accommodate the babies for the first few months.

It would have to be.

Rosie walked to the end of their bedroom,

"What do you think John; we could build a stud wall here, with a door way, so when they move into their cots they have a little sleeping area. It can easily be taken down once the extension is built?"

She turned to John, who had a strange look on his face.

"John, what's the matter, you look terrible!" concerned, Rosie walked towards him.

John put his hands on his hips and dropped his head.

"John, you're scaring me!"

Instinctively, Rosie put a hand on her tummy.

"Is it the babies, are you having second thoughts?" she could feel panic beginning to rise inside of her.

Her husband lifted his head and shook his head, staring at his wife.

It was time.

He didn't want to have any secrets from Rosie.

They had so much to look forward to; he didn't want anything to tarnish it.

"Rosie, I've got something to tell you. Sit down."

Rosie felt the world slow down.

She'd read about this happening, you watched it on television shows, now it was happening to her.

"You're having an affair, aren't you?" she stated simply.

John looked shocked.

"No! Good lord no, Rosie!"

John hurried over to her, took her hands and sat her down on the bed.

"It's something I do Rosie. I've been doing it for years but I've not told you about it because I didn't know if you'd misinterpret why I do it."

He stopped, there was no going back now, and he wanted a clean slate between them, no more going behind Rosie's back.

Rosie took a deep breath.

Thank god he wasn't having an affair.

Something he did?

She suddenly had a thought.

"It's not that you wear women's underwear when you're stressed is it?"

John's face was a picture.

He stared at Rosie, his jaw dropped open in shock.

"You know about that!"

He exclaimed, jumping off the bed and facing her, completely aghast.

"How?.... When?..... For how long?"

"Your Mother told me before we got married," replied Rosie, utterly relieved that this was all John wanted to tell her.

John was blindsided by his wife's admission.

He thought she was the one that was going to be shocked, not him.

"You know about it......you know....I can't believe it. I thought you might leave me if you found out, but today...today after hearing our wonderful news I just wanted to be honest with you."

Rosie snorted and gave a short laugh,

"If wearing women's pants is the worst thing you're going to throw at me in this marriage John, then I'm a lucky woman." John looked at her, not believing she was being so understanding.

"Really, you're really ok with it?"

Rosie tried to explain to her fraught husband.

"Look love, it's really not a big deal. You obviously didn't want me to know, which I understand, and I'm not needy enough to feel I have to know everything about you and why you do things. You wanted to keep it private and I respected that."

She finished simply.

John sat back down on the bed and faced Rosie.

It was important she knew why.

"Did she explain why, how it all started?" he asked anxiously, "You have to know I'm not a cross-dresser or have any other leanings.....and I'm certainly not aroused by wearing them."

"I know....I know," Rosie said gently. "Your mother said that your father always wore silk pyjamas and had bought you some for your tenth birthday and you loved them. She said as soon as you put them on you felt calm and relaxed."

John was nodding, remembering that first Christmas.

He took up the explanation.

"I would, I just loved the feeling of the silk on my skin. It was so soft, so comforting, I would whine and moan if they had to be washed and poor old mum would promise that she would get them washed and dried in one day so I was never without them. From then on, I'd get silk pyjamas and boxers for birthdays and Christmas. Then one year when I was seventeen, one of my sisters, as a joke, bought me a pair of silk panties,"

John paused and looked at Rosie,

"You know I prefer boxers that fit properly, I hate a breeze."

He gave a nervous laugh.

Rosie grinned and kissed him.

"I know love, you prefer the fitted design."

"I do," John shrugged, "I just do.....but let me be clear, it's plain silk pants only, ok? I'm not into thongs, lace or bows!"

Rosie threw back her head and laughed.

"Christ John, I really thought you were going to tell me there was someone else for a split second."

John grinned at his wonderful, understanding wife.

"Not a chance love, not a chance."

The weight off his shoulders was tremendous. Why hadn't he confided in Rosie earlier on in their marriage?

He was such an idiot!

He placed a hand on Rosie's tummy and gently stroked it.

Rosie looked down at her husband's hand on her tummy, slightly in awe of herself and what her body had decided to do and said simply,

"Twins....."

John nodded and replied softly,

"I think that's what they said?" and, emotionally spent but gloriously happy, they fell back on the bed laughing.

The rollercoaster ride for that day had come to an end.

Sally

It was a Saturday morning, just before the summer holidays and Sally was on her way back to bed with a mug of tea.

She smiled to herself at the muffled gunfire she could hear coming from Eddie's bedroom.

Obviously it was never too early in the morning to blast a zombie.

Back in bed, she opened her laptop to check her e mails and read the news. Whilst the laptop thought about warming up; Sally cast her mind back over the summer term.

Thanks to Sue's help and guidance she had managed to grow a glut of large, red tomatoes.

She and the children had spent many an afternoon making pizzas, tomato salads and tomato and cheese bread. They had tasted delicious, all the better for being home grown.

Jack had passed his lifeguard training and finished his GCSE's. He was going to study A levels in September.

Chris had finished college and was now job hunting and Eddie was just entering the phase in life where your friends are more important than your family.

Then there was Nick.

Steadfast, reliable Nick, whose only purpose in life was to give Sally and the boys everything they needed.

He really was her rock.

Sally clicked on e mails.

There were twenty two, probably all junk mail Sally thought to herself.

She picked up her mug of tea and took a sip.

She was about to place the mug down on the bedside table when an e mail caught her eye.

It was from the People's postcode lottery.

Sally froze.

Her arm froze, still holding the mug of tea, poised in mid air, the mug tipping ever so slightly.

Without taking her eyes off the e mail, in case it disappeared, she put the mug of tea down and with the other she found the mouse pad and directed the cursor to the orange unopened envelope.

She clicked onto it and held her breath.

What day was it....Saturday.....it was definitely a Saturday.

Her eyes flashed over the now opened mail.

Her eyes caught the words.....CONGRATULATIONS!!!!!........WON.......£25,000 ......amount debited......bank.......28 days....

Sally screamed.

"OH MY GOD!! BOYS!!"

Eddie opened his bedroom door.

"Mum, is everything alright, I heard you over my headphones?"

"EDDIE! WE HAVE WON £25,000........£25,000!!!"

Silence....then,

"NO WAY!! JACK, CHRIS, MUM'S WON LOADS OF MONEY!!

In ten seconds, two more bedroom doors opened and in another ten seconds, three dishevelled teenagers clambered onto Sally's bed, pushing and shoving each other like puppies to get a look at the laptop.

Sally wordlessly turned the laptop around to face her sons.

It was ironic really, the only other time all boys were on her and Nick's bed was at Christmas time.

Well, this WAS one heck of a present.

"It does say that, docsn't it?" Sally asked, suddenly doubting what she'd read, and now, the very existence of the e mail.

"Yep! There it is in black and white," confirmed Chris,

"Wow Mum, £25,000, what are you going to do with it?" asked Jack, his mind whirring over all the items a sixteen year old could buy with a percentage of that.

"What's the postcode lottery Mum?" questioned Eddie.

His turtle beach headphones were still perched on his head, albeit askew with the microphone flicked up at his ear.

"Um, it's, it's a....I'm sorry love I can't think...."

Chris helped his Mum out,

"It's a lottery, Ed, that's won on your postcode. A computer randomly picks it out, and if it's your postcode, you win. Monday to Friday its £1000, but on a Saturday, it's £25,000. That's it briefly Mum, isn't it?"

Sally nodded then her eyes widened......

"Anna does it too! Anna does the postcode lottery as well; I've got to ring her!" Anna lived three doors up from Sally so they shared the same postcode.

The postcode lottery was Anna and Sally's favourite conversation mood lifter.

If either of them were down they would start the 'What would you do if you won the postcode lottery" conversation?'

Sally grabbed her phone.

"Anna? Anna, hi, it's me, have you checked your e mails? No, do it now." Anna was confused,

"Hang on; hang on, is everything alright?"

Sally could hear Anna walking to her tablet which she kept on her pine dresser.

Sally could barely contain herself,

"I shall just say 'Postcode lottery'."

The line went quiet.

"NO!" it was Anna's turn to scream.

"Yes!"

"OH MY GOD! IT'S HERE! JOHN! JOHN! We've won £25,000 on the postcode lottery!"

Sally started to cry.

Anna started to cry.

"Congratulations Anna," sobbed Sally,

"You too, Sally, you too."

The friends both hung up to start celebrating with their families.

Sally put the phone down and dried her eyes.

"It's still there boys isn't it?"

The three brothers all rolled their eyes at each other.

"Yes Mum," they replied in unison.

Sally leant over and hugged each of her sons in turn.

"Oh boys, I can't quite believe it!"

"Will we get any of it?" asked Eddie, in his direct, thirteen year old manner.

"Ed!" rebuked Chris, "Don't be so rude!" he then turned to his mum, "Will we though?" and gave her a wink.

"Yeah Mum, don't forget who your favourite son is!" grinned Jack, who immediately disappeared beneath his brothers' bodies as they wrestled him in to a position of submission.

Sally shifted herself to the edge of the bed to make way for the wrestling trio and lifted the laptop up to prevent it being rolled on.

"I'm sure there will be a little deposit made into your savings account," Sally offered.

The fighting ceased momentarily and three groans came from the mass of teenage arms and legs.

"Savings accounts!"

"Boring!"

"You know Playstation 4 is now in the shops?"

Sally freed herself from the duvet and left the boys to it.

Picking up her phone she texted Nick to call her when he had a moment.

Two minutes later, her phone rang.

"Hey Sally, everything ok?" asked Nick,

"I'm just phoning to see if you fancied getting a takeaway for tea tonight, Chinese, Thai, anything you fancy,"

Nick frowned into the phone.

Sally didn't normally phone to see what he wanted for tea, and he couldn't remember the last time they had had a takeaway, they were just so expensive!

"What about the money, love, it's a bit extravagant isn't it?"

Sally couldn't keep it to herself a moment longer.

"Usually, yes, but you'll never guess what. This morning, I got an e mail from...."

Sally paused for dramatic effect,

"The People's Postcode Lottery!"

It was Nick's turn to freeze on the spot.

He could feel his own heart beating, banging on the inside of his chest wall.

"You're kidding me Sally?"

"No I'm not, my darling man! Our postcode came up and as it's a Saturday the prize is £25,000!"

Nick nearly dropped his phone.

"Oh my God Sally, no way! Are you sure?"

He shook his head.

"Oh my God, I just can't believe it?"

Sally and Nick didn't win sums of money like that, other people did.

Four weeks ago, Sally had found an old lottcry ticket in her underwear drawer, checked it and they'd won forty seven pounds and fifty two pence.

That was the largest amount of money they'd ever won, nothing like this amount Sally was talking about.

Sally had started to cry again,

"I'm not joking Nick, I'm not. The boys have double checked I'm not hallucinating and the wonderful thing is that Anna and John do the lottery too and they've won the same amount."

Nick sat down heavily.

This would make their lives, for the next couple of years, so much easier.

Driving lessons for the boys, cars, car insurance, he could finally afford a Veluxe window for their loft which he was boarding out, as somewhere for him to escape to, on his day off, when Sally was working.

Relief swept over him.

"I can't quite take it in love," he said softly down the phone,

"I know Nick, I know, things like this don't happen to us," replied Sally, drying her eyes, "apparently the money goes into our account in twenty eight days."

Nick nodded into the phone,

"Well, how about Chinese tonight then?" he said softly

"That sounds perfect," Sally tearfully smiled into the phone, "I love you Nick,"

"Love you too, Sally, see you soon,"

Nick pressed end call and took a moment.

He surveyed the depot.

Lorries were leaving and arriving at the depot, drivers were checking their loads.

Everything was exactly the same as before Sally had called, but wasn't that the sun coming out?

Well, it certainly had on his family today.

When James had mentioned in passing to Sue that he was eager to take Lottie home, as his house was ready for some chaos in it, in reality, he had had no idea how much chaos her arrival would create.

Lottie quite simply turned his quiet, sedate, ordered life upside down.

Every day was timetabled around Lottie's needs, her mealtimes, her walks, her naps and allowing time to clean up after her.

This must be what having a child is like, James thought to himself, as he bent to wipe her damp and muddy paws with an old towel.

Yet James loved every single moment of having Lottie in his life.

Numerous times throughout the day she would make him laugh out loud with her puppy antics.

She would lie at his feet, chewing one of his old slippers, as he ate his supper, when he worked at his computer, or as he watched the news in the sitting room.

She was such good company.

The crates that James had bought with such good intentions were folded up and placed in the garage, as neither Lottie nor James saw the need for them.

Lottie quickly became toilet trained, mainly due to the fact that she had three short walks a day and quickly learnt that that was the time to do it and, at night time, she slept on an old blanket on James's bed, both snuggled into each other for company.

If she became restless during the night, James would take her downstairs and let her out to do her business, dry her paws, and then carry her back upstairs to finish their night's sleep.

Lottie would lick James on the nose as if to say, 'Thanks Dad', turn around on the spot, as dogs do, to get comfortable and when satisfied with her position, would fall asleep until morning.

On a school morning, James would get up early to take Lottie for a walk.

After breakfast, the pair would make their way to school, where Lottie would spend the morning in her basket in James's office.

If James was teaching she would sleep in her kennel in the outside area adjoining James's office. At lunchtime, James would take Lottie for a walk across the fields, to stretch their legs and then she would sleep during the afternoon.

Once home, Lottie would get a burst of energy so James would play fetch and tug of war with her. When she she'd had enough James would go over some basic puppy training commands with her, reinforced with little pieces of cheese.

Supper time would follow for both of them, then one final short walk before bedtime.

James thrived on having Lottie love and care for.

Slowly but surely over the summer months, James could feel himself gradually coming back to life.

He had a purpose in his life now and he would always be eternally grateful for the day he got lost on his walk, that first day of the Easter holidays.

And of the rest of his life.

Phoebe didn't attend Sebastian's funeral.

She was still recovering from her injuries, but also felt it was taking her duties as wife, a step too far.

She wasn't sorry Sebastian was dead.

He had almost killed her.

She left it to his family to explain away her absence to the few work colleagues who had attended.

Whilst in Marbella, Gabriella had contacted Sally on Phoebe's behalf in an email and explained Phoebe's situation without giving away too many details.

She had apologised that Portia wouldn't be coming to Sally until they were back home and Phoebe was settled in, back at her parents, but said they would of course still pay her for her space.

Sally had been shocked to hear about Phoebe's accident and wished her a speedy recovery and reassured Gaby that payment for Portia's place wasn't necessary.

Sally read about Sebastian's death a couple of weeks later.

How awful, she had commented to Nick.

Phoebe and Portia were having a terrible time of it.

Sally sent a sympathy card to Phoebe's home address with note saying not to hesitate to call her if she needed anything, anything at all.

One bright, summer's day, a month after Sebastian's funeral, Paul and Celeste took Phoebe for a drive. They had something they wanted to show her, a new beginning.

They drove to the village of Chudley, the neighbouring village of Pentcroft.

A change of scene to put a little distance between Phoebe and her old life, but not too far from the friendships she and Portia had made.

They drove into the village square and pulled up outside a period property opposite the doctor's surgery.

Paul turned the engine off.

"Right ladies, let's get out and stretch our legs."

Phoebe frowned at the back of her father's head.

She knew him well.

He was up to something.

Stretch their legs?

They had only been in the car half an hour.

Celeste had an air of suppressed excitement about her and she wouldn't meet her daughter's questioning glances.

"It really is a beautiful day," commented Celeste, to no one in particular.

Paul stood by the car and reached into his trouser pocket.

He pulled out a key and walked up to the doorway of beamed frontage cottage.

He placed the key in the lock, turned it and opened the old, heavy front door.

"Shall we?" he said, and held the door open for Celeste and Phoebe to go inside.

Celeste led the way, through a beamed hallway into a cosy, sundrenched sitting room that looked out onto the square.

It housed large squashy sofas covered with throws and cushions.

Floor and table lamps were dotted stylishly around the room and a large wood burner stood proudly in the fireplace.

Enveloped in the house's warmth and light, they made their way through a doorway that led to a gorgeous, open plan, kitchen diner.

The kitchen was bespoke and designed in the style of a traditional Shaker kitchen, which in itself was stunning, but the show stopper was a Smeg cream range which sat adjacent to a matching cream fridge.

It was subtle, classy and homely.

The dining area housed a similar styled dining table with six chairs and sat along the back wall was a velvet, aubergine coloured Chesterfield sofa which seemed to gloat at its sumptuousness against the simple clean lines of the kitchen.

A door off the kitchen led to a quarry tiled utility room housing a washing machine and tumble dryer and a stable door led outside to a large, courtyard area, big enough for entertaining.

Upstairs there were three double bedrooms, an en suite and a family bathroom.

Phoebe forgot to wonder what her parents were up to and followed her mother around the house, her eyes taking in the lathe and plaster walls, the low ceilings, the uneven floors and odd shaped doors.

Back downstairs, Phoebe found her voice.

"Dad, you haven't bought this to rent out have you? It's going to get ruined, it's just gorgeous!"

Phoebe could not stop staring at all the unusual features.

"No love, not quite." Paul glanced at Celeste, who nodded, ever so gently.

"Let's go through to the sitting room," said Celeste.

Phoebe moved to the window seat and sat down.

"It's so quaint isn't it?" and turned around to find both her parents smiling at her.

"Do you like it Phoebe?" questioned her mother gently.

Her daughter still looked so fragile to her; she had been through such a lot lately.

Phoebe gave a low laugh,

"Like it Mum, it's simply stunning, but not in a harsh way. It.....it's like coming into a house that....that....cuddles you for want of a better word, and it feels so safe...." Phoebe looked back out onto the square, "It just feels so safe."

It was completely different to the house Phoebe had shared with Sebastian which had had harsh, cold surfaces, marble floors and mirrored walls.

Paul walked towards his daughter and took her hand.

Phoebe looked up at her father; not daring herself to believe what she thought was going to happen next.

It did.

Paul placed the key gently in her palm.

"Welcome home love, welcome home."

Phoebe stared at her parents, her throat threatening to close as she tried to fight back the tide of emotion rising up in her.

It was going to be all right.

She, was going to be alright.

Unable to stop them, Phoebe began to unashamedly sob.

"Oh Dad.....Mum...." and she threw herself into their open arms, not unlike when she was a little girl and had fallen over and hurt herself.

They all stood, as a family, crying together but for very different reasons.

Paul and Celeste, out of love and gratefulness that their only daughter would now be safe and secure, and Phoebe, out of sheer humbleness that she was that lucky to have the parents she did.

A triangle of existence built on love, gratitude and selflessness.

Phoebe kissed and hugged her father, then her mother, then stood back and looked at them both. Her face awash with tears, she struggled to speak to them.

"I just don't know what to say. You both stepped in when I needed you and quite literally saved my life. You have now given me and Portia a new home and a fresh start in life."

She bowed her head.

"How will I ever repay you? How can I ever begin to pay you back?" She raised her head and looked around her new home, "It's just so beautiful!"

"There's no need, my love, we have it to give and you are our daughter. You have had a terrible time over the past three years, Phoebe; don't underestimate the damage that you have suffered, not just physically, but even more so, emotionally," her mother explained. "Now, on to nicer things to discuss my love. We have filled the house with furnishings as we didn't want you to have to think about anything initially, except living as you and Portia, just being, but feel free, when you're ready, to change anything you wish. This," Celeste waved her arm around the room, "was just to get you started."

Phoebe gave a watery smile and surveyed her surroundings.

Her mother's taste was impeccable.

"Mum, it's perfect! It's just what I would have chosen," replied Phoebe, truthfully.

Her mother glowed with happiness that at last, her daughter's life could begin.

"How about another look round then we can have a spot of lunch at that pub that was on the right as we drove into the village...The Fox, I think it's called. I've only heard good things about it." remarked Paul.

Mother and daughter walked around the property again, arm in arm, Celeste pointing out little features and details. Phoebe soaked it all in as they walked.

Paul watched the two of the three most important women in his life, walk around the property.

When he had found out the extent of the abuse suffered by Phoebe, at the hands of Sebastian, it was all Celeste could do to restrain him from visiting Sebastian in hospital and finishing the job.

As usual, she made him see reason and convinced him that the leather bound photo album would result in the desired outcome.

Thank god the bastard had topped himself.

It had definitely saved him the job.

Twenty minutes later they were seated in the quaint surroundings that was The Fox.

Phoebe sipped her wine and placed it on the wooden table.

"Mum, Dad, when Sebastian's estate is finalised, I'll be able to pay you back what it cost you to buy my new home?" she said, looking from one parent to the other.

Her Dad put down his menu and reassured his daughter.

"Phoebe, your Mother and I feel that your new home should have no ties to your old life. It's a fresh start. We can easily afford it and I know you're struggling with what you think is a very expensive present, and we love you for that, but don't forget, darling, that your mum and I, although we had a nice little property business, we inherited your grandfather's restaurant when they retired. When we sold it, after they passed away, we made a lot of money from it, and we were very grateful for that. It's just the natural order of things. Wouldn't you do the same for Portia?"

"God, in a heartbeat" replied Phoebe quickly,

"Well, there you go then. Now, what are we having to eat today ladies?"

Phoebe ordered avocado and prawns and sat back and sighed, a sigh of pure gratitude.

She was a very lucky woman.

Walking back to the car, Phoebe looped her arm in her Dad's whilst her Mother stopped to look in an estate agent's window.

"Always looking for potential, your mother, always looking for potential," commented Paul, admiringly.

Phoebe looked at her astute mother and took a deep breath,

"Dad, it's time I got back on my feet now, work-wise I mean. I need to feel useful again. I've spent the last three years having to worry about my appearance, my clothes, my makeup. I was just a show pony! I don't want to return to that way of living. It's empty, shallow and dissatisfying, and I certainly don't want Portia growing up thinking these things define you as a person. So, what I'm asking you is, would you consider taking me on? Teach me the ropes of property development, how to run it as a business? I'd obviously need to start at the bottom of the ladder and I don't mind getting my hands dirty.........."

Phoebe stopped talking and watched her father's face break into a big grin.

He turned to his only child, kissed her cheek and said, "Welcome aboard Phoebe, welcome aboard."

Maggie dried and styled her hair and carefully applied her makeup.

She tried not to acknowledge it to herself but deep down she was looking forward to this evening.

Her parents were going to babysit Adele to allow Maggie and Dean the opportunity to discuss her progress this term and ask questions that may not be appropriate for Adele to hear.

The door bell rang and she heard Adele run to the door.

"It's Daddy!" she squealed, "Can I open it the door Mummy?"

"Yes love," called Maggie, down the stairs.

She listened to the loving exchanges and felt a warm glow inside. She picked up her purse and hurried down the stairs.

"Hello Dean," Maggie stopped momentarily on the stairs.

Dean looked great! He'd had a haircut, showered and had obviously put on some aftershave.

"Hey Maggie, you look nice," he commented, taking in her beige belted shirt dress with matching sling back shoes.

They smiled shyly at each other.

Adele looked from one to the other and started jumping up and down on the spot.

She wanted to hear what the teachers had to say about her,

413

"Hurry up, hurry up or you'll miss my parents evening!" she protested. Maggie and Dean laughed,

"Ok, ok," Maggie opened a door off the hallway, "Bye Mum, bye Dad, thanks for looking after Adele, see you later."

"Bye dear, have a good evening, take your time." her mother called.

That was an odd thing to say, thought Maggie, then she turned to Adele,

"Bye love, we'll see you soon," Maggie bent to kiss Adele on the cheek and followed Dean through the front door.

When they heard the front door close, Maggie's parents looked at each other and nodded.

"Fingers crossed pet, fingers crossed!" said Maggie's father.

Adele's time slot arrived and Maggie and Dean had their fears allayed regarding how their separation had affected Adele. The teacher reported that Adele's work had remained at a constant level and she had displayed no signs of negative behaviour. A divorcee himself, he then congratulated them on their positive handling of their separation.

"It's a hard road to navigate, separation, when there are children involved, I'm sure you'll agree, and sometimes, it's very hard not to bring negativity to the table. However, I can reassure you that not once has Adele come into school after a weekend and mention any rows, disagreements or hostility."

He smiled at the couple and shook both their hands.

Thanking Adele's teacher for his feedback and time, they made their way back to the car, Maggie, with a sense of sadness.

"Do you fancy a drink, Maggie?" Dean asked her, once back in the car. Maggie's heart leapt then sank almost simultaneously.

"That would be lovely, Dean, but I better get back, I don't want to impose on Mum and Dad, they're already doing so much for us."

Dean smiled and gave a sideways glance,

"I think they're kind of expecting you to be late....." he said and waited. Maggie's eyes widened as the penny dropped,

"Did you.....have you already...?" Dean grinned and shrugged his shoulders,

"Guilty as charged!" Maggie blushed and smiled at him,

"Then I would like that very much, Dean, I'll just ring Adele though and put her out of her misery."

Dean started the engine and drove away from St Michael's school and out of the village.

He was going to remind Maggie of how good they used to be as a couple.

He hoped with all his heart he could.

Having ordered a drink each, they sat in the cosy bar, slightly awkward with each other at this sudden shift in their relationship.

Dean didn't waste any time, he had wasted enough already.

He placed his drink down and cleared his throat.

"Maggie, first of all I would like to apologise for the way I left. You were obviously unhappy too, but I feel now I took the coward's way out. I just left. Instead of talking things through with you, adult to adult, and I'm sorry, you didn't deserve that."

Maggie shook her head,

"Dean, we were both so fed up with our lives, I don't think either of us were thinking rationally. We couldn't see the wood for the trees," replied Maggie gently.

Dean loved her for being so fair, not assigning blame.

She had been all year.

He then asked the question he needed to know the answer to, but didn't want to hear, just in case it wasn't the right one.

"Are you seeing anyone else, Maggie?"

He held his breath, what if she said yes?

"No Dean, I'm not."

Dean looked up at Maggie and found her looking at him, her eyes full of love.

He was almost home.

"Maggie, I've never stopped loving you, or wanting to be with you. I just felt trapped, not by us in hindsight but by our situation. Our lives are so different now, we each have a future on our own but I would be honoured if you would consider spending the rest of your future with me."

He reached into his jacket pocket and pulled out a long velvet jewellery box.

Maggie couldn't have wished for this night to unfold any better.

With shaking hands, Maggie opened the box. Inside was a gold necklace, nestling within it was a gold heart shaped locket.

"Open the locket," Dean said softly.

Completely overwhelmed, Maggie eventually managed to open the locket.

Inside, was a tiny picture of an old photo booth photograph they'd had taken when they first met.

Inscribed inside were the words,

My Love, Then, Now and Forever

Dean xxx

Maggie started to cry, smiling through her tears,

"It's beautiful Dean, just beautiful....the necklace, the locket...the words."

Dean moved closer to her and held her hand.

"I don't want you to think I'm a flight risk, Maggie. I won't ever bolt like that again, you have my word."

He leant in toward Maggie, their lips barely touching.

"What do you say Maggie, will you be my then, now and forever?"

Maggie felt she was floating on air.

She kissed Dean ever so gently and replied, "I will. Then, now and forever," she repeated.

Dean pulled her onto his lap and bestowed a kiss on her lips filled with love, passion and promise.

Now he was home.

The day of the Summer Fair arrived and it promised to be sunny and dry all day.

The PTA were up bright and early putting up gazebos, setting up tables and chairs and making sure the stalls looked as inviting as possible.

Sue and James were busy setting up the stall selling produce from the gardening club.

They were going to man it with help, on a rota basis, from children who attended the club.

They had a colourful array of produce to sell ranging from sweet pea plants, peas in their pods and runner beans to strawberries, raspberries and tomatoes.

The stall was simply groaning with freshly grown produce.

It had been decided by the PTA, in support of the gardening club stall, to erect the Pimms stall next to the gardening club stall to encourage people to buy some produce along with their Pimms.

"Well, isn't that a stroke of luck, Sue, we can just reach over and have our glasses topped up without having to walk anywhere! Wonderful!"

Sue laughed, James seemed so happy these days,

"Ah Mr Young, you can always see the positives in a situation!" James put on a mock serious face.

"Well, you have to, Sue, you have to, life is too short!" he laughed without any meaning or sadness attached to his words.

In no time at all, the gates opened and St Michael's Summer Fair was declared open.

It appeared as though everyone from Pentcroft and the surrounding villages had turned out to enjoy the stalls and events on offer.

There was maypole dancing, a gymnastics display, pony rides, tractor rides, plate smashing and the trusty coconut shy, to name but a few.

The stalls were endless.

"Hello there, Sally, how did your tomatoes taste?" asked Sue, on spotting Sally, as she handed change to a parent.

"Delicious Sue, just delicious! Can we do carrots next year?" Sally grinned,

"Absolutely! Enjoy your afternoon." Sue smiled,

"Hi Millie, hi Darius, have you lost your two already?" asked Sally admiringly, as she spied the pair looking settled for the afternoon, sitting at a table by the Pimms stall, drinks and strawberries and cream in front of them.

"Yes, and hopefully they won't be back until the end, cheers!" laughed Darius and raised his plastic glass.

Millie looked more pragmatic, "I think we're safe until the money runs out. Are you going to join us Sally?" and Millie pulled out another plastic chair from under the table.

"It's the only reason I'm here," Sally joked and, having bought her drink she sat down and viewed the fair with pleasure.

"It's a perfect day, isn't it?" she commented.

It really was a lovely sight to see children, parents and grand children enjoying themselves they all agreed. Mille then picked up her pot of strawberries and spooned some cream into her mouth.

"Isn't it wonderful Maggie and Dean are back together?" she said, now spooning up a strawberry.

Darius nodded in agreement,

"He's such a nice bloke, a really honest, nice bloke."

"It's lovely, really lovely that they're back together as a family," said Sally with feeling.

She had been thrilled when Maggie had told her that they were making a fresh start.

"Oh here they are!" exclaimed Millie, "Maggie, Maggie, over here!"

Ten feet away from them were Maggie and Dean, hand in hand, with Adele skipping along beside them, long brown plait swinging as she did so, happiness radiating out of the trio.

They smiled shyly, waved and made their way towards the table.

Dean was now living at Maggie's parents too.

It had again been Maggie's parents suggestion.

They liked Dean, he was a good father to Adele and they knew he loved their daughter and when they had separated they had partially blamed themselves for not helping them more, financially.

"Can I get you a drink guys?" asked Darius, already on his feet with his wallet out.

"No, no, that's fine, we'll get...." Dean started to protest.

"Nonsense, sit down and let me get you hard-working people a drink. Sally, a top up?" asked Darius already relieving Sally of her cup. Sally mildly protested but hadn't really got the energy to protest too much, she was too relaxed.

"As long as I don't stagger out of here drunk, it's not great for business really, being seen out drunk and disorderly," pondered Sally,

"Oh I'm sure it would be fine," grinned Millie, "It's not as if you're pushing a pushchair around, now is it?"

"Good point, good point." Sally laughed, and then Adele suddenly let out a squeal,

"Drew! Hi, Drew," Adele waved excitedly at Drew who was having a fantastic time at his school fair. He felt very grown up visiting the stalls by himself.

"Adele, hi, do you want to come and smash some plates with me?" Adele looked up at her parents with beseeching eyes,

"Can I Mummy, Daddy.....please?"

"Go on then, have a good time and don't leave the school premises."

Maggie watched Adele skipping alongside her friend. She had been on cloud nine ever since she had found out that Daddy was going to come back and live with them, they would be a family once more.

"Sally! Millie, Darius......oh hi Maggie and Dean, how ARE you all?" John and Rosie came walking towards them at a very slow pace.

Rosie's body was protesting heavily at having to carry around twins on such a hot day.

Sally jumped up to fetch Rosie a chair. Rosie eyed it doubtfully.

"I don't know if my fat backside is going to fit into that!"

"Don't worry about it, love, there are more than enough of us here to pull you out of it," teased John.

"How are doing Rosie?" asked Millie.

Rosie looked so uncomfortable, bless her.

Rosie grimaced, "There are not enough words to say how I feel, Millie. A woman's body is a feat of engineering if you ask me! How on earth my stomach and pelvic floor are keeping these babies in, I'll never know!"

Everyone made sympathetic noises.

"How long have you got until you're delivered Rosie?" asked Maggie in awe. Surely it must be next week, Rosie's tummy looked huge.

"Nine weeks, I'll be thirty seven weeks," she said grimly, "Hi Luke, alright my love?"

"Hi Mummy, may I have 20pence please? I want to have a go on 'Spin the Chocolate', they've got Crunchies!" his brown eyes lit up.

"Course you can my love, here's a pound, good luck!" Luke couldn't believe his luck.

"Thanks Mum!" and off he scooted in case his mum changed her mind.

"How's Luke dealing with all the excitement?" asked Sally,

"Ok for now," replied John, "I think the hard part will be when there are two crying..."

"Parents!" interrupted Rosie, bursting out laughing.

Everyone joined in laughing with Rosie and John nodded in weary agreement.

"You're not wrong there love!"

"Well," said Millie, "now we're all together, Rosie, we'd like to throw you a baby shower. John can transport you, by whatever means you are most comfortable in, to my house. We were thinking Saturday October 6th, a week before you're delivered. What do you think Rosie?" Rosie's face lit up, with pleasure.

"Ooooo.....a baby shower, that sounds lovely!"

Rosie beamed a smile around to everyone.

"Thank you very much everyone. I'll look forward to that!"

"Thally! Thally!" called a little girl's voice, Sally turned in her chair and gave a broad smile,

"Portia! Hello....how lovely to see you!"

Sally got up out of her chair to speak to Phoebe whilst the others chatted about work and babies.

"Hi Sally, what a great fair!" enthused Phoebe.

"They do tend to push the boat out for the summer one," replied Sally.

She looked at Phoebe as Phoebe took in the stalls and events.

She looked well, really well.

She had lost that tense, pinched look she used to have.

"Phoebe, come and sit with us and have a drink,"

Phoebe looked at group at the table and thought what a fun time they seemed to be having.

"Thank you Sally, I will. Come on, Portia darling, would you like some strawberries?"

Whilst Portia happily tucked into strawberries and cream, dressed down in denim shorts and a plain pink t-shirt, everyone said very jovial, 'hellos' to Phoebe and the conversation turned once again to work.

While Darius was in middle of telling another one of his humorous work related tales, Millie turned to Phoebe. "Do you have any plans for the future Phoebe, or are you just going to be for a while?" asked Millie gently.

What she really meant was 'recover for a while'.

"Well, I've started working for my Dad, he's a property developer and I'm really enjoying it." she replied, and she was.

Her life was so different now; she sometimes had to pinch herself to check she wasn't dreaming.

Sebastian really was gone; she lived in a cosy, old house with the occasional cobweb and covering of dust.

At weekends, she wear an old t shirt and jeans, trainers and no makeup and if Portia's chicken was dry, or the sausages a bit burnt, no one hit her.

She truly felt reborn.

She turned to Sally. "Sally, are you still able to have Portia on a Wednesday during the holidays?"

"Yes, yes that's fine, Phoebe," replied Sally,

"Thank you, Sally, Gabrielle likes Wednesdays as her day off, so that's great."

"What sort of property does your father develop?" asked Darius. His ears had pricked up when he had overheard what work Phoebe was involved in.

Dean shot him a look; he knew what he was thinking,

"All price brackets really, flats, starter homes, family homes and top end properties," answered Phoebe, deftly catching a strawberry that had escaped off Portia's spoon.

She carelessly wiped her hand on her jeans.

"Well, if you ever need a high spec job done, I would be happy to give you or your father a quote." He then nodded towards Dean, "or if you ever need a bespoke kitchen made, Dean here is your man, I can personally recommend him."

Dean smiled shyly and took a sip of his Pimms.

Wow! That was decent of Darius, passing over a potential job to him.

Dean caught Darius's eye and nodded his thanks.

"Ok, that's always good to know, I'll bear that in mind." She turned to Rosie,

"Rosie you must be due any day now?"

"No! I'm just fat and carrying twins!" and she pulled a long suffering face.

"Oh, congratulations, Rosie! Sorry, I've been a bit behind the times recently but I'm getting back on track now," she smiled apologetically.

Rosie smiled warmly at Phoebe.

"Listen, can you come to my baby shower in October, Saturday the 6th in the afternoon, is that right girls?"

"Yes, that's right, Rosie. Phoebe, I'm giving out invitations over the summer holidays, you live in Squire square now, don't you?" asked Millie,

"Yes, that's right, just opposite the Doctor's surgery, the one with the black beamed frontage.

"I know the one, it's a beautiful property," Millie said admiringly,

"Thank you Millie, I really love it there. It's a lovely peaceful spot. The next girls' night we have must be at mine."

Millie smiled and looked at Phoebe thoughtfully.

She had a tiny scar on her left cheekbone.

She has had a terrible time of it lately, she thought to herself. She leant forward and handed Phoebe a plastic cup of Pimms that Darius had placed in front of her and picked her own up.

"Cheers everyone, here's to good friends and good fortunes!"

"Cheers!" came the resounding reply.

The afternoon sped by and Sue and James were congratulating themselves on having sold nearly all their produce.

"I don't know if it's me, Sue, but the sales of our produce seemed to increase as the affects of the Pimms took hold on our generous parents," he mused,

Sue laughed.

"I think that had a lot to do with it!" Sue stopped tidying for a moment and listened.

There was a crackling of a loud speaker being switched on.

"James! It's the raffle!" Digging deep in her jean pocket Sue pulled five strips of tickets.

"Right oh," James took out his wallet and pulled out ten strips. "Good luck, Sue!"

"Good luck, James!" Ten minutes later and the raffle was well under way. There were numerous prizes donated not only by the parents from St Michael's but local businesses too.

"Number 371 on a pink ticket.....2 tickets to see Miss Saigon, what a wonderful prize..." the voice announced, "371......anyone?"

Sue gave a tiny scream,

"James! Oh my goodness!.....it's me!....I'm 371!...." and completely forgetting herself, she ran off to the raffle stall calling, "371? That's me...I've got 371!"

James smiled as he watched Sue collect her unexpected prize.

Her face was beaming as she hurried back to their stall.

"Miss Saigon tickets! What a prize, James! I've just got to find someone who loves musicals as much as me."

Sue looked out over the stalls, thinking.

"Julia would come but it's not really her thing...."

She then checked herself and smiled at James. "Oh well, plenty of time to sort that one out."

"I'll accompany you Sue, if you can bear my company for the day," James said suddenly.

Sue looked at James and her mind went blank. James?

427

"Look, I'm a bit of a West End bod, I've seen them all," he shrugged. "Don't tell anyone but I'm a sucker for a spot of singing and dancing," and he deftly bent down to pick up some tomatoes that had found their way on to the floor.

Sue thought quickly to herself.

She sensed no underlying motive.

Just two people who enjoyed each other's company and shared a similar love of musicals.

"That would be lovely James then, we could make a day of it." she suggested. Well there was no point going all that way without taking in some sights, she thought to herself.

"Oh yes, lunch in Convent Garden and taking in a spot of mime. I haven't done London for a couple of years now come to think of it."

The pair continued with their tidying of the stall, discussing their favourite musicals and plays.

Two friends, having survived the rollercoaster ride of loss and grief, who were looking for nothing more than friendship and companionship.

Later that day, Millie and Darius sat on their patio enjoying the last of the day's sunshine.

"Happy darling?" asked Darius, rubbing his wife's hand as they sat, just enjoying being.

Millie shifted a bit in her garden chair and thought before she answered her husband.

"I am Darius....I am....it's just, well....we've been very lucky haven't we, when you look back on our lives together, we really have been very blessed."

Millie was thinking of Phoebe, Maggie and Dean primarily and the trials and tribulations they'd gone through before their lives finally got on an even keel.

"We have Millie, yes, but how I see it is, if you keep your head down, work hard and treat people and friendships with kindness and respect you won't go far wrong," he replied rather philosophically.

Millie frowned at his words. "But it's not that simple, is it? Phoebe had done nothing wrong and look how she's suffered over the years. Maggie and Dean are good, hard working people and although their life is turning around slowly, they're still not there yet, in their own little home, are they?"

Darius rubbed his forehead; he had consumed far too much Pimms that afternoon to be having such a deep conversation.

He turned to his wife.

"I know love, life isn't fair sometimes and luck does play a big part in it, it has to be said."

Millie went quiet for a moment, lost in thought.

She put down her wine glass and turned to face Darius.

She wanted to run something by him.

One evening, a couple of weeks later, Millie and Darius invited Maggie and Dean around for a Chinese takeaway.

They had used the excuse that they wanted to go over any work issues. Were Maggie's hours fitting in with Adele? How would Dean feel being the main carpenter on a kitchen job that was coming up?

Issues that there was never time to talk about at work.

That was what they told Maggie and Dean, anyway.

Millie wanted the young couple to feel relaxed and comfortable so, while they waited for the takeaway to arrive, they sat round the large kitchen table, drinking wine and beer chatting about the children, school and properties.

When a natural silence fell, Millie and Darius looked at each other, then back at Maggie and Dean.

Maggie and Dean, sensing a slight change in the atmosphere, looked at each other, then back at their bosses.

They weren't, but something....there was something being left unsaid.

Darius broke the tension.

"Right guys, I'm just going to come out with it. You two are always talking about buying a property at auction, am I right?"

Maggie and Dean nodded blankly.

Darius continued,

"Well, in two weeks time there is a house going to auction in Tilbury, guide price of £70,000, two bedrooms, huge garden, loads of room to extend should you want."

Dean and Maggie nodded knowingly and wearily and looked at each other sadly.

"We know about that one Darius," replied Dean, "But it's probably going to go for a lot more than that. We've got £40,000 saved but getting a mortgage arranged will be tricky, accounts wise, as I've just got into a new form of employment."

Maggie smiled, "Thank you, though for looking out for us, we think a couple more years at Mum and Dad's, Dean will then have nearly three years accounts and we'll be in a really strong position to get a mortgage."

Millie looked at the hard working couple and was reminded of how easy her life had been to date.

"We'd like to help you buy it," said Millie

The word hung between the two couples.

The young couple didn't make a move, or a sound.

Had they heard correctly?

Had those words actually been said?

"Pardon?" said Dean, cocking his head to one side, not trusting his sense of hearing.

Maggie just stared at Millie.

She'd heard them.

Were they really offering to help them on the road to owning their first home?

Millie continued. "We would like to help you buy the house. We will pay for it, if we win it, help you organise a mortgage, then when it's been arranged, you can pay us back. We will have it all drawn up legally. We won't ask for rent, you won't have to pay anything until you have your mortgage arranged so you can keep on saving."

Maggie and Dean sat at the table, quite literally stunned.

Then they found their voices.

"Why would you do that for us?"

"Oh my God, you can't possibly do that!"

"It's just too much, no, no..."

Dean's voice suddenly rang out, strong and clear.

There was only one answer.

"Thank you, but we can't accept your offer I'm afraid. It's just too much!"

He looked from Darius to Millie.

"Thank you.....thank you so much for your kind offer but it REALLY is too much."

Darius poured everyone more wine and beer.

"What are you struggling with Dean?"

Dean put down his beer and said quietly,

"It's simply too much. Too generous, too much money, too kind and not paying interest! I couldn't sleep at night! I'm not a sponger."

Darius nodded at this passionate speech, of course, the man had his pride.

"Dean, I understand, I can see it from your point of view but it's a short term loan, just until your mortgage is in place, and you will get a mortgage, we've done our homework. Now, how can we help you guys, get this house in a way that you're happy with."

Maggie looked at Dean, then back at their hosts.

"If you are serious in your offer, and it is an incredible offer, we would need to start paying you back straight away."

Dean nodded slowly

"With interest!" Maggie added.

Darius looked at the pair, so conscientious, so proud, and turned to Millie, it was her turn.

"Look guys, let me explain our thoughts behind this offer. You are two lovely, hardworking people who just aren't getting a break. We have had lots of luck in our lives, and just want to give something back. Darius's aunt passed away last year, she had no children and left Darius and his siblings a large sum of money each. It's just sitting in a building society. We're not giving you the money; you're just borrowing it so you can pay for a house at auction in the time frame they stipulate. I can see why you want to start paying it back straight away, fine, but let's just agree on a nominal amount so you can both sleep at night."

Dean and Maggie looked at each other.

Listening to Darius and Millie's explanation, their offer began to sound more reasoned and business-like than they had originally thought.

Millie continued, "I look at you two and just want to help you get what you truly deserve. Everyone deserves a little bit of luck in their lives."

Once again, Dean and Maggie looked at each other then back at Millie and Darius.

"Are you absolutely sure?" questioned Dean.

"One hundred percent Dean," Darius held out his hand to Dean, "Deal?" Dean gave one last look at Maggie, who gave a tiny nod with the barest hint of a smile.

"Deal!" and they shook heartily on it.

Much back slapping from the men and crying and hugging from the ladies followed.

The celebrations were interrupted by the sound of the door bell.

"Food!" exclaimed Darius, "Well that's great timing, I'm starving!"

Everyone bustled round getting out plates, bowels, serving spoons and opening more wine.

The evening was spent going over bidding tactics, maximum bids and what to look for in the legal pack.

Two weeks later, Maggie, Dean, Darius and Millie sat nervously in their seats waiting for their lot to come up.

Maggie and Dean were desperately trying to remain calm but the possibility, all be it a fairly slim one, of owning their own house was making it almost impossible to do so.

The lots came and went and finally it came to their lot.

"Lot number 32, a two bedroomed property in the desirable village of Tilbury, in need of modernisation, may we start the bidding at £70,000....£70,000. Thank you,. .....thank you, lady to the left. Do I see £75,000?.....thank you.....Gentleman to the rear...."

Dean put his paddle down, sweating profusely with nerves.

"Do I see £80,000?......."

Maggie gulped, the price was rising in increments of £5000. They had agreed to bid no more than £150,000.

"Thank you to the lady on the left, £105,000."

Millie and Maggie craned their necks to see who they were bidding against.

It was a woman, fine boned, with long dark hair. She flicked her hair back over her shoulder.....it was Phoebe!

Dean put his paddle down.

He was on the verge of passing out with the amount of adrenaline that was being pumped around his veins.

"You're doing well mate, you're doing well."

Darius gave him a reassuring nudge in his arm. Darius could see how people got carried away at auctions, it was addictive.

It was like wanting to win a race.

"£125,000, thank you madam."

Someone dropped a paddle.

Phoebe turned her head at the noise.

She caught sight of Millie, Darius, Maggie and Dean.

"Do I hear £130,000?"

Dean shook his head, Darius elbowed him,

"Come on mate, you said 150 was your maximum."

Dean had lost his nerve,

"It's not going to happen. I can feel it. It's just not going to happen."

The experienced auctioneer offered,

"Would it help if we now went up in thousands?" Darius grabbed the paddle and raised it.

"Thank you sir, £126,000 , do I hear £127,000?"

The auctioneer looked at Phoebe, then around the room.

Phoebe's mind was processing what she had seen.

Maggie and Dean were bidding on the same house as she was.

They were desperate for a house whereas she just bidding to add to an already bulging portfolio.

"Going once," the auctioneer looked at Phoebe again,

"Two bed roomed property going for a steal at £126,000, going twice,"

Phoebe looked round at Millie, Maggie, Darius and Dean and smiled at the four faces now all staring anxiously at her.

She looked back at the auctioneer.

Everyone deserved a bit of luck.

Phoebe shook her head.

The hammer sounding made everyone jump.

"SOLD for £126,000 to the man or men at the rear."

The foursome jumped up out of their seats and hugged one another.

Maggie and Millie were opening crying and Darius and Dean man hugged and furiously shook hands.

"Thank you Darius, thank you, so very, very much." Dean said in a low voice, feeling surprisingly choked up.

"Happy to help out Dean, happy to help out," replied Darius.

He was thrilled.

It was theirs.

They all bustled out of the auction room to pay the deposit and fee and congratulate each other.

"Hey guys," called a voice,

"Hi Phoebe," smiled Millie.

Maggie and Dean were excitedly thumbing through the property details.

"Change of heart on the bidding?"

Millie looked at Phoebe quizzically.

"I know, I'm such an idiot! I was bidding on the wrong house! What has my poor father let himself in for? The one I should have been bidding on is further down the list. Right, if you'll excuse me I need to visit the ladies...congratulations guys...."

Phoebe called over to Dean and Maggie, and then she disappeared to find the toilets.

Maggie hurried over to Millie,

"Did she say why she stopped bidding?"

"It was the wrong house apparently," replied Millie, scanning the lots still to go.

She frowned and checked the list again.

There were no other houses for sale that day.

Millie closed the brochure and smiled to herself.

She really did know the nicest people.

"Good Lord, love! Do you think we've got enough balloons?" called Darius, as he made his way through the hall into the kitchen.

Pink and blue balloons, with matching coloured curly ribbon cascading down, adorned the house, along with baby inspired banners and bunting.

The house had a tiny sense of hysteria about it in Darius's eyes.

Millie swung round from the plate of hor d'ourves she was arranging, a worried expression on her face.

"What? Don't you think it's enough, do we need to rush out and get some more?"

She pushed past him and looked left into the hall then hurried through to the sitting room, passing a critical eye over the decorations.

"I just don't want it to look tacky."

Darius shook his head at his anxious wife,

"Enough? Millie, it looks like we're auditioning our house for the role of that house in the film UP!"

Millie shot him a withering look.

"Look, I know it's not the contemporary look you favour but in case it had escaped your notice, we're having a baby shower and balloons are a necessity. Now, unless you are going to help, scram!"

"Hello.....hello...?" called a voice,

"Sally? Oh great, come through and see if you think I've done enough food. Darius, take Sally's present into the sitting room and put it on the coffee table."

Darius fixed a good natured smile onto his face and offered it to Sally who grinned in return and gestured to do what Millie had asked.

He obediently turned on the spot and made his way through the throng of balloons to find the coffee table in the sitting room.

Gradually, the house began to fill with friends, work colleagues and relations.

Half an hour later the guest of honour arrived.

"Make way......make way.....wide load entering......wide load, coming through!"

"ROSIE, JOHN! Welcome to your baby shower!"

Millie hugged them both, and led them through to the sitting room.

Everyone cheered at their arrival.

"Rosie, you look wonderful," remarked Darius, kissing her cheek and taking her hand ready to guide her to her throne for the afternoon.

"Thanks Darius, I'm just terrified I'm going to trip and fall over. I'd never get up again you know, and I'm not joking!" Darius snorted,

"Well, there's no need to worry Rosie if you do," said Darius under his breath, "Millie's bought so many bloody balloons that if you did, you'd bounce straight back up again!"

"Darius!" Millie was standing right behind him.

"Oh darling, there you are, now what can I do to help?" he replied innocently.

Rosie smiled to herself as she gingerly lowered herself into her chair.

Millie and Darius, you just had to love them, they really were made for each other.

The afternoon was just the lift Rosie and John needed to see them through the last week of Rosie's pregnancy.

At thirty six and a half weeks pregnant, she was beside herself with discomfort.

She couldn't wait for the planned caesarean next week.

The stud wall was up. The twin basinets stood by their double bed. Car seats, travel cots and other baby paraphernalia filled the downstairs.

Their house was as ready as it could be for the arrival of twin babies.

Rosie was coming to the end of opening huge pile of presents. Everyone was laughing at a pair of bibs that said, 'That's my twin....' while the other one said, 'No, that's my twin..' She leant forward to pop them on the coffee table when she stopped, her face registering shock.

The bibs dangled from her hand.

"Oh no." she said quietly.

Everyone looked at Rosie, and then started to move towards her, something was wrong.

"What is it Rosie?"

"Is it the babies?" John, back from a visit to the toilet, rushed over to his wife.

"Rosie, what's the matter?"

Rosie's panic filled eyes met her husband's.

"I think my waters just broke!" Everyone immediately sprung into action.

"Darling, we need to get you to hospital," urged John, pulling his wife to her feet.

Darius took one of Rosie's hands.

"John, I'll get Rosie to the car. You phone the hospital and let them know you're on your way, they'll need to get organised."

"Right, yes, good idea!"

John reached into his pocket for his phone and hurried out the sitting room into the kitchen.

"Come on Rosie, let's get you to your car, my love, those babies are on their way."

Millie hurried down the stairs with a couple of towels to place on the front seat of the car.

"What about your hospital bag?" Sally asked, following Rosie and Darius out to the car.

"It's in the boot of the car, has been for the past two weeks."

Rosie was concentrating on getting to the car as quickly as possible.

Her waters breaking threatened to make things a little more difficult than if the babies had waited until their timetabled delivery next week, in hospital, on an operating table, under the control of the obstetrician.

"Shall I come with you?"Sally offered, "The journey....just in case?"

John looked at Sally over the roof of the car, potential roadside deliveries flashed through his mind.

"Yes! That would be great!"

"Don't worry about Luke, he'll be fine here," reassured Millie, as she tucked a blanket around Rosie's legs.

He was upstairs with Drew, oblivious to the drama's unfolding downstairs, playing Lego Star Wars on the Xbox.

"Thank you Millie," smiled a nervous looking Rosie. "John will call his parents at some point and he'll let you know when they'll come and collect him."

John started the engine.

"Thanks again Millie, for everything...the shower was fabulous!"

Millie leant into the car and hugged her friend.

"You are welcome love, now off you go, you've got some babies to deliver."

Everyone was gathered on the drive to wave them off.

An air of tense excitement filled the air.

The babies were on their way.

Rosie and John's babies were delivered without any more drama at 6.33pm and 6.35pm by caesarean section on Saturday 6th October 2013.

Their daughters weighed 6lb 7oz and 7lb 9oz respectively.

John and Rosie's parents arrived and so, after popping her head in to congratulate them all and admire their tiny, gorgeous daughters, Sally left them, to celebrate the arrival of the long awaited, new additions to their family.

She called Nick from the canteen and waited with a much needed cup of coffee for him to come and pick her up and take her home.

She looked around the faces milling around the cafeteria, displaying a multitude of emotions, and wondered what stories laid behind them.

Her mind wandered back to the people she knew in her life.

Millie and Darius's marriage had survived a rocky patch and strengthened because of it and they were now both equals in their marriage.

Maggie and Dean had, through sheer determination to better their lives, forged new careers and, with a little help and a bit of luck, now had their own home together.

After years of trying, Rosie and John were now new parents again, created on the foundations of a rock solid marriage, where acceptance of each other, for better or worse, was at the forefront.

Phoebe was now free from an abusive marriage and was well on the way to forging a new life for herself and Portia, with the help and support from her beloved parents.

James was rebuilding his life with the help of Sue and Lottie, his dog, and in turn had given Sue the opportunity to feel useful again and be involved in the community, and Sally?

Sally took a sip of her coffee and looked out of the cafeteria window.

Nick was just drawing into the car park.

Sally and her family had had the edge taken off their financial situation.

For the first time in their life they had a financial cushion.

She stood up and made her way out to car park to meet Nick.

She waved and smiled as Nick drove towards her, pulled up and stopped the car.

"Everything alright, love?"

Nick leant over and kissed his wife's cheek.

"Wonderful Nick, just wonderful, the babies are gorgeous!"

Sally had never felt more positive about her friends and family's future than she did today.

Caroline watched the prospective tenant walk around the house.

He had divorced from his wife two years ago and then worked abroad for eighteen months.

He had come back and bought a house on a new housing development being built just outside Stentbridge and had just taken up the post of Consultant Cardiologist at Barley Heath hospital.

Caroline knew the development. It was a development for the wealthy.

He needed a room for six months until the house was completed.

They went upstairs to the room Dean had rented.

Dean.

A rare good, decent man.

The good ones were always taken, she thought wistfully to herself.

"I'll take it." said the man.

He turned to look at Caroline and held her gaze.

Dropping his eyes he thought to himself, one thing at a time Colin, one thing at a time.

Twenty minutes later Caroline shut the front door behind him and a small smile hovered over her lips.

New beginnings...?

Maybe.....just maybe.

To being Inspirational.........

In the year 2000, my friend, Alison Tosh and I, were both pregnant with our third child. Born two months apart, both babies were born healthy boys. We were so blessed. Arran was Alison and Stephen's first son, Oliver was my third.

On June 7th 2014, Alison's son, 13 year old Arran Tosh, died - just six days after being diagnosed with a brain tumour.

There are no words to describe sense of loss that imploded on their family and reverberated throughout their extended family, friends and colleagues.

'Inspirational' was a word used to describe darling Arran, by all who knew him, myself included. 'Mature beyond his years' was another. Arran's unselfish actions towards his peers, friends, family and fundraising were quite simply, inspirational.

One Saturday afternoon, after busking in Sudbury, Arran took the donations he had earned singing and playing the guitar into a local charity shop and donated them to cancer research; a charity close to his heart as his Auntie had suffered from breast cancer.

As a mother of three sons, I bow my head in shame. Without a shadow of a doubt my sons would have put the money towards an Xbox game or to download players for a virtual football game.

This is not the time to tell Arran's story though, suffice to say by my donating 20% of the profit from the sale of each copy of *Community Chest*, to the Smile of Arran trust, I am attempting to do something inspirational, like Arran did on a daily basis, helping others in their time of need. Maybe at forty six I've left it a little late, but better late than never, I'm hoping.

Thank you so much for reading *Community Chest*, I hope you enjoyed it.

Georga x